# SAREE

Also by Su Dharmapala

*The Wedding Season*

SU DHARMAPALA

# SAREE

**SIMON &
SCHUSTER**

London · New York · Sydney · Toronto · New Delhi

A CBS COMPANY

First published in Australia by Simon & Schuster (Australia) Pty Limited, 2014
First published in Great Britain by Simon & Schuster UK Ltd, 2014
A CBS COMPANY

This paperback edition, 2015

Copyright © Su Dharmapala, 2014

1 3 5 7 9 10 8 6 4 2

Simon & Schuster UK Ltd
1st Floor
222 Gray's Inn Road
London WC1X 8HB

www.simonandschuster.co.uk

Simon & Schuster Australia, Sydney
Simon & Schuster India, New Delhi

A CIP catalogue record for this book
is available from the British Library

Paperback ISBN: 978-1-4711-4190-4
eBook ISBN: 978-1-4711-4191-1

Printed and bound by CPI Group (UK) Ltd, Croydon, CR0 4YY

MIX
Paper from
responsible sources
FSC® C020471

Simon & Schuster UK Ltd are committed to sourcing paper
that is made from wood grown in sustainable forests and supports the Forest
Stewardship Council, the leading international forest certification organisation.
Our books displaying the FSC logo are printed on FSC certified paper.

*In ever loving memory of my father,*
*Piyadasa Dharmapala.*
*I still miss you so very much.*

# CONTENTS

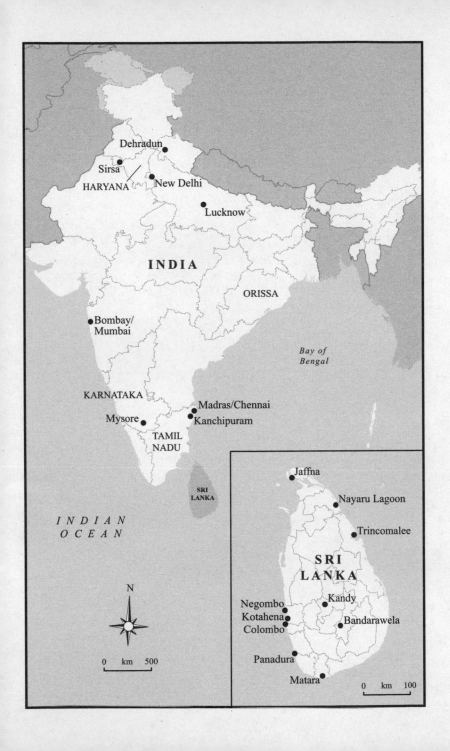

# Saraswati

There is a small park outside the town of Sirsa in Haryana, India. It is near the corner of the rough, dusty, potted road that forks off to Ottu. You might miss it. The turn-off for the park, that is. For that corner, shaded by a large banyan tree, has long been the haunt of the most impolitic of youthful gangs. Only this gang is slightly different to the Mafioso-style street-dweller you'd find in cities like Delhi, Mumbai or Kolkata – for it is a gang of young male bulls.

They are typical for Indian bovines, really: all angles, skin and bone. Their fine, almost fragile appearance belies their strength, agility and intelligence. They sit in the cool shade of the tree – mooing dispassionately, complaining of the poor quality of grass in the neighbouring fields, swatting flies way with a bored flick of the tail – waiting for their prey. A human in a hurry.

All pretence of lethargy is abandoned, however, at the sight of their quarry: a bronzed, saree-swathed woman with a large bale of cotton precariously balanced on her too-delicate head and neck. They watch carefully. For it is easy enough to mistake the figure of a woman reflected in the waves of heat rising from the arid ground with those shadows cast by large, fluffy clouds overhead.

It is the unmistakable tinkling of bells strapped to the ankles of field workers that gives the whole game away. The woman would know of the dangers posed by these militant bovines.

Of course she would. Local legend would have warned her. But the rapidly sinking sun and the desperate need to deliver her load to the cotton depot a little way over the hill to earn a few meagre coppers to feed her hungry children would have strengthened her resolve. Maybe they won't notice her. Maybe they won't charge.

As night will follow day, the herd allow the woman to go a few feet past the corner, lulling her into a false sense of security, just before the youngest gang member bellows out his war cry. And in a flash, they charge.

The woman, clutching her precious load of cotton on her head, starts to run too. Maybe she'll make it through the rapidly closing doors of the depot before the young bull impales her with his horns. Maybe she won't, and her bale will be abandoned by the wayside as she saves her own life at the expense of her children's empty bellies.

So, if you are brave enough to out run these bullish thugs and drive past – fast – in your new Maruti, you may find the park.

Once you get there, rest for a moment. Under the large *kikar* tree that stands guard like a sentinel to the west. Sit. Quieten your mind. Feel the pulsing of the mighty Saraswati River that once flowed all around. Tha thump. Tha thump. Tha thump. The rush of her flow that once brought wisdom and grace from the very roof of the world.

Then open your eyes and look. Carefully. She hides among a clump of turmeric plants or maybe even among the foliage of a *bhrami* tree. A little statue. No higher than your waist. A holy remnant of the great Harappan civilisation that thrived in the surrounding Indus Valley some four millennia previously.

She sits on a simple dais, a worn boulder acting as altar for the odd person who remembers she is still here and brings her an offering – Saraswati of the Sirsa Plains. The mother of the Vedas. She who needs no consort, for she is the one who is whole in and of herself.

It is difficult to make out the detail, but she sits on a lotus in full bloom. Of the four arms she is usually depicted with, only two remain. One hand holds a lute, the other, papyrus, because Saraswati is the patron goddess of the arts, and of wisdom forever lost to antiquity.

Of the remaining two hands, one lovingly caresses a peacock – the goddess's totem animal and chariot. And the other hand – well, it is hard to say, but she holds out her arm like a weaver about to cast her first pass. Full of purpose and passion. For she is also the patron goddess of the weavers. Those who create something out of nothing.

But there is intent in her eyes. What is she weaving? Who are the threads on her loom? Will she hide the main colours on the first pass, only to bring out beautiful patterns later? Or will she brutally cut those threads that serve ill and bring not joy? What is her design?

Come now, let's follow just a few of her threads as she weaves her endless saree of life, for we all start at one end and finish at another. We are all connected in this garment, threads on her celestial loom of humanity.

# The Knot

Colombo, Sri Lanka, 1981

No one had ever called Nila Mendis beautiful. That title belonged to her younger sister, Rupani, doe eyed and fair skinned – the jewel of her mother's heart. Nobody had ever called Nila smart either. That was her elder brother Herath, who was studying to be an engineer at Colombo University. No one had even described her as vivacious – no, all ebullience had been inherited by her other brother, Manoj, who seemed to use his gifts down by the street corner swindling shopkeepers or flirting with the girls who attended the convent down the road.

All earthly graces seemed to have escaped Nila's inheritance. Aunties, uncles, grandparents, neighbours and even her own parents murmured complaints, behind smallish hands that could hardly muffle loud voices. 'Oh, Nila,' they despaired, 'your parents simply don't have the money for a big enough dowry!'

Nila's fate would have been thus sealed, had Mrs Helma Vasha, their elderly Burgher neighbour, not taken an interest in the young child, who was all too often found at the well, crying at the slights daily heaped on her head. 'Come now, child, help me with my sewing,' Mrs Vasha would say as she led a sobbing Nila away.

By and by, the childless Mrs Vasha taught Nila everything she knew. She taught the young girl to sew by seaming saree remnants and offcuts. 'Never waste, child, learn to darn and draw life together by the tiniest of threads.'

She also taught Nila how to tat using a simple bobbin to make lace from hessian string taken from old gunnysacks. 'It doesn't matter what you start with,' Mrs Vasha insisted. 'It's what you make of it.'

Not that Nila's mother appreciated the time the good lady spent with her daughter as the years flew by. 'What good will sewing do her when she is married?' Vera Mendis snapped at Mrs Vasha once Nila reached a marriageable age of twenty-two. 'I'd rather she learn to spilt wood or shell coconuts. Looking the way she does, she cannot expect to find a rich husband who will let her spend her days making lace or decorating cushions!'

'It doesn't matter how you dress a pig,' her brother Manoj had jeered the day Nila wore a frock she'd made all by herself. 'A pig is still a pig.'

So Nila took her family quite by surprise that Thursday evening when she shuffled into the house holding her saree by bunching the yards of fabric together in her fists.

'What? You? A job? Doing what?' Manoj had asked incredulously, loungeing lazily on a planter's chair.

'It's actually an apprenticeship,' Nila called out as she dragged the tangled blue chiffon through the house, undoing the whole mess with relish in her room. 'At a saree mill.'

Unused to wearing saree for a full day, Nila had managed to step on her hem several times, despite Mrs Vasha's expert pinning, and the whole thing had almost come apart on the train.

'How did you get it?'

'Mrs Vasha's cousin has a friend at the mill,' Nila replied coming back into the main room that served both as a living and dining room.

'*Shah!* I didn't know Mrs Vasha found jobs for people. Maybe I should ask her to find me a job!' Manoj mocked. 'So tell me, what kind of place is this? Is it a bunch of old hags sitting around weaving? You'll fit right in!' he laughed as Nila went over to open the ornate armoire in the corner next to the dining table.

'They are all probably prettier than her,' Rupani giggled nastily from her spot at the head of the table, before looking archly at Manoj, 'but at least she's got a job. Something you haven't managed.'

Manoj stood up abruptly to pull Rupani's ear but was intercepted by their father, Mervan.

'Rupani does have a point. What happened to that interview you went to at the port?' Mervan asked, standing up to retie his threadbare sarong at his hips.

'Shiva Dhanapalan, he was a year ahead of me at school, got it.'

'Tamil?'

'Yes.'

'What about that job at the cement mercantile?'

'It's owned by a Tamil family and they don't hire Sinhalese.'

'This country is going to the dogs,' Mervan observed sourly. 'What about the job you went for at that rubber factory in Kurunagala? Have you heard back from them yet?'

'The job was given to the son of one of their businessmen in town,' Manoj replied glumly.

'What are you looking for, girl?' Vera asked Nila irritably when she moved aside the plate of dried fish Vera had been cleaning.

'That tablecloth I made last year,' Nila replied, setting down a stack of bedsheets and pillowslips.

'The large one with the ribbon you threaded through the bottom edge?'

'Yes.'

'I gave it to Rupani to make into a dress for temple. It's far too large for our little dining table,' Vera said offhandedly. Nila looked over at Rupani, who was indeed hemming a shapeless shift she'd fashioned from Nila's work.

'But Amma!'

'Don't you talk to me in that tone of voice!'

'But Amma, I needed that tablecloth! They asked me to bring samples of my work on Monday!'

'Why can't you take the other things you've made?'

'Like my blouse?' Nila cried. 'The one that Rupani accidentally poured tea all over the other day? Or the pillowcases that Manoj and Rupani used to catch fish down by the canal?'

'No need to get angry with me! If that tablecloth was so valuable, you should have said.'

Nila took a deep breath and sat down on the old mahogany chest by the doorway to the kitchen. 'Can I please have some money for some cloth, then?'

Vera grudgingly reached for the drawstring purse she kept tucked in the waistband of her underskirt.

'Amma, the *modalali* told me to remind you that there's still ten rupees outstanding from last month's grocery account.' Manoj stood abruptly with his hand outstretched to collect money for the local shopkeeper.

'Give the man five rupees and tell him I will settle the rest by the end of month,' Vera replied, rummaging for coins. As Manoj took off into the inky darkness, Nila knew he would not return till the early hours, half cut and reeking of beedee.

'Amma, I need a rupee for that botany trip next week,' Rupani piped up.

With a sigh, Vera tipped what was left in her drawstring purse into Rupani's outstretched hand as Nila's heart sank.

'Amma, what am I going to do?' Nila asked.

'How should I know? Maybe it's better you didn't go for this job at all!' Vera growled. 'Men don't like marrying women who have worked!'

Nila slumped on the old chest. This was always the way. She'd no sooner get an opportunity to escape her family than it was dashed away. Like the time she had been forced to miss her interview for teacher training college because she'd been needed to nurse Manoj through his first hangover.

'You think only of yourself, Nila! Your brother is dying and you want to go to an interview!' Vera had screamed.

Then there had been the time Nila had been asked to accompany the elderly Mrs Gamage from across the street to India on a pilgrimage. The older lady had said that there would be several wealthy people on the pilgrimage too who were looking for permanent companions. Only no one had been able to find Nila's birth certificate in time for the passport to be made. Several months later, Nila had found it among Rupani's things.

And just last month her mother had insisted she not accept a position as a trainee nurse at Colombo General Hospital.

'No decent man will want to marry a woman who has already seen another man naked. It is not respectable!' her mother had insisted.

Nila was trapped between respectability and an urgent need for respite from her home and family. And a job at a saree mill had been perfect. No one could fault that. Sure, she could ask Mrs Vasha for the money, but the widow was barely making ends meet herself. Just the other day Nila had found out that the old woman been reduced to taking her heart medication every second day instead of the prescribed daily dosage.

As she leant forward, holding her head in her hands, the lid of the chest she was sitting on creaked, sparking an errant thought into an idea. Nila jumped to her feet, threw open the lid and knelt down in front of the old box.

'Have you gone mad, girl? There is nothing in there for you!' Vera barked as Nila started to unpack the crockery.

'Look at all that dust!' Rupani sneezed as Nila sent clouds of it into the air.

What Nila was looking for was at the bottom of the camphor-lined ark, in among the yards and yards of moth-eaten sarees put in to cushion the crockery from unexpected bumps.

'Amma, may I have this?' Nila triumphantly asked her mother, lifting an old white cotton cloth from the very bottom.

It was a remnant left over from Rupani's layette, fragranced with dried jasmine – six yards of soft, white, fluffy cotton fabric – so fine that it was transparent, yet strong.

'Nila, this is old! Look – it's covered in stains!' Vera cried.

'I will work with what I have. May I have it?'

'As you wish,' Vera said – thinking Nila quite mad – as she went into the kitchen to see to the evening meal.

The day was young and cool but the cloudless sky above held the promise of the searing heat to come. As Nila walked up from Panadura station to the saree mill along the river road, her arms throbbed with pain and her legs tingled with discomfort. She had been up at the crack of dawn to draw forty pails of water from the well behind the house to fill the earthen jars that provided water for her family. She'd only had a quarter of an hour to get ready before her two-hour journey from Kotahena on the north side of Colombo to the little seaside town of Panadura some twenty miles away to the south.

Unused to wearing saree and without the help of Mrs Vasha so early in the morning, Nila had had to drape her saree herself. The result was poor, held together by innumerable pins, and she could barely take a step forward without tripping and falling. She had to kick the pleats out of the way as she walked so as not to step on them, which meant she wasn't walking to the mill but rather shuffling along at pace.

'*Aiya*, can you let me in? This is my first day,' Nila said a little breathlessly to the watcher at the gates of the mill.

'What's your name?' the man asked brusquely.

'Nila Mendis.'

The man tore his eyes away from the road to look Nila up and down with disdain before opening the large rusty gate. Nila paid him no mind – she was used to being dismissed for her dumpy figure, unfashionably dark skin and the odd-shaped eyes that sat on her face at angles to each other.

The saree mill was a large old Dutch house built at the turn of the eighteenth century to house the visiting members of the van Rickles family, whose interests stretched from Persia to the Solomon Islands.

Once the Dutch left Ceylon in 1802, the house had been taken over by an administrator from the British East India Trading Company, a perpetually sunburnt bachelor who felt more at ease with the natives than with his own kind. He preferred to catch the weekend packet to Ceylon than risk the matchmaking mamas of the Madras social circuit.

Nadesan Nair, a shrewd young Tamil, often accompanied the memsahib to his island retreat in Ceylon. Nadesan had started working for the British man as a valet, but worked his way up to become his chief native clerk in the Madras. While the ageing trader saw peace and solitude in the river, and the estuary just beyond – both teeming with fish, crabs, prawns and the seabirds that preyed on them – Nadesan saw unbridled opportunity.

The river was, in fact, perfect for washing and dyeing sarees. The cool brisk sea breeze would make small work of drying thick hanks of cotton even during the wettest of humid monsoons. The wide verandahs that encircled the house were perfect spaces for weavers. Protected from the elements, they could work the heavy looms in comfort with the silk and cotton feeder threads running the full length of the house.

And the ballroom that had once been the glittering salon was a spacious enough for artisans to embroider or block print sarees. The library at the back of the house could be converted into a change room, complete with ornate mirrors, so that the saree makers could see how their work would be transformed by the female form.

So when the old man started making noises about wanting to move back to England and see his motherland before he died, Nair had made him an offer he could not refuse, for he had been saving half his salary for many years.

Nair had moved to the island with his widowed mother and young wife. In Ceylon he would make his fortune unencumbered by the caste pecking order; caste did not seem to matter as much on the Buddhist island. The daring enterprise nearly went bankrupt several times in the first twenty years – the first lot of sarees sold to the *modalalis* of Kandy had all arrived in their stores moth-eaten and mildewed – but more than a hundred years later, the fourth generation of Nair saree makers were still the *chetties* of the mill.

Nila shuffled along nervously and stood with the chattering group of sixteen or so young women and men who were waiting outside the mill.

'I am so glad I got this job,' one girl babbled. 'My father died two years ago, and my mother could really do with the money.'

'What are you good at?' another girl asked coolly. She was dressed in a crisp pink chiffon saree that was meticulously ironed and draped. The *potta* was carefully pleated and pinned to her shoulder and cascading down her back in a narrow stream. 'I won the Gampaha district batik dyeing competition two years running. You may have heard of me. My name is Renuka Weeraratne.'

She looked around to see blank stares but was interrupted by a petite, bouncy country girl filled with dimples and smiles. 'I do macramé. I have been selling my work at the Nuwara Eliya craft market for some time now,' she giggled.

'My mother won't let me sell my work. She says that common people don't appreciate its artistic value,' Renuka said.

'So are you planning on keeping all the sarees you make here, then?'

'Yes, actually. I am getting married next June and my mother thought it would be lovely if I could do all the sarees for my trousseau.'

'Why? Can't your family afford to buy them for you?' a third girl asked brazenly. She was dressed in a pale floral saree that glowed next to her dusky skin. Unlike Renuka in her pink chiffon, she'd only pinned one edge of her saree to the back of her shoulder, letting the *potta* cascade over her like a fine sheen of water.

Renuka's eyes narrowed and she opened her mouth to deliver a stinging rebuke, but quickly shut it again. For while everybody had been distracted getting to know each other, nobody had noticed the big wooden door of the mansion swinging open.

A tall woman in a purple saree stood before them, holding the heavy mahogany door wide open. 'Come through,' she said in a deep, melodious voice, and they all filed in obediently.

'*Kaalai va nakkam, Aibuwan*, welcome to Nair & Sons Sarees – the only full-production saree house in Ceylon. My name is Gauri Nair and my father owns this company,' the woman said, inclining her head gently towards a framed picture of a bespectacled old man with many Shiva stripes of holy ash on his forehead.

'You are here because you may have the talent to be a saree maker. A master saree maker. To be a master, you must be able to design, weave, dye, work and drape a saree. Five skills – *pancha dakshata*. You will be taught all those skills here in the next six months and you will need to master all five of them before the exhibition in September. There are only four positions with the mill on offer and you need to win a place in the exhibition to earn one.'

Miss Gauri bowed deeply to a fair-skinned middle-aged woman who'd just come through an anteroom from the back of the house.

'Guru Lakshmi is our master designer. She will show you how to transform that picture in your head into fluid fabric.'

'Is this the new group, Gauri?' the woman asked.

'Yes, Guru,' Miss Gauri replied.

'Just make sure they are in time for the pooja,' Guru Lakshmi sniffed. She looked pointedly from the large clock

behind Miss Gauri to the road outside and then back at Miss
Gauri. The guru sniffed again before gliding away to the salon
behind her. Nila counted five students in the back room, waiting
eagerly, their sharpened pencils poised over large design boards.

Miss Gauri turned on her heel and walked off briskly, the
members of the group scurrying behind her like mice. Out on
the verandah, she nodded towards a bald dwarf dressed in a
white sarong and tunic.

'Now, Guru Sindhu here will teach you how to spin and
weave,' Miss Gauri sang, picking up a puff of raw cotton from a
large bale. 'He'll teach you the magic of the *baana* and *thaana* –
how to treadle a loom and create cloth from fluff.' A coterie of
barefooted weavers click-clacked away on the verandah, their
rhythmic slapping adding the bass to Gauri's melody.

The guru was too busy threading a large complicated loom to
give the new group anything beyond the barest of nods, though
he too looked briefly at the road and back at Miss Gauri.

She danced away again, leading the group out through the
house and down to the river, where sarees of every hue were
being dyed in great vats of pigments over open fires. 'Guru
Hirantha here is our dye master – he'll teach you how make
the colours of the sun from the fruit of the earth,' Miss Gauri
called out. She pointed to a hulking bare-chested man who was
stirring a vat with a massive paddle. It was a hypnotic sight –
yards and yards of fabric gently boiling away in the vats, iridescent blues, bright magentas, ruby reds and eye-watering yellows
all competing for attention against the verdant backdrop of the
emerald river – and a few of the students stood transfixed.

'Come along now,' Miss Gauri sang out, smiling, and made
her way towards a small clearing near the river. In the centre of
the clearing, surrounded by thick green shrubs, was an amphitheatre with the statues of the gods Saraswati Devi and Lord
Ganapathi on a central dais. 'There is a formal shrine in the
house,' Gauri said, 'but this is where I love to pray. I feel closer
to her here.'

'Her? Surely you are praying to Lord Ganapathi?' Renuka asked, pointing to the elephant-headed god.

'No, Saraswati Devi is our patron goddess. She takes care of artists, weavers and musicians – those who create something out of nothing. We start every morning with prayers in the main temple but try to come down here every few days to pray to her.'

'I am coming here to learn how to weave sarees, not to become a Hindu,' Renuka muttered as the group moved on. 'Tamils are like that, you know – they like to make everyone like them.'

'I come from Kotahena – I have no problems with Hindus,' Nila said, distracted. She'd been almost dumbstruck by the beauty of the statue of the goddess. Carved from white marble, it was almost lifelike. In the flickering early morning light, Nila had imagined that the goddess smiled at her.

'My best friend is Tamil. We grew up together. They are no different to us,' said a girl in a yellow saree as they all made their way back into the house. 'My name is Devika, by the way.'

'I am Nila.'

The little dimpled country girl who had spoken earlier introduced herself too. 'My name is Punsala,' she said.

There was no further time for introductions as Miss Gauri led them into a large shrine room on the eastern side of the house, where Guru Lakshmi, Guru Hirantha and Guru Sindhu were already seated facing the stone deities. They were joined by another woman, tall and svelte.

'This is Guru Sakunthala, she will teach you all the skills of embroidery, block printing, appliqué, lace making and saree blouse stitching,' Miss Gauri informed them, but she sounded vague now, her eyes straying towards the gate. The members of the group had started to mimic her, ducking and peering around each other for a glimpse of the road, though nobody quite knew who they were looking for.

'I will have to introduce you to your draping master later,' Miss Gauri finished quietly.

Everyone sat on the floor, as with a very audible grunt of displeasure, Guru Sindhu bowed his head deeply and started his chant, first addressing Lord Ganapathi.

'*Om gam Ganapataye namaha! Om gam Ganapataye namaha! Om gam Ganapataye namaha!*'

Nila wasn't usually given to serious religious practice. Members of the Mendis household visited the local Buddhist temple each full moon, for Poya, but did not disturb its saffron-robed officials at any time in between. Nila was pleasantly surprised now by the rhythmic beauty of the Hindu chant of praise. Her eyes closed of their own volition, her body swaying as the tempo changed and the more melodic dedication to the goddess Saraswati began.

'*Om aim maha Saraswatyai namaha! Om aim maha Saraswatyai namaha! Om aim maha Saraswatyai namaha!*'

Nila was so carried away that she didn't notice the deep rumbling noise of the motorcycle as it roared up the river road. She didn't even notice the loud backfiring until the chanting in the temple died away, and was the last to join the rustle and tussle to get a good view of the commotion.

Out the front, just inside the mansion's gate, a tall, broad-shouldered man dressed in a riding jacket and a crisp, low-slung white sarong helped a young white woman alight from the monstrously large machine. To the scandalised horror of everyone watching, the woman flung herself at him, pulling his head down to kiss him on the lips.

'*Deyo Buddhu sale!*' Punsala shrieked.

He gently disentangled himself from her before firmly sending her on her way out through the gates of the mill to the little track that led down to the tourist huts on the beach just beyond.

'What a rake!' Renuka said under her breath.

As he turned around, he shrugged off his jacket to reveal his

Saliya Brahmin thread – a thick white cord encircling his right shoulder and muscled torso. On his left shoulder was a large tattoo of a spider bearing a lotus on its back.

'Handsome devil!' Devika whispered to Nila.

'That is your saree draping master,' Gauri sang as the man drew close. 'My brother, Guru Raju.'

If Saturday mornings were Nila's favourite time of the week, it was surely because the afternoons were the time she liked the least. Week after week, month after month, for nearly two years now, Saturday afternoons were when prospective grooms came to the Mendis household to inspect its wares. And week after week, month after month, year after year, young men would turn their eyes away from Nila and look besottedly at her sister instead.

'So is your mother going to send Anoja to me this afternoon?' Mrs Vasha asked as Nila walked through a decidedly large hole in the stick fence that separated the two houses. Mrs Vasha always referred to the younger Mendis sister by her given name, Anoja, instead of her nickname, Rupani, which meant *beautiful*. It'd been Nila herself who'd coined the nickname after seeing how pretty her sister was as a baby, but Mrs Vasha bristled whenever she heard it, saying the young girl had enough airs as it was.

Nila sighed. 'No, she says she needs Rupani's help with the tea things.'

'What utter nonsense! Anoja wouldn't know the pouring end of a teapot from the end of a broomstick! The only reason your mother keeps her there is to see if one of your grooms will offer for your sister instead!' Mrs Vasha harrumphed as she sat down on the concrete step at the back of her kitchen next to Nila.

'Well, almost all of them have,' Nila said.

'The only reason your mother has not parted with Anoja is that none of them have been wealthy enough!'

'I thought the Obesekera boy's family made a respectable offer,' Nila said as she picked up a clove and wrapped the pointy end in faille tissue. This was their Saturday ritual – Mrs Vasha would help Nila wrap cloves for the grooms while discussing their potential. Nimal, Mrs Vasha's skinny servant boy, loitered about sweeping the garden, stopping periodically to scratch his wormy bottom or to finger his slingshot.

'No matter how much I feed him, he does not put on weight,' Mrs Vasha muttered as the lad went about his business. 'But you're right, it was a *very* good offer for your sister! The Obesekera family is a very respectable family.'

'But poor. Their land has been pawned to educate the relatives, who are all in government jobs.'

'Think about the respectability, Nila. To be a Mrs Obesekera of the Obesekeras of Ragama. What a fine thing it would have been!'

'Respectability won't pay for gold bangles or pretty sarees,' Nila pointed out gently as she laid out the wrapped cloves.

'It was her duty to accept. To help your mother, at least . . .'

'But she is young. The fear of being unmarried has not yet overcome the fear of not marrying a rich man – one who can afford many servants.'

Mrs Vasha grunted as she reached out for another handful of cloves to wrap. 'What is your view on the lad coming today? Are you hopeful, or will you call for Anoja even before the tea is served?'

'Oh, Mrs Vasha – I am always hopeful, and I don't always resort to Rupani to distract my suitors,' Nila chided. 'I was utterly hopeful, even when the matchmaker brought the Devasinghes' proposal. Hopeful that Siridasa Devasinghe would turn up sober! But alas, no – he fell asleep in an alcoholic fog no sooner than he'd slipped off his smelly slippers and sat down in Father's chair!'

Mrs Vasha laughed.

'I was even hopeful when the *kapuwa* brought the Edira-singhe proposal . . .'

'Surely you don't mean Gunawardene Edirasinghe?'

Nila nodded, smiling.

'When did this happen, Nila? When? But how could your mother even entertain the idea . . . why, everybody knows . . .'

'It happened while you were away in Nuwara Eliya visiting your sister, and yes, everyone from here to the turnpike at Nugegoda knows that Gunawardene Edirasinghe was dropped on his head by his ayah as a baby.'

'Your mother would marry you to a tree! Are you quite resigned to never marry, then?'

'Does it matter, as long as I can pay my way? Did you know that the English word *spinster* used to refer to a woman who could live independently because by spinning she could earn a living equal to that of a man? I like that idea.'

'And especially so since your favourite class is spinning and weaving?'

'Guru Sindhu is a genius!' Nila said. 'He understands each fibre, each fabric and each thread that goes into each saree! He understands how the *baana* and *thaana* should be threaded, depending on whether you are weaving a saree for a matron or a young lady . . . and . . . and . . . and he is so kind!'

'You are quite taken with him, then?'

'As I am with all the teachers!' Nila confessed. 'It's just that Guru Sindhu told me quietly the other day that I would be his choice for one of the four places on offer!'

'Well done! Oh, I am so happy for you! I can't wait to see your mother sit up and take proper notice of you when you bring in five hundred rupees a month!'

'But Mrs Vasha . . . I am not doing so well in the other classes,' Nila told her anxiously.

'I thought everybody loved your work!'

'Not all,' Nila said, remembering her first day at the saree mill.

Nila had found herself in a group with four others: Devika, Renuka, Punsala and a young man from Kandy called Rangana, who had terrible scars on the right side of his face. Their first class had been with Guru Sindhu, the dwarf weaving master.

'It's better that you are in small groups,' the guru said. 'I hate teaching big groups. I never know if my students quite hear what I am saying or if they can even see me! Today I will cover the basics of fabric making. We'll spend the first two weeks on spinning and the rest of the next four months on weaving. We leave the last month for you to work on your exhibition piece.'

The guru spent the next two hours describing the fibres used in making handmade sarees – cotton and silk – and the varying grades and qualities and where they came from. 'Now, you were told to bring some samples of your work – show me what you've brought.'

One by one, each of them brought forth their offering. Renuka volunteered first, of course, taking out a large bundle of batik murals and hangings from the large carry bag that she'd been carting all over the mill. She laid her work out on the only table in the room as if she were exhibiting at a grand fair, flourishing each piece, laying some on angles while draping others to great effect. Once she was done, she invited all to see, smiling coquettishly as everybody showered her with admiring *shahs* and *aahs*.

'Excellent use of colour and shading – excellent!' the guru said. 'You are a very talented young lady. Talented indeed!'

Punsala went next, shyly presenting a range of macramé toys and a hanging vase she'd made. 'Oh, but this is just wonderful,' Guru Sindhu cried. 'See how she's used different thread of different weights and stretch for the different animals? A peacock is of course proud and stiff, so she's used the heavy raffia. Whereas an elephant – it is majestic, while still being gentle and kind – so she's used a soft cotton! This shows the child has a good understanding of her base material!'

The Guru beamed with pleasure. 'Devika, what have you brought for us?' he asked.

Wordlessly, Devika pulled out a hessian-covered scroll from her bag. The hessian was so dirty and stained that Mrs Vasha would hardly use it for rags, Nila thought dubiously, as Devika gently unrolled the parcel on the floor. Without much fanfare, the young woman passed around piece after piece of delicately hand-painted silk. 'The oily hessian keeps the silk supple by not letting it dry out and the dirt traps in more of the moisture,' she explained.

If Renuka's work had elicited exuberant praise, then Devika's work drew thoughtful silence – for each piece was subtle as it was beautiful. And when Punsala expressed fear of soiling the work with her dirty hands, Devika protested, 'What is the use of beautiful things if they cannot be touched? They must be practical, not just beautiful!'

'Mistress Devika has just expounded the key principles of saree making. There is no point creating a beautiful saree if it cannot be touched or handled – indeed, it is a garment that *needs* to be handled,' Guru Sindhu said with a grave little smile. 'And Guru Hirantha will be pleased to have you in his class, Devika. I think you just may be skilled enough to take on *kalamkari* – an ancient saree painting technique. Each saree is made in seventeen steps and its trademark glossiness comes from being soaked in milk and resin.'

'Guru, I don't think I belong here . . .' Rangana stammered uneasily. 'I don't even know why they asked me to come,' the young man said, rising to leave.

'Why, *puthay*? What talent do you possess?'

'None. My old dance master knew someone here and he got me the job.'

'Ah! I know about you. You were the dancer who got

injured in the Kandy Perehera festival last year. *Puthay*, have
your injuries healed?'

'Yes . . .' Rangana replied, looking away. 'I am healed,
but . . .'

'But you can still dance, yes?'

'Of course!'

'If you could show us but a few steps?'

'I won't dance to amuse some silly girls!' Rangana roared as
everybody leapt back in surprise.

'I don't see any silly girls here,' the guru said.

'These girls *are* silly. You've got Miss Queen there with her
batik, another who likes to pull strings, and a third who likes
to paint on cloth! All silly girls!'

'Not silly girls, talented girls.'

'I don't see anything creative – they are just mimicking what
they've seen. There is not a single original thought in any of
their *kohu* heads!'

'Each of us starts by copying, Rangana. You copy the
masters until you yourself are masterful.'

'I am a master! A master of my craft!'

'Show me, then,' the guru said curtly, turning away to give
a sharp clap. 'Show me that you are a master of something!
Because right now you are behaving like an arrogant fool.' The
guru clapped again, his back to the dancer, and kept clapping,
with a sharp staccato beat. A goading beat.

With a grimace, Rangana took off his shirt and firmly retied
his blue sarong around his lean hips. Nila had to smother a
gasp of horror at the sight of his mangled body. The scars
that covered the right side of his face extended to his torso
and arms; tortured skin and flesh showed up black where the
rivers of hot oil had gouged their path downwards. He'd had
an accident with flares dipped in oil, which had meant to be the
centre piece of the pageant.

Rangana moved fluidly into first position as the guru turned
around, his outstretched arms forming a perfect arch; then, as

the guru kept clapping, he moved into second position, then third, his dancer's body moving sinuously to the beat, not stopping till he reached the final position, the eighteenth, and finished gracefully, his chin jutting out arrogantly.

'There is very little difference between a dancer and a weaver . . . the movements need the same grace and versatility,' the guru said. 'It requires the same dedication, *puthay* . . . And practice!'

Rangana nodded curtly and looked away.

'And now, quickly, to the final member of our group, before I send you to see Guru Lakshmi . . . your name is Nila, is that right, *puthay*?'

To say that Nila was intimidated would be a lie – she was terrified. She could never make anything to match the beauty of Devika and Renuka's work – or Rangana's dance. She pulled out Rupani's layette that she'd embroidered over the weekend and steeled her heart for the smirks of derision.

'Guru Sindhu! Guru Sindhu! I am so sorry!' Guru Lakshmi said loudly, bustling into the room. 'I have to finish a commission today, so I need to start my class a little early. Can you please send the group through?'

Renuka cast a single dismissive glance at Nila's work before following Guru Lakshmi through the door. Punsala looked torn but followed Renuka. Rangana stood a little aside to stretch his scorched muscles. Only Devika waited with Nila to hear what Guru Sindhu had to say.

He took the saree and held it up to the light, turning it this way and that, smiling at the delicate hand embroidery and the ribbon detailing Nila had used to hide the discolouration. As he inspected the fall of the saree, feeling the weight of the decoration used to create the dramatic floral motif, his face broke out into a beatific smile of joy.

'*Puthay*, did you do this by yourself?'

Nila blinked.

'Are your parents Saliyas?'

Nila was confused. What was a Saliya?

'Guru Sindhu – please send the rest of the group through,' Guru Lakshmi called irritably.

'Just a minute! Nila, do you know where this cloth comes from?'

'It was an old cloth that has been in the family for many years.'

'This is from the Bombay cotton mills – it is impossible to find such fine cotton today. Most of the mills were dismantled after Independence.'

'Guru Sindhu – I am waiting!'

Rangana slipped his shirt back on and hurried out of the room.

'Now tell me, who taught you how to—'

'Guru Sindhu, I really can't wait any longer!'

Guru Sindhu let out a sigh of exasperation. 'We'll chat later. Go, *puthay*, go,' he said, hastening them out the door.

If Guru Sindhu had been full of praise, Guru Lakshmi was utterly dour. 'What is the point of looking at any work that has not been properly designed,' she grunted, not even deigning to look at the students' proffered samples.

'Flow and structure,' she told them. 'You have to define what you want your saree to do before you even start thinking about fabric, colour, embroidery or any such silliness! And practise. You must practise designing to be any good at it. Flow and structure, flow and structure.'

The third and final class for the morning had been with Guru Hirantha, the jolly dye master. He explained the colour wheel and took everyone through the basics of dyeing, including the history and sources of the dyes used at the mill.

He smiled and inclined his head towards Nila with respect when he inspected her work, but he was effusive in his praise of Renuka's batik, marvelling at her skill. 'Oh – we are going to have fabulous fun, Mistress Renuka, you and I, yes we are! To have someone else interested in dyeing – this will be fun!' he giggled.

Miss Gauri made an appearance again at lunch to discuss their sleeping arrangements and allocate them to rooms at the large boarding house next door.

'But I wasn't planning on boarding,' Nila said to Devika in horror as Miss Gauri handed out room numbers. 'I didn't even know you could board.'

'I have to board,' Punsala said. 'It takes me eight hours each way. Besides, this is the first time I have ever been to Colombo. I am so excited. I can't wait to have some adventures!'

'I don't have a choice either.' Devika shrugged. 'I came down yesterday and stayed with my uncle in Moratuwa – but I can't stay with him all the time.'

'My parents won't let me board,' Renuka drawled from the next table. 'They are organising for my old ayah to stay with me in a house here in town.'

'Nila Mendis.' Miss Gauri smiled as she came around. 'It says on your form that you live in Kotahena. It's about a two-hour trip from here, is it not? You may board or come from home each day. I would advise you to board, but it is up to you.'

Nila inclined her head, not quite sure what to say. Her mother would never consent to let her board. Who would help her with the housework? There was no time to think about it, though, for the next class started immediately after lunch, in the cool shade of the eastern salon of the house.

'I am so sorry,' Guru Sakunthala apologised as they arrived. 'It will be most difficult for you to concentrate after that fine lunch of rice and sambar – so why don't we allow ourselves a little rest before we start, hmm?' She gracefully sat down on one of the half-dozen or so planter's chairs scattered around the room and closed her eyes. Unsure quite what to do, Nila, Devika and Rangana followed suit. Renuka, however, sat primly on her chair, though she did close her eyes.

'Now wasn't that lovely?' Guru Sakunthala murmured, rousing her class from their slumber after about fifteen minutes.

'I find these brief breaks very refreshing. At least it's better than trying to push through with a class of glazed-eyed students who are barely taking anything in!'

The guru proved to be as practical as she was beautiful and wise. She took the group through the various saree embellishment techniques, ranging from silk painting to block printing, from embroidery to cutwork design with gold thread. 'We'll also spend four weeks on the principles of saree blouse design,' she told them.

Her inspection of their samples before the next class was only brief. She'd allotted the same amount of time to it as the other teachers, but Renuka monopolised the time to such an extent that no one else got a look in.

'I want to become a master embroiderer, Miss Sakunthala. I studied under a few embroidery teachers in Kandy, but I need to learn so much more! Do you offer private classes? My parents would be more than willing to pay! Please have a look at my batik – do you think the skills would transfer?'

The final class of the day was with the colourful Guru Raju. Unlike the other classes, it was not held with the smaller group of five but with the much larger group of sixteen. Some at the mill gossiped that Guru Raju had arranged it this way to avoid spending too much time there. They said he preferred to waste his days in idleness and dissipation down by the beach, where fishermen's huts were set up as backpacker hostels, filled with exotic Western women with their hippie clothes and fair skin.

'So this is our group of novitiates?' Guru Raju drawled as he strolled into the large room at the back of the house. 'Don't call me Guru, by the way. It makes me feel old!'

'Now, let's look at the saree draping techniques we have on offer here,' he said as he carefully looked over the girls in the group. Normally, Nila would have felt very self-conscious being inspected so carefully, but Guru Raju's gaze was detached and academic, and with her many pins and poorly draped saree it wasn't as if she would be singled out for attention.

Which was why she nearly jumped out of her skin with surprise when Raju tapped her on the shoulder as he went past, indicating that she should join Devika and Renuka at the front of the room along with two other girls, Ramini and Mala, whom she had met at lunch.

'Let's look at the Ossareeya drape of the saree first,' he said, indicating that Ramini and Mala should step forward. 'An excellent saree drape to preserve the modesty of the wearer, though not very practical if one is in a hurry or needs to do any serious work. Legend has it that the pleats we see on the outside were attempts made by noble Kandyan ladies to mimic the wide-hipped dresses of the Portuguese women who first visited Ceylonese shores in the sixteenth and seventeenth centuries.'

He went on to dissect the style in which the two women had draped their sarees, complimenting and critiquing in the same breath.

'Now let's move onto the most popular way to drape a saree – the classical *nivi* style. Here we have three women who've attempted it – each with a very different interpretation.' Raju laid a gentle hand on Renuka's shoulder. 'What's your name, *nangi?*'

'Renuka,' she said, looking at him coquettishly through the corners of her eyes.

'Renuka has a very traditional interpretation. It is precise and proper. It does not reveal anything about who she is or what she brings to the world.'

Though his voice was soft and quiet, it was plainly a criticism, and Renuka looked stunned.

'Now, this young lady here,' Raju said as he moved over to Devika, 'has a more interesting way of styling her *nivi*. While she does have the confidence to wear her fall without a pin,' he said as he stood behind her, 'she is quite sloppy at pleating and tucking in.' He turned Devika around to demonstrate.

'And to our final model,' he announced as he moved to stand behind Nila. She was sure he could hear her heart rate accelerating with fear at the thought of what he would say about her.

'If I had to characterise this drape in two words, it would be ignorance and fear. See how she's tried to draw her saree so that it accentuates shape, but then left the drape gaping? Now that is ignorance.'

He pulled at her fall. 'And fear! Look at how many pins she's used to pin her fall into place – I am counting six just from her bustline to her shoulder!' he said.

Renuka let out a loud guffaw of laughter and a few others tittered along with her.

'Can you even walk, *nangi*?' Raju asked Nila, noticing the stiffness of the drape around her legs. There was another ripple of laughter, and he turned to glare the class into silence. 'This young lady just needs to practise. And that is what we're all going to do now. I want you to pair up and drape each other's sarees!'

And with that the first class in saree draping started in earnest, Nila and Devika automatically pairing up to practise on each other.

'And that is where I am having trouble,' Nila explained fretfully to Mrs Vasha. 'I need to practise, but how can I when I barely get home in time for dinner and then I am up just a few hours later to draw the water and make rotis?'

'How about when you come home? You are home by six-thirty, aren't you?'

'Yes, but then I have to help make dinner, which takes us well past eight-thirty!'

'Have you asked your mother if you could board?'

'I did, but she insists that she needs my help at home.' Just then she heard her mother's call from the kitchen step.

'Nila! Nila! Where are you, girl? You'd better come in and get ready before the groom comes!'

'Nila, leave it to me,' Mrs Vasha announced as Nila stood up, collecting the cloves and tissue. 'I will make sure you are allowed to board.'

'Mrs Vasha, what are you going to do?'

The old woman gently reached up to smooth out the frown on Nila's brow and patted her cheek. 'Haven't I always looked after you, hmm?' she whispered gently.

If ever there was a class for quiet conversation, it should be design class run by Guru Lakshmi, the taciturn art teacher. But that would require bravery and boldness beyond Nila's ken, for Guru Lakshmi not only discouraged conversation by her glacial stares but also had a nasty reputation for violence meted out with a simple hand fan.

Her carved wooden fan looked innocuous enough – why, a carved sandalwood hand fan was the pedestrian possession of every housewife on the island from Galle to Jaffna, and young children were known to associate its cooling breeze with afternoon naps – but in Guru Lakshmi's hands, it was a weapon of torture. Poorly drawn lines and sloppy designs earned their creators sharp whacks across the head. Missed homework was rewarded with sharp raps over the knuckles. And conversations in class, oh my goodness – well, they resulted in sharp slaps that left indentations of the carvings on the cheeks of both interlocutors!

It was equally difficult to talk during the dyeing class. Handling the heavy paddles of the dyeing vats and measuring precise quantities of dye required concentration. Notwithstanding, the noxious fumes made any real dialogue as uncomfortable as it was downright hazardous.

But Nila did not want to wait till lunch to share her news with her best friend, so it would be the noisy yet convivial weaving class in which they finally spoke, albeit between the slap slap of the looms. She'd been running late that morning and had already missed prayers and design.

'*Bung*, what's going on?' Devika demanded as soon as Nila slipped onto the bench of the adjoining loom, coming from the direction of the administration office.

'Has anyone told you it's rude to be so demanding?' Renuka said. There were four looms in the long corridor with a fifth just around the corner. 'My mother says that only people from low birth are demanding – because it is their way to survive!'

'And didn't your mother also explain to you that it is rude to interrupt another's conversation?' Devika snapped.

'I am being allowed to board!' Nila told everyone excitedly as she unwound the cotton she was using as weft for her boat shuttle. Nila was working on a toile for a cotton day saree.

'But I thought you came from a respectable family!' Renuka said, feigning concern. 'Isn't your father a postmaster? Or were you lying just to give yourself airs?'

'Can you mind your own business?' Devika said. 'This conversation is between Nila and I!'

'I was only asking because I am concerned. Anything could happen in that boarding house!'

'What exactly? There are locks on the doors and a night watcher.'

'But you come from a respectable family, Nila,' Renuka protested again, staring down her nose at Devika and Punsala.

'Are you saying that we're not respectable?' Devika cried, and Punsala's eyes flashed fire.

'It is barely past nine in the morning and you girls have already given me a headache!' Rangana shouted. 'Shut up!'

Before the girls could reply, the weaving master arrived and soon they were caught up in their lesson, with only the odd glare being exchanged behind his back.

'I know most of us like to think of a saree as a garment of glamour,' Guru Sindhu said, 'made of pure silk or the finest brushed cotton, but that is a newfangled thing. No, sarees should be made for purpose. Neither pure silk or soft cotton would be of any use to the *respectable* women who work the rice fields to fill our bellies,' he said, giving Renuka the briefest of glances. 'Women who work the field are in as much need of good sarees as the ladies who sip tea and gossip in their salons,' he went on, treading the loom and adjusting the counter-weights. And then the dwarf started to dance.

For weaving was indeed dancing for the tiny master. He was too small to command the loom seated and it would be too onerous to work the pulleys and levers turn after turn with his misshapen body. Guru Sindhu had instead taught himself to weigh the loom such that he climbed the entire frame and used his weight to move the fabric forward, his arms pushing the shuttle forwards and backwards as if he were strumming a sitar. Up and down the little man moved – fluid, supple fabric the fruit of his motion.

'Now your turn.' The dwarf bowed to invite his students to take up the challenge of weaving as he had done.

'So, what made your mother change her mind?' Devika demanded as soon as Guru Sindhu's footfalls became a soft echo.

'It's who rather than what . . .' Nila grunted as she threaded her bobbin through and pushed the lamms backward and forward to tighten the weft of her fabric.

Early on Sunday morning just as the family had finished their bed teas, Nimal, Mrs Vasha's young servant boy, had ambushed Vera Mendis in her dressing-gown. '*Nona*, my Madame wants to know if she may visit you this afternoon for tea?' the boy had yelled from the rain stoop as he scratched his wormy bottom.

'Of course she may,' Vera replied loudly, all confused. Mrs Vasha usually just asked Vera through the open window of the living room if she could pop over.

She was certainly taken back that afternoon when Mrs Vasha came a visiting, not through the holey fence at the back

of the house, which was her usual practice, but through the
front door, with Nimal settling his wriggling rear on the rain
stoop like a loyal page.

'*Aibuwan, aibuwan,* Vera, you are well I assume?' Mrs
Vasha asked very politely as she slipped off her heeled saree
slippers and walked into the house. The elderly Burgher lady
was dressed in an elegant cream and gold saree with her silver
hair up neatly in a precise bun. Her fair skin was dusted with a
fine sheen of lavender talcum, not that her fair skin needed any
lightening; her Dutch and Portuguese ancestry giving her the
fair complexion envied by millions.

Vera nodded vigorously, suddenly feeling decidedly gauche
in her pale green at-home as her mind flashed back to a scene
in this very room some thirty years previously, when she had
first met Mrs Vasha as a coltish nineteen-year-old bride.

'I have come here today to discuss an undertaking of a
serious nature,' Mrs Vasha said. 'Nimal, why don't you go and
put your slingshot to good use? I believe Mrs Mendis can't
reach the *jumbu* on the top branches of her tree and there is
some ripe fruit up there.' As the little boy left the room, she
turned to Vera again. 'If you don't mind, I shall sit down. I am
not as young as I used to be.'

Vera jumped to clear the settee of the clothes she had been
sorting for mending, stuffing Mervan's torn loincloths in
between the husk-filled cushions.

'I won't object to a cup of tea, my dear,' Mrs Vasha said.
'I believe my boy told you I was coming for tea?'

Vera turned, completely rattled, looking around for Nila or
Rupani to order them to do her bidding, only to see both girls
rush off to the kitchen.

'Now, as you know, my sister lives in Nuwara Eliya. She
is closely acquainted with the Ranasinghes of Bandarawela.
You must know of them, of course? Everybody does. They
are an old tea family. You came from Bandarawela originally,
didn't you?'

Vera opened her mouth to respond, but Mrs Vasha cut her off. 'The particulars don't matter, I suppose,' Mrs Vasha drawled condescendingly. 'It's just that I received a letter from my sister on Friday asking me if I could board their youngest daughter with me. She's just received an appointment as a teacher at the convent and this is such an easy distance to the school. But as you know, I am barely managing myself, so I thought it best that I find somewhere else for her to board. She is such a lovely girl, Piyasili Ranasinghe, so well educated and accomplished. Her parents will only let her down to Colombo for the week and they expect her back home each weekend . . .'

Again, Vera opened her mouth to respond, but Mrs Vasha cut her off again. 'Did I mention that Piyasili will have her ayah come down to Colombo with her each week? Such a well brought up girl, her parents would never hear of her coming to town all by herself without a chaperone.'

Vera shifted her weight from foot to foot, desperate to get a word in, but Mrs Vasha continued like the rising tide washing against the port of Colombo.

'The family will be happy to pay handsomely for their daughter to board with a respectable family. They mentioned that they would not even consider paying less than 500 rupees a month.'

Vera put her hand to her throat – it was almost half of Mervan's monthly salary.

'There is a small problem, though,' Mrs Vasha said as Nila came out with the tea things. Her eyes lit up mischievously as they met Nila's over the steaming brew. 'I doubt young Miss Ranasinghe is used to sharing. She has a room all of her own at her father's house, complete with an attached bathroom.'

Vera's demeanour changed rapidly, scowling.

'I can see you are not happy about this,' Mrs Vasha observed, draining her tea rapidly. 'Clearly I have come to the wrong house. It's just as well I told Mrs Gamage from across the road that I'd visit this afternoon. She does have room to spare, and,

I hear that young Albert Gamage is coming back on holiday in a few weeks. What a lovely thing it would be if they were to, you know . . . meet, and something should happen,' Mrs Vasha said conspiratorially to Vera. 'I mean Piyasili Ranasinghe does come with a large dowry. Nearly one lakh, I hear. What a fine thing it would be for our young Albert!'

Vera grabbed Mrs Vasha by the arm as she turned to go, her look of undiluted horror assuring Mrs Vasha of her victory.

'It is agreed, then. I shall bring Piyasili tomorrow myself and help her get settled here,' Mrs Vasha announced, the fall of her saree trailing on the ground behind her as she left, Nimal wriggling and squiggling as he followed.

'So, I spent the rest of Sunday cleaning out my room. I was so tired I missed my alarm this morning. My mother would have evicted me yesterday, if I had anywhere to go,' Nila told Devika dryly as she wound her toile around the beam at the back of the loom.

'It is a pity we cannot share, our dorm room is already full,' Devika sighed, clasping Nila's hand.

'I think it is a pity that your mother is letting a stranger into your house,' Renuka said. 'Does your family really need the money so badly that they would throw you out in favour of some unknown girl?'

'No one wants to know what you think, Renuka!' Devika turned with a snarl but Nila caught her arm and jerked her back.

'Don't bother,' Nila advised.

Rangana spun around in his seat. '*Deyo Buddhuhamduwanay* – will you girls just shut up? Another word out of any of you and I will report all of you to Miss Gauri! Now look – because of you lot I have mangled my toile.' Cursing, he leapt to his feet and stomped away.

One of the many things Nila enjoyed about living at the saree mill was the quiet. For someone who'd grown up in Kotahena amid the constant din from the sailors coming off Port Colombo and the noisy calls of the spice merchant, it was blissful, and she was free for the first time from Vera Mendis's acid commentary.

So quite naturally Nila unfurled, learning to meet the world with a steady gaze and happy heart, and the world greeted her with equal felicity. At least two of her male classmates went off to their classes one morning scratching their heads after encountering her at prayer. Her features and figure remained unchanged, but there was something quite different about her.

The blossoming of her mind and heart were there for all to see in her work – in her luscious colours, vibrant textures and soft, supple cottons and silks. It surprised no one that she was Guru Sindhu's favourite student or that Guru Sakunthala felt it appropriate to drape an arm around Nila's shoulders as they discussed lace-making skills. Even Guru Lakshmi went so far as to say that her designs were not stupid.

So it was to Nila who Punsala turned for help the night before a big design assessment was due. 'Nila, please, could you help me?' she begged.

Together with Devika, Nila was attempting to drape on herself a voile saree. They were on one of the many verandahs encircling the house, working by the light of several kerosene lamps. The saree was a damned difficult one to drape. The floaty fabric was weighed down by poorly designed beading, so instead of flowing fluidly, it acted like a poorly constructed net, pulling here and there. Draping sarees on herself was the only skill Nila was nowhere close to mastering. 'For someone who can drape another with such dexterity, you are incredibly clumsy when it comes to yourself,' Raju had told her sarcastically. The harder Nila tried to get the line and fall of her own saree correct, the more frustrated Raju became. 'It is really not that hard,' he would growl. 'Tuck, pleat, drape and pin.'

So Nila went over to Punsala promptly, gladly leaving the voile in a heap on the burnished wood floor. She looked over the girl's drawing thoughtfully.

'Here . . . you need to add a few embellishments to balance the design. And you will also need to tone down the decoration on the *potta*,' Nila said to Punsala, taking a pencil and fixing the design herself.

'Oh my goodness, you are so right!' Punsala said. 'Thank you so much.'

'My pleasure.'

'I don't quite know how I managed without you in my life, Nila! You are indeed a treasure!' Devika teased as Nila returned to the task of draping her saree.

Punsala tidied away her things and plopped down on the floor to watch them. 'I'm bored,' she said. 'I hate being stuck in here.'

'Soon enough we'll be proper workers and we'll be able to come and go as we choose,' Nila chided.

'But this was not what I expected when I came here. I came to Colombo for adventure and now I am stuck in a temple!'

On cue, someone started chanting in the shrine room.

'Oh, it is not so bad . . .' Nila consoled.

'Not so bad? Dosai and sambar, sambar and dosai . . . I swear I am about to turn into turmeric-coloured gruel,' Punsala complained as her stomach growled audibly. 'Would you like to go out for some hoppers?'

Both Nila and Devika shook their heads. The gates at the mill closed at nine pm sharp, and it was just after half seven, so they would be cutting it very close to return in time.

'Oh, please, I am so hungry that I feel faint,' Punsala begged, standing to theatrically totter and lie down on the settee behind her.

'Oh, okay then,' Nila relented as she pinned her *potta*. 'But let's be quick.'

Punsala clapped her hands gleefully and the trio slipped out the side gate.

'Oh, how I love fish curry,' Punsala said with a dreamy sigh as they ate *malu ambul thial* straight out of the bowl-shaped hoppers. 'My mother can't afford to buy fish for us kids. We usually only ever eat *kiri hodi*.'

'After my father died my mum sold three of our fields and my brothers survive by working the two that are left. In the months before harvest, we all survive pretty much on *miyoka* and *pol sambol*,' Devika said.

Nila sat listening to her friends. Vera Mendis never felt they had enough money, but in truth her family was middle class, and so were their problems. She had never known poverty of the kind Punsala and Devika described.

'Well, well, well, I can't say that I am surprised to find you lot here,' Renuka observed as her ayah staggered behind her with a large platter of hoppers.

'Why? We need food just like everyone else,' Devika bit back.

'It's just that it is the last night of the fair, and I thought that kind of entertainment would appeal to people like you. Filling yourself up before you go, are you?'

'We will be going back to the mill as soon as we've finished,' Nila said.

'A fair with rides, music, dancers and *muruku*?' Punsala demanded wide-eyed.

'Apparently there's a two-headed baby in a bottle,' Renuka said.

'Two heads? Must be your sister, then!' Devika said.

Renuka glared at her but did not reply, muttering, 'I will not lower myself to your standard.'

No sooner had Renuka left than Punsala started. 'Can we please go? Please?' she begged. 'If we hurry we can just see the two-headed baby and come back.'

'But the gates close in forty-five minutes,' Nila worried out loud. 'It takes fifteen minutes to walk there and fifteen minutes to walk back. We won't have enough time.'

'Not if we run back,' Punsala persisted. 'I am sure the watcher will let us in if we are only a few minutes late.'

'Oh, come on, Nila,' Devika said. 'I am dying to see Renuka's sister.' In the end Nila had no option but to follow them.

Once they got to the fair, they had to wait in the interminable human crush and humid heat to see its main exhibit, the two-headed baby in a bottle. Buffeted in the queue by screaming children, sweaty fair-goers and opportunistic pickpockets, Nila wished a million times she'd stayed at the mill instead.

The disappointment was all the more acute when they reached the exhibit to find that it contained a photo of the two-headed baby, a clay model and a description of how it had been killed by villagers in central Russia where it'd been born.

'I cannot believe we wasted our evening for that,' Nila grumbled as they hurried back to the mill.

'I knew Renuka was setting us up,' Devika huffed.

To add to their woes, the intense humidity turned into a sprinkling of rain that heralded an oncoming downpour. The monsoon had started.

'Follow me,' Punsala called. 'I know a short cut along the beach road.'

Nila and Devika scurried after her with no question. They really didn't relish spending the night out in the rain or being forced to knock at the *chettie*'s house to face a grumpy Miss Gauri in her nightie.

So they crossed the railway tracks and hurried along the beach, where tourists were crowded into huts, singing and drinking beer despite the drizzle. But as the beach road turned towards the river, skirting near the estuary, everything changed.

By day the shanties looked innocent enough, with industrious fishermen mending their nets and wives tending their numerous offspring, but when darkness fell, the fishermen started drinking. Unlike the merry-making tourists a mere half a mile away, these men drank with the single-minded objective of obliterating their minds.

'I think we should go back through town,' Nila said as they skirted a string of poorly built mud huts.

'It's only another few minutes,' Punsala assured them, but they huddled together tightly as they picked their way through the village.

They were fast approaching the edge of the shanty when they heard male voices shouting, violent scuffling and a sudden uproar. Punsala instinctively turned to look for the source of the noise and froze.

'We need to keep going,' Nila insisted, trying to pull the girl along, but she was motionless, transfixed by what was happening just past Nila's shoulder in the clearing.

'Rangana,' Devika called out as she followed Punsala's line of sight. 'Is that you?' She went tearing into the clearing.

Indeed it was their classmate Rangana. And he was being pummelled into mush by a wiry tattooed man while others jostled and pushed around them.

'What are you doing to him?' Devika demanded.

'What does it look like we're doing to him?' the tattooed man growled, punching Rangana hard in the stomach. Rangana doubled over, unable to stop a grunt of pain escaping his lips.

'Let him go!' Nila cried. 'He's our friend! Let him go!'

'I'll let him go all right,' the man said sweetly, 'once you have paid his debts . . .'

'You have debts?' Nila hissed at Rangana, but the tattooed man punched his mouth before he could answer.

'You can't drink *ra* for free.'

'You drink?' Devika demanded.

'But we have no money,' Punsala interjected, fear making her voice quiver. 'We can't pay you.'

'Then he'll just have to shed more blood. He's quite well used to pain,' the man said, punctuating his words with a series of heavy blows.

'We could bring some money tomorrow . . .' Nila said, then turned away, unable to watch anymore. 'I have some put away.'

That got the man's attention. He dropped Rangana into a heap and padded up. Nila would struggle later to recall exactly what happened next – she remembered only that it happened very quickly. One moment the three girls were standing there in the muddy lane and the next they were surrounded by men.

'I want the tall one,' the tattooed man goaded, looking slyly at Devika and flicking his switchblade open with a casual skill.

'Let the girls go – this is between us!' Rangana yelled, standing up with difficulty.

'No!' the man roared as he lunged.

Quick-thinking Nila, who was standing closest to the man, swung around with her saree fall, the beading on the fabric making it act like a net, flinging the blade out of his hand. She had bought them a moment, but if the situation had been tense before, now it was deadly, for the man pulled a gun out from under his shirt. '*Balli!* You'll be the first to go!'

'I don't think so,' Guru Raju drawled, cocking a shotgun.

Nila looked up to see the draping master.

'*Demala*, there is nothing for you to do here,' the tattooed man said. 'This is none of your concern. Take your *thosai* face and get back to the sewer where you belong with all your mother-fucking kind.'

'They are students at the mill and they are my concern,' Guru Raju said. ' Let them go.'

The man cocked his gun, but before he could pull the trigger, Guru Raju fired, taking aim at the coconut tree just beyond. The bullet grazed the thug lightly above the left eye. 'Next time I won't miss,' Raju warned. 'I will kill you and the police will thank me for it!'

Maybe it was the talk of police that made the thug stand down, or maybe it was the light trickle of blood that dripped down his face past the corner of his mouth. But he did lower his gun. Just enough. Guru Raju jerked his head at the students, indicating that they should leave. As he followed them, he tossed a handful of notes in the muddy laneway. 'This should cover his debts and then some!'

Panadura, Moratuwa, Ratmalana, Mount Lavinia, Dehiwala . . . Nila counted each of the stations on the train line back home with a heavy heart each Friday night. Each station meant she was closer to home, but there would be no welcoming smile or cheery cup of tea to greet her. Home she went nevertheless, carrying in her bag little treats for Rupani, consoling herself with the thought that her return to the mill was only two short days away.

Even so, Nila was completely taken back by the greeting she received on this particular Friday evening. Her mother barely acknowledged her as she came through the front door, saying only that she should go straight through. Piyasili Ranasinghe – the usurper of her room – would be dining with them, along with her playboy planter brother, Sunil, who came down each weekend in his shiny Ford to pick up and drop off his sister. The whole family were already seated at the dinning table with a large spread of rice and curry before them.

Rupani had been steadily flirting with Sunil, batting her doe eyes and sighing winsomely at everything he said. 'Oh, Sunil,' she would giggle, 'tell me all about tea planting. I have such an interest in horticulture! I tend all the plants here in our garden.' To Nila's dismay their mother would not call her lie or point out that Rupani would sooner walk on hot coals than tend the garden for fear of spiders and insects.

After changing out of her travelling saree and washing off the grime of the road at the well, Nila waited for her mother to call her to join their guests for dinner. Having been dismissed so summarily, Nila did not dare risk her mother's temper by presuming she would be welcome to dine with them. As she waited, she heard snatches of conversation.

'*Shah, putta*, I am so glad to hear you showed that Tamil bugger a thing or two,' Mervan said when Sunil told them how he'd caught out a thieving employee.

Manoj obsequiously offered to refill Sunil's empty *arrack* glass with more liquor: 'It's a local brew but superb.'

'*Anay, putta*, please have more *paripu*. You have such a long drive ahead of you. Rupani cooked it for you especially,' Vera lied, ladling another helping of lentil curry onto Sunil's plate.

It sounded as if the family was settling in for a long night of conversation when Mervan started reminiscing about his days as a young postal officer during the war. 'I rode from Colombo to Trincomalee carrying telegrams for the admiralty that Easter Sunday when the raid happened . . .'

So, following a habit of a lifetime, Nila slipped into Mrs Vasha's house in search of sustenance.

'I suspected I'd see you soon,' the old lady told her, pushing Nila to the dining table. She set a plate down in front her and filled it with creamy *pol kiri hodi* and some crusty bread.

'Do you know what is going on over there?' Nila asked, jerking her head in the direction of her own house before taking her first mouthful of the spicy coconut curry.

'Sunil Ranasinghe brought Anoja some milk toffees last week and this week he brings her an invitation to visit with them on the estate for the Uva Planters' Ball. Your parents are discussing the trip with Sunil and Piyasili.'

'Does Sunil like Rupani then?'

'I doubt that Sunil likes your sister any more than he likes the cows he keeps for milk,' Mrs Vasha said sceptically.

'But an invitation is serious . . . maybe he is in love.'

'Or maybe Piyasili likes to have someone silly to laugh at with her rich friends.'

'But surely Piyasili would not be so cruel, or toy with Rupani's affections like that.'

'I wouldn't put anything past Piyasili – a slyer girl I have yet to meet. And the Ranasinghes are known to be shrewd people. As the eldest son, Sunil knows better than to marry a girl with no dowry.'

'But an invitation like this . . . for a whole weekend. Why would anyone suggest such a thing if they did not have honest intentions?' Nila asked between mouthfuls of curry.

'Who knows why rich people do anything?' Mrs Vasha said. 'There is more news, though, my dear. Piyasili's parents have found her a suitable boy to marry and she will leave soon.'

'I hope Amma won't insist I stop boarding!'

'Don't worry about that. She's asked me to find another boarder for her. She has got used to the money. But enough of the Ranasinghes for now – tell me about your week.'

Nila recounted tales from her week at the mill, careful to avoid mentioning the trip to the fair but describing for Mrs Vasha the foibles of her classmates and the commissions they were working on.

'But we stopped working on Thursday. We spent much of yesterday and today cleaning the mill and readying the shrine.'

'Why?'

'It's Navaratri next week and we have a special dedication to the goddess Saraswati, so we clean everything and make sure our looms and cotton are all tidy before the festivities begin.'

'Hindus, I suppose,' Mrs Mendis observed, but was cut off by a sharp rap at the open door. 'Why it's Mrs Gamage and young Albert! How are you? When did you arrive, young man?' Mrs Vasha greeted them enthusiastically, kissing young Albert full on the cheeks not just once but three times.

'This morning on the flight from Bombay. I left London four days ago!'

'But I didn't know you had someone here,' Mrs Gamage said, peering around to see Nila.

'Oh, it's only me,' Nila said with a smile, waving them off as she went to wash her hands and put the heating coil in the jug for tea.

'Nila is like a daughter to me . . .' she heard Mrs Vasha explain to the Gamages as they sat down and made themselves comfortable.

'We were going to visit with your family but we saw that they already had some visitors,' Mrs Gamage told Nila when she returned with the tea.

'Yes, that was the boarder my mother has stay during the week, and her brother.'

'Why, Nila? Why does your mother have a boarder?' Albert asked. A studious, serious young man several years older than Nila, he had a gentle manner and kind heart.

'Didn't I write you about it?' Mrs Gamage said.

'No, Mother.'

'*Amma* . . .' Mrs Gamage corrected, patting her son's arm with a smile. 'Yes, Mrs Mendis has a boarder now that Nila is a girl with a job!'

'Where, Nila? And what do you do?'

'She works at a saree mill in Panadura – she is a saree maker,' Mrs Vasha said, beaming with pride.

'I say! Well done, Nila, well done! What is the name of the company?'

'Nair & Sons Sarees.'

'Tamils?'

'Yes.'

'You have to be careful with Tamils,' Mrs Gamage started, only to be cut off by Albert.

'But Panadura is a little far, *nay*?'

'That is why I board during the week, Albert. I come home every Friday night.'

'I always did say you were a girl with talent, never mind what you looked like,' Mrs Gamage said.

'Amma!'

'Well it is the truth, *nay*? Nobody thinks Nila is pretty. Mrs Weerasinghe from down by the canal, may her soul rest in peace though she was quite a nasty woman, used to say that Nila was positively ugly. She often wondered whether Nila had been switched at birth!'

There was a moment of stunned silence before Albert stuttered, 'Amma! You can't say that . . .' just as Nila started to laugh. Hard. So hard that tears coursed down her cheeks.

'It's quite all right, Albert. Really,' Nila said, giving Albert's arm a reassuring pat. 'Mrs Weerasinghe used to say it to me all the time. Once she even went as far as to enquire after the hospital I had been born at, only to find out that my mother had me at home!'

'And I always used to say to Mrs Weerasinghe that you were the kindest, gentlest girl in all of Kotahena, no matter what you looked like,' Mrs Gamage insisted. 'Though I must say you are looking very well indeed. Your skin is much improved – are you using that *kohomba kolla* and lime mixture?'

'No . . .'

'So you are using Fair & Lovely then? Oh, my niece uses that and she is at least three shades lighter now. My sister married a Tamil, you know, and they are darker than us. I even told your mother to buy your sister a jar of Fair & Lovely—'

'I don't think Anoja needs any Fair & Lovely,' Albert protested. 'She is just perfect as she is!'

'That is very sweet of you, Albert, to say that about my sister,' Nila replied with a smile.

'A very gracious girl indeed, and so kind-hearted! I remember her always playing with kittens and puppies,' Albert reminisced, while Nila said a silent prayer for the souls of the dogs and cats who were drowned in the river by Manoj as soon as their adorable youth had passed.

'And such a sweet disposition, too,' Mrs Gamage said, looking indulgently at her son.

'Then are you going to try your luck with Anoja?' the shrewd Mrs Vasha asked.

'Mrs Vasha . . . it is not appropriate!' Mrs Gamage protested.

'No, no. Let the boy answer honestly. We might as well have it all out in the open. What are your plans, Albert? Have you come home to find a bride, now that you have graduated?'

Albert hesitated, glancing at Nila. 'I have been offered a job as a hydro-electric engineer in New South Wales . . .' he said.

'Wales? In the UK?' the old woman asked.

'New South Wales is in Australia, Mrs Vasha.'

'But Australia . . . that is very far away, *nay*?'

'Yes, twenty hours by plane. I leave in six weeks. And I hope to take Anoja away with me as my bride,' the young man declared, his Adam's apple bobbing in his throat.

An uneasy sensation stirred in the pit of Nila's stomach.

'Well then, you'll just have to put your best foot forward,' Mrs Vasha said. 'She could not wish for a better husband than you.'

'And what is this talk of husbands?' Vera Mendis declared as she marched into the house with Rupani in tow. Though she started when she spotted Albert and his mother in the living room. 'A very good evening to you. I didn't know you were back in the country,' she said coolly.

'I just arrived this morning. From Bomb—' Albert replied before being rudely cut off by Vera speaking to Nila.

'Nila you are needed at home at once!'

'You'll never guess, but Piyasili Ranasinghe has just invited me for the weekend up in her parent's tea estate and I will need sarees. Nice cotton sarees for the day, at least two chiffon sarees for the evening and a grand silk saree for the Uva Planter's Ball!' Rupani squealed.

'In my day, young women weren't allowed to wear silk sarees until they were married!' Mrs Vasha grumbled.

'You should be able to borrow some sarees from the mill,' Vera commanded. 'But you'd better come home now and teach Rupani how to drape a saree. You got paid today, *nay*? We'll go into town tomorrow and get a few blouses stitched. Lord knows she's never worn saree before!'

With that, Vera and Rupani marched out, expecting Nila to follow them. Nila hesitated for a moment, feeling their rudeness keenly. They could have had Mrs Vasha stitch the saree blouses for a fraction of the cost of using the tailors in town but had chosen to arrogantly slight their good friend.

But follow them she did, pausing to kiss Mrs Vasha's wrinkly cheek and quietly slip a twenty rupee note into her hand for her heart medication. Nila was sure that Rupani's desire for new things would not be curbed by something as trivial as buying Mrs Vasha's medicines.

The air was heavy with incense and the sweet, sticky smell of jasmine and marigold. The shrine room was packed with the hundred and fifty or so mill workers and would have been insufferably stuffy, but for the uplifting fragrance of lotus, trucked in from the northern city of Anuradhapura, its blossoms covering every surface.

'The dinner went well. I thought the *idali* was a touch too hard, but the *sambar* was delicious, if a little too tangy,' Guru Lakshmi proclaimed in the sacred area behind the main altar. She was in the company of the four other gurus, all dressed in crisp new white sarees and sarongs. 'The *vadais* were not up to scratch either. Who were the cooks this year, Raju? Or are we cutting back on catering costs as well?' she added.

'Oh, Raju has better things to do than worry about the catering. How is that white girlfriend of yours? Does your father-in-law to be know that little white bunny?' Guru Hirantha asked.

'Oh, leave Raju alone – you all know it is Gauri who organises the catering. And it's the same people who were here last year,' Guru Sakunthala told her.

'All the same, if you keep carrying on with these white girls, Raju, the owner of Kanchi Silks will not want you for a son-in-law and what will happen then?'

The inscrutable Raju ignored the chattering, his eyes focused on the *pusari* organising all the implements for the pooja – the *vibuthi*, the camphor, the incense and the milk fresh from the udders of a new mother cow, who was tied to a coconut tree out the back of the kitchens.

'That is none of our business,' the Guru Sindhu growled.

'Sure, it is our business. More and more women prefer factory-spun sarees these days, and we'll lose our jobs if we don't embrace new technologies,' Guru Hirantha snapped. 'And partnering with Kanchi Silks is our best means of surviving. They can mass-produce sarees while we do the high-end designer work.'

'But that would mean shutting down a significant part of our work here in Sri Lanka,' Guru Sakunthala fretted.

'We might have to do that anyway,' Guru Lakshmi said sharply, 'since the new generation of management seems more interested in chasing skirts than running the business.'

It was only Raju's rolling eyes that betrayed the fact he'd heard the whole conversation.

'Whatever may come, we need to decide who we are going to offer places to . . .' Guru Hirantha said with a sigh.

'Why? So we can let them go them later, when we are forced to close the mill? That is cruel!' Guru Sakunthala said.

'We have more than enough work for four more people here at the mill for the next two years,' Raju said, speaking for the first time. 'And if the exhibition in Kanchipuram goes well, we'll have enough work for ten more for another three years.'

'And then there won't be a need for Raju to marry the daughter of Kanchi Silks,' Guru Sindhu pointed out wryly.

'Who are your nominees, Sindhu? I love the creativity that Renuka brings! What talent! What modesty! What decorum!' Guru Lakshmi said.

'I would rather choose a caged, starved viper!' Guru Sakunthala cried in horror. 'She is always goading the other students and trying to start trouble!'

'My picks are Rangana, Devika, Seevan and Renuka,' Guru Hirantha said.

'Yes,' Guru Lakshmi said, 'Rangana has improved enormously over the last few weeks. I gave him such a rapping with my fan a few weeks ago that it's finally knocked some sense into him!' She gripped her fan tightly to her bosom, glaring at Guru Sakunthala.

Raju smiled. He had told no one of the incident down in the shanties or the long conversation he'd had with Rangana the following day, man to man.

'I agree with you on Rangana, Devika and Seevan – but surely you must consider Nila,' Guru Sindhu said, with Guru Sakunthala nodding to second his nomination.

'That ugly frump?' Guru Lakshmi huffed. 'Did you see what she was wearing today? A grey voile saree. A voile saree! It made her look like a dumpy oil cake. Only a slender debutante can carry off a voile! That girl has no understanding of beauty!'

'How can you say that? That girl has a better intrinsic understanding of design, flow, colour and fabric than anyone I have ever met,' Guru Sakunthala said hotly. 'And Guru Sindhu says her weaving is second to none.'

'Lakshmi, I thought you said you loved her design work and that she had an exquisite eye for detail,' Guru Sindhu said.

'Don't get me wrong – I think Nila is an exceptionally talented young lady. She can design as well as the best student I have ever met, but she doesn't know how to bring it all together. Look at her now!' Guru Lakshmi said, ducking her head around the main shrine to spot Nila in the crowd. 'Look at her saree draping. It is truly atrocious. Why, I can see her underskirt peeping out the whole way!'

'But Raju says she does a superlative job draping sarees on other girls,' Guru Sakunthala said, only to be interrupted by Guru Hirantha.

'I agree with Lakshmi. As much as I like Nila's work – and her dyeing skills are second only to Devika in this group – she just can't put it all together. Imagine taking someone like that to an exhibition! Nair & Sons would become the laughing stock of the entire island!' he said.

'I think Rangana, Devika, Seevan and Nila should be offered roles,' Guru Sindhu said again. Guru Sakunthala inclined her head delicately, indicating her assent.

The decision was at a deadlock, splitting the faculty along ethnic lines, for while Gurus Sindhu and Sakunthala were Sinhalese, Gurus Lakshmi and Hirantha were Tamil.

'Well, that is decided then. We'll offer places to Rangana, Devika, Seevan and Renuka,' Guru Lakshmi crowed triumphantly. 'You agree with us, don't you? What do you say?' she demanded of the Tamil Raju.

Raju waited till the sadhu lighted the sacred flame before he replied.

'It is too early to make a decision. We need to see the pieces they produce for the exhibition to make the final choices.'

'Surely you'll want to make a decision before that. It is the sensible thing to do. That's how we've always done it before you came back.'

'So that all the other students can waste their time doing work that will be of no consequence, Guru Lakshmi? No. That is not fair. I won't make my decision before the exhibition,' Raju returned firmly.

'Fine then,' Guru Lakshmi sniffed. 'When will Gauri announce the theme for the exhibition?'

'The Monday after we return from the Uva Planters' Ball in Bandarawela. The exhibition will be on the twenty-first of September and the winners will leave with me for India on the evening flight. That way they can visit the saree houses in India before they start their work proper.'

'You are giving them seven weeks? We've only given them six in the past!'

'It gives the students who'll be going with me to Bandarawela enough time.'

Guru Lakshmi sniffed nastily again before dramatically swinging her *potta* around and following the sadhu, who'd started to toll the bell for the pooja. She was followed by Guru Hirantha.

'Raju, can you take Nila up to Bandarawela next week? That girl is talented, but she needs to learn taste,' Guru Sakunthala hissed as she went past.

'Nila is an exceptionally talented young lady. She has a gift for the *baana* and *thaana*, Raju. And she has a good heart . . . a pure heart. We need her,' Guru Sindhu murmured softly before he picked his place in the chant.

Nila wondered how much longer Devika and Rangana could continue arguing. It had started as soon as they'd left the mill. They were halfway to Ratnapura now and they'd barely stopped to draw breath!

'*Gani*, listen here. I am a man from Kandy. My ancestors are from Kandy. My ancestors' ancestors are from Kandy. It is faster to get from Panadura to Bandarawela through Kandy than it is to get from Bandarawela to Ratnapura!' Rangana repeated for only the twentieth time.

'It may be faster but the road is much more windy and there are more mountains!'

'That may be the case but the road through Kandy is better!'

'But going on the Kandy road means that we go through Colombo and we don't want to sit in traffic through the city!'

'What would you know? You're just a farmer's daughter from Matara!'

At that point, Nila reached from the back seat to pinch Rangana on the ear.

Guru Raju was driving the three of them to Bandarawela – to the very harvest ball that Nila's sister Rupani was attending with Piyasili and her brother Sunil. When Rupani had found out Nila would be there, the row at home in Kotahena had been beyond belief.

'The only reason she is going is so that she can ruin me!' Rupani had screeched.

'The only reason I am going is that the Nairs have been going to Bandarawela to dress the mothers and debutantes for twenty years!' Nila told her.

'Amma, no man will want me if they know my sister looks like her! Look at her! And they will question my respectability if they know I have a sister who works!'

'Don't go. Tell them you can't go!' Vera had commanded. 'Tell them you are needed elsewhere.'

'Amma, I have already tried telling them I'd much rather not go, but Guru Raju won't take no for an answer. And I will lose my job!'

'Upstart of a Tamil!' Rupani had snapped.

Vera looked uncomfortably at Nila. She could not risk losing her elder daughter's direct income or the indirect income they earned by renting out her room, but her sympathies were with her younger daughter. Then she had an idea.

'You will not speak to your sister. You will not look at your sister. You will not claim any relation to your sister! Do you understand me, Nila?' Vera demanded.

Nila had been appalled at the request but had acquiesced. It wasn't as if she could say no to her mother – or Guru Raju.

'We leave the day before to go to Bandarawela so we can arrive rested and relaxed. That way we are best prepared to deal with a day of hysterics and hijinks,' Raju had insisted to Devika, Rangana and the red-eyed Nila who'd tried several times to beg off going up to the ball.

'And we set up a saree stall in the foyer of the Bandarawela Grand Hotel. Women inevitably change their minds about the sarees they want to wear and there are seamstresses who are prepared to stitch saree blouses at a moment's notice,' Miss Gauri had added. Only everyone was taken by surprise as Nila stifled a sob and bolted out the room.

Guru Raju had rolled his eyes and look an askance at his sister. Did he really have to take her with him?

Gauri narrowed her eyes and gave him a menacing nod. Yes. Gauri adored Nila. The girl was kind and gentle as she was talented and intelligent.

Raju shrugged wearily. He was already exhausted. Never in his experience had the drama started *before* the ball. First, the mill's Volkswagen kombi van had broken down. After spending an afternoon down with the mechanics in Panadura, Raju had to concede it could not be fixed in time. He then wasted several more hours trying to find a van to hire before resigning himself to driving the old crank-handle Ambassador up the mountains.

The view from the mountain road was spectacular. Even the most prosaic of souls could not fail to be moved by the splendour of the steep slopes covered in a velveteen blanket of tea bushes, flecked with the brightly coloured sarees of the tea pickers who darted in and out of the hills. But three hours into the journey and not a single word about the stunning scenery had been uttered. Not a single mention was made of breathtaking vistas that presented themselves at every bend or turn. No. Rangana and Devika would insist on arguing about the road.

However, just past Poruwadanda, as the road started to climb more steeply and wildly, the squabbling had stopped, though it was a mixed blessing indeed. For the two protagonists had finally found something they had in common – carsickness. Then Raju had to stop the car at regular twenty-minute intervals so that either or both of them could regurgitate their breakfast. He had to crank start the car each time they stopped.

'You don't suffer carsickness, then?' Raju asked Nila thankfully after Devika and Rangana had drifted off to sleep in the back seat.

Nila shook her head.

'This is beautiful country, isn't it?' the guru said.

Nila was silent. She found the handsome draping master intimidating and his obsession with appearances superficial. The constant parade of beautiful young white women was annoying as well. It gave rise to an inordinate amount of gossip among workers, students and teachers alike. Nila would much rather work on her weaving than keep tabs on the foot traffic over the narrow bridge that connected Guru Raju's bungalow to the mill.

'Are you looking forward to the ball tomorrow? I hope Gauri told you to pack a nice saree – the planters usually don't mind if we join the dancing later.'

'No,' Nila replied, rapidly blinking back tears.

'You don't like dancing?'

Nila shrugged. She had never had the occasion to dance, her parents choosing to take Rupani and Manoj to parties or weddings.

'So, tell me about yourself, Nila. I know you have two brothers and a sister. Are you close to them?'

Nila shook her head stonily.

Raju tried again, telling himself that this would be his last attempt to get through to the girl.

'I saw you at the store the other day when your sister came to visit you. It was very nice of you to buy her first saree. A

very special day for a young lady, when she gets her first saree.
She is very beautiful, your sister.'

Tears collected in Nila's eyes and she looked away. Yes,
she'd bought Rupani her first saree. More than that, Rupani
and her mother had insisted that Nila pay for two further
sarees. Rupani had known exactly what she wanted for her
visit to the Ranasinghes: 'Nice cotton sarees for the day, at least
two chiffon sarees for the evening and a grand silk saree for
the ball!' Nila had loaned her sister her own cotton sarees, but
the chiffon and silk they had purchased new. This had eaten up
what had been left of Nila's savings, so much that she didn't
even have money for her train ticket back home the following
weekend.

Raju gave up. There was no getting through to Nila Mendis.
He would second the nomination of Renuka at the faculty
meeting. For while Renuka was vicious as a viper, she did have
a spark in her, something Nila desperately lacked.

The Grand Old Hotel in Bandarawela was abuzz. Everybody
and everything was quivering with excitement. Even the flying
cockroaches knew better than to show their ugly faces that
evening, hiding away in nook and crevice to return to exas-
perate the cleaning staff after the party. Plantation families
from all over the hill country and the crème de la crème of
Colombo high society had been pouring into Bandarawela for
a fortnight now, and tonight was the height of the tea harvest
festivities.

By early evening a large contingent of older gentlemen
had retired to the downstairs bar to nurse tumblers of scotch,
needing a break from the hysterics and hijinks, but a whole
battalion of younger men remained, and had taken station near
the foot of the grand staircase. They were there to watch the
debutantes as they made their way down the ancient stairwell.

For there was money riding on it – on which of the young ladies would take a tumble swathed in a saree for the first time. And there was money on who would show the most leg while engaged in the delicate task of hitching her pleats to step down the first stair.

There was also another wager afoot, but this one was discussed only in sly whispers, for the boys were petrified – truly petrified – of being caught by their wives or mothers. Why, if the stakes of the wager were to be revealed, well, it would most definitely result in a scolding of the severest kind, or goodness knows what! All that could be discerned, even by the nosiest of waiters, was that it involved Piyasili Ranasinghe's new friend, the flirtatious Miss Anoja Mendis.

But above stairs, the Mendis name was being used in quite a different way altogether. For Nila Mendis was being feted by all and sundry. Several harried lady's servants were employed in the task of simply hurrying her from one dressing-room to the other!

Nila's rise to fame had come as something of a surprise. The group from Nair & Sons had set up their annual stall that morning and waited for customers as usual. Raju did most of the selling while the others assisted him. That was until Nila helped sell a saree to one of the more elderly ladies who'd come in.

The matriarch of a large rubber plantation family, she'd long since relinquished bright colours in favour of whites and beiges as an emblem of her widowhood. 'Raju told me she never buys anything,' Devika had hissed at Nila as the old woman walked up. 'He asked me to ask you to deal with her.' Raju had been assiduously ignoring Nila since their stony ride to Bandarawela the day before.

Nila approached the older lady and waited for her to speak first. 'I am not looking for anything,' the older lady had snapped, so Nila kept a respectful distance while still shadowing her through the stall.

'Do you have anything in white?'

'Do you need a saree for temple, madam?'

'No, I need a white saree for tonight!'

'I do have some white sarees that are suitable for temple or funeral wear, but I don't have any that would be suitable for a grand party.'

'What about that silk saree hanging there? That white one with the silver border? Are you blind?'

And with the practice born of dealing with the elderly Mrs Vasha, Nila was able to gently guide the lady away from the garish white drape with delicate humour. 'Oh madam, that would sooner suit a Bharatanatyam dancer than a lady!'

'Why should I buy *any* sarees when I am one foot in the grave?' the old woman growled, tossing her jewelled hands in the air.

'Because then you'll be well dressed in your coffin. Do you want the gossips to say that they had you dressed in rags?'

'Oh, if only that is all they would say! They'll say I was a crotchety, stingy old woman!'

'Well, are you?'

'Crotchety or stingy?'

'Stingy. All old people are crotchety. How can anyone be cheerful when their joints hurt?'

'Ha! You are a funny girl. I like you!' the woman had laughed. 'Of course I am stingy. How can a person not be stingy if they have people constantly asking them for money? *I need a new a new car! I need two new servants! We need more equipment for the plantation!*' she said, mimicking her whiny offspring. 'They'd leave me to die if I didn't hold the purse strings.'

'Oh madam, why not spend a little money on yourself, then?'

'At my age? No. They'll say I am wasting their inheritance,' the lady muttered.

Nila understood. The old lady was lonely. Lonely despite living in a household with a large extended family.

'Madam, I am not going to tell you to buy a saree. I think

the saree you have on right now is pretty enough for tonight. But let's have a look at some sarees for fun,' Nila suggested kindly.

For the next half hour, Nila and the old lady simply enjoyed themselves looking at the various sarees – touching their soft silk, playing with the beads that made up the *potta* and inhaling the fragrance of the sea still clinging to the yards of fabric.

'You know, Miss Nila, when I was a young girl my father took my family down to Hambantota for a holiday by the beach,' the old lady reminisced as Nila selected a soft white saree with an aquamarine wave motif from a pile that had been set aside for the young debutantes. Nila had noticed the lady's eyes straying over the saree several times. 'I spent two whole months there. It was the best time of my life,' the woman confided as Nila draped the new saree over the one she was already wearing.

'Was it just the holiday by the beach or was there anything more?'

'Since you ask, yes. I fell in love with a young man who used to catch the bus every morning for school. I never met him – I didn't even speak a word to him – but his face was so kind. Years later I saw a *sahastara karaya* when my husband was visiting the whore who used to be my maid. And he told me that I had seen the face of my true love but never spoken to him.'

'What do you think, Madam?' Nila asked, turning the woman gently around to the mirror.

The years fell away. Hidden below the gnarled and wrinkled body, a sweet young girl showed her face again. The old lady held her hand to her heart. She no longer had one foot in the grave, for Nila had draped her a young woman's saree. Modest yet hopeful; demure and pure.

'Why, Mrs Hettiarchie, I haven't seen you look this well since your eldest son's wedding!' an acquaintance called out from the foyer as Nila gave her a spontaneous kiss on her papery cheek.

'Young lady, I will have this saree and four more, and let them say I am wasting their inheritance!' the lady cried, fishing out a crisp five hundred rupee bill from her purse.

Having observed Nila at work, a few of the ladies who'd been chatting with Devika about sarees abandoned her. They found her flippant and not willing to listen. They did not wish to be served by Raju, either. Chatting with someone so handsome could raise the heckles of jealous husbands. And Rangana – well, Rangana was a surly young man who just told them what to wear. And these women already had enough of dictatorial men in their lives. As they unburdened their sorry hearts, Nila found sarees that suited them best.

For the harried mother of two sets of twin boys, she chose a blue-grey chiffon. 'I haven't bought a new saree in five years!' the woman complained in between yelling at her boys to stop sliding down the handrail of the grand staircase. 'Well then, this saree should suit you,' Nila advised with a gentle smile. 'See, it only costs a hundred rupees. And at that price, do you really care if you put a hole through the hem running after your boys?'

For a woman trying to woo her husband back from his mistress, it was a red Kanchipuram silk with erotic temple motifs. Nila advised her to pleat her saree only seven times for good luck and advised her to wear it without an underskirt. 'I've heard it drives men crazy when their wives have nothing on under their sarees!'

'Is my *potta* right, Nila? Is it finishing just at my hemline?' Devika asked hurriedly as Nila put the finishing touches on her friend's drape. All the ladies had had their sarees draped and Nila could hear the music wafting up the stairs.

'It is perfect, Devika. Go. Have fun!'

'Aren't you coming?'

'In a bit.'

'Are you sure? I could help you with your saree.'

'I'll come down in half an hour or so,' Nila lied. 'Let me rest for a bit.'

Devika glided over to kiss Nila on the cheek. 'You deserve some rest. You draped sarees on at least twenty-five ladies.'

'Thirty, actually.'

'We'll see you soon,' Devika called as she rushed down the stairs.

Nila tidied the room, picking up discarded clothes, packing away the safety pins and the lengths of cord used to tighten the waistbands of underskirts, humming to herself. She could only imagine the beautiful ladies downstairs, swirling around in their mesmerising sarees – cerulean blues, ruby reds, golden creams and dark greens sparkling under the crystal chandelier.

'You've done a splendid job today, Nila. You truly have,' Raju said from the door as Nila half-jumped out of her skin. 'Oh, I'm sorry, I didn't mean to scare you,' he apologised, strolling in.

'Thank you,' Nila said, looking away. Nila wasn't usually much affected by the handsome draping master, but that night, Raju, the perennial devotee of sarongs and singlets, was dressed in a crisp grey suit with a white shirt and blue tie. For the first time, Nila understood why he had so many of his female students swooning.

'Aren't you coming down?' he asked. 'Many people want to meet you. I've been asked to book you for several weddings.'

'I am a little tired – I'll come down later.'

'Oh, come now. This is silly. Come with me while people are still sober enough to meet you properly,' Raju said. Even from across the room, Nila could smell the sour fragrance of *arrack* on Raju's breath.

Nila hesitated. 'I really don't feel up to it . . .'

'Come now, don't be silly.'

'No, thank you. I need to rest before I come down.'

'Don't be coy. Please come.'

'No, Guru Raju, I can't.'

'Go and get dressed now! I have two families who'd like to invite you to dress their wives for parties next week! Go!' Raju commanded fiercely. He'd had enough of Nila's silly missish ways. It was one of the many things that frustrated him about local girls. They hid behind false modesty that helped no one. And Raju needed to get these rich businessmen on his side to ensure the survival of the mill, and there was no better way to get to them than through their wives.

Nila stared at him for a moment before padding around to a screened-off corner to drape her saree. The much detested grey voile. Nila had finally learned to drape it on herself, though she was still by no means an expert. She did the best job she could, decided it would pass, and returned no more than ten minutes later.

Raju looked up and saw red. 'This! This is what you wear! I'll be the laughing stock of the whole ball! I spent the whole day listening to you advise women on colour, texture and fabric, and you wear this! You don't need to *try* to look ugly!'

Nila reeled as if she'd been punched. She didn't know what to say.

'Don't tell me you don't have any other sarees to wear! We give you an allowance so that you can buy at least one saree a month from the mill. What are you doing with that money? Are you selling the sarees on the side? Are you trying to increase your dowry so that someone will marry you?'

Nila stepped up and slapped him neatly across the face.

'Enough! No, I am not selling my sarees for a dowry. My sister, the one whom you thought so beautiful, took all my sarees. Every single one of them. So that she could come up here and get herself a rich husband,' Nila cried. 'She left me this one because it was ugly.'

'But I just saw your sister . . .'

'Yes, she is at the ball. But she and my mother insist that I not speak to her. At all. Apparently my ugly face could scare away her suitors.'

'Nila . . . I'm sorry.'

'Just go away, Guru, please . . .' Nila cried, turning away to hide the tears pouring down her face.

'I don't know what came over me . . .' he whispered. 'Please forgive me.' Only Nila would not look at him. After a tense moment, he turned and left.

Nila collapsed on the narrow bed, sobbing as if her heart would break at all the injustices that had been heaped on her since the birth of her beautiful baby sister. What could she do? She could not change her face.

When she finally looked up, exhausted, she found Raju sitting across from her on a chair. 'Surely I can meet these important clients tomorrow?' Nila asked with a hiccup.

'You can indeed,' Raju replied softly. 'I went down to look at our stall . . . You were so good today that there's hardly any sarees left for me to give you.'

'You don't need to give me a saree.'

'I will organise for you to have some new sarees as soon as we get back to the mill,' Raju said, standing up. 'Don't argue with me. It's the least I can do to make up for my rudeness,' he said, brushing aside Nila's protests. 'But now I want you to come downstairs and see how happy your customers are in their new finery. As someone who drapes sarees, I know one of my greatest pleasures is watching my models parade around in them.'

'But I can't go down looking like this . . .'

'Come with me,' Raju said holding out his hand. 'Come. Trust me. No one will see you.'

He was wrong. As the guru led Nila into the hall outside, they saw a couple skirting away to a deserted part of the hotel. It was Rupani and Sunil.

Sunil started visibly. 'Isn't that your sister?' Nila heard him say.

'No, it isn't,' Rupani insisted, dragging him away down the corridor.

'I'm sure it is your sister,' Sunil said.

'Even if she is, that ugly woman is nothing to me!' Rupani cried.

Raju looked embarrassed, but Nila dismissed what had happened with a slight shake of her head. 'Where are we going?'

'It's a secret,' he said, pulling her along by the hand. Raju and Nila went down the deserted grand staircase, around the corner of the ballroom and up a rickety flight of stairs. 'I have been coming to this ball since I was a child,' Raju said. 'I found this old balcony when I was about six and I spent the whole night watching the party. No one can see us from here,' he reassured Nila as he pulled her onto the narrow landing overlooking the ballroom.

Nila peered through the railing at the magical scene below, hundreds of women dancing in their alluring sarees. 'Oh, they are so beautiful,' she whispered as she watched them twirl and whirl under the twinkling lights.

'No, they are not.'

'Excuse me?'

'They are not beautiful,' Raju insisted. 'Show me a woman you call beautiful.'

'What about her, the one in the cream saree,' Nia pointed out.

'She has bad teeth. Do you see how she covers her mouth when she laughs?'

'What about her? The one with the large earrings and the diamond necklace?'

'The only reason she looks pretty is because her rich husband can buy her a king's ransom worth of jewellery. She has a squint in one eye and crooked nose.'

On and on it went. No sooner had Nila pointed out a beautiful woman had Raju dissected her imperfections. Nila was soon running out of beautiful women to point out when she pointed out Piyasili Ranasinghe to Raju.

'Her beautiful? Truly Nila, can you not see anything? That girl is vicious. Vicious like the rest of her family. Look at the lines around her mouth and the nasty glint in her eyes! No, she is not beautiful at all! Oh Nila, there is so much more to beauty than a symmetrical face and a pleasant figure.'

In that cramped, dark opera balcony of a bygone era, Nila and Raju finally started to talk. For what seemed like an eternity. About family. About life. About beauty. And by and by, Raju was able to draw out the story of Nila's life.

'Would you trust your parents to choose the saree you should wear on a night like tonight?' he asked quietly. Raju had draped his coat over her shoulders to protect her from the cool draught.

'No, of course not! They don't know the first thing about form or fluidity!'

'Do you trust them to do the best thing by you?'

'No!'

'Then why do you trust them when they say you're not beautiful, Nila?'

Nila was silent. As the band struck up the final song, Nila and Raju descended the narrow rickety stairs.

'Oh, Nila! I have been looking everywhere for you! Come quick!' cried Devika as she came tearing around the corner. 'Everybody is shouting.'

'What's wrong?'

'Your sister . . .'

The narrow street that led to the Mendis household was in many ways typical of all lodging quarters afforded to the families of postal workers in Kotahena: dingy slapped over with a veneer of respectability. Though the latter could not really disguise the former.

The series of identical houses had been recently white-washed due to the efforts of the Good Wives Society, but middle-class poverty meant that the single coat of paint was already green with tropical mildew. The houses' poor wiring sang in the heavy monsoonal downpour, hissing and sparking, and made the simple task of walking across the street a health hazard.

'Does Nila Mendis live here?' Devika called out to the first lady she found looking out her window that wet and miserable evening.

'Across the road,' Mrs Gamage called out.

So Devika strode confidently and knocked on the door of what looked like a deserted house.

'Who is it?' a distant voice asked from inside.

'My name is Devika. I work at the saree mill with Nila. She hasn't been for a few days. Is she well?'

'She is busy,' the voice called back.

'Will she be returning to the mill?' Devika asked. When no response was forthcoming, she repeated her question again.

'No,' the voice came back eventually.

'Madame, this is very silly. Can I come in and see Nila, instead of shouting through the door like this?'

'Please go away.'

'But Nila is a very talented saree maker. She's got to come back.'

There was silence.

'Mrs Mendis? Is that you, Mrs Mendis? Please let me in,' Devika shouted through the slats of the window.

A few of the neighbourhood ladies were now standing at their doorsteps watching the commotion.

'Mrs Mendis, please let me come in and talk to Nila. Maybe I could even help with Rup—'

Vera Mendis opened the door with a snarl. 'Get away from my family now!' she snarled, broom in hand to shoo away her unwelcome guest.

'But Nila—'

'Nila nothing. This whole situation is entirely Nila's doing!'

'It wasn't Nila's fault! How could it be?' Devika protested, only to be pushed off the doorstep. 'Just tell Nila that the theme for the exhibition is the river,' she said. 'The river!' she then shouted into the house, for she was sure that she saw Nila peering at her through the shadows, two dark orbs at an odd angle to each other, glistening with tears.

'Get away with you now!' Vera shouted at Devika, running at her as if she were a demon.

'So you've decided to join us, have you, Miss Mendis?' Guru Lakshmi said snidely as Nila slipped into her seat in the design class. It was Tuesday morning, two weeks after the Harvest Ball in Bandarawela, and the first time that Nila had returned to the mill.

'I had understood you were too ashamed to show your face in public,' the guru said as Nila shoved her bag under her seat. 'And that all my efforts at teaching you were to be a complete waste.'

'No, guru. It was just that . . .'

'Everyone knows what happened at the harvest ball. I am so glad it was your sister and not you, or I would have had words with Gauri. We would have had to dismiss you. Such a shameless girl your sister must be!'

'I heard she lured him . . .' Renuka whispered to the girl next to her, just loud enough to be heard.

'That was *not* how it happened!' Devika said sharply. 'I was there.'

'Do you think we are going to believe the words of a nothing girl like you against those of Sunil Ranasinghe? He is a respect-able man from a respectable family!' Renuka said.

'You don't even know the Ranasinghes!' Nila pointed out.

'Of course I know the Ranasinghes. They are a famous up-country family.'

'Men will be men. And if your sister were a decent woman, she would have known better,' Guru Lakshmi pointed out. 'Anyway, you'll have to catch up with two weeks' worth of missed lessons and your share of commissions. You've been lucky that Devika has been kind enough to carry some of your load.'

'Oh, I am so glad to see you, Nila,' Devika squealed as soon as they left the class. 'I honestly thought your parents would never let you come back.'

'And how can your mother blame you for anything?' Punsala chimed in as Nila looked up and down the corridors in wonder.

'What is this?' she asked, pointing to the looms set up along the length of what used to be a deserted corridor, each of them covered over with a large dust cloth.

'We're all working on our exhibition pieces,' Devika explained. 'We've set up these looms to work on them and use the other looms to work on real commissions.'

'But why are they covered up?

Before Devika could explain, Guru Sindhu came bustling up. 'Ah yes, the watcher told me you were back. Good. Very good. Now, Nila, I need you to come with me. Since your most excellent work at the harvest ball in Bandarawela, we've been swamped with commissions. Two hundred sarees have been ordered by a *modalali* in Nuwara Eliya alone,' the man said with a joyous little skip to his step as he pulled Nila along.

'This of course has meant that all the looms have been taken up for real work and we've had to pull out some old looms for the students to work on for their exhibition pieces.'

'Is there a loom for me?' Nila asked with a worried frown.

'No, but when the watcher told me you'd come back, I went searching for one,' the dwarf said as he went into the old wood storage hut near the kitchens. 'You were quite lucky the cooks hadn't got to this yet for firewood. It's an old loom – or rather two old looms. The frame on this one is broken but the bed on the other isn't. So if we put them together, we'll get a working one,' he explained as he and Nila pulled the old decrepit looms into the tiniest of spaces left in the corridors.

After several hours of fiddling, they managed to get the thing assembled, though the bed kept falling off and the lamms were so brittle that Nila could crumble the aged wood in her hands. 'Thank you,' Nila said to the weaving master as he looked on worriedly.

Soon, though, it would be Nila's turn to worry. As she hurried to the dyeing hut she was accosted by both Miss Gauri and Guru Sakunthala. 'You have no idea how happy Raju will be to see you. We've had ten bookings for you to dress brides. Here are some pictures of the brides and samples of their sarees – you'll need to study them before the weddings and the first one is tonight!' Miss Gauri said, piling a box of photographs and swatches into Nila's arms.

'Nila, you have to have lunch with me in my office today and the rest of the week,' Guru Sakunthala said as soon as Miss Gauri walked off. 'You haven't learned how to pearl bead a saree and you certainly don't know how to do cutwork. You may need these skills for your exhibition saree.'

'Here, you'll need to finish these three dyeing commissions by Monday next,' Guru Hirantha said distractedly as Nila walked into the dyeing hut. 'We've been so behind on work since you went away.'

As Nila set down the box of samples on the ground and picked up the heavy dyeing frames to heft out to the river, she felt a sudden urge. An urge to swim out to the middle of the river's fast flowing emerald heart and never come back.

How could she catch up with everything here at the mill and still do all the work that needed to be done for Rupani's grand wedding?

Nila had no time to do any design work or even think about her exhibition saree for Guru Raju collected her as soon as she'd finished tea, to go and dress a bride whose auspicious time for marriage had been set for eight in the evening. 'I was going to come over to your house today and speak to your parents if you hadn't returned,' he said as soon as they were on the road. 'How are you?'

Nila shrugged. How could she explain all that had happened without exposing the ugliness of her own family?

'And if it is not too bold of me, how is your poor sister?'

'Engaged.'

'Excuse me?' Raju started. 'Was your father able to bring Sunil Ranasinghe to heel?'

'No, my father could not bring Sunil to heel. He came home with a swollen face and bruised ribs for all his efforts to bring young Master Ranasinghe to account for his misdeeds.'

'Who is Rupani marrying?'

'Our neighbour Albert.'

'How did that happen?'

So she explained the events of the past two weeks, telling the guru what she could and leaving out the rest.

'After Father came home from Bandarawela announcing that he could not make Sunil marry Rupani, she became quite hysterical. She blamed me, as did my mother.' Nila's bruises had healed now and she did not want to confess how badly her mother had beaten her.

'How? Why?' Raju asked, outraged. 'Didn't both your mother and Rupani insist that you not speak to her the whole weekend?'

'That was indeed the problem. I spoke to her and interfered.'

'I am very confused. Of course you spoke with her – she was hysterical . . .' Raju's voice trailed off as he remembered the unpleasant events of the night.

They had found a dishevelled Rupani screaming and clinging onto Sunil in front of a crowd of amused onlookers. 'You said you'd marry me!' she had cried. 'Don't do this to me! You have ruined me!'

Sunil had pushed her away and she had landed in an ungainly heap, bruising her head against a windowsill.

'Marry a slut like you? I don't deal in damaged goods!'

Sunil and his cronies had hooted with laughter.

Together with Devika, Nila had taken Rupani back upstairs and tidied the girl up while Raju called for a doctor to come and administer a sedative. Rupani had slept all the way back to Colombo in her sister's arms.

Nila sighed. 'Rupani told my mother that if I hadn't interfered Sunil would have married her and that the fuss I created was what drove him away.'

Raju snorted with disgust. 'Your mother must be mad. I would not want a daughter of mine to marry a womaniser like Sunil.'

Nila gave him an arch look and smiled.

'It's not what you think, and I certainly don't take advantage of innocent girls. So how did this engagement to Alvin come about?'

'Albert. He's our neighbour and has been in love with Rupani since she was a child. So when she took ill with hysteria, his mother offered to take my mother up to Kandy to visit the Temple of the Tooth to save her life.'

Rupani had been crying and wailing in bed for days on end, lying listlessly facing the wall, but no sooner had the invitation been issued than she had miraculously mended. 'I think a trip to Kandy is exactly what I need to lift me out of the doldrums,' she had declared, drying her eyes.

So what had started out as a quiet pilgrimage had rapidly developed into a royal tour, when Albert had generously offered to hire a car for the trip and to foot the expenses at the guesthouse. And as generous as Albert was, Rupani was just as committed to taking advantage of his kindness. She'd insisted on stopping three times during the trip for tea and treats.

However, Rupani made it clear that she took no pleasure in Albert's company. 'Rupani, white sarees really suit you,' Albert complimented Rupani nervously as they visited the Holy Temple. 'And I had no idea you were such a devout Buddhist.'

'Well, Nila bought me the saree and I know all my prayers because I went to a Buddhist school,' Rupani replied in a bored voice. 'And can you hurry up? I want to go for a ride on the lake!' Rupani had snapped at Albert when he'd been delayed helping his elderly mother around the Holy Temple compound.

This rude behaviour had continued until the third morning of their week-long visit to Kandy, when Nila overheard a hushed, tearful conversation between Rupani and her mother in the early hours of the morning. 'Amma, my monthly courses are late. What am I going to do?'

'I think a quick marriage to Albert is all there is left to do.'

With that, Rupani's behaviour changed dramatically, so much that Albert spoke to Mervan as soon as they returned to Colombo. That very night, dusty and wearied from all the travel, Albert had asked for Rupani's hand in marriage.

'Their marriage could work out. They could be very happy together,' Raju said. 'He clearly loves her.'

'Rupani will never know of moderation or manners if she marries Albert,' Nila said sadly, 'nor will Albert know anything of love or affection.'

'At least Rupani's child will have a name,' Raju said.

It was late when they arrived back at the mill after the wedding, and starting to rain. 'I think there's someone waiting for you,' Nila told Raju with a smile as she spotted a golden-haired goddess dressed in a tie-dye frock waiting impatiently in the darkness by the footbridge to his bungalow.

'I'd better go,' Raju grinned. 'But you work on that saree for the exhibition.'

With that Nila hurried to the corridor where Guru Sindhu had set up the broken loom for her. She took out the bags of raw silk she'd bought from the mill store earlier in the day and started to treadle the loom, using the heavier yarn for the *baana*, so that the saree would weigh downwards to flatter even the heaviest of Rupani's friends.

Threading the loom took a lot longer than it should have, though. The breast beam kept falling off, bruising Nila's legs, and even the heavy cross frame came loose and nearly split her head in two. By two in the morning, Nila had barely started the first heavy shedding and twisting that would reinforce the plain end of the saree when the batten fell over, nearly crushing the tips of her fingers. The wind had blown rain onto the verandah, soaking almost half of Nila's store of silk yarn, and she was starting to feel very defeated.

'By all that is holy, what are you doing with that old banger of a loom?' Raju asked quietly as Nila sat there sucking on her fingers.

'Weaving a saree, I hope,' she mumbled from around her fingers.

'You aren't planning on weaving your exhibition piece on that old thing, are you?' he asked as he picked up a scrap of cloth and wetted it by holding it out to the rain. 'Give me your hand,' he said, and gently cooled her throbbing fingertips with the cloth.

'It's the only loom available.'

'But—'

'Guru Sindhu searched and searched. This is the only loom left.'

'Maybe one of the other looms will come free soon,' Raju said. 'It's a bit too early to start weaving when you haven't even designed what you'll be weaving. And what is this?' he asked, picking up the raw silk. 'Surely you weren't planning on making it with this!'

'I was planning on making Rupani's bridesmaids' sarees with this,' Nila said, snatching the hank of silk away.

'When is the wedding?'

'In five weeks. The afternoon of the exhibition.'

'What if you win? What'll you do then?'

'Is there a chance I could win?'

'Anything is possible if you give it a good chance!' Raju growled. 'But if you waste your time weaving sarees for Rupani's silly wedding, then you won't have a chance at all.'

'I am not wasting my time—I am doing what needs to be done.'

'Are you mad, Nila? You have a very good chance of getting a position here at the mill if you do well. Do not be silly and throw it all away for a sister who neither values nor loves you!'

'I am not doing this for Rupani. I am doing this for my parents.'

'Why? Because they love and care for you?'

'No. Because they have raided my dowry fund and even taken a mortgage out on my father's pension to pay for this wedding. If me making eight sarees for Rupani's bridesmaids means that there'll be enough money to buy rice for an extra month, I will do it!'

'But you understand that you'll be of more service to your parents if you get a job here!'

Nila's eyes flashed, but Raju saw that her mouth was trembling, and he paused. She had lost a worrisome amount of weight over the past few weeks and lines of exhaustion marked her face. Not to mention that she'd helped him dress an entire bridal party just a few hours ago. The girl was so tired she was barely making sense.

'Fine then,' he said softly. 'I'll take care of it.'

'No, please don't even think of giving us the sarees. Rupani wants them dyed a particular shade of orange to match something or other.'

'Don't worry about,' he repeated. 'I will take care of it. You go to bed and get some sleep.'

'But—' Nila said hotly, ready to keep weaving for a few hours yet.

'Go to bed, Nila, and get some sleep,' Raju whispered softly. Nila opened her mouth to argue, but the weaver's seat fell off the loom with a loud clatter and a cloud of dust, startling them both.

Nila sighed, hanging her head in defeat.

Anxiety clawed at Nila every time she went past the corridor where her broken loom should have sat. For it was not there. Disappeared. Without a trace. Someone had thought to sweep the space, so even the dust from the rotting wood was gone.

The likely culprit had vanished too. He must be off with one of his doxies, Nila thought grumpily as she walked around the mill looking for the missing loom. And it wasn't as if she could simply ask Guru Sindhu for another loom, because there wasn't another loom to be had.

'Have you started on your designs yet?' Devika asked Nila bluntly at morning tea time.

'No.'

'Then I suggest you make some time, cause if you don't, Guru Lakshmi will disqualify you and then you will be in serious trouble.'

'But I don't have any time.'

'Skip weaving – you are almost as good at it as Guru Sindhu!'

'What am I going to use as inspiration?' Nila asked, exasperated.

'It's the river, remember? There's one right behind you!'

There had been a dramatic change at the mill in Nila's absence. Since the theme for the exhibition had been announced, it was as if all the students had gone mad. Within the space of two weeks, friends had turned into foes. They poked and prodded one another, trying to discover each other's designs, looking for ideas that they could cunningly appropriate for their own exhibition pieces.

Renuka had often admitted in the past that she was not interested in a career at the mill, but she was one of the most competitive. 'I don't need the money, but the prestige would make my in-laws proud,' she'd drawled.

Even bubbly Punsala had become dour and secretive. She had peeked into Nila's empty design book over morning tea the day before while keeping hers firmly tucked under her seat. 'My mother really needs me to get this job,' she'd snapped when Nila looked puzzled.

So Nila took Devika's advice and skipped her weaving class. Instead she went for a long walk down the river to where it emptied into the estuary and the delta beyond. If inspiration was required, then it was there in a bountiful quantity.

Nila had never had the time to visit the many pools along the river. These little ponds were teaming with lotus now – red, white and hues of green in between. The larger pools were home to young birds, including a *watha rathu malkoha* whose red face peeked in and out of the reeds that housed its nest and chicks.

Nila could not help but laugh as she saw five young otters and one who had to be the mama otter all living in the trunk of an old *kos* tree that had fallen over into the river. As the harried mother lay in the sun scratching herself, her young ones took turns somersaulting off an old overhanging branch and diving neatly into the water below.

So it was with joyous heart and peaceful mind that Nila returned to the mill to sketch her design. She sat by the steps of the amphitheatre to the outdoor temple and drew. And sketched. And pencilled. In the margins were her notes for the saree.

It would be woven from silk dyed in an emerald hue with silver thread being incorporated in every third weft row to give the fabric brilliance. The plain end would be reinforced with tassels. The embellished bottom border would have a playful cursive motif inspired by the family of otters. In their honour, Nila made it a recurring panel of five key elements. And the *potta*, well, that's where Nila truly let her heart sing and her drawing hand fly. She drew the lotus pond with its multicoloured flowers – the heart-wrenching line and grace of buds peeking through the muddy interior and the flowers in full bloom that would eventually fade away.

Nila stopped only when Devika came in search of her for lunch. 'Well done!' Devika crowed when Nila showed her the designs. 'These are truly amazing. I can't wait to see how you weave this!'

'I was planning on pearl beading the lotus flowers.'

'I hope you have enough time to do all this,' Devika warned with a worried frown.

'It should be fine,' Nila said. 'Hey, have you seen Guru Raju?'

'Not you too! I thought you were immune to him!'

'No, it's just that . . . oh, never mind. We'll see him in draping class later today anyway,' Nila said as she turned towards the boarding house.

'Where are you going, Nila? The dining hall is this way,' an exasperated Devika said, pointing in the opposite direction.

'I'm going to put these in my room. I don't want to get curry on my designs. I am having make-up classes with Guru

Sakunthala and she usually brings lunch for us to share.'

'Where is my loom?' Nila asked Raju summarily later that afternoon in class.

'In my bungalow – you can work there.'

She looked around to see if anyone had heard him. 'No, I can't. Someone could see me!'

Raju couldn't help but smile. 'Then come after seven in the evening and use the footbridge to cross over to Guru Sindhu's bungalow, and then you can just step over the stream to my place,' he said.

'No, I won't! It's not appropriate to visit a guru.'

'So why do I see you, Rangana and Devika often visit Guru Sindhu to drink tea on his verandah? If you work on your saree in my bungalow, you will be able to keep it hidden.'

'I see no need to be so secretive about what I am designing!'

'Oh really? Then why was it that Guru Lakshmi was showing me designs for sarees with a lotus motif *pallu* just before? Apparently Punsala handed in her designs early. One had a cursive motif with a recurring five element panel.'

Nila looked over at the diminutive Punsala, who was chatting with Renuka, in stunned disbelief.

'I only needed to glance at the design to see your style. But Guru Lakshmi thinks that Punsala has improved dramatically under her tutelage and this is the evidence. So I suggest you come over to my bungalow tonight to work and store your designs there.'

Nila nodded quietly.

Nila, Devika and even Rangana had visited Guru Sindhu's little bungalow many times. The little dwarf weaver loved to entertain and would cook his famous spicy potato balls with yoghurt dipping sauce for his favourite students. 'Eat, eat,' the little man would urge them as he shuffled around his quarters fetching a stool or a cushion to make everyone comfortable.

So Nila was quite confident crossing the little footbridge to get to Guru Sindhu's bungalow, but she definitely had butterflies in her stomach when, with her design cartridges and pencils clasped to her chest, she took a large step across the tiny stream that separated Raju's home from the others.

'Raju! I am here, Raju!' Nila called through the back door and waited for a moment. She called again and was met with silence. Glancing anxiously around her, she spied the local fishermen rowing down the river in a flotilla, their evening journey lit with a multitude of kerosene lamps. In a few moments they would come by and Nila's secret would be blown out faster than a coconut lamp in the monsoon, for many of the fishermen were friends with the watcher at the mill.

Nila darted anxiously into the house without invitation, only to be met on the other side with the bulk of Raju's chest. 'I am so sorry, I am so sorry. I just didn't want to get caught,' she babbled nervously.

'I was on my way to open the door,' the guru said.

'Did you still want me or shall I come back later?'

'Yes, yes, of course. I was just tidying up. Come through,' Raju said.

As they made their way through the little kitchen that held his bachelor tea implements and cooking utensils, Nila was struck by the raw and acrid smell of linseed oil. 'What is that?'

'Oh nothing,' he evaded as he led the way to a living room with a large divan in the corner spread with a light quilt made of old sarees. Several kerosene lamps lit the warm lime-washed interior and on the other side, through a small indoor court-yard, was a small shrine to the goddess Saraswati and Lord Ganapathi. A freshly lit oil lamp indicated that Raju had probably finished praying just moments ago.

'I closed the doors in case anyone thought of peeking in,' he explained, pointing to the shuttered windows and doors. 'I know a few keep tabs on whoever comes over the footbridge.'

'You are aware, are you?' Nila asked with a little smile.

'Yes, I am completely aware. You could drop a hint or two to some of the girls that it's pointless peeking into the bungalow early in the morning. My friends rarely stay the night.'

As Nila came into the room proper, her breath caught in her throat. What was this? Where had she come to? No one at this mill, Nila was sure, knew of this. 'What are these, Raju?' Nila asked, looking at the hundreds of stacked canvases in the room.

'My paintings,' he said.

'What do you mean? I thought you were a saree maker.'

'I am a saree maker because I have been taught my trade from since I was a babe. But what I want to be is a painter,' he explained. 'I was studying art in India when my father fell ill last year, so I came back to help Gauri with the mill. The agreement is that if we can get a good showing at this exhibition in India, then I can concentrate on my art.'

'Oh, is there a particular style of work you do?'

'Are you interested in art, then?'

'Yes, it was my best subject at school. Do you do portraits? Or perhaps landscapes?'

Raju hesitated for a moment, turning slightly pink before clearing his throat, and said, 'Nudes, actually.' He picked up a canvas and turned it around to show Nila.

Unlike the other people who'd seen his work, Nila didn't giggle, titter or look away uncomfortably when confronted with the naked female form. Instead she looked at the painting at length before turning around to pick up other canvases and setting them the right way around so that she could look at them. 'But they are all of *suddu* women.'

'Local women, both Tamil and Sinhala, won't pose naked for me. *Anay bay aiyo! Mata ladji aiyo!*' Raju mimicked the coy local lasses feigning embarrassed refusal. 'I just can't convince them that I am only interested in their bodies.'

Nila giggled. 'I can see your problem.'

'I mean that I am only interested in *painting* their bodies.' Raju couldn't help but smile sheepishly. 'It is so difficult to find any halfway cooperative models. The ones who do cooperate want my . . . oh, it doesn't matter. You are not here to talk about my painting – you are here to design your exhibition piece.'

'But where is my loom? Rupani's bridesmaids' sarees, what am I going to do about them?'

Raju took her hand and led her to a chair by the tiny dining table in the alcove. 'You design while I weave,' he commanded as he walked to the other side of the room and pulled a loom out from behind a silk screen. 'I spent the day putting this together,' he explained.

Raju had indeed repaired the loom. He'd hammered the frame together with new wood to replace the rotting beams and had properly bolted the whole thing together with fresh steel screws. As Raju threaded the frame, Nila sat at the table to design. She started half a dozen concepts as Raju took time and care to stretch the hundreds of fine two-ply silk threads along the length of the machine to create the garment.

But Nila rejected each design she came up with, crumpling cartridge after cartridge on the floor with exasperated sighs. She wasn't going to revisit the lotus concept. And using the concept of fish seemed too trite. She already knew that Devika was using the rocks that the river cascaded over upstream as inspiration for her *kalamkari* masterpiece, so that wasn't an option.

'Why don't you take a break?' Raju advised as he started to twist the first two rows for the plain side of the first saree, and Nila looked up from her work a moment to watch him weave. He was dressed in his customary sarong but had discarded his singlet in the muggy night heat. His muscles bulged and ripped as he pushed the battens forward and back, moving the weave along at a tremendous pace.

Nila had always been entranced by Guru Sindhu's weaving style, seeing the magic the dwarf made as he danced. But watching Raju weave was different: he commanded the loom. He was its master and the garment he created was at his beckoning. His towering height made it easy for him to push the battens forward and back and the strength in his legs meant the force he applied on the foot pedals was incredible. He could create a saree with a higher thread count per inch than Nila ever could, making the fabric denser and richer. Two-ply silk yarn went in one end and glorious supple fabric rolled out the other.

Soon Nila returned to her task, though a little reluctantly at first. She stretched her mind far and wide seeking inspiration for her theme. Finally she thought of the beautiful waterbirds who lived in the estuary, and she sketched away for about an hour and a half until Raju, who'd taken a break to make them both cups of tea, came back and sat next to her.

'I'd give up on the waterbirds. I am not giving anything away here when I say a few students are going down this path.

In the first week, before things got tense, students were showing each other designs, and I saw at least three or four takes on *rathu demalichcha* alone.'

'This is just so frustrating. I had it all pinned down. I knew my design. I cannot believe Punsala would steal my work.'

Raju gave a weary sigh and shook his head. Thunder rolled with an ear-splitting crack as the heavens opened and rain started pouring.

'Is it always like this?'

'Unfortunately, yes. A few years ago one student called the police on another and we had a fistfight in the court-yard. Another year all the students put their work under lock and key in their suitcases, but just before designs were due someone found out that you could pick the cheap locks with a kitchen knife. That year we had to restock the kitchen with cutlery.'

'Why? Why do people behave this way?'

'Poverty, Nila, it's poverty. Most of the students who come here are poor. Do you think a rich man would send his child here to learn? Saree weaving is not respected as it once was. We weavers no longer enjoy the status we once had along with healers and blacksmiths.'

'But how can they be so dishonest?'

'I sometimes think that it is easy to be honest only when your stomach is not cramping of hunger, or to hold on to your integrity if you don't have to send your children to work as servants in someone's kitchen.'

'I know, I know,' Nila agreed with a gentle shake of her head. 'But I thought Punsala was my friend.' She stood up to gather her design tools. 'I think I'll call it a night,' she said. 'I'll go for a walk down the river tomorrow after class and perhaps that will inspire me.'

'Leave them here – it'll be much easier,' Raju said, taking her pencils out of her hands. 'It'll save you having to bring it all back tomorrow. And I'll walk you to the boarding house.

I doubt any of the spies are out this late at night,' he said, unfurling a large black umbrella.

Raju wasn't quite sure what it was, but when Nila put her little hands on his forearm to stop slipping on the old wooden footbridge, he felt a strange jolt in his heart. The uncomfortable feeling of his pulse accelerating was so unfamiliar to him that he didn't even realise he'd opened his mouth to say, 'Nila, wait for me behind the outside shrine tomorrow. I'll walk with you down the river.'

The relentless rain ceased briefly after lunch but started again and went on right through the afternoon. Nila could hardly see ten feet past her nose, for the monsoonal downpour made everything grey, and a trip scouring the river seemed more and more unlikely.

When classes ended, Raju walked past Nila to mutter, 'I think you'll have to give up on your plan to find inspiration down by the river,' and she nodded – but just after dinner, as the crows started flying towards the mountains to seek their evening refuge, there was a burst of evening sun so bright, so odd for that time of day, that Nila felt obliged to use it for whatever it meant. She hurried out the side door, slinging a light shawl around her shoulders.

She walked past the shrine on the river, going the long way to the river track instead of taking the short cut past the dyeing huts, and pausing briefly to find a dry lamp to light an offering. It had been weeks since anyone would have been able to light an offering here, because of the rain. Nila closed her eyes and recited her prayer to Saraswati.

'May your grace light my way,' she finished softly, opening her eyes. Perhaps it was the fading evening light filtering through the treetops above that made her see it, but Nila could have sworn she saw a smile flickering on the goddess's marble face.

So perhaps it was Saraswati, too, who guided Nila upstream instead of down, past the small rapids and eddies that marked the river's course as it headed inland. It led her through the dreaded shantytown, though by daylight it didn't look so bad. Children ran around naked while mothers washed their vegetables at the outdoor well.

Further upstream, past Panadura town proper, Nila kept walking and found a series of market gardens, the reedy vegetables showing stunted growth, for the sun hadn't really shone in weeks and weeks. Another ten minutes along, Nila came upon a village, bustling with evening activity.

Her eyes took in tiny details that would escape most, like the fluttering saree of a new bride as she walked to her in-laws' house with the evening shopping, and the faded gold of the tattered garment an old beggar woman wore that exactly matched the coat of a scrawny dog loitering nearby.

The unexpected burst of sunlight had given Nila an hour to explore up river, but it faded as suddenly as it had arrived. Shopkeepers rushed about pulling in large bunches of *kurumba* while yelling at the dawdling customers to hurry up as errant drops of rain started to splatter. Nila turned to hurry downstream, only to find a long paddle sticking out of a coconut-tree-hull canoe barring her way.

'Something told me I'd find you here,' Raju said, standing up to offer Nila a hand. 'Come on, get in, it'll be faster home this way.'

It would indeed have been a faster trip back home, had Raju not had to stop several times as wave upon wave of heavy rain came upon them. 'The canopy of trees in this next inlet will give us some shelter,' Raju called out over the heavy downpour.

And it did give them some respite, sheltering them from the worst of the rain for about a quarter of an hour. 'Thank you yet again for rescuing me, Raju,' Nila said. 'You seem to have made a habit of it. I am in your debt.'

'Actually, Nila, I am in your debt,' Raju replied seriously, holding Nila's eyes in the twilight. 'I cannot believe the way I spoke to you in Bandarawela. It was impossibly cruel. Think of this as my atonement.'

'You didn't say anything that wasn't true, Raju. You weren't to know about my family situation, and you are quite right, I am not beautiful or even pretty, and what I was wearing didn't flatter me.'

'All the same, I said it to hurt you and that was not right.'

Nila smiled to accept his apology. 'How did you think to find me up the river?'

'I came looking for you when the sun came out, but Gauri came and wanted to chat with me about something. By the time I got away from her, I walked past the outdoor temple and saw the lamp you'd lit. I figured you were upstream.'

'Well, thank you,' Nila replied as Raju pushed off again, guiding the slight craft through the fast eddies and currents of the now rapidly flowing river.

Observing her white knuckles on the sides of the craft, Raju soothed her gently. 'Relax, Nila. I grew up on this river, remember? I learned to swim in that waterhole,' he said, pointing to a little pool across one of the banks. 'And I got the worst hiding of my life for stealing *kurumba* from that estate!'

Raju pulled into the stream between his house and Guru Sindhu's and jumped up the embankment to help Nila up, then ushered her into his bungalow. He pulled a few towels out of an armoire, tossing them to Nila along with a soft, old white saree. 'Sorry, I don't have anything else you can change into,' he apologised, showing her the way to one of the smaller bedrooms.

It took Nila no more than a few minutes to wrap her long hair with the towel and change her saree, but when she came out, Raju was on the other side of the small courtyard attending to his evening prayers, lips murmuring his love for the goddess Saraswati as he lit the oil lamp and wafted incense over her figure.

As he bent his head in prayer, Nila was struck by his beauty. His were eyes softly closed and his concentration as he chanted was absolute, his body rocking with a gentle rhythm. This was no disbeliever paying lip service to the Holy Mother – he was her true child.

'I missed my evening prayers,' Raju apologised as he returned, lighting the kerosene lamps without much ceremony. And it was then that she saw it, behind some of the canvases of nudes. A painting of the goddess.

'That is Saraswati Devi, isn't it?' Nila asked, pointing to the painting.

'Yes. It was part of a series I did many years ago.'

'Why did you always paint her in front of a river?'

'Because she is the river goddess. *Sara* means flow and *wati* means to have. Saraswati is literally she who has flow.'

'Tell me more,' she commanded, her heart thumping in her chest. This was what she'd been searching for.

Raju was pleased by her interest, and pulling out some large books on Indian art history, he invited Nila to sit next to him on the divan. Late into the night they talked, about the goddess, about the river and the forces that held the world together.

'By immersing the fires of ignorance in her waters, she brings wisdom and light. The consort of the Lord Brahma, she was able to tame his wandering mind. She is also the protector of practising Buddhists,' Raju explained.

'So she is herself the river yet she has no fear of fire?'

'Her power and grace is more omniscient than the fires that fan ignorance and hate.'

With that Nila started to design, into the wee hours of the morning as Raju weaved. Her creative process was punctuated by cups of tea strengthened with Horlicks and snacks of salty Maliban biscuits that Raju brought her. 'Designing on an empty stomach leads to weak line and form,' he teased. And when Nila showed him the final designs before he walked her across to the boarding house, he knew. He knew that he'd finally met a kindred soul who understood beauty; its elusive and transient nature and how it could make the spirit soar or crush it with equal efficiency.

'Oh Nila,' he said as they walked across the bridge. 'I can't wait to see you weave this. Magic doesn't come from the loom. It comes from the heart.'

Perhaps it was because his own heart and mind were so full that Raju didn't hear the sound of a branch breaking in the mango tree just beyond the courtyard. Maybe he could be forgiven, for mango trees were wont to shed their limbs in the heavy monsoonal rains, but had he lifted his kerosene lamp a little higher than was required to light his slippery path, he would have seen him, even in the pouring rain. Hiding in the shrubs below the mango tree.

The tattooed thug from the shantytown. The thug who'd spent the last six weeks in jail, thanks to Raju tipping the police off. The tattooed thug who'd followed Raju and Nila all the way along the river and had watched them work together throughout the night.

It was barely past four in the morning when the shrill alarm went off. It was difficult for Nila to drag herself out of bed, for she hadn't lain down in it until well past midnight. She brushed her hair out of her eyes and shook the sleep from her head.

She knocked at Manoj's bedroom door and went in, holding her nose against the sour stench of soiled clothes. 'Wake up, Manoj, we have so much to do,' Nila pleaded, shaking him. 'It's quarter past four and Rupani's engagement guests will be here in a few hours.' He rolled over and snored.

Giving up after a few minutes, Nila made her way down to the well by herself and sighed. 'How did Amma get all these?' she asked herself softly, spying the shadows of the forty or so urns that would need to be filled with water for the guests.

She slipped on her rubber slippers and splashed the pail into the well.

Nila had been drawing water for close to an hour when Nimal, Mrs Vasha's servant boy, came through the holey fence with several breakfast rotis. 'Do we have to organise those chairs that the lorry just dropped off as well?' the little boy asked, his voice worried.

'Yes,' Nila replied with a sigh as she heard the noisy clanging of a deliveryman dragging foldaway chairs through the garden. 'Don't worry, I'll do the lifting – you just move them around,' she assured the boy, who was the size of a six-year old despite being at least fourteen. No matter how well he was fed at Mrs Vasha's house, his early years of malnutrition could never be overcome.

The rest of the morning flew, with Nimal and Nila working together to set everything to rights for the engagement. It was only after they had shifted the four-tier engagement cake into place that she turned to the task of getting herself ready. Not that she had any space for it! Quite literally no space for her to stretch her arms to pleat her saree!

For Rupani and her eight chattering bridesmaids were getting ready in the bedroom, allowing no one else in front of the mirror – and when one of the girls tried to make a sliver of space for Nila before the narrow polished glass, Rupani growled at her. 'Don't worry about it! It's not as if anyone will be looking at her.'

When Rupani emerged before the assembled guests she looked beautiful, her pretty face and figure flattered by the saree Nila had bought for her. There were many admiring comments and whispered compliments. But the guests' admiration soon turned to disgust and indignation at Rupani's behaviour. When Albert slipped the ring on her finger after the reading of the banns, looking as if he would burst with happiness, she shrugged his tender hand away. Family, friends and neighbours looked away, embarrassed and appalled by her abominable gesture. They were even more horrified at the way she spoke to her elderly mother-in-law to be afterwards, rudely ordering her around.

'Someone should give that girl a good thrashing,' more than one guest muttered.

'That girl does not need to get married. She needs to learn some manners,' others harrumphed.

Nila overheard these comments as she slipped in the room to stand behind her mother and felt ashamed for her younger sister.

'Is that Nila?' an aunt who had travelled from Badulla asked. 'Has she done something to her hair? She looks so different.'

'Nila Mendis certainly has the figure for a saree,' a male friend of the family commented slyly.

'Who knew she was hiding those curves beneath those frocks,' his companion replied, only to earn a scowl from his wife.

Nila had not changed at all in any real sense, but the months spent at the mill had given her confidence. She knew her worth now, which lent a calm confidence to her natural kindness and warmth. So it was she who was the true host of the festivities, ensuring all guests were graciously welcomed and properly attended to, and in return they positively showered her with praise and attention.

'Child, come and sit down next to me and tell me where you got that saree from,' aunty after aunty begged. Vera's sister from Badulla insisted that she spend at least half an hour by her side. 'I am stuck in Badulla with ten children,' the woman pleaded. 'Tell me the latest fashion for sarees or I will go insane!'

Nila was dressed in a silk saree of cream and lilac that glowed next to her dark skin. It was one of the half a dozen or so sarees that had appeared miraculously on Nila's bed the day after she'd returned to the mill. She and Devika had several blissful hours in their dorm room as she finally learned the skill of draping a saree on herself properly – how could one not, when gifted with such yards of beautiful silk that begged to be worn close to the skin?

'Oh, could you teach me how to drape my saree like yours?' the younger female cousins implored Nila at every turn, for she'd draped her six-yard silk dream in the Orissa style, with the *potta* wrapped around her bust before it was brought over one shoulder. It was an uncommon drape that created the illusion of length, drawing attention away from Nila's dumpy waist.

'How are you doing at the saree mill?' uncles asked as they sidled up to speak with her. 'What's the name of the place, *duwa*?'

'Nair & Sons.'

'Tamil?'

'Yes, Uncle.'

'Do they treat you well?' a short balding gent demanded. He was dressed in a suit that reeked of mothballs.

'They treat me very well,' Nila insisted. 'I want for nothing.'

'*Shah*, your parents must be so proud of you, Nila. It's not easy to get a job at the moment. Both my sons have finished their senior exams and neither one can get a job,' another uncle scoffed, pointing out two dejected-looking men skulking in the corner.

'It's jolly good of these Tamil fellows to offer you a job,' the man in the mothball suit said. 'They usually only ever employ their own kind.'

'Uncle, I could not agree more,' Manoj said, butting rudely into the conversation. 'Every time I apply for a job it gets given to a Tamil bugger. Someday someone is going to have to tell the blady bastards that this is our country!'

'But, Manoj, you know that is not fair,' Nila chided gently. 'Murali Senerathnam got the job at the cement company ahead of you because he passed four GCE O-Levels instead of two. And George Dhanapalan has worked at his father's ware-houses, so it made sense that he be offered a job at the mercan-tile.'

'But what about our father?' Manoj fired back. 'He has been passed over for promotion so many times that it is a joke. They keep giving all the top posts to Tamils.'

'Yes, they treat us like second-class citizens in our own country!' the gentleman with the unemployed sons said.

'There are an equal number of Sinhala and Tamil workers at the mill,' Nila protested, though she knew there were tensions between the two groups. Some of the younger Tamil workers had maps on display in their dormitories depicting the northern half of Sri Lanka being towed by gunship to Tamil Nadu. Though the older Tamil workers growled at them, they seemed to be fired by an inexplicable zeal to split the island apart. Guru Lakshmi loved to play favourites, too, pitting her Sinhalese students against Tamils, firing jealousies and stoking hate. But Nila had always put that down to the guru being an unpleasant person – it had nothing to do with her being Tamil.

'See, Uncle, give a woman a job and she develops a smart mouth. Careful you don't get ahead of yourself, Nila, or I'll stop Amma from letting you go to that job at all,' he threatened, earning a chorus of approval from his audience.

'But Amma won't listen to you, younger brother,' Albert drawled jovially joining the group. ''Cause Nila is older than you and deserves respect for at least getting a job. Something you haven't achieved yet!'

This elicited muffled giggles from some of the men as Manoj opened his mouth to reply before thinking better of it.

'There is really nothing wrong with working with Tamils,' Nila persisted. 'They are no different.'

Her brother sneered at her and walked away.

'That is entirely correct, *nangi*,' Albert agreed. 'The *suddas* made *achuru* wherever they went. Look at the mess India is in. One third calls itself West Pakistan and the other third calls itself East Pakistan, with India stuck in the middle. What a disaster!'

'That is not the fault of the *suddas*,' one of the uncles told him. 'It's the fault of the blady stupid Tamils. They want to rule the Sinhala and take all the jobs and money and power for themselves!'

'No, Uncle, that's not true,' Albert said. 'Sinhala and Tamil people have lived in harmony together for thousands of years. The *suddas* created this whole problem by promoting Tamils ahead of Sinhala.'

Nila had heard these arguments a thousand times, and as the conversation took its predictable route, she glanced out the window into the street to see a feeble-looking Mrs Vasha walking weakly back home. Turning to follow her, she thought she saw someone familiar talking to Manoj on the street.

Who was he?

Nila normally didn't pay much attention to Manoj's thuggish companions. They were usually of a similar breed – swindlers, hard drinkers and time-wasters. So it was only when Manoj's companion turned to face the house, doubled over with laughter, that Nila recognised him.

Why was Manoj talking to the tattooed man from the shantytown?

It was a very unusual sight that greeted the workers and students that Monday morning: Raju at the gate of the mill. All dressed in white *and* without one of the *suddis* who were his habitual companions. As he welcomed both students and workers back from the weekend, they could not help but wonder whether the tables had turned on him and *he* was waiting for someone to arrive – so much so that a few of the girls who secretly fancied themselves in love with him waited just beyond the central courtyard, watching, plotting and hating. They nearly fainted with relief when it became clear that Raju had been waiting for Nila, automatically taking Nila's heavy weekend bag from her and walking with her. It was not as if he would fall for that fright.

'Could you come to my bungalow at lunch?' Raju had urgently asked Nila at the gate. 'I really need to tell you something important.'

'I have something important to tell you too!'

'What is it?'

'You first!' Nila insisted.

'No . . . no. What I need to tell you will take time,' he'd replied in a low tone that barely concealed his excitement.

'I have my lessons to make up with Guru Sakunthala and then I have lessons with you,' Nila muttered, trying to think of a solution. 'I can come with you now if it's really important. Guru Sindhu is not a stickler for time.'

'No, that's okay. I'll see you this evening. Try to get away a little early if possible.'

Nila nodded her agreement as she took her bag back from him and climbed the steps to her room before morning prayers.

And as the day progressed, Nila was forced to ponder the truism that a day would linger if something exciting is to happen at the end of it.

First Guru Lakshmi would return the approved designs for the exhibition; but that was not before she caustically critiqued each and every design and the designers who produced them.

'Ingenious Devika, ingenious,' the lady had drawled handing the large design cartridge over to the beauty. 'The rocks on your *kalamkari* had better be smaller than those in your head for this design to work at all. And please don't go for emerald green; emerald green with milk resin will make the saree look more like an outfit worn by aliens in those American films you see in Colombo.'

'And Nila,' she'd drawled nastily. 'You have made some very good designs. But remember it is gift of the Goddess to bring to fruition. Not that you will be able to do it, seeing that you don't have a drop of Saliya blood in you.'

Then Miss Gauri came up and handed everyone extra commissions. 'I am so sorry,' she apologised. 'We got three new orders this weekend.'

'When will we have time to weave our pieces for the exhibition?' several students cried in protest.

'We'll be cancelling saree draping lessons from now on. That'll give you at least an extra ten hours a week,' Miss Gauri explained.

It was well after dusk before Nila could escape to Raju's bungalow. She didn't even have to knock on the door, for Raju was waiting for her.

'Oh, Nila, you won't believe it,' he said, taking her hands in his own. 'I received a letter from Tambimuttu *mama*! He has shown one of my paintings to a good friend of his. A famous art teacher in London. And he wants to see more!' He picked Nila up and swung her around.

'Wait a minute,' Nila laughed. 'I don't understand a word you've just said. Who is Tambimuttu?'

'Meary James Tambimuttu; he is one of Sri Lanka's greatest poets and my *appa*'s friend. Surely you've heard of him?'

Nila, who'd been educated entirely in Sinhala, shook her head.

Raju rolled his eyes. 'Never mind, then. But he is friends with an art teacher by the name of Lucian Freud in London. Freud is a very famous painter.'

'And this Lucian wants to see some of your work? Have you picked anything to send him yet? And is that why saree draping was cancelled?'

'Yes,' Raju confirmed. 'If not, I would have insisted Gauri cancel dyeing. There is only so much you can learn about boiling cloth in vats of colour,' he said, leading Nila into his living room. 'I have selected a few works already but I am not happy with any of them.'

Nila moved to look at the stacks of paintings that Raju pulled aside.

'They just don't seem quite right,' he said with frustration. 'I thought I'd redo them. Use these for sketches.'

It was clear that he'd already started – the room was pungent with the sharp smell of linseed oil, mixed with the headier aroma of oil paint.

Nila had seen his paintings before but hadn't had a chance to study them, too busy chatting with Raju or working on designs herself, but now she looked at them carefully. The sarees Raju had painted his models in had a luminescent beauty, begging the viewer to reach out and caress their soft folds. The women too were beautiful, their limbs draped languorously across his day bed, or posing by the river or down at the beach, and yet . . .

'You can see something isn't right, can't you?'

'Yes. It's as if the sarees and the models don't suit each other,' she agreed. 'It's strange. You've chosen the right saree for the right woman and the drapes are exquisite. But something is not quite right.'

'I have thought of maybe weaving a new saree and finding a model for it, but I know that it is stupid.'

'Have you thought of finding a new model first perhaps? Find a saree to suit the model rather than the other way around?'

'That's difficult, Nila. I really like to get to know my models when I paint them and that could take up to six weeks. Tambimuttu *mama* wants my paintings before I head off to India for the exhibition. And that gives me barely three weeks.'

'Have you thought of approaching some of your old models?'

'Perhaps,' Raju said, looking at his paintings.

'Anyway, I'd better start weaving the rest of Rupani's bridesmaids' sarees,' Nila said.

'All done. I even managed to dye the lot yesterday, see.'

Over by the corner there was a stack of sarees, all soft and sinuous, and in a shade of pale orange that could have been stolen from the evening sun as it set into the inky depths of the Indian ocean in Panadura.

'How can I ever thank you?'

'Just win at exhibition,' Raju grinned. 'The sooner we have a good showing in India and get enough commissions, the sooner I will be able do this all the time!'

'I guess I should get to work, then,' Nila grinned in return, the thought of telling Raju about the thug from the shantytown completely slipping her mind.

So as Nila threaded the loom with the complicated pattern for her exhibition piece toile, Raju painted. Chatting, laughing and sometimes stopping to play music on the old gramophone. 'You've never heard jazz?' Raju demanded. 'Louis Armstrong? Miles Davis? John Coltrane?'

'Is that an American car? Like the Cadillac?'

Raju laughed on his way back to his easel. 'You have much to learn my young friend, much to learn.'

'So how did you do it? Learn so much?'

'I went to school in London before I went to India. My father sent me there to be educated in 1962. A friend and I went to New York by steamship for six weeks.'

'You have seen so much,' Nila sighed wistfully. 'I haven't been any further north than Anuradhapura. I am sure you'll become a famous painter one day.'

'I don't know about famous but I'd like to be good though. I'd love for the world to see what I see. The beauty comes in all different shapes, forms and how we define it.'

'Thank you, thank you, Raju, for sharing so much with me.'

Together they worked. Her weaving and him painting as the monsoon rains intensified. Their friendship borne initially out of Raju's guilt for his cruel words in Bandarawela turning into companionship of the minds. In Nila, Raju found a friend

without pretense and in Raju, Nila found an intellect she
wanted to explore.

'I knew it, I knew you'd like Amaradeva,' Nila teased. 'His
music is *boring*. My father loves it. But the sitar makes my
head hurt.'

'I guess you are a fan of Rukmani Devi then. All gloss no
substance,' he teased back though he did go and put a vinyl
record on for Nila to sing along to.

By the end of the week, Nila had made great progress with her
piece, while Raju was still struggling.

'What am I doing wrong?' he demanded as she brought
him a cup of tea. 'Inspiration comes so naturally to you!' he
complained, pointing to Nila's toile – though to call the two-
by-two tapestry a toile would be a great injustice, for it was a
study in poetry.

In its creation, Nila had broken almost all standard conven-
tions in saree making. While she had reinforced the plain end
of the toile, she'd left the bottom threads loose and unwoven,
which was where her genius shone through, as she tatted the
repeating pattern freehand. The *potta* had a peacock feather
design, threaded through with tiny beads of steel, which Nila
hoped to finish that evening. She would start the embroidery
the following day, using iridescent blue silk dyed using indigo
and silver. It would be a masterpiece.

Nila stood next to Raju and critically assessed the paintings
he was working on. There was energy there, yet something was
lacking.

'What's inspiring you, Raju? I know what's inspiring my
saree. It is the goddess Saraswati. I feel her in everything I do.
I see her everywhere. I feel her.'

'Light, I love light.'

'Then show light, Raju. All I am seeing here is the saree
you've painted on her.'

'I love sarees. I love how a saree flows. How it shapes and how it caresses. I also love how a person can define themselves in it. You make a saree into what it is. The most beautiful saree in the hands of an unskilled person is useless. Likewise, the prettiest woman may wear the prettiest saree and still be ugly. It's what's inside that matters.'

Nila stared at him for a moment.

'I adore women,' Raju confessed. 'I like the shape of their breasts and I love the way sarees mould their rears.'

'Perhaps then you need to focus on women. I see the sarees you've draped but you haven't spent much time on the women themselves.'

'I need to paint from life. I need a muse – a new model. Someone who can help me break this,' Raju said. 'You have good taste, Nila. Come down to the beach with me. Help me find a model.'

Nila shook her head. 'I'm busy. I have to finish my toile.'

'You've made good progress. Just quickly. We'll go down for hoppers by the beach tomorrow and come back as soon as I've found a model.'

'Oh, Raju, I haven't even started the embroidery!'

'Come on. I'll buy you a *faluda*. I'll even get them to put an umbrella in it for you,' he pleaded. The sickly sweet milk concoction with rose essence and caraway seeds was Nila's favourite, and he knew it. 'Please? I really need your help.'

And how could she say no, after all he'd done for her?

The hopper hut Raju took Nila to was very different to any other Nila had ever been to. The cleanliness alone was enough to mark it as the province of foreigners. There were no dead cockroaches crushed under the huge pots of boiling curry and there was electricity – a single light bulb providing illumination for the deft hopper makers as they churned out crisp bowl-shaped pancakes one after the other. There was even a guitarist playing soft music on a raised platform that acted as a stage.

'Here, let's sit here.' Raju pointed to a table on the edge of the beach area, where they could see everyone. Quite a few of the tourists were sprawled around on chairs, sucking on cigarettes.

'My father worked for a *sudda* before Independence and said that all he ever ate was roasted meat and boiled vegetables. No spices, no pepper, no nothing. Do you think that is why *suddu* people are so skinny?' Nila asked, glancing at several white people who were ravenously munching away on the bowl-shaped breads, tucking into the chicken or fish curry as if they'd never seen food before.

'Remind me to tell you all about the munchies,' Raju smiled as the waiter brought them two tall glasses of *faluda*.

A few of Raju's friends came to talk, looking curiously at Nila as they greeted him in languages she didn't understand before lapsing into English. Although Nila understood English and spoke it well, she struggled with the Scottish brogue or the nasally vowels of South California, especially when they were slurred by the effects of LSD.

Though it may have been just as well, for Raju's friends' comments were very suggestive. She was looking quite well, fashionably dressed in a bottle-green paisley print saree, and when Raju explained that she was his student, not his girlfriend, a few expressed an interest in her themselves, to his evident horror. Eventually they were left in peace, though, and began a careful survey of the women on the beach.

'What about that one?' Nila asked. 'The one in that white dress by the coconut tree.'

'I painted her two months ago. She is the one draped in that blue saree.'

'Really? She looks different with her clothes on,' Nila stated, tilting her head to look at the girl again. 'Well then, what about her? The one with the beautiful hair?'

'No, not her,' Raju said wrinkling his nose. 'I went out with a girl who looked just like that when I was living in the UK, and her father ran me off with a shotgun from her room.'

'Why?'

'I am Tamil and she was an English rose.'

'What about her, then?' Nila pointed to another woman. This one was quite a beauty, with pale blue eyes and long blonde hair. She was dressed in a wraparound skirt made of a saree with a crocheted halter-neck top. She was lying on a hammock strung between two coconut trees, one long leg hanging over the edge as she swung to the music.

Raju took a long look at her before shaking his head slowly. 'Too beautiful.'

Nila rolled her eyes. 'Excuse me, but don't you want to paint beautiful women?'

'No, I want to paint real women. Women who have worked. Women who are passionate. Women doing what they need to do to get on in the world. Women dressed in beautiful sarees.'

'Okay, what about her, then?' Nila said dryly, pointing to an older woman who was not dressed like a hippie and had something quite schoolmarmish about her, primly eating her hoppers.

The guitar music had finally given way to a more upbeat tempo. Someone had brought out a set of drums and a bass guitar, and an impromptu jamming session began. The vocalists were at best mediocre and the quantities of marijuana the other musicians had smoked meant that poor improvisation was the order of the day.

'So, are you going to ask her?'

'She wouldn't take her clothes off for me, I'm quite sure of it,' Raju said.

'What about her, then?' Nila asked. 'Or her?' Girl after girl. But no sooner had she pointed a woman out than Raju would find something wrong with her or worried about the saree he'd drape her in. Finally she convinced him to ask a girl or two, but they were all heading down to the beaches further south that weekend.

'Oh, Raju, I give up, I really do. Why don't you find a saree that you want to drape on your model and then we'll find the model,' Nila sighed.

The fact that it was Poya, the full-moon holiday, two weekends before the exhibition threw almost all the students into a panic. There were those who were panicking because they genuinely needed the extra time. Then there were those whose exhibition pieces were well advanced and could afford the four-day weekend, but who would lose the chance to spy on the work done by others. And then there were those who were just panicking because they could.

Which was why Miss Gauri found it difficult to get anyone to help her that Friday afternoon. Packing and labelling two hundred sarees was a large task and Nila was the only one who volunteered. 'I could not have done this without you,' Gauri sighed thankfully as she and Nila folded the last heavy silk saree and packed it into a display box.

'No problem at all.'

'Are you sure you don't mind catching the late train? Won't your family be worried about you?'

Nila looked away. How could she explain that she would rather spend the rest of her days at the mill if she could? That she'd finally found a true home?

'Did you find what you were looking for?' Gauri asked of her brother as Raju strode into the mill store, all grumpy, dusty and sweaty.

'No,' he grumbled. He took in the tiredness around Nila's eyes and the hair flying out of her habitually neat bun and was angry with his sister. She should have asked one of the male students to help her instead of imposing yet again on Nila.

'Do you even know what you're looking for?' Gauri teased.

'No,' he growled.

'My brother the frustrated artist,' Gauri said to Nila with a cheeky smile. 'Since he can't find the perfect girl, he is looking for the perfect saree! Like in the Vedas, he thinks the gods will bestow the perfect woman on him if he finds the perfect saree!'

'Not the perfect woman, Gauri, the right woman,' Raju said. 'But the right saree would be a good start. I have spent the day trawling through our warehouses in Colombo and even made myself a laughing stock with the saree sellers by visiting boutiques that don't carry our work. I have looked at hundreds of sarees, but none were right. I want something classic, none of this hours of beading and endless design. You can hardly see the woman these days for the amount of decoration on her drape!'

'Why not find a simple saree, then?' Nila suggested from the corner.

'Where would I find one?' Raju asked wearily. 'I've looked everywhere.'

'Why don't you try the cupboard in the administration block,' Gauri suggested, absently ticking off items from her inventory list. 'Appa used to store old sarees they weren't able to sell in there.'

'I have nothing to lose,' he said, and took off still muttering to himself.

Nila checked the time, and after saying a quick goodbye to Gauri, she too hurried away.

The heavy load of bridesmaids' sarees she was carrying weighed her down and she only just made the train to Kotahena. A mere hour and a half later, she wished she had missed it – for when she reached home, there was no one there. Not a single welcoming light. Not even a note stuck on the door. Nila didn't bother knocking on Mrs Vasha's door, for she knew the elderly lady was visiting her sister up in the hill country. There were no lights from the Gamages' house across the street either. It took Nila a good fifteen minutes of knocking on neighbours' doors to find out where her family was.

'So sorry,' the harried neighbour apologised. 'I was supposed to meet you, and take the bridesmaids' sarees from you,' she said, snatching the heavy parcel from Nila's hands.

'Where are they? My parents, my brother and sister? And the Gamages?'

'They went down to the beach in Bentota for the long weekend. Your sister said she needed a little holiday before the wedding, so Albert hired a car and Manoj went along for the ride.'

'Where am I supposed to stay?' Nila wailed.

'I don't know,' the neighbour replied as she locked the door behind her.

Nila looked up and down the street, wondering where she could spend the night. Normally, there would be at least half-a-dozen families who would gladly take her in, but they all seemed to have deserted the capital city for Poya.

Checking her purse, Nila discovered she had enough money to buy a ticket back home to the mill – no more, no less – but even the rail system conspired against her that night, for she heard the last train leave as she rushed into the station.

'*Nona*, would you like to sleep on my bench?' an old beggar woman offered. The old lady in question was coughing up blood and spitting it where she sat, so Nila shook her head, though she was tempted by the kind offer. Then, within a blink of an eye, some thieving ruffians snatched her large hessian tote containing a week's worth of unwashed knickers and smelly brassieres. To add to her mounting woes, Nila no longer had any underwear left! She spent the night at the old station, hungry, cold and terrified.

Nila only gave full vent to her emotions when she finally reached the mill just before dawn the next morning to find the gates locked. Sobbing hysterically, she clung to the wrought-iron grilles. 'Nila? Is that you?' Raju called into the darkness, putting away his rifle. Hearing a noise, he'd thought that one of the crocodiles from the estuary had got a goat.

Delirious with exhaustion, Nila could barely raise her head as Raju swept her up into his arms and rushed her into his bungalow. 'What happened?' he kept asking as he tested her forehead for a temperature.

'No one . . . at home,' was all Nila could mutter as she fell into a dead faint, but not before seeing the nubile, full-bodied woman with dark eyes and skin rise from the tumbled sheets on Raju's bed.

Nila would never forget the sound of rain on the roof of Raju's clay tiled bungalow – the heavy thump thump, ceaseless and relentless. The rain coloured everything a dull shade of green, reflecting the emerald river around the mill.

As Nila slipped in and out of the clutches of an exhausted sleep, she heard snippets of conversation between Raju and the dusky beauty.

'Who is she?' a shrill voice demanded.

'. . . not important . . .' she heard Raju say.

'Well, I didn't come here for this kind of thing . . .' The argument had shifted somewhat.

'Leave then!' Raju snapped in return.

'You'll have to explain everything to my parents!' the female voice shouted. Nila heard the woman storm out into the rain, and the heavy thud of Raju's footfalls as he raced after her. After hours of tossing and turning, Nila fell into a deep slumber again, to waken just as dusk was darkening the evening sky.

Raju had put her to sleep in the very bed left empty by his lover. She sat up abruptly and found herself naked under the quilt. She blushed furiously – how could she ever look Raju in the eye again? Since she could not find her clothes, she gingerly donned the light cotton robe Raju kept for his models as she padded into the main room, thinking only of a speedy exit.

'What are you doing?' Raju asked as he came in through the back door, leaving his black umbrella on the back stoop. He had two big hessian bags in his other hand.

'Looking for something to wear.'

'I went to your room and got your clothes,' he explained, holding up one bag. 'And something for us to eat, too,' he said, holding up the other bag.

'I'll leave as soon as I get dressed,' Nila replied, taking the bag of clothes and disappearing into the bedroom. 'Thank you so much for everything you've done,' she called out as she dressed. 'I'll get Rangana to help me move the loom when he gets back.'

'Why? You've been working so well here.'

'I really don't want to cause any more trouble,' Nila explained, coming into the room looking for her slippers.

'Aren't you staying for dinner? You haven't had anything to eat for two days!'

'That's fine, Raju, really. I'll pop into town to get something.'

'In this rain? Don't be an idiot!'

'But I don't want to be any trouble,' Nila said. She headed for the front door before changing her mind and tracking through the house to the back. There would be a few students still at the mill and she'd rather not get caught leaving the guru's bungalow.

It was only as she made her way through the small living area that it hit her – the tangy fragrance from the light papery dosai and the soupy sambar Raju had laid out. It was like being felled by a falling coconut. Her stomach growled quite audibly. She nearly swooned when Raju pulled out several piping hot *urdu vadai* from a paper bag.

'Sit,' Raju commanded, pushing Nila onto a wooden chair and setting a plate in front of her.

'Thank you,' Nila replied weakly as she ate, dipping pieces of the crisp pancakes in the soup.

Raju waited a good ten minutes before he interrupted. 'You'll be happy to know I have found the perfect saree. You were right – I needed something simple. And I found it in the cupboard, just as Gauri suggested.'

'When was it made?' Nila asked between mouthfuls.

'I can't figure that out. The fabric is old, but the work on it is quite new. And I can't figure who made it either.'

'Haven't you asked your sister?'

'My sister took off to the beach not long after you left – though I think all the holiday-makers will be severely disappointed,' he said dryly, gesturing to the sheet of grey-green rain outside. 'Now tell me what happened, Nila. You told me you'd be back on Monday. The saree I peeled off you was foul. I tossed it into the cook's fire.'

Nila stiffly explained what had happened.

'And they didn't tell you or arrange for you to stay somewhere else?' Raju asked, incredulous.

'It was my fault. I normally get home early. They probably waited for me as long as they could.'

'Nila, there is no excuse for abandoning your child. Never!

I'd sooner rip my own heart out.'

'But it wasn't so bad . . .'

'Really? Where would you have gone, had you not had the mill to come back to?'

'Well, I did. It doesn't matter,' Nila said as she stood to leave.

'Don't you want to see the saree? It is perfect!' Raju said, feeling a deep stab of pain at the thought that she might go.

'I'd better get back. You probably want to get back to painting anyway,' Nila said, flicking her hand in the direction the easel. On the canvas was the rough outline of a young woman who bore a striking resemblance to the woman she'd seen last night.

'Please, Nila.'

Nila did not want to see the saree. She was afraid that he would, in a moment or two, look into her eyes and see. See her love for him. And the pity that was sure to follow would render Nila wretched beyond belief. But she could not say no. Not to Raju. So she took a deep breath, sighed, and turned slowly towards the simple wooden frame in the corner.

He led the way, lighting kerosene lamps. 'It is a truly beautiful saree, Nila,' he said. 'The person who created it struck the perfect balance between adornment and letting the fabric speak for itself. There is a youthful naivety about it, yet the styling is so sophisticated. The person who made it must have a beautiful soul. A pure soul,' he continued, as he lit the lamp nearest the frame and moved away so Nila could see it.

For a moment Nila couldn't speak. Her heart stopped. For in front of her was the saree she'd made as a sample for her first day. The sample that Miss Gauri had taken into her possession before saree draping class. Her first attempt at saree making.

'What I'd give to meet this person!' Raju said rapturously.

'Maybe you already have,' she said with a broken smile. 'That was the saree I made for my first day sample.'

As she turned to walk away, he caught at her arm and stopped her. 'What is it, Raju?' she asked, looking up, and before she could protest, he kissed her.

'No, Raju, no!' She squirmed away.

'Why not?' he demanded.

'I don't want to end up as just another woman in your bed! How dare you!'

'Is that your problem? That I am a womaniser?'

'Yes! There is no love here,' Nila yelled, tears starting to course down her face.

'You may not love me, but I certainly love you,' Raju replied, his voice catching in his throat.

'How can you? I am not beautiful! I am not even pretty! I am ugly,' she cried.

'No, Nila, you are not ugly. The person who created that saree could never be ugly!' he replied, gathering her into his arms and kissing any part of her that he could, telling her that he loved her over and over again. 'I cannot live without you, Nila. I knew for sure this morning when I found you at the gate. I was so scared something had happened to you. I would have died, Nila. I would have died.'

'Raju, you love many women. What you feel for me will pass,' Nila protested, trying to break free from his embrace.

'Nila,' Raju said, holding her face by her chin and looking deep into her eyes. 'When I turned eighteen I took my vows as a Hindu priest. It is a privilege only open to Brahmins and Saliyas. I can only sleep with one woman. My wife.'

'But what about—'

'I have never slept with any of them,' he whispered. 'I have never been with anyone,' he insisted as he carried her to his bed in the alcove.

Surfacing from sleep for the second time in as many hours, Nila stretched languorously, feeling the gentle sting between her legs that had never been there before. She didn't even need to turn her head to hear Raju's heartbeat. It was just there, just below her ear, as he held her tightly. Slow, steady and dependable. Yet Raju's uneven breathing told her that he was awake, and suddenly fear gripped her. Would he regret what they had done? What would happen to her?

Before panic could claw away at the joy of Nila's most perfect night, Raju shifted, sensing that she was awake. 'Wasn't that beautiful, darling?' he demanded, turning so that he was cradled between her thighs, his lips just over hers, his proud, jutting manhood telling Nila that their passion had far from burnt out. And if their first time had been beautiful, the second could only be described as exquisite. There was no fear this time, just unbearable joy, as they took turns trying to out-pleasure each other, giggling and laughing as they discovered each other's bodies.

But panic did claw at Nila when she woke for the third time, in the early hours of the next day just before dawn. Raju was not there next to her and the coolness of his side of their narrow bed told her that he'd left some time ago. This gave Nila the time to let terrifying thoughts come to the fore. What was she going to do? She certainly couldn't demand Raju marry her. She loved him too much for that. And she knew objections would come from both their families. She was Sinhalese and he was a Tamil.

Unable to lie still, Nila curled over to bury her head in Raju's pillow, inhaling his fragrance, the smell of the camphor and sandalwood he used for religious rites. The rain had stopped, but in the dark light of dawn she could see that the rain clouds were not far away. The end of the monsoon had not yet arrived.

'Hey, what are you thinking?' Raju asked as he padded into the room and sat down on the bed next to her.

'Raju, what are we going to do? This can never work. Our families will kill us.'

'Shh . . . come, come with me,' he said, pulling her up.

'But Raju!'

'Trust me,' he replied, as he took her into the main room and helped her to dress in a plain white cotton saree. He draped it on her like a lover who knew her body, all the secret nooks and crannies of pleasure. When he was finished, she helped dress him in his dhoti – not a sarong, but the garment of the Hindu priests.

'Come,' Raju said, pulling her out the front door and over the little footbridge. He hurried her along the muddy track by the river to the outdoor temple, where he carefully helped her down the narrow set of stairs to the amphitheatre, made slippery by the rain. Nila stopped and held her breath.

The entire temple was lit with hundreds of little oil lamps. In the centre was a small dais bearing just a handful of flowers, some sandalwood and camphor. In the fathomless darkness that marked the moment between night and day, Nila could not say if she'd strayed into a magical dream.

'It's not extravagant, Nila, I'm sorry,' Raju apologised as he led her to the altar. 'But it's enough for marriage.'

'Raju, your family will hate me and mine . . . and I don't know what they'll do to you!'

'Nila, neither your family nor mine will be able to do anything to us.'

'They will – they'll track us down and hurt us,' she cried.

'Not to India, they won't,' Raju said with a smile. 'We'll stay in India until they calm down – and if they don't, we'll either remain in India or move to London.'

'But what about the saree mill? It is your birthright!'

'No, you are my birthright. Everything else I could lose and I wouldn't care a jot.'

'What about your father, Raju?'

'My father will be angry for a while, but he loves me too much to stay that way for long. He will come around. Especially once you give him a grandchild,' he whispered. 'So promise me, Nila, that you will be mine. In this life and for the next seven.'

So she did, following him around the sacred fire seven times. As Raju recited the ancient verses that bound them as husband and wife, he strung on her a simple gold pendant on the white cord he wore habitually around his chest, the symbol of his priesthood. 'It's not much, but I will drape you in gold when we get to India,' he told her.

As he tied the simple *mangala sutra* around Nila's neck, he stared deep into her eyes. 'I promise to protect our home and our family,' he said.

'I promise to be true and loyal to you,' Nila vowed in return.

They recited the seven ritual pledges to each other before the beatific Saraswati and the tender Lord Ganapathi, the gods being the only, yet most powerful, witnesses to their nuptials.

Just as they finished the last of the fourteen sacred rites, the sky above thundered. The peace was over. Raju and Nila ran through the pouring rain to their bungalow, and there they would remain cloistered for the next two days. Not that they minded. What use were fancy hotels or exotic locations for honeymooners so desperately in love with each other?

Raju's only living parent was his father. His mother had been taken by the malarial epidemic of 1968 while he was at school in the UK.

'You couldn't come to see me all weekend? You could not even come on Monday. It takes you till Tuesday to make an appearance. It takes no more than five minutes to walk from there to here,' the old man snapped gruffly from the divan. Old age and a series of strokes had left the once robust saree maker partially blind and paralysed from the waist down, but Shiva Nair still knew his mind.

'I told you about the paintings that Tambimuttu Mama asked me for. I have been working on them. And what's the point in coming here anyway? You are always asleep,' Raju teased, gently picking up the old man and taking him to the dining table.

'Humph! Enough cheek from you, you young rascal! And I don't care what you do, as long as you don't mess around with any of those foreign women!'

'So you don't mind him messing around with local women, then?' Gauri asked with a laugh as she came into the dining room, where the servants had set a table laden with fragrant idali, pungent *paripu* and coconut chutney.

'He should be not messing with any women at all! His marriage to the daughter from Kanchi Silks has been all but agreed to!'

'I never agreed to a marriage with Shanthi Govindarajan!' Raju growled.

'But if the situation here changes, we need a base in India we can move to quickly!' his father replied. Despite his afflictions, old man Nair still had his finger on the pulse of local politics. 'I don't trust J.R. Jayawardene. He is an oily, two-faced love merchant. He will destroy the relationship between Tamils and Sinhalese before he is through.'

'The Tamils and the Sinhalese are capable of getting on just fine,' Gauri said slyly. 'Don't you agree, Raju?'

Raju turned to stare at his sister. His mouth was full of food so he could not respond.

She gave him an arch look before continuing. 'Some of our most talented saree makers at the mill are Sinhala. Take Nila Mendis, for example. I saw the toile she made for her exhibition piece. It is truly exquisite.'

'Lakshmi and Hirantha had some misgivings about her, didn't they? Didn't Sindhu and Sakunthala ask you to take her under your wing, Raju? How is that going?' the old man asked.

'I think he's taken her more than under a wing,' Gauri smirked mysteriously, but before anyone could ask her what she meant, she deftly turned the conversation to innocuous topics such as the horrible weekend she'd had down in Bentota with her friends, and how they'd spent the whole time indoors with everybody's tempers becoming increasingly frayed.

After dinner, Raju helped his father into his night sarong and left him in his room with the old gramophone playing some Duke Ellington, then went to find his sister.

'How did you find out about us, Gauri?'

'Renuka. She came to me this afternoon and said that she had spotted the two of you down by the hopper hut on the beach one night last week. She hadn't thought much of it until she spotted you again chatting by the shrine room yesterday. She was worried that Nila had taken a leaf out of her sister's book and would trap you into marriage.'

'So what did you say?'

'That I wasn't worried. That my brother was a smart man. Then she started on about favouritism, so I told her that you would not be on the panel this year, since you are focusing on other projects. I have organised Mr Pantipuram to be on the assessing panel instead. *Ana*, Renuka is dangerous. You will need to watch for her.'

'I will. And I will tell Nila too,' Raju agreed. 'But what do *you* think? About Nila and me?'

'I think it is a crying shame that you put a stupid white cord around your wife as a *mangala sutra*,' Gauri said. She went to the sideboard and pulled something out of one of the drawers.

'I went into town and got this today,' she said, pouring a gold chain as thick as her little finger into Raju's outstretched hand. 'I'm dying of embarrassment that my new sister has no gold to speak of!'

'You like her?'

'I adore her! And I am just glad that with her being your wife, I won't have to pay any extra wages!'

'Oh, Gauri!' Raju laughed. 'How do you think he'll take it?' he added seriously, jerking his head in the direction of their father's room.

'He'll rage for a few weeks, maybe even months. But he loves you too much. And he will love her. He won't be able to help himself.'

'She is exquisite,' Raju sighed.

'Well, go enjoy your exquisite wife. It's dark enough for her to sneak into your home now!' Gauri laughed.

Nila had, of course, been a virgin before she got married. The only knowledge she'd gleaned about what went on behind the closed doors of a bedroom between a man and woman had been from the snatches of conversations she'd overhead from the ladies who came to Mrs Vasha's house.

'Thank goodness he leaves me alone a few days a month. Monthly courses are a saviour for that alone, if not anything else,' a middle-aged mother of six had complained.

'I don't want to get married,' a young Burgher bride-to-be had cried to her mother while Mrs Vasha fitted her wedding dress. 'It will be painful.'

Which was why Nila was quite confounded by what was happening between Raju and herself. For her it was pure pleasure – and yet something that needed to be done time and time again to be truly enjoyed. Sometimes slowly, sometimes fast and sometimes just before Nila slipped out of Raju's bungalow to head to her room.

Indeed, Nila had been so concerned by the disparity between what she'd known the act to be and what she shared with Raju that she'd voiced her concerns to him. 'Maybe we are doing it wrong.'

He'd smiled before slipping out of their bed to return with a stack of Indian art books he kept on the top shelf of his bookcase. Flicking through the heavy tomes, they'd found more ways to give each other pleasure than they had ever thought possible.

'I had no idea,' Raju had gasped in wonderment as Nila tried something they had seen pictured in most of the books.

'But you are delicious,' Nila had sighed from down there after she was all done.

That was when he told her about Renuka. 'Just as well she only saw us down by the shrine room,' Nila giggled, slipping out of bed to start weaving. 'Imagine her reaction if she'd seen us down by the trees beyond the river!'

When Raju had spotted Nila by the river dyeing sarees, he'd hurried to the water's edge. 'Come with me,' he'd whispered roughly, luring her to the copse of trees just beyond. When the female workers dyed cloth in the river they wore no underskirts, and Nila only had to slightly tug at Raju's sarong for it to come apart. 'Men who wear pants are stupid,' Raju had muttered as he pushed her against the large *kos* tree and entered her in one fluid motion. They had shuddered to release in a burst of sunshine, the salty sting of the sea breeze caressing them, the soft fabric of Nila's potta teasing Raju's bare chest.

Their passion was incandescent yet earthy, spilling over into every part of their lives, filling them with a creative force that neither had experienced before. While Nila weaved at the loom, Raju painted her, naked except for the saree she herself had created, draped over her body. His paintings had a new sensuality – he had suckled at those round breasts, knew the taste of the briny juices between her legs. The sound of her heartbeat was his mantra. He painted his lover with the same joy he took in pleasuring her.

Nila's saree making had taken on a sensual quality too. As she sat at the loom she felt the pressure of her foot on the pedal, the shift of the lamms and bobbins, and fell into an easy, assured rhythm. There was just one frustration. 'My saree is not as beautiful as it could be,' she complained to Raju.

'Students aren't given the best materials,' Raju agreed as Nila started to freehand tat the lace along the bottom edge using steel bobbins. 'We never know whether what they create will be a complete waste of time. I'll get you the better beads and embroidery threads tomorrow.'

'Don't, Raju. I want to be selected on my own merit, like everyone else.'

'You aren't going anywhere anyway. Your place is here with me.'

'But I want to know I earned my place here fairly. Not just because I am your wife.'

'What will you do if you don't get offered a place?'

'Work on it until I am. I don't expect anything for nothing, Raju. I want to work until I deserve it.'

Raju stared at her for a moment. 'Fine then,' he said slowly. 'But when we are in Madras, we'll go to the silk market and buy the finest silk to re-weave this saree. There is a town just south of Kanchipuram where you can buy beads, too. Diamonds from Australia and sapphires and rubies from here in Sri Lanka.'

'Why, Raju?'

'Because I will re-weave this saree for you, my darling,' he said, delicately touching the design boards that lay against the wall next to the loom. 'And you will wear it when we celebrate our marriage. It doesn't matter that we'll cross the fire seven times again.'

While Nila could not believe her luck in having married such a passionate man, it was his kindness that truly overwhelmed her. He had insisted on driving her back to her parents' home the weekend after their marriage.

'I will wait for you at the Sri Ponnambalavaneshwarar temple for an hour,' Raju insisted as he helped her out of the car in Kotahena. 'I'd rather you not go at all, but that would tip them off immediately. But if anything is amiss, you come back or get a message to me somehow. I won't let anything happen to you.'

'Nothing will happen,' Nila insisted, touching him gently on the arm.

'I won't feel safe until I have you safely by my side on the plane!'

By the middle of the following week Nila was intensely grateful that she had Raju's bungalow to escape to. Rules were relaxed so that the students could work exclusively on their exhibition pieces. Some students had quit the mill altogether. 'I won't come back until the morning of the exhibition!' Renuka had huffed, bundling her woven saree into a large bag.

Others stayed on, but they succumbed to frequent bouts of hysteria in varying degrees of intensity. It was not uncommon to see girls sobbing in corridors or for the young men to rage out into furious arguments. Raju and the watcher took it in turns to break up the fights, which scared Nila witless.

'What if one of them hit you?' Nila worried after an altercation so nasty that Raju, Guru Hirantha and the watcher had all had to step in to calm the frayed tempers.

'I'll just step out of the way,' Raju teased. 'Not even two weeks married and she's already starting to nag!' he exclaimed to Devika.

'I hope the two of you aren't going to be like this the whole time we are in India,' Devika said.

Nila had confessed her secret to her best friend and invited her to work on her exhibition saree in the calm quiet of the draping master's bungalow. Devika's blue-green *kalamkari* masterpiece was nearly finished, but the final stage required inking with a steady hand, something that was near impossible with jealous classmates around.

'I am afraid we'll be like this for the rest of our lives,' Nila laughed, turning back to her embroidery. She was working on the peacock motif, slipping sequins and beads along the threads at precise intervals to shimmer and shine in the light.

'Seven lifetimes at least,' Raju protested. He was applying

the final lacquer over his canvases before taking them down to Colombo on Friday.

He was sending Tambimuttu a series of three paintings of Nila to show Lucian Freud: one of her weaving at the loom, the evening light playing on her hair and skin, another of her dyeing fabric in the river, the dampness seeping through her saree, and a third showing her lying supine on their bed.

Now that Nila was mistress of her own home during daylight hours , she had finally met Gauri. Properly. As a sister-in-law.

'I can't tell you how happy I am that he chose you, *thangachchi*, and not one of those silly white women,' Gauri had said joyfully, adroitly slipping an extra charm onto Nila's *mangala sutra*.

'Gauri, stop weighing my wife down with gold – she will hardly be able to stand,' Raju joked as his sister gave Nila more gold bangles.

'You must stop, *akka*,' Nila protested, for Raju had taken the opportunity to visit the gold merchants in Colombo on Friday night for yet more gold – delicate earrings, chunky rings and thick bangles – all of which he'd taken pleasure putting on her on Sunday night before making up for their two days apart.

To Nila it all seemed too strange to be true. She who had received so few gifts in her life seemed now to be drowning in abundance. Even her parents had given her a few trinkets in honour of Rupani's nuptials. 'We can't have you looking like a beggar,' Vera had remarked sourly at the gold shops in Pettah on Saturday morning.

'But no one will be looking at her,' Rupani whined. 'And if you don't buy her any, I can get that extra pair of earrings.'

In the end, a compromise had been struck and Nila was given a gold chain and earrings, though more copper than gold. 'Make sure you're there on time,' her mother had said. 'And if you are late, don't bother coming at all.'

If the truth were indeed to be known, Nila was considering

not returning at all. She had finally realised that, other than blood, she had nothing in common at all with the people she called her family. The time she spent with them at home that afternoon with her parents and siblings did not change her mind, and the evening was no better.

'I hope Malinthi from down the road is not planning on wearing that hideous saree to my wedding,' Rupani had prated on.

'I saw Albert take his mother to the doctor this afternoon,' Vera had sniffed. 'You'll have to put a stop to all this wasting of money, Rupani. I don't see why she needs a doctor when I only ever see an apothecary.'

'Look, these Tamil bastards have completely taken over Jaffna,' her father complained listening to the news on the wireless in the background. 'Someone better trash the bloody buggers!'

Nila had to bite the inside of her cheek to stop herself from crying out her abhorrence to his views.

'Here, Father,' Manoj smirked, handing Mervan the evening paper. 'See, on page ten, some lads in Negombo doused the Hindu *pusari* with petrol and set him on fire.'

'They should give those lads a medal,' Mervan laughed.

Nila felt sick to the stomach. 'I haven't seen Mrs Vasha this weekend,' she said, excusing herself, choosing not to stay and share the meal of rotis and curry she'd spent the afternoon making for them.

Mrs Vasha looked unwell, terribly unwell, asleep in her planter's chair and her breath rattling slowly. She started awake at Nila's approach. 'I am just tired, my dear. It's all this travelling,' the old woman said, dismissing Nila's grave frowns. 'So what is that around your neck, child?'

'A gift from my mother,' Nila replied, bending over so Mrs Vasha could inspect the necklace.

'It's cheap and tacky, that's what it is. You are their eldest daughter and should be respected as such!'

When Nila told her what had happened the previous weekend, when she had found the house – and the street – deserted, Mrs Vasha almost had an apoplectic fit. 'It kills me that they treat you like that. Something could have happened to you!'

'Something did happen. Something amazing and wonderful,' Nila said, sitting down close to the old woman so that she could tell her the story. She held a finger to her lips to beg for her silence, gesturing over her shoulder to her parents' house. 'They cannot know. He is Tamil.'

'But married, Nila? To the son of the *chettie* of the mill?'

'Yes. He loves me and I cannot imagine my life without him.'

Nila gently pulled out the proof, in the form of the thick gold chain and the ornate pendant of her *mangala sutra*, tucked away in her brassiere. Next to the copper that Vera Mendis had bought her daughter, the gifts from the Nairs stood out like peacocks in a pen full of common chickens.

'What sort of a man is he? Does he treat you well? What are your plans?'

'He is a painter. An artist. He treats me like a queen,' Nila assured the old woman. 'And he says you are to come and stay with us in Panadura when we return. We will move into the *chettie*'s house and I can look after you.'

'Is there any chance I can meet your young man before you leave for India?'

'I hope so. As it is, we'll struggle to do everything before we leave. The exhibition at the saree mill will be over by midmorning, so I should be home in time for the wedding. We need to be at the airport by six.'

'You are like a daughter to me. I must know more about this man before I let you go off with him,' Mrs Vasha begged.

Nila sighed. Mrs Vasha had been more of a mother to her than Vera Mendis had ever been, and she owed her this. 'Maybe he could sneak into the wedding. No one ever notices who is actually there. You will love him, Mrs Vasha. He is a wonderful man.'

'I am sure I will. All the same child, I just need to meet him.'

The morning of the exhibition dawned bright. The rain had been less frequent over the last week, and just the day before, the wind had changed direction to come from the north-west instead of the south-west, pushing the monsoon clouds out over the Indian Ocean instead of inland into the island. And so it would remain for the next nine months until monsoon started yet again.

Nila had spent the night uneasily. It'd taken her till near midnight to put the finishing touches to her exhibition piece while trying to help Raju pack for their journey to India.

'But do we have to take my designs for the saree? We hardly have any space left!'

'Darling, how are we going to find the silk to match if we don't take the designs with us?'

Even so, her dreams were plagued by elusive demons of fire and blood. She woke several times before finally falling so deeply asleep in the early hours of the morning that she'd missed the alarm to sneak back into her quarters.

'It's lovely sleeping in with you,' Raju had murmured sleepily as Nila sat bolt upright in their bed. 'Wait till everyone heads off to prayer before you head into the mill. No one will notice where you've come from.'

And everybody was too busy to notice indeed. You could have brought a two-headed cow into the compound and no one would have raised an eyebrow. There were people everywhere by the crack of dawn. Extra cooks had been brought in to help the regular staff to make celebratory cakes and tea, and professional saree models had been driven in from Colombo.

Nila took her time getting dressed in their bungalow, wearing a cream silk saree with a bright red border. She'd selected it from the mill store the previous week and had managed to finish a simple sleeveless blouse the other night.

As Nila was pleating the fabric, the largest pleat at the back and the smaller finer pleats at the front, she looked up at Raju, who was tidying up their home. 'Who was she? That girl who was here that morning I came back from Kotahena.'

Raju looked up, confused.

'You know. The girl who was here? You even drew a rough outline of her.'

Raju looked very uncomfortable. 'She was a prostitute.'

'Excuse me?'

'She's a *devadasi*. I needed someone who wouldn't be too modest to take off her clothes.'

'But she spoke of her parents – do they know what she does?'

'I hired her from them.'

Nila was speechless for a moment, then felt suddenly grateful. Though her parents had never treated her well, they had never demanded that of her.

'Congratulations,' Miss Gauri said melodiously once everyone was seated in the indoor temple, the only space large enough to hold everyone.

'The students you see here today have completed a gruelling six-month apprenticeship. Of the sixteen of you who started, only twelve remain. That is a testament to your tenacity and skill,' she smiled. 'The arrangements for this morning have been explained to you previously. When your name is called, your model will walk across and display your work and you will need to answer any questions the panel may have for you.

'At the end of parade, the panel will take a few moments to decide the top four designers, who will be awarded positions here at the mill. The winning saree makers leave with Guru Raju to attend the exhibition in India this very evening.' She paused to draw breath. 'I shan't try your patience any further – we'll start now with Punsala Abeywardene.'

As the first model sashayed across the temple floor, the diminutive Punsala hesitantly fronted up to answer the judges' questions about 'her' design. Not that she had actually done Nila's design any justice, heaping insult on injury by poor execution. The motif was badly woven, with the edges fraying, and the colour she'd mixed up had turned out a virulent lime green instead of the colour of young shoots that Nila had imagined.

There were two students after Punsala before Rangana's name was called. Everyone stopped their fidgeting to watch as the graceful model pirouetted and ducked as she walked. The saree Rangana had created shimmered and glowed in every shade of green and blue, depending on the angle the light caressed it at. It was as if the model was walking through alternating waves of the sea and river. 'I made every fourth thread silver to give it brilliance,' Rangana explained. 'And yes, those are fish – the *rathu kailya* you see in the river.'

Next up was Devika, and her piece was so electrifying that it even elicited an involuntary '*Shah!*' from Mr Pantipuram, the head of fine arts at Colombo University. 'I mixed Indian ink with a ground green crystal to get the bright deep green,' she told the judges. 'And that is the temple motif from the river temple in Kelaniya.'

After Devika came Renuka. She'd spent a great deal of time discussing how she wanted her saree displayed when they'd all been dressing their models, pulling the model into a corner and showing her pictures of how she wanted her to move. And it paid dividends and then some. For as the model walked onto the temple floor, she released the length of *potta* like a rolled-up carpet that unfurled as she made her way across the floor. When she reached the judging panel, she twisted her shoulder to display what was on the fall of the saree – a tapestry of life on the river.

'Of course, I could not have done it without the help of my most excellent teachers. I will forever be in your debt, Guru Lakshmi,' Renuka cried, tears dramatically streaming down her face.

Then came the Tamil student named Seevan. His saree was spectacular too – he'd dyed it a stone grey, but with silver beads threaded through which gave the impression that his fair-skinned model was cloaked in a garment made of granite.

A whisper went through the crowd – the competition this year was very stiff.

Then it was Nila's turn. The chattering immediately stopped, even before Nila's model appeared. For almost everyone had to take a second look to confirm that it was indeed Nila Mendis standing before them. Her saree was flattering and the drape faultless, her hair carefully put up in a bun. Colour matching the bright red border of her saree was painted on her lips. More than that, Nila looked radiant. Blissfully radiant. She glowed with an inner happiness that showed in the delicate smile on her lips and the bright twinkle in her eyes.

Nila's model was halfway across the temple floor before anyone actually noticed her, but when they did, the entire room fell silent. First there was disbelief and then there was awed reverence.

'Why have you chosen golden-white when the rivers are rarely that?' Guru Hirantha asked her.

'Golden-white is the colour of the goddess Saraswati,' Nila replied with quiet confidence.

'Why the goddess Saraswati?' Guru Lakshmi asked.

'She is the river goddess,' Nila replied as her model pirouetted to show the spectacular fall of lace and the green-blue peacock embroidered on the *potta*. The totem animal of the goddess.

'How did you execute that border and lace?' Guru Sakunthala quizzed her. 'I have barely mastered the skill of freehand lace making myself.'

'My grandmother taught me,' she replied. Grandmother was the name many gave to Saraswati.

There was no need for any further questions. It was clear that Nila was a master saree maker.

After the final students had presented their work, the panel retired to discuss their selections and tension gripped the room. The field was very strong – who would be selected and who would be rejected?

The members of the panel were gone a long time, and eventually the students learned that there had been an altercation between them. Guru Lakshmi was now insisting on Raju being brought into the discussion. He'd been sitting to one side, enjoying the show. Gauri and Raju then had a brief chat, Raju suggesting a compromise that Gauri agreed to. As the judges filed back into the room, she turned to the crowd and raised her voice to announce the winners.

'Devika Goonethilake,' she called out as everyone applauded. There were no surprises there, nor was anyone surprised to hear that Rangana and the Tamil student Seevan had been selected.

'Nila Mendis,' Gauri called next, but the words were barely out of her mouth before Renuka jumped to her feet.

'I protest!' she shouted. 'Nila Mendis has cheated!'

Gauri looked to see who had caused the disturbance. Before she could speak, Renuka interrupted her again.

'Didn't you hear what I said? Nila Mendis is a cheat! She's been cheating all along!'

'That is a serious accusation – how has Nila cheated?' Guru Sindhu asked, speaking for the first time.

'She has cheated because she has received help from Guru Raju!'

'I have not helped Nila to design or weave this saree,' Raju protested. 'I deny it categorically!'

'But do you deny she is your whore? That you sleep with her?' Renuka screamed, quite deranged.

'I don't deny that she is my wife,' Raju replied hotly.

'Renuka, you foolish girl, you should have waited before making such wild accusations,' Gauri growled. 'I was about to call out your own name. The panel strongly recommended we make an exception this year, and offer a fifth role here at the mill. It would have been yours.'

'We will no longer be making you that offer,' Raju said, his voice low and deadly, 'since you have called my wife a whore.'

Renuka hesitated. 'But this mill belongs to your father,' she protested. 'I will take my objection to him,' she cried, turning to go towards the large house.

'No, the mill belongs to me,' Raju said, drawing himself up to his full height as the *chettie* of the mill. 'My father handed me the deeds of ownership a year ago. I would rather it be left to Gauri, but it is mine. So I order you to leave my mill at once.'

Renuka had miscalculated badly, expecting the other students to rally behind her. As she turned to go, genuine tears streamed down her face. 'We'll see who wins at the end!' she called as she stepped out into the scorching sunlight.

It had not been easy to take leave of the mill. Once Renuka had left, pandemonium reigned. Raju and Gauri had bundled Nila towards the *chettie*'s house, hissing in her ears that everything would be all right.

Raju had rushed in to break the news to his bed-bound father – he'd rather the old man hear the news directly from him than the many gossips at the mill – but he found Shiva Nair already seated on the verandah with a steaming cup of tea and a beaming smile.

'I gather the exhibition was a bit tumultuous this morning,' he grinned.

'Yes, Appa,' Raju replied, and cleared his throat nervously.
Turning to Nila and Gauri, he motioned them to sit down, only
to realise that everybody – students, teachers and workers –
had followed them to the large house and now stood crowded
around, unable to tear their eyes away from the unfolding drama.

Raju shrugged and turned back to his father. 'Appa, I have
made a decision about who I want to spend the rest of my life
with. It is not Shanthi, but this wonderful young woman . . .'

'Named Nila Mendis?' the old man chortled.

Nila sat on the floor next to Gauri, her eyes downcast.

'Come here, child,' he commanded, and she cautiously
approached the old man.

'Sindhu has spoken so highly of you that I can only thank
the gods that my son saw sense and married you!'

'It took him long enough,' Guru Sindhu smirked, walking
around to stand behind the old man. 'I knew Nila was perfect for
you, Raju, the minute I met her! Why, I even told your father!'

'You knew?' Raju accused his father.

'Of course I knew – I gave you an entire weekend with her
after your marriage ceremony as a wedding present, didn't I?
I had hoped I could meet her before you left for India, though!'

The planned exhibition celebration turned into an
impromptu marriage celebration with cakes and iced coffee.
'We'll have a proper celebration when you come back,' Shiva
Nair crowed, holding onto Nila's hand as Raju and the other
students piled their luggage onto the newly repaired van for
their drive into Colombo.

The plan was that Raju would see the group safely to
the airport before accompanying Nila to Rupani's wedding,
meeting Mrs Vasha and then making a safe escape to India.

'Blessing be on you, my precious children,' the old man
called, and everyone at the mill cheered as Raju drove off in the
kombivan with Devika, Rangana and Seevan in the back seats
and the bridal couple in front.

So it could well have been pure joy that blinded Nila to the risks of taking her husband into the treacherous lair that was her family. Danger was the last thing on her mind when they slipped into St Lucia Cathedral church hall, where the wedding was being held, only a little late.

The danger didn't even occur to her when Raju cheekily joined the greeting line to congratulate the happy couple, thumping Albert cheerfully on the back when he couldn't quite place the man. 'We met at Cambridge, old boy – at Cambridge,' he said. Nila smiled with pride at the dashing figure her husband cut as more than one woman turned her head to follow the darkly handsome man across the room.

May be the danger should have occurred to Nila when she finally spoke to her mother, halfway through wedding celebrations. 'Wait till I get my hands on you, girl,' Vera had growled through clenched teeth, but Nila thought she was angry because she had been late to the wedding.

Nila should have probably have known it when her brother Manoj looked at her and mutter nastily, 'We'll have a fiery celebration tonight!' There was a menace in his voice she should have picked up, but Nila was too used to ignoring her brother.

She should definitely have known something was afoot when her relatives, especially her aunt from up country, refused to look her in the eye. She should have noticed the thunderous facial expressions of her male relatives and the pitying glances of her aunts.

But Nila's heart was too suffused with joy to see – joy at seeing Raju seek out Mrs Vasha and spend a good hour in her company, fetching her glasses of iced coffee and making sure her plate of snacks was never empty, allaying any fears she might have of relinquishing Nila to his care. 'I love her more than life itself,' he'd assured the elderly lady. 'And you must promise me that you'll come stay with us. Our children need a grandmother.'

'I'll slip out now,' Raju told Nila half an hour before the bridal couple were supposed to leave on their honeymoon. 'I will meet you at the Hindu temple around the corner.'

Nila would spend most of her life trying to figure out what went wrong – how the fates could have been so cruel to her. What evil thing had she and Raju done to deserve what happened to them?

For as the newly married couple were farewelled amid a rain of rice and shiny silver confetti, Mrs Vasha took a bad turn. Nila and several of the local ladies rushed to her aid, carrying her to a small anteroom as she struggled to breathe. A doctor was called for, but by the time he arrived half an hour later, the old woman only seemed marginally better. Well enough to insist that Nila leave for the airport immediately. 'Go child,' she whispered urgently. 'Have a happy life, my dearest – you certainly deserve it. He is a good man.'

The last thing Nila expected when she ran out the door of the church hall into the bright afternoon sunshine was to find her husband trussed up, with an angry mob led by her brother encircling him. And next to Manoj stood the tattooed thug from the shantytown in Panadura.

'This is the filthy Tamil who raped my sister,' Manoj yelled at the mob. Raju looked terrified as Nila ran to him, only to be intercepted by the strong arms of her mother just a few feet away from her husband.

'You have brought shame and dishonour on our family,' Vera screamed, slapping Nila across the face.

'A marriage to a Tamil is no marriage at all,' her father spat, slipping the belt off his pants. 'They are our enemies. They are less than filth. Consorting with filth makes you filth,' he roared, raising the leather strap again and again at her, the heavy buckle hitting her on the forehead and splitting her scalp.

Nimal, Mrs Vasha's little servant boy, came running into the fray trying to help his mistress's friend. Manoj felled him with a single punch across his scrawny jaw.

Raju pulled desperately at the ropes that held him down, trying to free himself and save his wife, but he couldn't. His screams of outrage were muffled by the cloth stuffed into his mouth and would haunt more than one person there in the years to come.

Blood ran down Nila's face as her mother took her by the shoulders and shook her. 'I never thought you capable of such treachery. When Manoj told me that his friend had seen you with a man at the mill, I didn't believe him,' she said, pointing to the tattooed thug. 'But when a fine young lady came to me in tears this morning and told me that you were this man's whore – that you sneak into his house at night to lie in his bed and pose naked for him as he paints – I knew it was true!' she cried.

Nila fell to her knees at her mother's feet and sobbed. Renuka had taken her revenge, its consequences deadlier than she could ever have expected.

'I am sending you off to Badulla with your aunt,' Vera spat, dragging Nila up by the hair and thrusting her into her diffident aunt's arms.

'Raju! Raju!' Nila screamed. Her split head throbbed, making her dizzy, and she could barely see through cut and swollen eyelids.

'Raju? I will give you Raju!' Manoj shouted as he brought forth a can of petrol and doused Raju with its contents, tearing the *potta* off Nila's saree to drape it around his neck. 'We'll make it a little like suttee,' he taunted. 'Only in reverse. You Hindus like that. Burning alongside your beloved?'

Raju tugged at his bindings like a madman now.

'Is there anything you want to say, *Demala*?' the tattooed man asked, ripping the stuffing out of Raju's mouth and leaning in close to his face.

Using the last of his strength, Raju brought his head crashing down on the thug's forehead, the headbutt disorienting them both for a moment. Then the thug laughed, struck a match and tossed it at Raju's head.

Raju looked up to see a bloodied and near-comatose Nila being bundled off into a car. 'Seven lifetimes and more!' he screamed.

The last Nila saw of her husband was him being lit up like an unfortunate lantern at *Vesak*; a halo of red, orange and blue as the saree draped around his neck caught fire first before the petrol took hold of the heat and started burning the flesh of his body.

# The First Drape

Nayaru Lagoon, Sri Lanka, 1982

His voice trailed off. What was the point of speaking if nobody listened to you?

For most of Mahinda's life, conversation had occurred around him or above him. As if he was not even there.

'Yes, he is a very intelligent boy. He must go to Jaffna for further studies.'

'It is a tragedy that has befallen his family, but he must continue with his studies!'

'Of course he must go to university. He will be the light that shines on this entire village!'

It was as if his mind, body and soul did not belong to him but rather to the village he was born to.

And today was no different. The out-of-town examiners whose job it was to listen and assess him as he did his final oral exam were too busy looking out the window, watching the fisherman on Nayaru Lagoon. Karthik, from the far shore, had had a good morning. He'd pulled in cage after cage of live seafood: prawns, crabs and lobsters from the lagoon's azure depths. Mahinda could almost hear the examiners' stomachs rumble with hunger and the convulsive swallowing of saliva. Their meagre teacher's salaries could not afford such delicacies. The catch was destined for the tables of rich businessmen further up north in Jaffna or the coconut plantation owners south in Trincomalee.

The headmaster, the saintly old Sir Poornaswarmy, beamed at Mahinda, encouraging him to go on, and he did, raising his voice just a little. After a moment or two the examiners turned their attention back to him, but the chief examiner muttered something under his breath. Not many understood, and even those who did thought maybe they had misheard him. Except for Mahinda, who was close enough to both hear and understand. *Para Demala*. Filthy Tamil.

Within a blink of an eye, Mahinda switched from Tamil to faultless classical Sinhalese. His subject was Sri Lanka's name.

'The island's first recorded name was *Tambapani*. Golden sands. Though our precious island has an even more ancient name. A name bestowed on it by the greatest epic known to human literature – the Ramayana. It was the Indian sage Valmiki who coined the name *Lanka* – the resplendent isle . . .'

'That was very good. But I wouldn't get my hopes up about getting into university,' the chief examiner drawled arrogantly when Mahinda was finished.

'Oh, I think he has every chance of getting into university,' old Sir Poornaswarmy objected. 'He has done all the extra-curricular subjects and is the top in the district.'

'But they are standardising exam results again now.'

'That is just wrong!' the headmaster spluttered. 'We checked. We checked with the education board before our lad came back to the village. They said that standardisation was over!'

About ten years earlier, in the early seventies, the government had introduced a policy designed to ensure that students from all districts were equally represented in university placements. Until then, most places had gone to English-speaking Tamils from the north and east and Sinhalese from the towns and cities. Now results were standardised across the island and there was a district quota system. Affirmative action had had a discriminatory effect; Tamil students from the north had to do better than rural dwelling Sinhalese students to get into the same courses.

'No, it isn't. The decision to reintroduce the policy was made last week,' the examiner told him.

Mahinda said nothing. He knew the man was lying to aggravate the old school master.

As the bell tolled to indicate the end of the examination period, Mahinda pushed his rusty old bike along the narrow strip of palmyra trees that ran from the road to behind the school hall and waited by the filthy waterhole. A waterhole inhabited by a flock of nervy waterfowl.

The waterfowl had just cause to be nervy, though. Had it not been for the plentiful supply of fish remains that floated down the little stream behind the school they would have long sought a different home. For the students took delight in tormenting the poor creatures. It wasn't uncommon for fire-crackers to be lobbed at the birds from the makeshift science laboratory under the coconut tree. And one full moon, some of the more enterprising villains had brought in a half-filled clay pot of *ra*. Had it not been for the headmaster, who kept a close eye on his charges and knew when they were up to no good, all the birds would have perished of alcohol poisoning.

Mahinda watched the village teachers as they packed up and waited patiently for the chief examiner to finish his duties. It was clear from the stiff smiles on his teachers' faces that even they found the examiner irritating. When the man finally stepped out into the sunshine, Mahinda struck, jumping on his rusty pushbike and riding straight at the waterhole, as fast as he could go, lobbing large pebbles like grenades and then swerving hard to avoid landing in the murky water as he swung around.

'Quaark! Quaark!' the birds screamed as they took flight.

'*Iskolay Mahathaya*, look where you are going!' Mahinda yelled as the chief examiner bolted to evade being run over.

As the man rushed back to the safety of the schoolroom, he ran into the path of one of the heavier waterfowl. The terrified bird defecated liberally over the man's bald pate.

'You did that deliberately!' the examiner shouted. 'I will make sure you fail!' Not that anyone took much notice. They were too busy laughing at the sight of the sticky grey-white goo dripping down his head and his ears.

Mahinda rode off, not looking back. A whole three months of blissful freedom beckoned before he might be required to go to university.

'Mahinda *putta*, you do our district proud,' farmers called from their fields as he rode past. On one side of the narrow bunt, tender green rice plants were planted in neat furrows, and on the other side, maturing tobacco plants topped with bright pink flowers. The heady woody fragrance of tobacco flowers mingling with the sea spray gave Nayaru its unique fragrance.

As he rode through the little group of shops that served as Nayaru's trading hub, the *modalalis* tossed ripe rambutans at him. They smiled as he caught the fruit with one hand while steering his bike with the other.

'Be like him when you grow up,' young mothers advised their boy children as they played in the sand by the lagoon. Their hearts swelled with maternal pride at the sight of him, tall and lanky, with the promise of the man he would become. His intelligent eyes shone bright from under his heavy brows, his skin darkened by years of working under the hot sun in his father's fields.

As the road turned south, Mahinda screeched his bike to a dusty halt when he saw the *gamanayaka* strolling across from his hut to greet him.

'*Puttar*, I don't have to tell you the dreams of this village are riding on your shoulders,' the old man said. 'Achiamma and

I have been doing *abishekam* for you all week. By the power of Lord Ganapathi, may you be the star that shines on us all.'

Mahinda looked at the ground, unable to meet the village headman's kindly eyes or acknowledge his wife's generosity. *Abishekam* – libation with fresh milk of the stone statues of the gods Lord Ganesh and Lord Shiva in the small village temple – took devotion and time. And most of all, love.

'Off you go, *puttar*. Have a rest now. And enjoy your holidays.'

Mahinda gave the man an embarrassed little bow as he pushed off again and continued his journey home. The young man didn't stop for long once he reached the half-mud, half concrete house he called home, though. His brothers and sisters rushed to greet him as he came through front gate.

'Can you take me down to the lagoon to swim?' 'What does the word 'obfuscate' mean?' 'Can you mend my *bonika*?' three of the six of them demanded in unison. Mahinda took a moment to answer their questions, reaching out to push back his youngest sister's glasses on her button nose before making his escape. 'I'm home now for a few months, I'll teach you all manner of things,' he said, before darting through the house to pick up the reel he'd whittled from a piece of driftwood.

'Are you going already?' his grandmother demanded, cutting him off at the doors to the kitchen.

'Yes, I haven't been for months now and it could all be a mess . . .'

'Why don't you give it up?' the old lady grumbled, handing the boy a decidedly chipped cup of hot tea. 'The island is haunted. They say the moths are actually spirits of dead people.'

'Pfft,' Mahinda scoffed as he swallowed the dark brew in one mouthful and made his escape. He had a great deal to do before the tide turned and he needed to hurry.

Everybody in these parts knew about the copse of trees that jutted out into the middle of the lagoon like an island but nobody ever really wanted to go there. It wasn't just the rumours about ghosts – the lagoon itself was teeming with sea snakes. Mahinda saw half a dozen or so in deeper waster as he splashed across sandbar, then picked his way carefully around the little stinger crabs that scurried around at low tide and got to work immediately. He hadn't visited in some time, so the brisk sea breeze and the elements had done their worst. The little hut Mahinda had fashioned from some old corrugated-iron sheets was a mess: the pupae baskets all upended and fallen branches everywhere.

He was busy sorting through the baskets of cocoons when he heard her bell, carried on the evening breeze as the wind changed direction.

'I thought I'd find you here,' his mother said, carefully alighting from her bicycle, her eyes bright and cheery. 'What did you do your oration on?'

'I spoke about Sri Lanka. The name Sri Lanka.'

'Did you talk about Ramayana? That it was in the Hindu epic that first referred to Ceylon as 'Lanka' – the resplendent isle. That it was the Indian sage Valmiki who coined the name?'

'Yes, of course I did. How could I forget the first story you ever told me?' Mahinda smiled. Mother and son worked together, chatting as they set the hut to rights.

It had been quite by accident that Mahinda and his mother had found the silk moths, here on this very island. A whole whisper of them, all white with grey markings. They'd come to gather firewood early one morning after a terrible storm had lashed the coast. 'They must have been blown in from India,' his mother had said, turning her face to the uncommon northerly wind.

A few weeks later they'd found a nest of cocoons where the moths had laid eggs. 'Why, I am sure we'll be able to throw some silk from these,' she'd told Mahinda with shining eyes as she spied the fluffy cocoons.

'For what, Amma?'

'For a beautiful silk saree. I would be a queen if I dressed in silk,' his pretty young mother had said, twirling around in the little clearing.

They had taken the cocoons home, but as soon as his mother dropped the golden pods in boiling hot water to throw the silk, young Mahinda had started screaming.

'They are dying, Amma! They are dying!'

Sure enough the pods were twisting violently, the larvae inside fighting desperately at being boiled alive in their self-spun enclosures. One cocoon even jumped straight of the cast-iron pot, landing in the dirt of the kitchen floor.

His mother had immediately scooped the cocoons out of the scalding water and hugged him to her breast. 'But I want you to be a queen, Amma,' he'd cried. 'I promise to make you a silk saree. I promise – but how can I?"

'What if we find a way, hmm? What if we find a way to get silk without killing the moths?'

That was how it'd all begun. Over months and years, they'd collected the cast-off cocoons and attempted to extract silk from them. At first, his mother had just humoured the little boy, amused by his interest in the project, but as he became older, she saw real ambition in his eyes. Every day after school, he would experiment with ways to collect the silk, his little pink tongue poking out of the side of his mouth.

When he was ten, she took him on a long bus journey to Jaffna to look at books on sericulture at the majestic old library. The little boy had bravely asked the chief librarian to explain some of the more obscure words in the books to him, which amused the straitlaced public servant no end.

'I could barely see the top of his head over the counter, but he demanded to know what sericin was,' the man chortled into his afternoon tea as he told his colleagues.

Back at home they had planted mulberry shrubs. 'Don't waste my precious fertiliser on those stupid trees,' his father had snapped, but his mother took a little of the precious urea anyway, to encourage the shrubs to grow.

And now they were almost there after fourteen years. They almost had the twenty pounds of cocoons they needed. Twenty pounds of soft gold fluff that Mahinda carefully kept in a hessian sack in the little hut.

'*Putta*, you'd better hurry and go home,' his mother urged, pointing to the rapidly incoming tide. When he frowned, she rushed to reassure him. 'Don't worry about me. I won't be far away.'

If there was ever a job that every lad in the village aspired to from when he could first walk, it was to be a village watcher. Fathers and elderly men were automatically exempt from this duty, so it fell to the fittest and sharpest young men to protect the village from dusk to dawn. From three treetop lookouts, these young farmers and fishermen kept a keen eye out for the elephants, leopards and wild boar that roamed freely within the dense jungle just a few miles away.

It was quite common to see a procession of little boys follow these strapping young men along the dusty red laneways of the village at dusk, their milk bellies sticking out over their tattered shorts as they followed their heroes, shoulders back and fearsome frowns on their faces. Fearsome at least until their mothers stepped out onto their doorsteps to call them in for dinner – then they ran home like the little lambs they were.

'Decided to come back, have you?' Vannan called from above as Mahinda clambered up the rough rope ladder. 'I didn't quite miss your ugly face but I certainly missed the food,' he teased, reaching for Mahinda's food parcel even before his friend made it onto the platform high above the ground.

'Who has been watching with you?'

'The dung-for-brains Govinda and then Badayana Bala. But I kicked him out after I caught him taking a watery crap off the side,' Vannan growled. 'I mean if you have to have a crap, at least crap in the direction of the jungle and not in the direction of the village! So I have been doing the watch on my own.'

'But I've been gone for six weeks.'

Vannan had already spread steaming bowls of idali, coconut chutney and drumstick curry out on the mat. 'Do you have any idea what it was like being stuck with those two buffoons all night? Govinda could not stop talking about his goats and Badayana Bala could not stop farting!' he said. He opened Mahinda's banana leaf–wrapped rice packet and grinned. It was filled with good village food: *kos* cooked in rich coconut cream, spicy *handalo* and *dambala*. The fresh jackfruit, fish and curried vegetables was a meal fit for a king. The boys sat and exchanged food, laughing and joking and catching up on the village news as darkness fell.

'So, how was it? Ammachi did *abishekam* for the entire four weeks,' Vannan asked finally, pouring himself and Mahinda a hot cup of black tea from a thermos.

'Not too bad. Tell Ammachi I will come around tomorrow to thank her. There are a couple of good bunches of *kurumba* on the tree on the south side of our field. I was going to take one to the *gamanayaka* and his wife. I'll bring a bunch for Ammachi too.'

'Just take a bunch for the *gamanayaka*'s wife. My mother would no sooner expect something from you than she would from me. Once you get to university, I'm sure she'll quite disown my brothers and I altogether and say that you are her son.'

Mahinda smiled. 'And how is the planting going? I saw some of your southern fields from the lagoon when I came in this evening. The field closest to the road looks a little sparse.'

'You aren't still going over to the island, are you? Haven't you given up on that crackpot idea yet?'

Mahinda raised an eyebrow. 'When have I ever given up on anything?'

'Did you hear back from the spinners in Trincomalee, then?'

'Yes, I did.'

'So? What did they say?'

'That I was insane. Here, look at this,' Mahinda said, pulling a letter from the waist of his sarong where he'd tucked it in. Vannan grabbed it and started reading by torchlight, but Mahinda didn't wait for him to finish.

'They say that it is not possible to spin fine saree silk from silk hankies,' he told his friend. He knew what the note said by heart.

'Why?'

'Because the silk is too coarse. You need to reel saree silk straight from the cocoons.'

'Maybe they have a point. You might have to give this up. Your mother died, Mahinda. She is not coming back,' Vannan pointed out gently.

'Vannan, I made her a promise and I intend on keeping it.'

And into the night the friends chatted, their conversation punctuated by eerie jungle noises as they kept watch, the call of elephants and the growl of leopards carrying in the darkness. They returned more than once to the problems Mahinda was having with his silk.

'See, when the moths leave their cocoons, they make a mess of it, almost ripping the cocoons in half,' Mahinda explained. 'We can't reel full lengths and that makes the spinning a little more complicated.'

'More complicated?' Vannan asked.

'Yes.'

'But not impossible.'

'I don't think so, but I'm not sure,' Mahinda said.

'Learn to spin the silk yourself, then.'

'I am having enough problems growing the damn worms – how am I going to spin the silk as well?'

'Mahatma Gandhi spun his own cotton.'

'He also took on the might of the British Raj and chased them out of India.'

'So you are admitting that us Indians are better than you Lankans finally?' Vannan goaded.

'You're a Tamil, you damn fool! You're no more Indian than I am!'

'Just come to Jaffna with me this weekend,' Vannan said. 'We'll see if we can buy a spinning wheel from the market. The trade winds have risen, so there'll be boats from Puducherry.'

Mahinda looked sceptically at his friend but then shrugged. 'Why not? I have taught myself almost everything about growing silkworms anyway. I shall teach myself how to spin as well,' he conceded. 'So, how are things going between you and Miss Shivani?' He knew the real reason his friend wanted to go to Jaffna.

Vannan shrugged. 'Who knows? All I know is that I need a good harvest in the next six weeks before I can even consider approaching her family.'

'Have you told your parents?'

'Are you mad? They would kill me! My parents will never consent to a marriage with a Karawe. The fisherman's caste! My mother would die! But with my own tobacco harvest, I will be able to stand on my two feet and not depend on them. I have even started thatching my own house on the field my *athappa* left me.'

Mahinda rolled his eyes. 'Just make sure you break the news to your mother after I leave for Colombo. I don't want to be here when the crying starts!'

'But you'll be there, right? You know, when I get married,' Vannan said.

'Err . . . let me think about it,' Mahinda teased. Vannan cuffed him over the head. 'Of course I'll be there, you fool! Who else will keep you from shitting in your sarong?'

He took Vannan in a head hold and they wrestled briefly before collapsing in laughter as the platform creaked, reminding them that they were dangerously high up in the air.

'Let's catch the bus to Jaffna next weekend,' Mahinda suggested. 'If I get a good price for the *kurumba* this week, we can even take in a film in town.'

'You mean you aren't sick of watching *Sholay*? How many times have we seen it?'

'Twenty? Twenty-five?'

As Mahinda stood to retie his loosened sarong, that was when he saw it, in the dark blue inkiness of the cool morning.

'*Machang*, what do you think that is?' he asked, pulling Vannan alongside him. 'There is something moving there, by the road.'

Vannan reached out immediately for the large rusty temple bell, its loud ringing reverberating through the peace of the early morning. 'It is not a thing, it is a boy!' he yelled as he slid down the rope ladder and ran towards the road.

Mahinda hit the ground mere seconds after him and followed close behind. They could hear the footfalls of the villagers rushing to join them, carrying lit coconut fronds to light their way.

'Get the *vedda*!' shouts rang out, and someone ran off to fetch the village healer.

'Who could it be?' people were already demanding even before Mahinda and Vannan reached the prone figure.

Mahinda's heart nearly stopped as he reached the lad. The leopards wouldn't have had much of a feast if they had indeed taken him. For the boy was emaciated. Bones stuck out at angles and his feet were covered with open sores, oozing pus.

Vannan knelt to gently turn the boy over, reaching for the flask of water he carried on the leather belt at his hips to pour some water into the child's mouth.

'Nimal, is that you?' Mahinda asked, as the breaking day gave him just enough light to make out the boy's features.

'I told his mother not to send him to Colombo,' Mahinda's *amma* raged as she paced up and down beside the little shack on the island. The news of Nimal's return had spread quickly. Once the *vedda* had taken charge of Nimal and shut the door to his healing hut, the villagers had automatically turned to Vannan and Mahinda to find out what had happened.

'What did Nimal say?' 'How did he get from Colombo to the village all by himself?' 'What happened to his *nona*?' Not that the boys knew any of the answers. Nimal had not said a single word. And judging from the grave concern on the *vedda*'s face as he had taken Nimal's pulse, no one might ever know the answers.

'I should have insisted your father him take in,' Mahinda's *amma* kept raging. 'I knew that Burgher woman could not be trusted. Came up north on holiday and took our boy. She was sweet enough when she promised his mother she would care for him. But all his mother really cared about was the fifty rupees she sent each month.'

'Amma, you can't blame her. Her husband drinks everything she earns at the market.'

'I know, I know,' his mother said. 'I just wish we could do something.'

'I wish that too, Amma, but how? The tobacco crop last year didn't fetch as much money as we'd hoped and we will need money for the start of school next year . . .' Mahinda's voice trailed away.

'*Putta*, you need to help people even if you have nothing to give,' his mother said. 'If you wait till you can afford it, then it is not charity but guilt.'

Mahinda closed his eyes and promised himself that if Nimal survived, he would find a way to help him.

'So, show me where you are up to,' his mother demanded, hitching her white cotton saree and sitting on a tree stump.

'We nearly have the twenty pounds we need, but we're no closer now than we were six weeks ago. The larvae have been munching on anything and everything while I've been gone, so their cocoons are all sorts of colours. Look, I picked this lot from Vannan's tobacco field on my way here and their cocoons are almost all red!'

'You aren't planning on throwing them out, are you?'

'But they won't take any dye.'

'Silly boy! You have silk that is already the colour women love! If I were you, I'd spirit a few tobacco plants here and see if you can get a few more of these red cocoons!'

'Amma, you missed your calling as a businesswoman!' Mahinda teased. 'Think how much wealthier we'd all be if you ran a shop instead of delivering babies?'

'And what about the women and children who would struggle without me?' she smiled. 'Besides, it was what I was born to do.'

'What? Ride from house to house in the middle of the night to tend to screaming women?' he grunted, hefting another load of coconut fronds to the shed and squatting on the sandy ground to strip the leaves from their branches.

After he'd torn apart a dozen or so branches, he arranged the sturdy but pliable wood in a circle, much like the spokes on a cartwheel, and started to weave. 'Careful with the edges,' his mother told him. 'Coconut fronds can give you nasty cuts.'

No sooner had she said it than a nasty thorn embedded itself under Mahinda's nail. '*Cheek*,' Mahinda grumbled, wincing as he tried to extract it. His mother promptly pulled a safety pin from her saree blouse.

'Come here,' she said gently, and eased the offending piece of wood out, humming a familiar lullaby.

'I'm not a baby, you know.'

'But you'll always be my baby. My first baby,' she smiled as she took her seat again, stretching back in the dappled sunlight to ease her wearied back. Being the midwife for the five villages around Nayaru Lagoon was not an easy job. Not only did she look after all the expectant mothers, but she also looked after the health of the children, at least until they were in grade school. It was to her that they came with their swollen bellies, emaciated and full of worms.

'I'll sit for another quarter of an hour but then I'll need to head off,' his mother told Mahinda as he sat weaving the new enclosure for the silk larvae.

'Can't you stay a little longer? I hardly ever get to see you.'

'One day I'll come to live with you and you'll long to see the back of me!' she laughed. 'So how are things going between Vannan and Shivani?'

'How did *you* find out about that?' Mahinda said, startled.

'I have my ways.'

'I have promised to go with him to the *kovila* for his marriage, but I'd much rather not be in the village when his mother finds out.'

'Chelvathy is not that bad . . .'

'Really? My ears haven't quite recovered from the time she caught Vannan and I trying beedee.'

'I hope your bum hasn't recovered either! I was so embarrassed. I am the village midwife and my son was caught smoking before he was even eight!'

Mahinda rolled his eyes as he sat weaving. 'Amma, can you blame us for trying tobacco? Both our fathers are tobacco farmers.'

'Tobacco farmers! Tobacco farmers? I'll give you tobacco farmers!' His mother gave his ears a nasty tug. 'You know smoking stunts your growth. I don't mind grown men smoking, but not young boys not old enough to wear long pants!'

Mahinda laughed. 'I can't believe it has been nearly ten years and you still haven't forgiven me!'

'Some things are just unforgivable,' his mother said, but he could see she was trying not to smile. 'That's good,' she said, looking at Mahinda's handiwork.

Within three-quarters of an hour, he'd woven a proper enclosure for the larvae. There was space at the bottom for shredded mulberry leaves, and a braided strap made from coconut leaves spiralled up the inside walls, creating a ledge on which the caterpillars could weave their cocoons.

'I think this design might just work,' Mahinda said. 'This way, I only need to feed them once a day, and because it isn't too deep, the mulberry leaves won't rot before I get the chance to change them.'

'Just as well, if you're going to Jaffna with Vannan tomorrow. You'll be able to leave them for the entire day and not worry about them until you come back.'

Mahinda cocked a surprised eyebrow at her.

'As I said, I have my ways of finding things out,' she explained. 'If I don't see you before you leave, can you please remind your grandmother to put an extra spoon of milk powder in the younger children's tea? They shouldn't be having tea in the first place. And remind your father about Prema's glasses. They need mending . . . And don't forget to look in on Nimal before you leave.'

'Yes, Amma,' Mahinda agreed as he watched her climb on her pushbike again.

She carefully wrapped her saree fall around her waist and tucked the end in nice and safe. She then hitched her pleats out of the way so that they didn't get entangled in the chains as she took off for the other side of the lagoon, turning back briefly to wave. The blue and white stripe along the hem of her saree proclaimed her profession from miles away. Farmers were known to set themselves down in ditches as she went past, such was the respect she commanded in the community. She was the one who was there at the start of each life in the village, and more often than not she was the one who dressed bodies for cremation.

It was an hour's walk to the bus stop from the far side of Nayaru Lagoon to the main road to Puttalam. Mahinda and

Vannan started early with lunches packed and water bottles filled.

'Nah . . . you have to put a squeeze of lemon into the *kurumba* to get the best flavour, you just lop the top off the coconut and squeeze a little in,' Vannan insisted as they skimmed pebbles across the lagoon.

'But you don't even drink *kurumba*. You hate the stuff,' Mahinda replied incredulously.

'That doesn't stop me from knowing how to best drink it.'

'And you always know how to do things better?'

'Of course I do. Wasn't it me who taught you how to climb trees better? And didn't I teach you how to swim, too?'

'Yes, by pushing me out of the *oruwa* in the middle of the lagoon.'

'It was embarrassing that a boy who'd lived by the beach all his life could not swim.'

'I was eight . . .' Mahinda pointed out wryly.

'Old enough, I say. You'd spent too much time tied to your mother's *potta* anyway.' Vannan growled. 'So what's the plan, *machang*?'

'I thought we'd go to the market first and take it from there. What time are we meeting your Shivani?' Mahinda replied, not quite looking Vannan in the eye.

'In the evening. Isn't that what she said in her letter?'

'How should I know what she said in her letter? She's your girlfriend, isn't she?'

'But you got the letter, didn't you?' Vannan retorted.

Vannan and Shivani's grand love affair was, by necessity, conducted primarily by love letter, with the occasional illicit meeting facilitated by sympathetic friends. Neither set of parents would consent to a match, both convinced of the superiority of their own caste.

'We Karawes are descended from seafaring warriors,' Shivani's father would proclaim to anyone who would listen. 'We don't grub about with sod-busting Vellalars. Stupid, that is what they are. Dirt for brains.'

Whereas Vannan's mother, a devout Hindu and strict vegetarian, cut the local Karawe fishermen a wide berth at the markets, sniffing sanctimoniously. 'They kill animals, you know. That's bad karma for seven generations. That's why they convert to Christianity. They think their new god can wash them of their sins. Not possible. That is why so many of their children are born with missing limbs or are retarded.'

So it was to Mahinda that Shivani would send missives, smuggled by a youthful network of similarly lovelorn friends.

'But I gave it to you without even reading it! The last time I accidentally read one I was sick for a week!'

'Humph!' Vannan started running, hearing the bus coming in the distance. Mahinda broke into a run behind him, but drew up suddenly when he spied a familiar figure approaching the bus stop from the other direction.

'Oh no,' he called, racing to catch up with Vannan. 'Badayana Bala is running to the halt too! Do you want to miss the bus?'

'Don't be a fool! We won't be able to get up there for another three weeks because of the harvest,' Vannan yelled back, only to slow down himself.

'What's wrong?'

'Mrs Subramanium.'

'What? Where?' Mahinda looked around in horror.

'At the bus halt.'

And sure enough, she was there – the woman who struck terror in the heart of every boy aged fifteen and up in and around Nayaru. Dressed in her bright blue and green saree, she lit up the country bus halt like a neon light. Mrs Subramanium, the district matchmaker.

'We'll catch the next bus, then?'

'But that's in another two hours! I won't risk being late to see Shivani,' Vannan said, speeding up again.

'Well, we're not sitting on the bus, then,' Mahinda insisted.

So Mahinda and Vannan completed the three-and–a-half-hour journey clinging onto the doorframe of the rusted Ceylon Transport Board bus, though the perilously overcrowded bus was already tipping over to its side.

'So, when are we meeting your lady love?' Mahinda asked. They had arrived at the central Jaffna bus terminal just after eleven o'clock and were making their way to the dusty park on the other side of the fort.

'A little after six. She is hoping to get away during her second cousin's wedding.'

'And where are we meeting her?' Mahinda asked, feeling alarmed. They sat down on a derelict park bench under a large twiggy *kikar* tree to have an early lunch. Vannan didn't answer, looking away as he unwrapped the banana leaf from around his parcel of food.

'Tell me we are not meeting her at the temple again?'

Again Vannan didn't answer.

'Oh man! No! I am not doing it again. I am not going skulk out the back of that Hindu temple so you can make eyes at Miss Shivani! There are elephants there and I stank of their dung for a week.'

'Relax. You don't normally smell much different,' Vannan muttered.

'Well, I'm not going, then. You go and see your princess all by yourself!'

'Oh, come on, *machang*! You know we can't get caught. I need you there!'

'Why? I stand there next to a hill of elephant turds while you sing silly love songs to your girl from around a tree! Why do you need me there?'

'Because while you are standing next to the dung heap, you can keep a lookout for Shivani's brothers!' Vannan said. Not that they were afraid of Shivani's brothers in any way – not if it'd be a clean fight. But born and raised the scions of a prominent family in Jaffna, they could rally the entire town behind them if they wished to.

'Then promise me you won't sing to her.'

'I make no such promises. She says it is my voice she's in love with.'

'Well, it certainly can't be your personality!'

'How about if I buy you some *muruku* before we go to see the film?' Vannan pleaded.

Now was Mahinda's turn to avoid his friend's eyes.

Vannan doubled his offer. 'Okay, I will even buy you an Aaliya brand ice-cream.' Mahinda still looked away. 'What's wrong, *machang*? Are you feeling sick? I knew I should have forced you to sit on your girly backside in the bus!'

'I'm not sick, you fool! It's just that . . .'

'It's just what?'

'It's just that I don't have money to see the film. I have 300 rupees for the spinning wheel but nothing more. And I'm not even quite sure that's enough.'

'What do you mean, you don't have money? I know you sold at least ten bunches of *kurumba* to the *modalali* yesterday. So what did you do with it?'

Again Mahinda looked away, concentrating on his lunch.

'You gave it away, didn't you? You gave it to the *vedda*! I knew it! I knew he'd pull you in, like pulling in the minnows from the lagoon!'

'What was I supposed to do? He came around and said that Nimal's mother couldn't pay for the herbs he needed.'

'Do what I do – offer to find the herbs for him!'

'Well, it's too late now, so there.'

'So what are we going to do? We can't spend the next six hours at the markets, especially if we don't have any money,' Vannan grumbled.

'You're so smart, why don't you come up with an idea?'

'Okay then, I'll find a way to get us into the cinema if you promise to come with me to see Shivani.'

'How? I know you don't have any money – your father hasn't finished his harvest yet. Mahinda looked down at both their food parcels, which contained no more than the bare minimum to save them from starvation – just boiled manioc with *pol sambol*.

'I have my ways.'

'Nothing that will get us into trouble, I hope. I cannot go to university if I have a police record,' Mahinda pointed out.

'Nothing illegal.'

'Fine, I'll come with you to see Shivani, then. Just tell me how you're going to get us into the cinema.'

'My mum gave me fifty rupees to do a pooja for you. I reckon we go to the back of the market and buy an old pooja offering for twenty-five rupees and use the rest to see the film.'

Mahinda felt embarrassed that Vannan's poor parents would rather petition the gods for him to go to university than spend their hard-earned money on food, but Vannan was adamant.

'Finish your manioc quick, *machang*. We don't want to miss the start!'

Not that they would have missed much had they been late anyway. The Jaffna Odeon across the way from the fort had been showing the same film for the past six years at a quarter past midday every day – *Sholay*, the story of two criminals hired to catch a ruthless bandit. Mahinda and Vannan knew the dialogue by heart, though neither could speak nor understand Hindi.

'They don't make them like they used to,' Vannan sighed contentedly several hours later as they left the smoke-filled cinema. Out in the fresh air, he rolled yet another cigarette with the finest tobacco from his father's farm.

'Those things are going to kill you,' Mahinda said, squinting against the bright sunshine, carefully watching where he put his feet. It was market day, and every farmer within a ten-mile radius had come into town to sell their wares. If one somehow avoided being run over by an overzealous bullock cart, one inevitably stepped in the patties the skinny bullocks left behind.

Vannan filched several rambutans from a passing cart. 'So what exactly are we looking for?'

'Idiot, it was you who suggested I spin the silk myself.'

'I guess it's a spinning wheel you'll be wanting, then,' he said. 'We'd better head down to the north end of the wharf.'

'I know, I used to live in Jaffna, remember!' Mahinda told him as they climbed on a bus heading towards Kankasanthurai on the north side of the peninsula.

Six months of the year, vendors from Puducherry in India used the calm seas to make the 150-mile journey to Jaffna. With a southerly breeze behind them, the distance could be covered in a matter of mere hours, making it an attractive proposition for the astute businessman.

Mahinda and Vannan hurried through the busy market, not bothering to look at the snake charmer or the bright tent of sarees, but they could not help but be transfixed by the firewalkers.

'Show your devotion to the Draupati Amman – she was with you when your soul was created and she will be with you when the world ends,' devotees called out as they rushed forth over pits of hot coals, their eyes glazed with religious fervour.

'We'd better keep moving,' Mahinda said to Vannan, pulling at his sleeve after what seemed to be an eternity.

The vendor they were looking for was the famous Mustafa Mohamadeen. 'Come one, come all!' the barrel-chested merchant called from the flap to his glorious tent, the tassel on his moth-eaten fez dangling over his bright blue glass eye. 'If you can't buy it from Sir Mohamadeen, it is not worth having!

'So what are you looking for today, young sirs? May I interest you in a cassette radio? A thousand rupees – very cheap. Or how about a new hoe? A fine new hoe for strong young farmers like you.'

'We are actually looking for a spinning wheel,' Mahinda informed the trader as they stepped into his sumptuous fabric-hung tent, a world quite different to that of the derelict fishing port outside.

'A wheel to spin yarn,' Vannan clarified.

'Why do you need to spin yarn? If it is cloth you need, why, I have it in abundance! I have silk, cotton, polyester, dupioni silk, chiffon, lace, wool – not that you need that in this heat – guipure lace, bombazine, brocade, bump, cambric . . .'

'No, I need a spinning wheel.'

'If it is a silk saree you are after, I have a better collection than those clowns over there,' Mustafa Mohamadeen replied, pointing towards another bright tent.

'No, we need a spinning wheel,' Vannan said patiently.

'What for?'

'To spin silk.'

'You fool, everybody knows you throw silk by reeling it straight from the silkworm's cocoon. Why do you need a spinning wheel if you want to reel silk?'

'Because I want to spin silk instead,' Mahinda explained.

'Why?'

'Why do you want to know?'

'Because I do,' the merchant told him.

'Because I want to create silk without killing the moth inside, okay? Satisfied?'

Mustafa Mohamadeen, the greatest trader south of Andhra Pradesh, stopped for a moment. And started to laugh. So much that his large belly jiggled and tears started to stream down from the corners of his eyes. 'What fool's errand are you on?'

'It is my own foolish errand, so show me your spinning wheels if you have them.'

'Of course I have them . . . come this way,' the merchant said, leading the boys out the back of the tent over a precariously unbalanced gangplank to the vessel that had brought him to Jaffna.

'Spinning wheels, spinning wheels,' Mustafa Mohamadeen muttered to himself as he pulled off tarpaulins from piles of junk on the deck. 'Here we are, spinning wheels,' he said finally, dragging several specimens to the fore. 'What type of a spinning wheel would you like? A double drive or a single drive? I even have some that are electric, though I would not recommend it here during the dry season. Your electricity is more off than on.'

Mahinda looked at the vast array of machines on offer, confused. Some were made of wood and some were made of steel. Some had their two wheels at interesting angles and others had strange pieces that stuck out. He looked at Vannan, who shrugged his ignorance. 'Which do you recommend?' he asked the trader.

'I would recommend a double-drive, foot-operated machine like this one here. It's a fine bargain for 1500 rupees.'

'Do you have anything cheaper? What about this?' Mahinda asked, pointing to a rusty specimen with one large wheel and another smaller one.

'That is 2000 rupees. Don't be fooled by the rust. It is a superb spinning wheel, look!' Mustafa said, giving the wheels a delicate nudge. Both started to turn, one clockwise and the other anticlockwise. 'An expert spinner could make a good thousand yards of yarn with this in a day.'

'What about an ignorant jackass?' Vannan asked, and Mahinda scowled at him.

'Well, young man, if you are a beginner, you can't go past this, the Saraswati 1000. Made 100 per cent in Hyderabad! 100 per cent! Look at its sleek lines. The wood is from the pine trees in the Himalayas. With this you'll be spinning like a Saliya within a week!'

And it was a handsome piece indeed, all pale pinewood gleaming in the bright Jaffna sun. Anyone could see that this was a premium piece of equipment.

'How much?' Mahinda asked softly.

'Three thousand rupees,' Mustafa Mohamadeen announced proudly, patting his belly.

'Err . . . perhaps not,' Mahinda said, backing his way out of the boat.

'Why, young sir, how much were you intending on spending?'

'About 300 rupees?'

'But I thought you were serious buyers!' Mustafa Mohamadeen was outraged. 'Off with you! I should set the watch on you for wasting my time!' he roared, running the boys off his leaky boat.

'Well, that is that, then,' Vannan said. Mahinda trailed despondently behind him as they made their way to catch another bus. In Nallur they made a quick stop at one of the seedier vendors that lined the road to the temple and bought an old offering plate for twenty-five rupees, giving the young *pusari* another ten to do the offering.

'We should have spent more money on the offering,' Mahinda muttered afterward. 'I have nothing else to spend it on now.'

'The gods don't need your money. Keep it for something worthwhile like food,' Vannan replied, smoothing his hair back and sniffing under his armpits as they made their way around to the elephant sheds at the back of the temple.

And there she was. Sitting warily on a coconut tree stump dressed in a bright pink saree, nervously watching everyone who came around the corner. Vannan rushed to stand on one side of a large palmyra tree while she coyly went to stand on the other side, both of them within earshot but not actually touching or seeing one another.

Shivani was all things required in a classically beautiful Tamil woman. Fair skinned and lusciously curved with bright eyes that could laugh merrily or just as easily be filled with winsome tears.

'Oh my darling Shivani, how I have missed you,' Vannan cried, then broke into the chorus of a familiar Tamil love song. *'Every moment of every minute I am apart from you, my heart bleeds with unending pain. You are the bow to my arrow and the sun to my moon and the milk to my tea.'*

If Shivani had been a halfway sensible woman, she would have demanded Vannan speak to her properly. But no, she would drag on the drama for a full half-hour, sighing, gushing and cooing in return. It was excruciating, and today's performance was no exception.

As always, their brief reunion ended in tears. 'I know you will find someone else to love! Someone your mother will approve of!' Shivani sobbed hysterically, clutching at the golden cross she wore around her neck. Her family had converted to Catholicism only to secure free education for her brothers. She was no more a Catholic than the sacred cow tethered to the gate of the *kovila*, but in moments of desperation, she would appeal for any form of divine intervention. 'I swear to Almighty God that I will kill myself as sure as I stand here if you stop loving me!'

'Oh my darling,' Vannan declared, 'I will surely follow you to the grave!'

'And only if the both of them were to die would I be free of this farce,' Mahinda muttered to himself.

'Till next time, my darling,' Shivani declared, then ran through the trees to the temple and out to the street beyond.

'Till next time, my sweet,' Vannan cried and came sadly to stand beside Mahinda. 'I think it's time we went back home.'

'Will you be able to hold back your tears until we get to the bus halt or do you want my hanky now?' Mahinda asked. Vannan punched him in the arm.

It was nearing early evening and they would need to catch the bus soon to get back to the village before the jungle animals took control of the roads, but Mahinda was hungry. 'Here, let's have some rotis,' Mahinda offered sarcastically, pointing to the a roadside stall. 'May it be a balm to your broken heart.'

As they squatted by the road with their rotis, Vannan droned on and on about Shivani. '*Machang*, you have no idea. She is a princess. She is a goddess. She is a queen. She is in fact a woman in a million. No, a woman in a billion. No, she is the only woman in the world like her!'

'Of course she is, you idiot! How could there be another woman exactly like her?'

'You are an arse! A complete and utter arse!' Vannan said, but he carried right on. 'Have you seen her eyes? They are so dark they reflect the universe.'

Mahinda wanted to point out that Vannan had probably never seen Shivani's eyes, for they never spoke face to face, but he couldn't get a word in edgewise. Vannan only stopped talking when a group of young men pushed past shouting and chanting slogans, so many of them it was almost like a parade, making their way to an open space next to the town hall.

'What are they saying?' Mahinda asked. He was bilingual but struggled to make out what the men were saying in their thick Jaffna accents.

'Bloody stupid fishermen,' Vannan muttered after listening for a few moments. 'Some Eelam nonsense. How are they going to unite the Tamil nation when the various castes aren't allowed to use each other's toilets? I can see it now. The great revolution brought to its knees by the fact that soldiers can't crap in the same toilet!'

'Let's go watch,' Mahinda suggested.

'You fool! They'll butcher you before you even set foot in the park!'

'But how would they know I was not a Tamil?'

Indeed, Vannan and Mahinda looked so similar that they could be mistaken for brothers.

'Have you seen the way you walk?' Vannan demanded.

'Of course I haven't seen the way I walk. How could I?'

'Because all Sinhala men walk like Tamil women. Watch!' Vannan said. He leapt to his feet before sauntering backwards and forwards effeminately in front of his friend.

'You really are an idiot . . .' Mahinda growled, but before Vannan could reply, they both saw Mustafa Mohamadeen lumbering through the crowds dragging something large behind him. He was heading straight for them, and when he saw that they had noticed him, he waved and beckoned them over. They made their way over to him, curious.

'I was packing my boat to return to Puducherry when my crew reminded me of this,' the trader said, wiping his sweaty brow before coughing and spitting by the roadside. 'I have spent the last half-hour looking for you. I had hoped I could find you at the bus halt.'

'What is it?'

'It is a charka.'

'A what?'

'A charka. A traditional Indian spinning wheel. The very model made famous by Gandhiji.' It was a large piece of furniture too, about four feet by four feet with two horizontal wheels. 'Look, when you are spinning, you'll have to pull this one to an angle,' the man explained.

'How much do you want for it?' Mahinda asked, feeling ill at the thought of the food they'd just spent their money on.

'Nothing. Take it. It's yours. It'd cost me as much in fuel to take it back to India,' the old trader replied, walking away.

'Does it come with instructions?' Mahinda called after him.

'Have a look at the bottom of the box.'

Mahinda could not quite believe his luck.

'So, how exactly are you planning on getting that home?' Vannan asled, looking at the large box sceptically.

Mahinda looked up to retort that a man who could heft ten bunches of *kurumba* could easily move this onto a bus when he saw Badayana Bala coming from the direction of the district hospital.

'Bala, *machang*! Is that you? I didn't know you came to Jaffna today!' Mahinda called out, much to Vannan's consternation.

'Did you have to do that? You knew I'd help you take it home,' he groaned.

'But this way I don't need to hear you carry on about Shivani anymore,' Mahinda whispered back as Bala squirmed his way across the street.

'*Machang*, it is this diarrhoea! Came to see the doctors yet again, but they can't do anything!' Bala replied, doubling over to demonstrate his intestinal pain.

As it turned out, it was just as well that they'd met Bala, for the box that the spinning wheel came in disintegrated even as they loaded it onto the bus, and it took three sets of hands to get the whole thing back to the village.

'Just make sure you wash the damn thing before you start spinning with it. You don't want anyone to catch diarrhoea from your silk,' Vannan muttered as he left Mahinda at his house amid a sea of charka parts.

Anger was apparent in every one of Mahinda's movements as he prepared to weave yet another enclosure for his silkworms. He dumped an armful of coconut fronds on the ground and hacked the leaves off with one blow.

'I heard you and your father had words this morning,' his mother said softly, coming through the copse of trees behind him.

'What is his problem? I am not behind on any of my chores and yet he will pick on me!'

'Mahinda, Mahinda . . .' his mother said, trying to grab his arms as he brushed past to start tending to a small grove of mulberry bushes.

'I can never do anything right! He will always find fault, won't he?'

'Mahinda,' his mother said, holding her hands out in supplication. 'You have done everything right by him. You will do so much more than your father and I, and his heart is bursting with pride. He is just sad to see you go.'

'But why does he always have to complain about . . . you know . . . about this?' Mahinda demanded in frustration.

'The simplest and easiest answer is that he doesn't understand—'

'What do you mean, he doesn't understand? Of all people, he should understand! Didn't he drag you up here from Matara so he could pursue his dream of becoming a farmer? We've all nearly starved to death because of it!'

His mother sighed. Yes, she and her husband had come up to the inhospitable north in the 1960s to build a new life, answering the call of the socialist government then in power. They had truly believed, like so many others, that it was only by supporting the drought-stricken north that a unified Ceylon could built.

'A separate village of Tamils, a separate village of Muslims and village of Sinhala people is not a nation! We need to learn to live together,' the populist politicians had called out in the villages and towns of the south. 'We'll provide you with free land! We'll rebuild the ancient tanks built by the great Sinhala kings and provide water for the great push north!'

Mahinda's father had thought frequently of poisoning his wife and family along with himself in the following years. The climate in the north was arid and unpredictable, and the government's support had been at best sporadic. Many had fled back south, especially when another drought hit in 1976, but Mahinda's parents had persevered.

'This is our home now,' his mother had reassured her husband. 'We can survive on what we have. We don't need much,' she'd insisted. She'd been an avid student of health sciences at school and knew how to dry and grind the fish that so were plentiful in the seas around Nayaru to increase the nutritional value of the rice porridge that was the staple diet of most farming families. She also supplemented their meagre meals with wild herbs filled with life-saving iron and other trace elements. So unlike most in the village, Kusumaveti Ratnayaka's children didn't display the obvious symptoms of malnutrition, such as rickets and scabies.

The success of her family could not be laid solely at her feet, though. The *gamanayaka*, a princely descendant of the Jaffna royal family, had been a man ahead of his time. He'd braved the ire of other village headmen around Nayaru by protecting and supporting the immigrant farmers from the south.

'No, he doesn't understand,' his mother repeated firmly again, laying a gentle hand on his shoulder. 'All your father ever dreamt of was to become a farmer. To live an independent life free from the big landowners. In you he sees more. You are about to leave and become an engineer! An engineer, my son! Respectability, wealth and a secure future! It is more than he ever dreamt of for his son, and he cannot understand that your dreams are different.'

Mahinda shrugged. He could not forget the way his father had spoken to him that morning.

'What are you doing?' his father had demanded when he saw the spinning wheel Mahinda was fiddling with.

'I'm trying to fix this spinning wheel,' Mahinda had said, and started excitedly to explain the whole plan.

'Why are you wasting your precious time with all this nonsense!' his father had roared, kicking the offending spinning frame. 'You barely have three months before you head off to Colombo and you want to waste your time on this cock-amamie idea? There's work to be done in the fields. And if you weren't so selfish, you'd help your brothers and sisters with their schoolwork.'

That last statement had really rankled, as he had been

spending every spare moment he had with his younger siblings, looking over their schoolwork and setting them extra tasks to do over the holidays. He'd also spent the better part of every evening being quizzed by his youngest sister, Prema, whose greatest ambition was to work at the Sinhala Dictionary office. She was working through the dictionary, her cracked horn-rimmed glasses perched on her button nose, asking everyone the meaning of obscure words. 'What do you think *noesis* means?'

'I want you to plough all the fields on the south side of the lagoon and get them ready for planting by the time you leave for Colombo,' his father had decreed.

'But that's more than ten acres to clear! I won't have time!'

'You'll just have to make time, then!'

So he'd ploughed all day, eating into the precious little time he had to tend to his silkworms. The tide had already turned when he finally made it to the island that afternoon and he didn't relish spending the night up on the watchtower with a wet sarong.

'Now I won't have time to figure out if this silk thing is even worth pursuing!' Mahinda complained bitterly to his mother. 'It was hard enough as it was – if you don't feed them regularly, they die, and if they don't die, some stupid bird eats them!'

Kusumaveti opened her mouth but stopped before she spoke. Wisps of hair that had escaped from the bun at her neck fluttered around her face, and she closed her eyes and turned, as if she heard something on the very wind. 'Duty calls,' she said softly. 'I'll have to go now, my darling. Can you please remind your father again that your sister needs new spectacles? I keep telling him, but he forgets.'

Mahinda nodded, and she went to fetch her bicycle, ringing the bell and waving as she took the long way around the lagoon. The merry sound rang in his ears a long time, but at length he returned to his weaving, marginally calmer now.

He managed to complete one enclosure and then picked several large clusters of larvae from the surrounding trees. No matter how much anyone might laugh at him, he knew the silk caterpillars were intelligent creatures. When he spent time with them, they started to recognise his voice, raising their pale white faces to him as he tended to them, looking at him curiously.

Yet caring for them was tricky. He couldn't just dump mulberry leaves in their basket and leave. He'd done that a few years ago and found that the worms would gorge themselves to death within a day. Slow and steady feeding was what was needed. Ideally, he'd come and refresh the bed of mulberry leaves every couple of hours.

Mahinda was so engrossed in sorting the silk cocoons that he didn't hear the uneven footsteps coming towards him until they were very close.

'Hey, is that you, Nimal?' Mahinda asked, squinting into the darkness of the forest.

The boy staggered forward.

'What are you doing here? Shouldn't you be resting at home?'

Nimal didn't answer but collapsed lifeless on the ground.

'Does he follow you everywhere?' Vannan asked exasperatedly as Nimal squatted by the edge of the field watching them. They were furiously hoeing the lowest section of Vannan's southern field with the briefest strokes possible. News was that Mrs Subramanium was back in the village and the entire male population had disappeared. Even the ne'er-do-wells who usually loafed around the village shops had found occupation.

'Yes,' Mahinda replied in between heaves of his hoe.

'Why? Surely he is annoying you! He's sure as hell annoying me!'

Mahinda smiled. Despite what he said, Vannan had brought Nimal some hand-me-down clothes from his younger brothers and was very much an accessory in ensuring that the boy had enough to eat.

'He doesn't want to go back home and he doesn't want to stay with us either,' Mahinda said.

'Why not? Your grandmother's *kiribath* and *pol kiri shodi* are famous all around Nayaru. Hell, I'd move in with you if I could!'

'How should I know why he doesn't want to move in? He doesn't speak.'

'So, how do you know he *doesn't* want to move in?'

'Because every time I ask him, he shakes his head and hides in the hut,' Mahinda said as he stopped to adjust the hoe.

'How do you know he even understands you?' Vannan asked. 'He doesn't speak, right?'

'*Malli!*' Mahinda called to Nimal, raising his voice. 'Can you go and get me the small flat stone by the well? I need to sharpen my hoe.' The little boy scurried with alacrity to the other side of the field. 'See, there's nothing wrong with his hearing. He just doesn't speak.'

Vannan grunted. 'So do you know why he no longer speaks?'

'All I've been able to gather is that he left Colombo after his *nona* died. He's seen some awful things. The other day, I went to the hut early to drop off his breakfast before I started on the north field and I heard him screaming in his sleep. About someone burning . . .'

'Poor boy.'

'I wish I could help him. It's fine that he sleeps in the shed now, but what is he going to do in a couple of months when the rains start?'

'He can move in with me and Shivani once we get married,' Vannan muttered.

'Why? So he can poke his eyes out with your blunt farming tools? It's bad enough that what he's seen has rendered him dumb but watching the two of you will surely make him want to go blind too!'

Vannan put his hoe down to punch Mahinda in the arm. Hard. At which point Mahinda put down his hoe too, to block the punch. Soon the friends were on the freshly ploughed earth, wrestling each other with wild abandon, putting each other in head holds and trying to rub each other's faces in their smelly armpits. They stopped only when Vannan managed to tug loose Mahinda's sarong.

'Hey, stop!' Mahinda protested, clutching at the near-threadbare garment.

'Why? Are you ashamed of the sugar banana you have hiding underneath there?'

'No more than you are of those peanuts you call balls,' Mahinda laughed back, standing up to give his friend a helping hand. 'Shivani is going to be utterly disappointed on your wedding night! Hey, what?' he demanded when Vannan stopped.

Vannan pointed to something behind Mahinda's shoulder, and he spun around to look.

And there was Nimal, frozen with terror, his eyes unseeing. Urine started to drip down his leg onto the red earth and the putrid odour of faeces filled the air.

Mahinda and Vannan approached him slowly. 'There's nothing to worry about,' Mahinda reassured the boy, touching him on the shoulder. 'We wouldn't really hurt each other.'

'No, I'd sooner cut off my own arm than hurt this good-for-nothing dung-for-brains,' Vannan said.

'Come, let's get you changed, hmm?' Mahinda said gently, and he took the boy down to the little stream by the lagoon to clean himself while Vannan collected their hoes and other equipment and went to fetch some clean clothes.

'Does he do that often?' Vannan asked later, when they were back in the shed.

'No – this is the first time.'

'He needs to be seen to. He needs help.'

'I know, I know,' Mahinda said. 'I spoke to the *vedda* . . .'

'The *vedda* is a bloody hack! I wouldn't let him tend to my dog, much less Nimal!'

'Yes, but even he recommended I take Nimal into Jaffna. So a proper doctor can have a look at him. If you are all right with it, I was thinking I'd bring him with us next week.'

'Yes, Shivani suggested that we meet at the fort in her last letter. She can steal a few minutes from her friend's engagement party around the corner,' Vannan said squatting in the shed. 'We can go the evening before and spend the night at my aunt's house. If we get to the hospital early, we'll be able to avoid the queues.'

'You and Shivani better get married before Shivani runs out of weddings to go to! How else will you meet?'

'Shivani will never run out of weddings to attend. We are Tamils, remember. There's a wedding to go to every second week. Speaking of doing things quickly, though, how are you going with your silk project?'

'Good and bad. Nimal is quite amazing,' Mahinda replied. 'See, he's been helping me with the silkworms. He's even woven some enclosures for me and keeps them well fed, look!'

In fact Nimal had made Mahinda's shed a cosy place. Despite his small size, the boy was a hard worker, and while Mahinda was out working in his father's fields, Nimal had taken to managing the silkworms.

'They aren't scrawny little maggots anymore, are they?' Vannan observed, taking in the healthy, plump caterpillars munching away on juicy mulberry shoots.

Had Mahinda been truly honest, he would have confessed to the heart-wrenching fit of jealousy that had gripped him when he'd found Nimal tending to his precious silkworms. How dare this boy touch his pets? The silk moths and their offspring were his charges! What if Nimal killed them with his inept handling?

'You have to be very careful with them! And don't handle them too much!' Mahinda had scolded.

But over a few days, it became clear that Nimal, with his fewer responsibilities, could care better for the creatures. Tend to their needs more attentively.

'The trick is to give them fresh shoots every two hours. And look at the size of the cocoons!' Mahinda said proudly, showing Vannan the gunnysack.

'So have you started spinning the yarn yet?'

'Well, that's the bad bit. As you can see, I've managed to put the charka together,' Mahinda explained. 'The pictures in the manual were pretty self-explanatory.'

'Thank goodness, or I wouldn't think you'd make much of an engineer!'

'I can spin cotton easily enough, but not silk,' Mahinda said, and gave his friend a demonstration, first spinning some cotton he'd picked up from the village store and then trying again with the slippery silk. No matter how he tried, the silk wouldn't pull as easily, and a knot formed at the eye causing the wheel itself to get stuck. 'I have washed and washed the silk, it just won't slip into the spinning line,' he complained.

Vannan leant in to feel the difference between the cotton and silk with his rough calloused fingers. 'The cotton is softer and more supple,' he said. 'Maybe you need to do something to the silk before you spin it. Process it somehow.'

'But how? And how am I supposed to find out? Since those damn fools burnt down the Jaffna library, there isn't anywhere I can find information!'

'Have you tried the university?'

'Of course not. Jaffna University is a Tamil Tiger stronghold.'

Vannan looked thoughtful for a moment. 'How about this? I'll come with you to the university, and if someone asks, I'll say you and Nimal are my deaf and dumb cousins from Batticaloa.'

'Don't be stupid – they'd kill us!'

'Don't you want to find out if this ridiculous idea of yours is worth pursuing or not?'

'Of course I do!' Mahinda said. 'But they'll know that Nimal and I are Sinhala and kill us on the spot. They're not stupid, you know!

'Of course they're stupid, you bloody fool! Think of the cause they're fighting for! To split in half an island the size of India's smallest fart! They'll never succeed!'

The Protestant missionaries who'd come to Nayaru Lagoon in the late 1700s and early 1800s had written to their families that they had found the Garden of Eden. 'This is God's own good earth. How can these heathens not believe in God when confronted with the majesty of his work?'

Even the hard-bitten northerners from Jaffna were known to holiday down in Nayaru, finding a peaceful balm for their souls in the calm lagoon and the gentle pace of village life, where each day stretched as long as the next with little or no urgency to shorten it. No one hurried. No one fretted. There were no buses to catch and no business to tend to that could not be sorted out the next day.

Even Vannan was known to stop and admire the lagoon reddened by the rising sun at dawn as he walked to his fields. He loved to match the stroke of his hoe with the rhythm of the waves on the beach beyond. 'The wind was high today, so I was able to clear twice as much land,' he'd joke.

So it was in the early hours as Mahinda walked to the island on the lagoon to take Nimal his breakfast. He stopped on the beach just as the sun peeped over the horizon, turning the salt water a deep shade of vermilion as a *sula sula* swooped across from the other shore. It sang a trilling song, its bright red webbed feet a stark contrast to its grey plumage as it ducked and weaved in the cool morning breeze.

For several breathless minutes it played, soaring high in the sky before plummeting dramatically down, neatly avoiding the water, only its feet trailing the surface, leaving a sweet ripple behind. It was as if it knew it had an audience and played to Mahinda's naive enchantment. Yet even the most committed of show-offs tire of their own antics, especially if they have just a single routine. So with a gleam of greedy anticipation in its eyes, the bird swooped towards the island, its beak already half-open, salivary glands leaking at the thought of juicy white moths.

Mahinda tracked its descent, spellbound. The only sound was the waves lapping at the beach beyond – which made the crack of the old BB gun from the trees even more disconcerting. In one instant the bird was swooping, and in the next, it was dead, its bright red blood staining the whitening water as the sun rose steadily in the morning sky.

'What did you do that for?' Mahinda cried horrified. 'I gave you that gun to scare away boars, Nimal, not to shoot innocent birds!'

Nimal looked angrily at Mahinda in return. Glare for glare. Stare for stare. Rage fairly emanating from his scrawny body. He refused to relinquish the gun even when Mahinda tried grabbing it from him. If Mahinda was outraged, so was Nimal! He tugged at Mahinda's torn T-shirt and pointed.

'What? What do you want me to see?'

Nimal thrust Mahinda into the clearing, which only the day before had been swarming with moths. One never hears the flapping of a single moth, but hundreds or even thousands of flapping moth wings create a sound almost as eerie as it is sweet. When Mahinda had visited the previous evening, the clearing had been buzzing, but now, it was strangely quiet. Not a single moth to be seen.

There were several dead birds on the ground, though. It looked as if Nimal had resorted to his trusty slingshot first, only turning to the BB gun after he'd depleted his stock of appropriately sized pebbles.

Even the worms were gone, judging by the upended enclosures. Sure, the fact that birds preyed on moths had been an issue before, but Mahinda had dismissed it as part of the cycle of life. They'd taken moths before, but never massacred them. What had happened this morning was war. A bloody battle. With severe casualties on both sides.

'Oh no . . .' Mahinda cried. 'What are we going to do?' he said, collapsing unceremoniously on the ground. A banana-leaf parcel dropped from his hands and landed in the dirt.

Nimal grabbed his breakfast, setting it carefully down on the rickety table in the hut before coming back out to give his friend's ear a vicious tug. He seemed to be saying that the situation wasn't hopeless, and that Mahinda should get up and get on with it.

'What? All right, so we still have the pods to depend on for new breeding stock – but even that'll take a good month!'

Nimal gave him pointed look.

'Okay, twenty to twenty-five days,' Mahinda conceded. 'But I don't have much time left. I have to head down to Colombo before February.'

Nimal gave him a withering look before pulling at his T-shirt again to drag him to the hut.

Mahinda had fashioned a little bed for the boy, high above the ground to keep him safe from night creatures such as the deadly scorpions and amphibious sea snakes wont to escape from the lagoon of a night. He saw now that Nimal had fashioned several storage containers from discarded fishermen's crates and stowed them under the bed.

'What have you got here?' Mahinda asked as Nimal pulled out two crates and gestured to them in the manner of a proud papa.

Mahinda peered over the edge to see his silkworms. All of them. In various stages of development, from tiny ones that were almost invisible to the large languorous ones almost ready to start spinning cocoons. All safe and snug. And as Nimal made a small cooing noise, the larger worms raised their heads in his direction and allowed him to stroke them. Leaning into his caress. Making it clear they loved and craved the boy's gentle touch.

Mahinda looked at the upended enclosures and back at Nimal and his worms, confused. 'Did you have time to save the worms before the birds attacked?'

Nimal shook his head and gestured that it was cold.

'You're going to have to try again, Nimal. I don't understand.'

Nimal sighed and looked at Mahinda as if he were a simpleton. This time he gestured to the sun in the east and then pointed to the west. Mimed the action of sleeping, and the cool of the night. To keep the silk larvae warm, he'd been collecting them in the evening and popping them to sleep under his bed.

'So you get them out and put them in their enclosures during the day and take them in at night?'

Nimal nodded, smiling, before turning to caress some of the worms again. He picked up those worms clearly starting to spin and put them in enclosures with other cocoons, so that they could transform together. His kissed his fingertips and rubbed them on their bellies before leaving them to their change.

Mahinda sighed. 'Even if we have silkworms, it's going to take a while before they're ready to breed. Anyway, the birds will attack again.'

Nimal gave an evil grin, pulled out his slingshot and waved it at Mahinda, as if to say that he'd be properly ready the next time.

'Oh, Nimal,' Mahinda grumbled. 'You're missing the whole point! I want to make silk without hurting the moths – but I don't want to hurt birds either!'

'And no, I am not a sissy,' he protested when Nimal started to mock him, prancing around like a girl. 'You are a Buddhist, you should understand . . .' Then he realised that Nimal probably hadn't had the same level of religious education he had. Or Kusumaveti's gentle mothering either.

'All life loves life. Everyone of us clings to our bodies as a mother clings to her newborn child,' he explained softly, echoing his own mother's very words. 'So to kill, to destroy another's body and to separate the *athama* from the *kaya* is wrong.'

Nimal pointed furiously into the air. Into the air that should have been buzzing with moths. He clearly loved the creatures – Mahinda realised it when he saw Nimal's chin give a telltale wobble, and a watery brightness to his eyes.

'Look, maybe we need to give this up altogether. I'll be leaving soon anyway and you'll need to go back to your parents.'

Nimal shook his head, digging his little toes into the ground and crossing his arms. There was no way he would return to his parents' hut. He'd escaped the horrors of what he'd seen down south only to walk into another living hell.

'So what will you do? While I am gone?' Mahinda demanded in exasperation.

Nimal looked proudly around him, gesturing to the enclosures and the healthy silkworms, and puffed up his chest.

'No, you can't! You can't live here all your life! The doctor said you needed to start mixing with people to help you to start speaking again.'

Nimal rolled his eyes.

'Yes, I agree with you that doctor was a bit of a hack, but you won't learn to speak hiding here talking to silkworms and moths!' Mahinda growled. He was still cross with the Tamil doctor who'd seen them at the public hospital. He had given Nimal the barest of attention. 'Sinhalese people speak too much anyway,' he'd snapped at Mahinda. 'There wouldn't be half as much trouble if they kept their mouths shut! So this is probably a good thing!'

It was just as well that the tiny but strong Nimal had been there with them or else Mahinda could never have managed to stop Vannan punching the man in the mouth.

Vannan had ranted all the way to Jaffna University, then got into an even bigger snit when they ran into Shivani's eldest brother, Theevan, whom Mahinda knew quite well from his days at Jaffna Central College. Mahinda knew Rajan and Geevan too, Shivani's middle brother and youngest brother. He was glad not to see them all together.

'Still friends, are you? And you even have an accomplice now!' Theevan had drawled, seeing Mahinda, Vannan and Nimal come through the gates.

'And why wouldn't we be friends?' Vannan had growled at his brother-in-law to be. Vannan had met Shivan's brothers through the district cricket tournaments.

'I don't imagine it was easy being told that the village headman chose a *Sinhalaya* over you to support through school.'

'The *gamanayaka* made the best decision,' Vannan said.

'How does it feel? To be treated like dirt?'

'I would eat dirt for this man,' Vannan said. 'He is closer to me than my own brother. I have no problem with a system that gives good village-bred boys a chance to get to university. You city mongrels can fight over Tamil rights all you like – it has nothing to do with me. Now get out of my way,' he'd pronouncd with fire.

'Careful you don't grow a big mouth, we have ways of silencing people now,' Theevan had threatened but quietened visibly when a few young men wearing the armbands of the Liberation Tiger of Tamil Eelam came past. Threatening violence was one thing, but seeing a young man who you'd played cricket with murdered in an instant was something else, which was would happen to Mahinda if he were identified as Sinhalese.

It had shocked Nimal to the core when they'd met Shivani later in the day and Vannan explained to him that she was Theevan's sister. 'Oh, don't worry,' Vannan had reassured him. 'She is nothing like him.'

'You can't stay here in the hut with the silkworms, Nimal. How do you think you're going to survive when I leave?' Mahinda demanded.

Nimal mimed the shape of a luscious woman, indicating Shivani, then mimed a plate of food and rubbed his belly, indicating the promise she had made to keep him fed.

'You sure you want to do this? Live here like a hermit and eat from Vannan and Shivani's?'

Nimal nodded enthusiastically, then grabbed a couple of empty cocoons from a nearby pile and stuffed them in his ears, laughing.

'It's just as well you have the cocoons, then. You're right, that is the only way to survive Vannan's singing,' Mahinda laughed in agreement.

There was something quite special about tobacco harvest. Rice was grown to feed the community, but tobacco, well, tobacco was grown to buy luxuries like cooking oil, soap, cloth and kerosene. So a good harvest meant smiles all around, laughter and bonhomie.

Laughter gave way to bliss when the Ceylon Tobacco Board truck left the lagoon, headed for Puttalam laden with cured leaves, so heavy that its chassis carved groves along the uneven mud road as it left the collection of shops that acted as the depot. The village farmers were paid for tobacco by the kilo and would rather see the truck drag its way to town like a pregnant bitch than wait for a second truck that may or may not come.

The village children would chase the truck, slow as it was, all the way to the main road, tossing firecrackers as they ran, their eyes bright and their skinny legs pumping as fast as they could to keep up. Then they would return home to a delicious meal of rich red rice, *paripu* and pepper fish before everyone in the village would take the afternoon off to relax. Even Mahinda's father was in a good mood.

Which was why, on that particular afternoon, Mahinda was able to sneak away, after all the ruckus had died down. His father was having a rare nap in the shade of the old *kos* tree in his coconut-string hammock, his brothers and sisters had all gone down to the other side of the lagoon to play with their friends, and his grandmother was visiting, sitting around with the other village grandparents and forensically examining the gossip of the last six months.

'I didn't expect to find you here,' Mahinda said as he spotted his mother kneeling beside Nimal looking at an enclosure full of worms.

Nimal looked up at Mahinda as if he were mad. He'd sensed something unusual moments before Mahinda had arrived. He could not describe to Mahinda the eerie coldness in the air or the strange sounds of a bicycle bell he'd heard.

'Babies care not for the tobacco harvest,' his mother smiled. 'Why, I am sure I delivered Nimal here just a few days after harvest some fifteen years ago!'

'Happy birthday, Nimal!' Mahinda congratulated his friend. 'Vannan and I will make sure we'll celebrate this week!'

Nimal looked terrified.

'Don't worry,' Mahinda chided. 'We won't do anything silly.'

'So, tell me. What have you been doing?' his mother asked, looking at the large pot they had set on three stones.

'Oh, so much!' Mahinda exclaimed, as Nimal's eyes followed him with concern. 'Don't worry. She is not like other grown-ups. She understands,' he explained to the boy.

Mahinda misinterpreted the boy's concern about him talking to thin air, thinking that Nimal was still shaken from the savage tongue-lashing they'd received in the aftermath of the bird-butterfly massacre, just days before. How were Nimal or Mahinda to know that the flock of *sula sula* were used by the fishermen to spot schools of tuna in the sea?

'Damn fool children! Damn silly games!' the head fisherman had roared. 'We didn't know what had happened. We've been out on the water for two days without catching a damn thing! Two whole days!'

The *gamanayaka* had stepped in, reaching out with placating hands, but had been rudely brushed aside. 'Silkworms! I'll give you bloody silkworms,' the barrel-chested fisherman had yelled, grabbing Mahinda by the front of his T-shirt. 'Families will starve because of your silliness!'

In the end, the man stomped off ungraciously, muttering that if Mahinda had not been earmarked for university he'd be used as live bait to catch fish instead. 'He'd be perfect to catch that shark that's been escaping my net for years! Three hundred pounds, I reckon.'

'We were making so many mistakes, Amma, no wonder the spinners in Trincomalee said they could not spin for us,' Mahinda explained, reaching out for an old exercise book. He'd carefully copied reams of information from the library at Jaffna University between its faded pages.

'The problem was that we were boiling it but not for long enough or hot enough. The spinners in Trincomalee spin cotton, and you only need to comb cotton to clean it of its impurities. To make silk ready for spinning, you need to boil it. Here, let me show you,' he said, picking up several larvae, all busy secreting silk from their open mouths.

'See, the silk that the *Bombyx mori* worm produces in its salivary glands has two components: sericin and fibroin. The fibroin is the stringy centre of the silk and sericin is the sticky stuff that binds the whole thing. A single cocoon has up to fifteen miles of silk!

'To unravel and spin silk, we need to boil it. Hot. To get the sericin really loose. No wonder the weavers in Trincomalee rejected the samples I sent them – as soon as they started spinning their spindles would have stuck! And if they tried to comb the impurities out, their combs would have stuck too!'

'And what is this?' Kusumaveti asked, pointing to a hank

of fibres hanging off a hook, a grey-white mass swaying at the slightest puff of breeze.

'It's some we did for practice a few days ago,' Mahinda explained. 'But it's not quite right. The thing is, Amma, we've been using coconut leaves to boil the water, but I don't think it's been hot enough. So I found an old *kos* tree in the forest and I have been hacking it and bringing it here. *Kos* burns hot. I hope to get the silk from all these cocoons today,' he said, showing his mother a stack of cocoons.

'Oh my goodness!' Kusumaveti crowed, eyes shining at her son's cleverness. 'I'm so proud of you.' She squeezed his shoulder. 'But now I will have to go – I'm needed elsewhere.'

'Can't you stay just a little longer, Amma?'

'My darling, one can never time the birth of a child. The head fisherman's daughter went into labour about five hours ago. She is young and strong and will need more time. But the basketweaver's wife is quite the way along. I suspect she'll have the baby any minute now and I don't want to be long away from her!'

'But Amma, there's five miles between their huts!' Mahinda cried aghast.

'Which is why the district pitched in and bought me a bicycle!' his mother smiled, climbing on the bike and waving merrily as she sped away.

'Well, we'd better get on with this then,' Mahinda said to Nimal, who was still looking at him in horror. To whom exactly was Mahinda speaking to? Was he insane?

'Come on,' Mahinda said ignoring the look of horror on the boy's face. 'Let's get on with it.'

So for the next quarter of an hour they set about getting everything ready for boiling the silk cocoons. In the past two weeks they'd made a healthy collection of cocoons, enough to warrant a large pot. Before they started, both Mahinda and Nimal squatted around an old chipped plate and pulled out their rusty pocketknives to scrape shavings from a couple of bars of Lifebuoy soap. This was the trick that Mahinda had not had the chance to share with his mother.

While Mahinda had gleaned a great deal from the technical books he'd found in the agriculture section of the library, it had been in the literature section that he'd struck gold. While Nimal and Vannan had wandered off to play cricket on the lawn in front of the library, Mahinda had wandered aimlessly in and between the high stacks, breathing in the musty fragrance of books decaying in the salty air, until a faded, silk-bound volume caught his attention.

It was a set of short stories about ancient Chinese pilgrims who had travelled to India to study Buddhism, grisly tales full of blood and gore in which pilgrims fought off vicious bandits and even nastier packs of snow leopards that tracked them from the peaks of the Himalayas to the fabled gates of the centre of Buddhist learning, Nalanda in Bihar. And as the protagonist in the first story lay dying in his bed, the head *arahant* came to his side to guide his spirit towards nirvana. It was in their dialogue that the precious nugget of information lay.

'Love and compassion are the reason we are born, and yet it is love and compassion that can free us from the unending cycle of birth and death, my son,' the wizened old monk had advised. 'Tell me of the place where you were truly happy, where you could be yourself and you were just loved as you are.'

'At my mother's house,' the dying pilgrim had wheezed. 'She was the silk mistress for Emperor Hsiu Tang and she earned the *bao* from our feudal lord for being the most skilful silk maker in all the Western kingdoms. But she was kindness itself. She was a devout Buddhist and refused to hurt her silk moths. So she used daikon juice mixed with soybean oil to weave her silk.'

Mahinda hadn't finished the story, so giddy with joy that he was. The juice of the fat white daikon radish was a strong alkaline and mixing with it soybean oil would have made a soapy solution. Maybe this was it. Maybe soap was the key that would help him spin the shorter fibres together. Soap had not been mentioned in any of the other books about silk processing.

Mahinda and Nimal finished scraping the soap and set the shavings to boil in the large vat of water. They were just about to drop half a hessian sack of cocoons into it when Vannan came tearing into the clearing, his eyes wide with terror. His body was coated with sweat and grime, and judging by the splatters of mud on his blue sarong, he'd just waded through his father's freshly irrigated paddy fields.

'You have to save me!' Vannan cried. 'Hide me quick!'

Mahinda did not think twice as he quickly grabbed some rope from the hut. He tied one end to a heavy rock and tossed it over one of the higher branches of an *angsana* tree, tugging hard to ensure that it was firmly caught on a branch. 'You climb,' he instructed Vannan. 'I'll keep it tense.'

In his hurry to scale the trunk, Vannan's sarong came loose not once but three times. He took a deep breath to calm himself before putting a foot on the fork of a low branch and hefting himself up higher with the aid of the rope.

'I heard that the Tigers had been recruiting in and around Puttalam, but I didn't realise they'd come as far down as Nayaru,' Mahinda said urgently as Vannan reached the midway branches. 'Don't worry, Nimal and I are right behind you. We are quite safe here.'

'It's not the LTTE, you damned fool!' Vannan called back. 'It's Mrs Subramanium! I'm not scared of the LTTE, but everyone is scared of Mrs Subramanium! Even the LTTE!'

'Holy hell, Vannan! Why didn't you say!' Mahinda yelled, loosening the rope so that Vannan landed on a branch heavily. 'Did she see where you were going?'

'I don't think so. My brother sounded the alert when he saw her umbrella in the distance and who can miss that stupid bright blue and green saree she always wears!'

Mahinda and Nimal made small work of pulling apart the hearthstones and dousing the fire, then fanned the smoke away in the brisk sea breeze. They'd both managed to climb halfway up two largish *angsana* trees and were hidden by their leaves when Vannan's mother came into the clearing following a largish lady dressed in an incongruously bright saree. From the vantage point of the trees, she looked like one of those colourful chameleons that could be easily found in the forest just beyond.

'You must be here, I know you are,' Mrs Subramanium called out loudly. Several birds from nearby trees took flight. 'I know you are not hiding up on the watchtowers and I know you aren't hiding by the school hall like you did the last time I came. And Mahinda Ratnayaka's grandmother said that he had come here, so I know you must be here too.'

Vannan glared at Mahinda through the canopy of the trees, clenching his fist with outrage. Mahinda rolled his eyes and shrugged. What could he do?

'Come now. The time for silly childish games is long past,' she called out.

Neither Vannan, Mahinda nor the mute Nimal made a sound, sitting tight on their perches. They could outwait her any day of the week.

'Well, we'll just have to wait for them to return, I guess,' Mrs Subramanium said, glancing about her. 'This looks like a boys' playhouse. *Cheek*, look at the nonsense these boys are collecting,' she observed, rummaging through the bag of cocoons with distaste.

'While I'm here, I might as well tidy up,' Vannan's mother said, walking into the hut to make Nimal's basic bed. Out of the corner of Mahinda's eye he could see Nimal screw his face up with outrage.

'Now look at this!' Mrs Subramanium commented, picking up a stack of Sinhala language periodicals that Mahinda had brought for Nimal. 'All comics!'

'I might as well take all these clothes home to be washed,' Vannan's mother said, picking up a few pairs of musty shorts and T-shirts and stuffing them into a bag. 'That boy Nimal has no one to look after him properly.'

'What's this?' Mrs Subramanium asked, picking up Mahinda's little copybook full of notes. 'Can't understand a word of it,' she sniffed, dropping it carelessly on the ground.

Up in his tree, Mahinda gritted his teeth.

'Oh, I don't know *what* these boys are doing,' Vannan's mother muttered. 'Look at this, just look at this,' she said, picking up the hook on which Mahinda had draped the silk he'd collected just a few days before. 'I've been looking for this hook all week! It's what I use to hang my pot for boiling clothes in!'

'Stop!' Mahinda called. 'Don't!' He climbed down the tree hurriedly and without much grace, pausing at the base of the tree to retie his sarong. 'That's the silk we collected the other day!'

Mrs Subramanium grabbed the hook of silk and held it over a puddle of mud. 'So, where is he?' she demanded, her eyes glinting. 'Tell me or I will throw this silk in the dirt!'

'Up here,' Vannan called, resigned, as he too slid down. Only Nimal held his perch high up in the canopy.

'Oh, my precious *putta*, I can't tell you how happy I am to finally see you!' Mrs Subramanium gushed, making the transition from threatening to congenial in less than a second. She handed the silk to a nervous Mahinda, who grasped it with both hands. 'As I was telling your poor mother, having a fully grown son is such a burden, a burden he is obliged to reduce by getting himself a good wife!'

'As I have said before, I am not interested in getting married.'

'Sure you are! You just don't know it!' she insisted, turning briefly to Vannan's mother, who was smiling. 'I have arranged marriages for everyone from here to Puttalam. I have all the eligible young men and women on my books. Both Tamil and Sinhala. Did you know I brokered the marriage for the daughter of the mayor of Puttalam? A fine young lady.'

Mahinda looked up at Nimal, who was clinging to the tree for dear life. From the mutinous set to his mouth, Mahinda knew he would not come down until the interlopers had gone. That might be some time, though. Vannan was like a silk moth caught in a spider's web. No matter how much he struggled, he could not escape Mrs Subramanium, but he would not give up the fight.

'So, I have proposals from all the good Vellalar families from Puttalam to Jaffna. I even have half the families from Trincomalee. I think Sanuja Jayaratnam is a fine young lady. You must ignore her buckteeth, though. No one is perfect,' Mrs Subramanium insisted, shoving a handful of photos at Vannan and ducking her head back into her capacious black handbag.

All the information about prospective brides was there in Mrs Subramanium's handbag. In neat faded files, colour-coded for caste and social strata. Gold for wealthy Vellalars, lime green for children of Muslim merchants and blue for the offspring of Karawe families. 'Blue for Karawes like the ocean they sail!' she joked. And the individual files contained information about the bride's age, Vedic horoscopes and photos.

Mrs Subramanium proposed one bride after another. As soon as had Vannan rejected one young lady, the next profile of another came up.

'I never give up, you know!' she insisted as she ferreted deep into her bag. 'And as soon as our Mahinda finishes his studies in Colombo, I have the daughter of a wealthy Sinhala *modalali* from Trincomalee all lined up. She is only eleven now but in six or seven years she'll be perfect! I told your father all about her when I saw him in Mullaitivu the other day when he was in town to buy your youngest sister's new spectacles.'

Vannan could not help but smile as Mahinda spluttered with horror. 'Did you hear that? She'll be ready in six or seven years!' he teased. Busy tormenting his friend, he almost missed the photo that accidentally fell out of the matchmaker's handbag.

'And who is this?' Vannan asked, leaning over to pick it up from the muddy ground. Mahinda saw a strange look cross his face. 'Who is this?' Vannan asked again, gently wiping specks of dirt from the image of the bride's face.

'Her name is Shivani and she is of no use to you,' Mrs Subramanium retorted, whipping the photo from his hand. 'Notwithstanding, I think I have a very good offer for her hand from an educated government clerk from Puttalam.'

'And why is a clerk from Puttalam better than me?'

'She is a Karawe,' the matchmaker insisted. 'Do you want to break your mother's heart? Do you? Marrying a girl beneath you?'

'Is that what you say to the Karawe families? That they are beneath Vellalars?'

'No, I lie to them that there are no higher people than the warriors of the sea,' she retorted.

'But she is the most beautiful creature I ever beheld,' Vannan insisted, taking the photo back and looking at it in the evening light.

'Are you sure your son is not blind?' Mrs Subramanium asked his mother. 'Half the girls I have shown you today are at least as pretty as or even prettier than her.'

'No, they are not. She is the most beautiful woman in the world!' Vannan declared.

'I would be the laughing stock of all the matchmakers in the land if I brought your proposal to her family.'

'And why am I such a difficult prospect? I am the eldest son. I will inherit the most land!' Vannan declared indignantly.

'Mrs Subram—' Vannan's mother tried to get a word in edgewise but was ignored.

'She is a Karawe!' Mrs Subramanium said. 'What will your children be? Neither fish nor fowl?'

'That is ridiculous and you know it. It would not be the first time an inter-caste marriage has been made! Or are you too scared? Scared to go and broker the marriage? Or are you just a second-rate matchmaker?' Vannan goaded.

Mrs Subramanium did not quite know what to say. She looked at Vannan's mother, who finally spoke.

'Mrs Subramanium, this is the first time he has even shown a slight interest in any girl. He has been rejecting all your proposals for the last two years. I frankly don't care if she is a Karawe. All I know is that with three farmer sons I need help in the kitchen. Broker the marriage, if you please,' she said. 'I don't really believe this caste business is of any use at the end of it all.'

Mrs Subramanium looked more than a little mortified. 'But . . . but . . .'

'Just present my son's proposal. That is all we can do.'

Mahinda finally started spinning late one evening, by the light of several kerosene lamps. Vannan had taken Nimal to do the watch with him, ostensibly because the silent boy did not give him a migraine, but in reality because he understood that Mahinda needed time.

The letter had arrived from Colombo University offering him a place. The engineering course would span the next five years. His father had burst out into uncharacteristic tears, as had the *gamanayaka*. Even Vannan's *appa* had cried. The sight of three grown men bawling like babies had alarmed Mahinda, who was feeling rather overwhelmed himself, but soon the men had pulled themselves together and retired to the *gamanayaka*'s porch to celebrate with a bottle of *arrack*. Vannan's mother was already busy making food for him to take to Colombo, though he would not be leaving for three weeks yet. She made things that would keep well, like packets of fried dried gourds and deep-fried jackfruit.

'*Puttar*, who will look after you? You will have nothing when you get to Colombo,' she had worried, bustling around her tiny kitchen in quite a tizz.

'I will be fine, Ammaci. I hear food at the university is top class,' he told her, trying to sound confident. She wasn't fooled, though. She saw the sudden brightness in his eyes and heard the tiny wobble in his voice.

He would desperately miss Nayaru – the simple village life and the sweet smell of ripening tobacco and sea spray. He'd miss his silkworms, his family and his friends. The only thing that cheered him was the fact that Vannan's proposal for Shivani's hand in marriage had not been dismissed out of hand. Shivani's parents, frustrated by her long reluctance to consider any of the proposals put to her, had agreed to a meeting.

'Any marriage, even one to a dirt-grubbing Vellalar, has to be better than having a spinster daughter,' her father had conceeded. 'Let him come. And if she likes him, she can marry him.'

An entire delegation was leaving Nayaru at the weekend to meet the family. Even Nimal had been roped in to carry the ceremonial platter of betel leaves despite his mute protests.

'My weedy younger brother is too large to carry one and Shivani is so excited to use you as a pageboy for our wedding. She thought you were so cute when she met you the other day. She has an outfit with a frilled shirt all picked out for you already!' Vannan said as he read out his latest letter from Shivani. Nimal did not look pleased.

Mahinda liked to see Vannan so happy, but he was tired of his gushing and his tone-deaf love songs, so when Nimal agreed to do the watch in his place, he was delighted. He couldn't take one more night-long treatise on the many perfections of Shivani Muttasingham without hitting Vannan over the head with a coconut and stuffing the husk in his mouth.

As darkness fell that night he had walked over to the hut on the island with eight hanks of silk ready to spin. It took him a considerable amount of time to assemble the charka. It was a sizeable piece of equipment, about four feet in length, consisting of one large wheel that sat at right angles to the main strut and several smaller interlocking wheels. Much like the model made famous by Mahatma Gandhi, it required the user to sit cross-legged to spin it.

The wheel was old, very old – the wood was a deep mahogany colour and scored with nicks and scratches that spoke of many years of service. It was also wont to get stuck. Mahinda suspected it'd spent so many years in the hull of Mustafa Mohamadeen's humid junk that it had warped out of shape.

So he spent some time sanding away uneven sections, tightening, adjusting and soothing the wooden parts first. He applied wood oil and polished the interlocking wheels until they glowed in the evening light. He then greased the parts that would not touch the silk, using an old rag to apply the fat. It was just as well Mahinda had an engineering bent or else he could never have got the thing working!

Then he worked the spinning wheel, watching the smooth wave and form of it, getting to know its foibles as he gently spun some cotton, rolling a combed hank in one hand while he turned the wheel with the other, the rhythm of the machine somehow in harmony with the sound of the waves breaking on the shore beyond the lagoon.

A little after nine, Mahinda stood up and retied his sarong. 'I can't put it off any longer. It is time to spin some silk. Either this thing works or it does not!'

But it did not work. He tried about half a dozen times and the silk would simply not catch. The more frustrated he grew, the slower he went, to make sure the silk fibres clung to each other, but then there was not enough tension to pull the thread through. Then he tried to spin it fast, but the silk did not catch at all and the central line broke.

After several hours he stood up and yelled his anger into the star-lit sky. 'I give up. This is not possible. Why did I even

start this stupid project?' He pushed the charka away, blew out
the lamps and strode across to the beach, intending to go home
to bed, but by the light of the full moon he saw that it was a
king tide.

'And now I'm stuck,' he muttered to himself. Sure he
could wade across, but he didn't like his chances with the sea
snakes. So he walked the length of the beach instead, looking
at the bright moon reflecting on the lagoon, full to the brim
with water. Gold on black. In the distance he could hear soft
chanting.

Why of course! Vannan's mother was doing yet another
*abishekam* to thank the gods for sending Mahinda to university.

'I'll do a special *abishekam* for you this time. Now that you
are to become a university man! And an engineer! You do us
so proud. You will need the help of the goddess Saraswati,'
Vannan's mother had told him.

The chant was unfamiliar – the Hindus in and around
Nayaru seemed to call more often on Draupati Amman and
the god Shiva than on Saraswati – but the soft breeze carried
the words to him. '*Yaa Kundendu Tushaara Haaradhavalaa,
Yaa Shubhravastraavritha, Yaa Veenavara Dandamanditakara,
Yaa Shwetha Padmaasana Yaa Brahmaachyutha Shankara
Prabhritibhir Devaisadaa Vanditha Saa Maam Paatu Saraswati
Bhagavatee Nihshesha Jaadyaapaha.*'

'May goddess Saraswati, who is fair and beautiful like the
jasmine-coloured moon and whose pure white garland resem-
bles frosty dewdrops; who is adorned in radiant white attire,
on whose arm rests the veena, and whose throne is a white
lotus; who is surrounded and respected by the gods, protect
me. May you remove my lethargy and brighten my life with the
light of knowledge.'

Mahinda did not quite know what came over him next –
maybe it was an enchantment – but as the words seeped into his
heart, his moths came fluttering around him in the moonlight

and guided him back to the charka, their gentle wings pushing him towards the shed. They hovered near his hands as he took up the silk and fluttered over his head as he bowed it in thanks. Then, repeating the prayer to the goddess Saraswati, he started to spin.

He sat spinning, and spinning, and spinning. First very slowly. But by and by, the magic of the goddess was revealed to him. The spiralling of a single fibre clockwise pulled the others along while another pulled anticlockwise. It was a dance. A dance of creation masking a dance of death. For when one created silk thread, the silk itself disappeared. To create one, one must inevitably destroy the other.

More than a few times Mahinda got stuck. The needle at the eye of the charka broke and he had to stop and refit the damn thing. But as dawn lit the morning sky like a newborn opening her eyes for the first time, Mahinda had beside him two hanks of spun silk in a lustrous shade of golden white, soft and supple enough to make the finest silk saree.

Mahinda had caught the bus from Trincomalee back to Puttalam at just past midnight and was back in Nayaru by daybreak. He could barely contain his excitement when he got off, running the full three miles back to his village from the bus halt. He didn't bother going back home – he wanted to share his news with people who understood him the best. Vannan and Nimal.

The first thing he noticed when he reached Vannan's parents' modest home was the lack of activity. At a little past six in the morning, the place should have been bustling, his brothers on their way to look at their fields, his mother setting the large handwoven mats out to dry freshly threshed rice.

'Is something wrong? Has someone died?' Mahinda called out, walking around the back of the house to the kitchen.

'They might as well have.' Krishna, Vannan's younger brother, was sprawled in the yard with a blackened eye and a split lip.

'What? What happened? Where is Vannan?'

'Like you give a damn about him!'

'Krishna!' Vannan's mother admonished softly from the door, her hands filled with cloths and a slimy green poultice for her son's blackened eye.

'If it weren't for Mahinda, we wouldn't be in this predicament!'

'What Krishna? What did I do?' Mahinda demanded.

'You! You and your people!' Krishna yelled standing up abruptly. 'Had the *gamanayaka* supported my *ana* through school he would have had everything. The girl he desires, the education he deserved and the standing in the community that is his birthright. Instead he was betrayed by his own kind for *you*! You should never have taken that bursary!'

'You know I didn't want it! I came back from school in Jaffna after my mother died intending to work with my father. You were there. You heard the discussion. All I have ever wanted to be is a farmer,' Mahinda cried out in frustration.

Krishna faced Mahinda square on. The boy had grown in the last few months, Mahinda noticed, and was now taller than him.

'That bursary was set up especially for my brother after you won the scholarship to Jaffna!' Krishna said. 'The village wanted to take a chance and see if my brother could get to university. But you gave up your scholarship and came back. Then the *gamanayaka* chose to give you the bursary instead, so you could continue studying. Why did you take it? You are no better than a common thief!'

At this point Mahinda lost his temper and pushed him. Just enough to get Krishna's attention. They were like brothers – he had known Krishna since birth – and as the older brother Mahinda was due some respect, so what happened next completely caught him off guard. Krishna swung a clenched fist at him.

Mahinda went sprawling on the ground, his lip split and the contents of his hessian shoulder bag strewn around him on the ground. He was too surprised even to react when Krishna picked him up him by the lapels of his shirt and shoved him against a wall.

'Do you know what they did to us?' Krishna said in a low voice. 'They insulted us and dishonoured our *appa*. They said we weren't worthy of Shivani! All because of you!' He slammed Mahinda so that his head hit the wall.

'My son is killing Mahinda! My son is murdering his brother!' Vannan's mother screamed, dropping the fresh poultice on the soft earth.

'I still don't understand what happened!' Mahinda yelled.

'Because of you they said we weren't good enough to join their family. They could not overlook Vannan's lack of education – and you are the one who took his place at university.'

'I may not even have got into university!' Vannan said, appearing suddenly behind his younger brother. He came to stand next to Mahinda, pushing Krishna away with the pointy end of his mother's broom. 'The *gamanayaka* chose Mahinda because it was more likely he would get in.'

'That's because the government lowered the entry requirements for the Sinhalese and made it harder for the Tamils!' Krishna shouted, pushing Vannan's weapon aside. 'Now Mahinda's father is walking around like a giant because his son has got into university and our *appa* was tossed out into the rain!'

'That didn't matter in the end anyway. Mahinda came back here and the quotas operate on a district basis, not a race base. Don't you see?' Vannan pleaded. 'Or have those damned LTTE fools got into your head too?'

'No! You don't see!' Krishna roared. 'You are on the Sinhala side. Every time you defend them or side with them, you spit on your own people! Ammaci, I am off to Puttalam. The Tigers are recruiting and I'll be damned if I will let my own kind be treated like dirt!' He turned and stalked off in the direction of the bus halt.

'*Puttar!* No!' Vannan's mother screamed. 'Vannan! Go after him! Save your brother!'

'Let him go,' Vannan said. 'He'll be back within a week. He's no soldier. He double hoes his fields to protect fieldmice.'

'So what happened?' Mahinda asked that evening as they watched over the village. After the dramatic exit of Krishna, the *gamanayaka* had seen fit to come and visit Vannan's parents and to console and counsel them at length about their son's desertion.

'The LTTE are a plague,' the village headman had said. 'They are taking dutiful children away from their parents and turning them into monsters. My second cousin's boy died in one of their training camps. They came and gave my cousin five hundred rupees and his body.'

'Isn't it worth it? To sacrifice your life for Eelam? To live like free men?' Kadal, Vannan's youngest brother, asked eagerly.

Vannan's mother struck like a cobra, pouncing to twist her youngest son's ears. 'Don't you even dare think about joining those hoodlums! Low caste thugs with no brains or education! Hasn't my heart been broken enough?'

'Owww!' Kadal yelled. 'Stop it!'

'Leave the boy alone, Chelvathy,' the *gamanayaka* said. 'You would not be able to stop him if his heart was set on it anyway. But let me tell you something. The LTTE are living in a fool's paradise. We Jaffna Tamils are less than twenty per cent of the population,' he said. Murgan tried to interrupt, but the headman held up a silencing hand. 'Yes, still less than twenty per cent of the population, even if we include the plantation

Tamils. It is stupid to expect that the Sinhala government will give us two-thirds of the coastline. Especially when there isn't enough space for the Sinhalese either.'

'So what do you expect us to do? Take all the injustices they heap on our heads lying down? The land that Mahinda's family farms used to belong to the Krishnapillay family and it was taken from them!' Kadal said furiously, all decorum forgotten now. 'They took our land! They have no right to be here!'

The *gamanayaka* shook his head sadly. 'My family have been on this land for over twenty generations. Before the Krishnapillays lived there, a Sinhala family lived there and a Tamil family before them. There have always been Sinhalese living in the north, just as there have been Tamils living in the south.'

'But what are we to do? How can we change things if we don't fight for our rights?'

'The Mahatma brought the mighty British empire to its knees by doing nothing. Absolutely nothing. We, as Hindus, are not worthy of his legacy if we cannot learn from him. All the top engineers, doctors, lawyers and public servants in this country are Tamil. The British made it that way. They gave us Tamils a better education. What do you think would happen if all our Tamil brothers stopped working? The island would stop too and the Sinhala government would be forced to take notice of us!'

'It is an old man's way!' Murgan mocked.

'It is an old man's wisdom. Mark my words, the bullets the LTTE turn on the Sinhalese, they will just as soon turn on us. Killing one man is the same as killing another,' the *gamanayaka* said. As he left to go home he looked weary, his movements stiff and slow.

'When Krishna comes home I am going to give him such a thrashing,' Vannan told Mahinda. 'I can't believe he would do this to our mother – and it's his fault Kadal was talking that way to the *gamanayaka*.'

'But tell me about your meeting with Shivani's family,' Mahinda insisted. 'What went wrong?'

'It all started well enough. Shivani's parents were quite welcoming. It was clear that we liked each other, and my aunty found that her husband and Shivani's uncle worked at the Jaffna council together. It was a bit of a surprise to Shivani's aunty what my family's caste was.'

'Such polite and respectable people *and* in the government service,' the old windbag had kept repeating over and over again, looking somewhat taken aback.

Neither side could ignore the fact that their children were clearly smitten with each other. Shivani was a deep shade of beetroot as she sat looking out the window and Vannan could not stop sneaking little peeks at her. It was clear that it was love at first . . . er . . . sight . . . or something like that, anyway.

So it surprised no one that after about three quarters of an hour Shivani's father made his first observation on seeing the glow of joy that so became his only daughter. Her eyes shone so bright that they paled the glistening jewels at her ears and throat. A gentle smile that he'd never seen had settled on her lips. Before long the families found themselves talking about the wedding, as if the other details had all been agreed. 'I suppose we could have the marriage services in both a *kovila* and the church, to satisfy both faiths,' Shivani's father had said.

'So, what happened next?' Mahinda asked.

'We were talking about a suitable time to fix at both the church and *kovila* when Shivani's brothers appeared, those stupid overgrown apes. They'd been off gallivanting somewhere and they laid into us straight away.'

'All three of them at once?' Mahinda said.

'Yes,' Vannan told him. 'And they weren't impressed to see me there.'

'I'd rather my sister be a spinster than be given in marriage to this Sinhala-loving dog!' Geevan had said, as Rajan muttered something about sullying their bloodline.

'But this is the only proposal she has liked,' Shivani's mother had pleaded, thoroughly embarrassed. 'This is what she wants. Let it be. Your father and I are happy for her.'

'And what will you do when this fool whores your daughter out to *Sinhalayas*? Will you be happy for her then?' Theevan had demanded.

'Which was when I felt it appropriate to stand up and punch the fool in the mouth,' Vannan admitted a tad sheepishly. 'That's when things really exploded. Insults were hurled all around, lots of pushing and shoving. Theevan said my family were uneducated farmers with dirt for brains, and that we weren't good enough for his sister. That's how Krishna got his black eye. Nimal scarpered and ran all the way to the bus halt – I've never seen him move so fast. And my parents sobbed all the way home.'

'So what now? What are you going to do?'

'Shivani got a message to me while we were still in Jaffna. She will run away sometime in the next week or so. We can get married and return to Nayaru and live far way from those apes.'

'Tell me when you need me and I'll go to Jaffna with you,' Mahinda said. 'As long as it's not tomorrow,' he added, a small smile playing on his lips. 'I have to go back to Trincomalee.'

'So the trip was fruitful?'

'More than fruitful. The spinning master has offered me a job.'

'What?' Vannan asked incredulously.

'I couldn't believe it either. He wants me to come down again tomorrow to discuss the possibilities. A government agent will be there and they want me to work with them to build a project around my production technique.'

'But what about university?' Vannan asked. 'The whole village is depending on you. Your father is depending on you.'

'But this may be something more. Something that no one else has done before,' Mahinda said.

'No one in this village has been to university before!'

'I know, but I love this. I love silk farming. I'm happy taking care of my silkworms, I love spinning silk yarn and I'm really excited about this opportunity! I thought you'd understand,' Mahinda said.

'No, I don't understand. I don't understand why you'd sacrifice everything for some cockamamie idea!' Vannan told him. Mahinda heard the anger in his voice.

'But you helped me! You encouraged me all along!'

'I've also encouraged you to steal *kurumba* from the village across the lagoon and taught you how to swim, but I didn't expect you to make a life out of either!'

'But this is more than a dream now. It's really happening.'

'Just stop. Stop now. It's just a dream – leave it at that. I've had to sacrifice so much for you. I could have been you! I could have been an engineer and married Shivani. Shivani's brothers would not have dared to treat me and mine like dirt if I'd got a place at university. So don't you dare! Don't you dare think of running off to Trincomalee!'

'But Vannan . . .'

'Mahinda, you listen here. When you came back from Jaffna after . . . well . . . I stepped aside for you. I am at least as smart as you.'

'But I didn't want you to step aside. When I came back I was ready to—'

'What? Grow silkworms?'

'Yes, to become a farmer like my father. I was ready to do it. I have never been hung up on becoming an engineer!' Mahinda protested fiercely. 'I told you, I told the *gamanayaka* and I even told my father. But no one listened to me!'

'How could we? You'd just lost your mother. You weren't thinking straight. This whole village is depending on you now. I am depending on you. Give up this childish dream and do what is right! It is what your mother would have wanted you to do!'

It was a quarter to midnight and Mahinda started to panic. He ran up and down the darkened main bus halt in Trincomalee in search of a bus but could not find one. Not a single one. He could find buses headed south, he could find buses going inland west, and he even found a bus that was going to take the circuitous route from Trincomalee down south to Batticaloa then on to Galle and Colombo. But he could not find a single bus headed north. Not one to Kumpurupiddi, not one to Nayaru and certainly not one to Jaffna. It was as if all roads to the north had been closed.

'What's going on? Why aren't there any northbound buses?' Mahinda demanded of one bus driver after another.

'Heard the weather is turning bad up north . . .' a few muttered before going back to their game of *booruwa*. Yet the air was still and there was no hint of a storm. The crows were nesting comfortably in town and hadn't returned to their homes in the mountains.

In desperation, Mahinda tried hitching a ride on one of the many lorries that carted vegetables and other essentials from the harbour in Trincomalee to Jaffna, but again he had no luck. All the truck drivers seemed to want to go around the long way, through Vavuniya to Jaffna. Mahinda would normally have agreed, as the road was quite good that way, but he wanted to get back to Nayaru sooner rather than later.

At a little after one in the morning, he walked from the bus halt and stood at the fork where the road veered off to Mihindapura. There were plenty of cars heading up north, but again no one was willing to give him a ride. Maybe it was the rather large sack of silk yarn he had strung across his back. All twenty pounds of it.

A few of the drivers heading up north through Vavuniya carefully looked him over before tossing out helpful advice if they judged him to be Tamil. '*Thambi,* we've been told to avoid heading up north tonight. Everybody is saying that our brothers are planning on giving the *Sinhalayas* in Kumpurupiddi a taste of their own medicine. Shipping them all back south on buses.'

'Just the *Sinhalayas* in Kumpurupiddi?' Mahinda asked in his best Tamil, shrinking into the shadows of the street lamps. 'No talk of it in Nayaru?'

'Do you have friends in Nayaru?' some asked. 'The *gamanayaka* in Nayaru is strong. LTTE will not go there!'

After several hours of waiting at the crossroads, Mahinda gave up. Maybe he could sleep in the doorway of the mercantile store across from the junction and try to catch a bus at daybreak. He opened his shoulder satchel to stuff his sack of silk in it and could not help but smile at the crisp white shirt contained therein. He reached out to touch it. His first brand-new shirt. Fresh out of the packet. Maybe he could wear it to Vannan's wedding.

Mahinda had arrived back in Trincomalee that Monday morning not knowing what to expect. 'Thank goodness you are here early,' the guild master had said, coming out of his office. 'No, this won't do,' he said looking Mahinda over. 'Here, try this,' he'd suggested, tossing Mahinda a brand-new shirt from his cupboard. 'Come quick, the government agent is waiting for us next door.'

What had happened next meant that Mahinda's head was still in a spin a good ten hours later.

'Come, young man, come,' the government agent had said, graciously inviting Mahinda into a room full of other officials. 'Tell me about what you are trying to do.'

'Err . . . I . . .' Mahinda had stammered, feeling rather overawed. He was a village boy, more used to ploughing fields than talking to powerful government officials.

The guild master stepped in. 'As I said, this young man has been able to cultivate silk moths. And we all know how difficult that is. The *Bombyx mori* moth is notoriously difficult even to keep alive. They are prone to disease and can die from drafts. But this boy has done it. He has successfully cultivated a whole crop of them and has the cocoons as proof, see!' He pulled a handful of Mahinda's pods from his pocket.

'Well done!' the government agent told Mahinda. 'We tried getting something like this going in Matale a few years ago and all the moths died after a cold frost in the mountains.'

'Didn't they also start a project a few years ago in Hambantota?' the guild master asked.

'That failed. The entire breeding stock was wiped out by a flock of swallows.'

'What about the other project in Hatton?'

The government agent sighed, whipping off his glasses to rub his eyes. 'The watchman confused mulberry leaves with *casa casa* leaves and an entire generation of caterpillars died. Then we had this nasty storm and the rest of the moths were blown somewhere else.' He looked at Mahinda again. 'This is what we'll do, son. You can sit with our chief sericulturist and explain to him what you've done. He can take over from there. This may well be the beginning of a viable sericulture industry in Sri Lanka!'

'And we have the expertise now to spin the silk too,' the guild master had gloated. 'This young man showed us how to get even the smallest fibre out of the cocoons.'

'*Shah!* Well done! Not that the short fibres matter. You just boil the cocoons whole and reel the silk directly from the pods.'

'No,' Mahinda said in a quiet voice.

'Yes, the finest silk is that reeled directly from the pods,' the guild master said, not quite hearing him.

'No,' Mahinda said a little more loudly.

'Excuse me, *putta*. What did you say?' the government agent asked.

'I won't teach you how to raise silkworms if you are going to kill them for the silk,' Mahinda said firmly.

'And why not? Silk has been thrown for thousands of years by boiling the cocoons,' the guild master retorted.

'I won't give you my breeding stock if you are going to kill the moths to get their silk.'

'Can you explain to me why?' the government agent asked. He raised a hand in the air, signalling to the guild master that he should wait to hear the answer.

Mahinda explained how he'd started and why he wanted to create the silk without hurting the moths. He went into detail about how Nimal raised them, keeping them warm overnight and feeding them every two hours so that they grew up healthy and strong.

'We, all of us, cling to our lives. What right do we have to kill silk moths just for their cocoons?'

'Do you have a name for this type of silk?' the government agent asked. Both he and the guild master were impressed by the boy's passion and knowledge. While Mahinda was a boy from the village, it was clear that he was about as shrewd and intelligent as they came.

'Err . . . *ahimsa* silk,' Mahinda replied in a confident voice.

'Well, I think we can find you some money for this enterprise,' the government agent said. 'We'll give you two lakhs for the first year to get everything together and 2500 rupees a month for you to set it up in your village in Nayaru. The *gaman-ayaka* there is a wise man. He'll support you with this project, I'm sure – it will benefit the whole district.'

'Two thousand five hundred rupees?' Mahinda whispered softly. Senior doctors in the public service didn't make that much money.

'We've just received a large amount of money from the government to develop sericulture here in the north-east and you came along at the right time. I understand you've been offered a place at the university in Colombo, though, so you've got some decisions to make. You can't do both. This project will be a full-time job. So, go home and think about it. I know what I'd do if I were you, though. Not many engi-neers get the opportunity to do work like this – and it'd be

ten years before you'd be anywhere close to making this kind
of money.'

Mahinda had barely been able to farewell the man, his head
had been in such a whirl. He spent the rest of the afternoon
spinning silk with the guild master before heading off to catch
a bus home. 'Talk it over with your parents. They'll see that
opportunities like this don't come along every day,' the guild
master said as he left.

He wasn't quite sure how he was going to break it to his
family that he wanted to become a silk farmer instead of an
engineer. But he knew in his heart that was what he wanted to
do. He could already hear the howls of protest from his father
and see the disappointment in the *gamanayaka*'s eyes. He was
still standing there by the road absent-mindedly feeling the
cotton of his new shirt and thinking about this problem when a
truck carrying a load of rubber tyres came past.

'*Thambi!* Heard you were looking for a ride north. To
Nayaru? Hop in. I'm on my way to Jaffna! I have to get there
before midday.'

Lulled by the gentle rocking of the old truck, Mahinda fell
asleep, using the satchel slung on his back as a pillow. His last
thought as he drifted off was that he really didn't feel ready for
the war he would have to fight when he arrived home.

It was the harsh sound of a rifle being fired that awoke Mahinda.
The sound ripped through the early morning air, cool and
sharp. He jumped out of the back of the truck without stopping
to think and hid in the ditch beside the road, his satchel still on
his back. It was half-dark, the sun not yet over the horizon. He
knew he was back in Nayaru because of the smell of tobacco
flowers mingled with sea spray, but there was something in the
air that was altogether different. Something burning . . . what
was it?

'These tyres are promised to a *modalali* in Jaffna!' the lorry driver protested loudly. 'I can't give them . . .' The rest of his words turned into a gurgle as Mahinda heard someone draw a knife across the man's throat.

He lay flat on his back in the ditch frozen with terror. The unthinkable had happened. The LTTE had struck Nayaru! What was happening to his family? His father? His grandmother? He lay there, breathing hard, unable to move. Then he heard a voice he knew. Krishna, Vannan's little brother. 'Get those tyres. We'll need to build a bonfire.'

Mahinda gritted his teeth and inched forward on his stomach, using his elbows. His family lived the furthest away from the village. Maybe they had escaped to the island and were safe up in the trees. He needed to get to them. Determination fired him as he crawled along the muddy paddy field, slowly, not making a sound. He climbed over the bunt and looked over his shoulder at the watchtower.

Badayana Bala lay at the bottom of the tree. Dead. He'd been shot in the head. Mahinda felt sick.

Making his way across the village was not easy. The whole place was crawling with LTTE cadres – skinny young men dressed in jungle fatigue shirts and sarongs with rusty rifles slung across their shoulders. They looked like young farmers and fishermen, not soldiers. And if Mahinda looked carefully, he knew he'd been to school with most of them, or at least played cricket with them at the district tournaments.

Stealthily he picked his way around the hamlet's outlying houses, his near-perfect knowledge of the village saving him from detection more than once. He knew to hide behind the cesspit near the fishermen's shacks because no one in their right mind would even consider looking for anyone there. Then he skirted around the edge of the shops and wove through the string of palmyra trees that led to the back of the school, near the waterhole. It was there, as he hid behind a clump of coconut trees that had once served as shelter for the science lab, that he witnessed the final chapter of the horror visited upon Nayaru.

The Tamil villagers had been corralled in the schoolyard. Judging by the state they were in, they had put up fight to protect their Sinhala neighbours. Even Mrs Subramanium was there, looking cowed and terrified. The *gamanayaka* and the old schoolmaster, Sir Poornaswarmy, were the bloodiest and most bruised of them all, despite their advanced age, both of them kneeling on the ground, their heads bent over in front of the other Tamil men. Marking them as the leaders. They were held in their positions at gunpoint by boys young enough to be their grandchildren. Their wives were sobbing with the other women, all crouched together.

'We've got a supply of tyres,' Krishna announced, coming into the clearing with several other cadres rolling the large tyres they'd stolen from the lorry.

'You filthy thief!' Vannan's mother screamed. 'I should have drowned you at birth. You are no son of mine. From now till the end of time, I will curse your name!'

One of the cadres came up and hit her in the mouth with his rifle butt. 'Stupid woman, Eelam is greater than blood. It is greater than your son!'

Mahinda saw something odd in the distance and squinted in the dim grey light to make out what it was. A pile of loose branches? Coconut fronds?

No, it was a pile of human bodies. All in a heap. Mahinda could just make out the arms and legs of the Sinhala village shopkeepers and farmers, with the corpse of the *vedda* right on top. He saw Nimal's mother's body, and her husband's, and Nimal's brothers and sisters too.

Men, women and children. All murdered. And in that instant, the sun peeked over the horizon and a ray of sunshine glistened off a bright object that had fallen to the ground. A pair of child's spectacles. There was only one child in and around the five villages of Nayaru who wore glasses. Mahinda's youngest sister, Prema.

He could not stifle his scream. The *gamanayaka* looked up with everyone else to see where the noise came from. '*Puttar!* Run! Save yourself!' the old man shouted when he saw Mahinda, using the last of his strength to stagger to his feet and run at the LTTE cadre who raised a rifle in Mahinda's direction. The old man took a fatal bullet in his chest.

Mahinda didn't think twice as he crouched down to grab a few large pebbles and lobbed them in the waterhole. The terrified birds flew shrieking into the air, providing him a brief measure of cover, and he ran.

Unburdened by heavy weaponry and fired by adrenaline, he easily outpaced the LTTE cadres, running through the familiar streets of the village and past the irrigated paddy and tobacco fields as the morning sun climbed higher in the sky. Even as he ran, he saw dead bodies, the mutilated carcasses of those who hadn't even made it as far as the schoolyard.

A few times the cadres took aim at him, but their bullets missed him as he zigzagged across the village and past his home, where the pools of blood in the front garden were the only sign of the evil that had occurred but hours before. He cut around the back of the house, hoping to lose the cadres as he waded across to the island, but they were close enough to see which way he had gone.

'He's going to the island! We've got him now!' they called to one another, and they splashed through the water holding their weapons above their heads.

But when they got to the clearing, they could not find him. They tore up the hut, upended all the silkworm enclosures and ripped at the silk yarn drying in the wind. They even shot at the tree canopy, netting nothing more than a few *sula sula* that were circling nearby. It was as if Mahinda had vanished into thin air.

Vannan appeared in the clearing. 'He can't have gone far,' he said. 'You go back through the other way to the village and I'll take the long way to find him,' he assured his fellow cadres. 'We'd better get a hurry on before the army gets here.'

'Not a single sound,' Mahinda's mother said to her son, sitting up in the tree canopy with him and Nimal. She held one hand over Mahinda's mouth, her other arm tight around him as he struggled furiously against her steel grip.

'He's got to be up there!' one of the cadres insisted, firing into the trees again.

'Don't be a fool. There's nothing up in the trees. Besides, how could he get up there anyway? He's probably back in the village now,' Vannan said. His voice carrying clearly through the like island

Vannan hung around for a few moments as the other cadres took off, splashing across to the other side of beach.

'I know you are up there, Mahinda,' Vannan called when they were out of earshot. He looked up into the trees. 'They've got Shivani, Mahinda.'

How could Vannan think he cared about some stupid woman when his whole family had been killed? His friend had betrayed him and Mahinda was maddened with fury, but his mother kept her grip on him, covering his mouth so tightly he could not cry out. Vannan called for Mahinda again, looking up into the canopy, but as the wind carried the first tendrils of smoke over to the island, he took off.

Mahinda and Nimal stayed up in the trees for what seemed like an eternity, coming down only when the smoke and the acrid odour of burning tyres and human flesh had completely blown away. Mahinda fell to the ground sobbing. 'What am I going to do, Amma? What?' he cried.

She let him sob his grief out in her loving arms, holding him gently for the longest time, until he was calm. 'The army will be here soon,' she told him. 'Actually I hear them now.'

And she was right. In the distance was the unmistakable sound of helicopters.

'Take Nimal here,' she advised, 'and go to my sister in Matara. She is a good woman and she'll look after him while you are in Colombo. Finish your studies.'

'What about you, Amma?' Mahinda asked as he scrambled

to his feet. Nimal had wordlessly gathered his meagre belongings up and came to stand next to Mahinda.

'My work is just beginning,' she replied with a beatific smile. And as Mahinda looked across the lagoon, he saw them. Villagers drifting across the water, being pulled to the island by an invisible force, their feet not even rippling the surface. Shocked and bewildered.

Nimal stared, unable to believe his own eyes until his mother came past, ruffling his hair gently before drifting off to find her murdered children.

'Have you always been able to see them?' he asked Mahinda as they waded across the lagoon, two living souls moving away from the island as the dead souls moved towards it.

'Yes. Ever since my mother died three years ago, yes. I came back to Nayaru for the funeral and found her here,' Mahinda told him, not even noticing that had Nimal spoken for the first time.

As they reached the shore, Mahinda turned to look at the island for the last time. On the edge of the beach he saw his mother first embrace his father, then crouch to reach out and embrace the children she hadn't held for so many years.

The harbour in Trincomalee was a mess. There were boats here, there and everywhere. Refugees mingled with soldiers, sailors, fishermen and Indian traders who'd been turned away from the port in Jaffna. More than one hundred Sinhala villagers had been murdered in and around Nayaru. The survivors, the few there were, were in a state of shock. But the entire Sinhala populace in the north and north-east was on the move.

The roads inland were deemed too dangerous, so the Sri Lankan government was providing safe passage on its naval vessels to the ports of the south – Galle, Hambantota and

Matara. From there people could travel overland to relatives. Restart what was left of their desolate lives.

Nimal had fallen asleep despite the pandemonium. Not that Mahinda could blame him. They'd hardly had anything to eat or drink in the past two days. Mahinda gently settled Nimal's sleeping body into a comfortable position, rolling up some old newspaper and tucking it under his head.

He stood up to stretch, which made him realise he was a great deal hungrier than he'd realised. Yet he had no money. He'd only been able to get a few rupees from his father's home and the copies of his letter allowing him university entrance.

He grabbed his shoulder satchel and made his way down to the trading vessels. Maybe he could barter his new shirt for half a loaf of fresh bread. The boats bobbing brightly in the azure blue sea were a strange sight, so at odds with the grey desolation in his heart.

He had no luck – no one wanted a new white shirt. There were so many people paying for safe passage with valuables such as gold and precious stones that a new white shirt held no currency. Mahinda was about to give up and go stand at the army ration point when he heard a voice call out.

'Hey, young sir! Is that you?' It was Mustafa Mohamadeen, the trader. 'How did you go with your spinning? Was the wheel I gave you any use?'

'You remember me?'

'How could I forget? The stupidest thing I had ever heard. To get silk without killing silkworms. I told the story to my friends in Karnataka. Professional silk makers. Sericulturists. They could not stand for laughing!'

Mahinda opened his bag to show Mustafa the precious silk he'd spun, not harming a single silk moth.

'Well, well, well . . . it is rare that I am proven wrong, young sir,' Mustafa said. He reached out and took the silk from Mahinda's bag and weighed it in his hand. There could be no doubt that this was silk of the highest quality, the threads fine and even with a bright lustre.

'Why, this silk is good enough to grace the saree loom of the most skilled Saliya in Karnataka! To be made into a saree worthy of a maharani!' Mustafa observed reverently.

'It's no use to me,' Mahinda replied wearily. 'I'd trade it all for my family.'

'How about one thousand rupees?' Mustafa asked. 'That is all the money I have on me right now, but I will send you another thousand rupees for it when I get to India.'

Mahinda looked down at the silk. There were no dreams left to dream. He was numb. He reached out a weary hand to take the money and handed the silk over. It would provide him and Nimal with a start.

# The Pleats

Kanchipuram, Tamil Nadu, India, 1983

tink I sleep. All my life. I tink I not even alive. I sleep when Appa gives me to Murukananthan from Kanchipuram. He gives 250 rupee he earn making twenty-five new dhoti for Guru Rameshwaran. Twenty-five dhoti take one year to make.

'Pilar,' he says. 'Go. I give nuttin more for a girl child. Should have drowned you at birt but your *ammaci* forgot. Before she knew it you be a year. Can't kill a child. Dey put you in goal.'

Murukananthan put brown string around my neck under banyan tree. Like cow. 'Mariamman' be carved into tree. 'We be married now,' Murukananthan he says and walks away. Twenty miles. To Kanchipuram. I never leave my village. I not know what past de big banyan tree in Guru Rameshwaran banana field.

We walks. Walks. Walks. My leg hurt. But we walks. We comes to his house before dinner. I too tired to see anytin. I knows it be bigger dan my father house. But my father house in village. Kanchipuram be big town. Houses close together. People close together. Noisy.

I sits on mat. I no wash my face or hair. I no eats. I hears his father. His mother. Two brothers and his idiot sister-in-law. Dey say Murukananthan gets good money for village girl. I sit den I sleeps. Murukananthan he roll on top of me. Push my saree and he inside me. Dey say I should have screamed. Pain. But I sleeps. I feel no pain. Good dere be blood on my saree or Murukananthan and his brothers kill me. Dey don't put you in jail for dat.

But I wakes up. Screaming. Ripping. Paining. Nine months later.

Dey give me my son. He still covered wit white slippery ting. Skinny boy wit curly hair. Bright eyes. Like god Ganesh.

'He be like de lotus dat come from mud,' de birting mother she says to me softly. 'He so fair dat he could be a memsahib child. Magic be in dis child.'

I looks at my boy. And he be magic. He beautiful. He not even one hour old and he smiles. Now I understand what dey say. Dat mothers love sons more dan God. I looks at my son and I wakes up. Like I see de sun for first time. So I gives him de name Laksman. After god Rama's brother.

'Oh so fancy name,' my *marmee*, Koddi, laugh. 'It your *pooroochen*'s job to give name. Not you, stupid girl!'

I don't say nuttin. I pretends I sleep. I keeps my Laksman next to me. Murukananthan gone to Calcutta. He put down train lines. It hard work. He gone for two months. Baby must have name. Cannot wait two months. How God know him if he dies? I want God to tink he be his brother.

'Stupid girl,' Marmee says when she sees I close my eyes. 'Eyes open but sleep in de head. My boy should got more money for sleeping wife.'

And money be de problem. See I grow up in village. No money no problem. You eat what you have. If no, you go to jungle and eat what dere. Wild manioc. Leaves of de *casa casa* tree. Roots. Mushrooms. Tummy full. But in town you buy everytin. You buy old rice. You buy rotten vegetables. You buy rotting manioc. Make you sick. You cannot eat paper money. And you cannot eat what you buy wit paper money. *Cheek!*

My boy I keep safe. I feed him my titty. Nuttin else. And giving him titty wake me up. When my milk run into his mouth, I wake up more. Funny pain in my titty. Like tickling. I loves my Laksman. He grow fat and strong. Not like idiot sister-in-law son. She give him rice water. He sick.

Murukananthan take me when he come back. I not fall wit child. I happy I not got child again. My sister-in-law have four child and all dies. She sits dere wit last dead baby. Baby boy. Dey take baby because it stinks. Like dead cow in jungle. She run after baby. My brother-in-law run after wife. My *marcel* run after son. Dey all run over by last bus from Madras.

My *marcel* get two broke arm. My brother-in-law get two broke leg. My idiot sister-in-law more idiot wit broke head. Dat when Koddi speaks. To me. Nicely. Like I no girl from village.

'Pilar,' Koddi says. 'You goes to work. You work or we die.'

'No,' I says. 'I no work. Murukananthan bring paper money. I no work.'

'Marcel no work. Ana no work. We be Saliyas. Cannot work wit broke arm and leg.'

My father-in-law and two brother-in-law make saree like my *appa*. In de hut next to house. Mornin and night. Click-clack. Click-clack. All day. Everywhere silk cloth.

'I Saliya too. What I care about saree?' I have two cotton saree. One my father gave day I marry Murukananthan. One Murukananthan bring me from Calcutta.

'Stupid girl. My son paper money not enough. Not to buy medicine. Not to buy food,' Koddi cries.

'Den *you* work,' I says. 'I not leave my son for you stupid family.'

She try find work. No one give her job. Dey say she too old. Not strong. She comes home. Sit and cry. 'My man die! My son die!'

Dat make me sad. I no want my man to die. I die if my son die.

De man who buy saree come to de hut. In big car. He big man. He wear pants not sarong. I look at him. And I look at him. He fat man. Big belly like he wit baby.

'Shamurgam,' he says to my father-in-law holding white cloth over nose. 'If you cannot weave sarees for me, how can I possibly pay you?'

'Only until he mends,' Koddi she cries. 'His leg mend and he be best Saliya in Kanchipuram!'

'I run a business not a charity,' he snaps. 'If you want money, you must work! I cannot pay you for sitting around all day.'

'But I needs money,' Koddi cries more. 'I needs money for medicine for my man and boy!'

'Then you'll just have to work,' de man says. 'My daughter is getting married soon. I need a strong woman to help with the kitchen work. You're too old, though, Koddi. What about that girl? The one in the corner?'

'She say she won't work,' Koddi she spits.

'If stupid girl don't work, throw her out,' my father-in-law shouts from bed.

'My man gives paper money! You no throw me out,' I yells.

'You man gone to Andhra Pradesh for two months. You dead before he back!'

Now I scared. I not know anyone in Kanchipuram. I cannot go back my village. I not know where my village be.

'But who look after my boy while I works?' I asks.

Big Sir sees my Laksman first time. My Laksman smile at Big Sir. Big smile. My Laksman like a snake charmer. Only he use smile.

'Bring him with you,' Big Sir he says softly. He even move his white handkerchief from his face to look at my boy. Dat is how my Laksman and I start to work every day in Big Sir house.

'Fast, Pilar, fast!' Koddi yells. It be early morning. It be raining for three days. I takes Laksman while he sleeps and puts in my saree. I tucks my *pallu* in tight wit him across my chest. I is careful – babies in my village dies cause dere mothers tucks em in too tight. I checks my Laksman. He be breathing. I checks all de time he be breathing. I nots see we leave our street.

I is scared. I never leaves street before. Marmee buy vegetables. Marcel buy rice. And idiot sister-in-law bring water.

I follow Koddi. I is very careful. Holes of water everywhere. Mud. Dirt. *Sani*. Street be busy. Peoples. Cars. Trucks. Dogs. Cows. Everybodies goes everywhere. Peoples goes to work. Peoples goes to temple. Peoples goes to market. I is so scared I cannots see Koddi. But I follows her saree. Blue wit gold. Even dat hard. Kanchipuram be city of saree. Everywhere bright sarees.

I suddenly looks up to see I be lost. I cannots see Marmee anywhere. I no breath. I no know how to get home. I no know how to gets anywhere. Dat when I hears it. When I sees it. Like goddess stand before me. All white. Statues going up into de sky. I stand dere. Also like statue.

Marmee comes and tugs my hair. Hard. 'What? Have you not seen temple before?'

I shakes my head.

'Dat be Kamakshi Amman temple. It be for Kamakshi Devi.'

I no know whats to say. De temple so beautiful.

Den we runs. 'We must gets to house before crow cries,' Marmee says.

Big Sir house far away from shanties. Dere be few peoples on de road. Dere be no *sani* on de road. Dere be no cows on de road. Dere be no dogs on de road. Dere only be big white walls.

'Walls so big I cannot sees de sky,' I says to my Laksman.

If de fence big, de house bigger. Maybe like king palace. Maybe God house. It be bigger dan all de houses in my village. We goes around to de back. We walks around de mango trees and to de kitchen. Kitchen in small outside big house. Kitchen house bigger than Guru Rameshwaran house in my village. It be busy. More peoples. Maybe ten or fifteen. All busy.

'Koddi! *Achaa!* You be sight for sore eyes,' big lady wit big nose-ring and many bangles cries. 'How you man? You boy? Gopal say dey cut you man leg! What you do now?'

I sees Gopal. He be skinny boy who live behind our house wit no front teeth. He lives wit six brother and father. No woman in de house. His *mam* dies when cow runs her down when she *sani* on road. His house very dirty.

'Gopal is idiot,' Marmee say. She make fist to hit Gopal but he walks into house fast. 'No, dey no cut my man leg. I takes him to Ayurveda hospital. I needs money for medicine.'

'Sir says he sees you. You bring Murukananthan wife work in *sangeet*.'

'*Achaa*, yes. Here she be,' Marmee says pushing me. 'Dis is Balini *baba*. You do what she tells you do. Balini *baba*, Pilar be stupid girl from village. You hit her if she no do what you want she do,' Marmee says. She turns to go.

'Here, take dis,' Balini *baba* says. She quickly wraps dosai in big banana leaf and puts in some *vadai* too. My stomach growls. I looks away.

'*Romba nanringa*,' Marmee says. Again and again. She kisses Balini *baba*'s hand. We only eats plain rice for days now.

'Pilar, come,' Balini *baba* says. She be kind woman. She takes me to another hut in garden.

'What dis?' I asks. Dere be hole in de ground wit bowl. Dere also be a big water bucket next to hole in ground.

'It is the toilet,' she says.

'What you do in toilet?'

'You *sani* and you pass water and you wash with water. Now,' she says, opening a cupboard. Dere be hundreds of sarees. White. All stacked. She takes Laksman. He awake now. He smiles. He got two teeth.

'First thing you do when you come here is you wash and you change. Go,' she says giving me bucket wit water and little square of white ting. 'Take it. It called soap. Dis what you do,' she says, making white ting fluffy under tap. She shows me how to wash. My hands. My feet. My face. 'Every two days, you must wash your body.'

'Whats?' I cries.

'You goes in here and you wash your body.'

'Buts I never wash,' I says. 'I only ever wash in river in village in dry season. When river not full.'

She walks to other side of room and turns shiny little ting on wall. Water comes out of hole in walls like rain. I goes to look and she push me in. Like dat. I screams and screams. '*Aiyhoo!*' Balini *baba* she laughs. I hear mens laughing from outside. Laksman laugh.

'Eh! Gopal, you bloody fool! Get out of here,' Balini *baba* screams. And laughing stop. I stops screaming. 'Now use the soap,' she says. It smell good. I comes out. I sees myself in shiny ting on wall for first time. Maybe I is not as ugly as Koddi says. My skin light like Laksman and I got big eyes like Laksman. I realise dat my Laksman, he look like me.

'Now you wears saree,' Balini *baba* she says, giving me a fresh white saree, underskirt and blouse from de cupboard. 'You go pass water you change saree. You go *sani* you change saree. You change saree when you go home. You change saree when you come back. You never wear saree from road into house. You never wear cleaning house saree for serving food. You understand?'

'Yes,' I says, draping in my saree. Dis be my first saree without holes. It soft. And clean. I go to take Laksman.

'You bring baby, you wash baby too,' Balini *baba* says and she put my Laksman into bucket. He screams now. I laugh. Balini *baba* wash him good wit soap. He come out very white. Like milk.

'If I didn't know it, I tink he be a baby from a respectable family,' Balini *baba* says softly. But I hears.

'He be smart boy, he be good boy,' I says, taking him and putting him into my *pallu*. He hungry now. He take titty.

And dat is how we starts working in de Govindarajan house. De biggest house in town. De house of Kanchipuram Silk.

works hard. I get to de big house every morning before crows wakes ands I leaves after Balini *baba* takes de bed tea to Sir and Madame and Missy. But I never sees Sir, Madame or Missy. Dey in house. I work in de kitchen and outside.

'Sridevi was de garden and kitchen girl,' Balini *baba* says. 'But she got coughing sickness so she gone back to village. Big Sir be big angry. He comes in and calls us all dirty filth. Says we must wash alls de time. Says garden and kitchen girl cannots come to house no more. Only garden and kitchen,' she whispers. She looks over shoulder to see if Sir be dere.

'Balini *baba*, so you looks after all house?' I asks. Bali *baba* strong woman I tinks.

'*Achaa*, no!' she laughs. 'Dere be Gopal, he does most of de heavy cleaning. Dat fool Henry, he drive Sir's car. Den his brother Thomas, he drive car for Madame and Missy. Venay and Gunay be de cooks. Den dere is Mr Krishnapillay – he be de Sir personal servant. Like Miss Sonali – she be de personal servant to Madame. Dey never speaks to us. Don't speaks to dem. And Mama Leela be Missy's ayah. Since baby, she looks after Missy.'

'She be very happy abouts wedding?'

Balini *baba* looks away. She not answer.

'But Missy pretty, yes? She is daughter of Sir.'

'Yes, Missy is very pretty, but . . .' Balini *baba* shrugs. 'But Big Sir and Madame dey nots happy abouts marriage.'

'Dey say it be biggest *sangeet* since maharajah time,' Gopal says, bringing boxes of glasses, and Balini *baba* tells me time for work.

And I washes glasses. Oh more glasses dan I cans count. I washes so much my fingers be like dry betel leaf. We puts glasses on racks and stack ems against kitchen wall. Nice and neat. Like a big wall of glasses. In de afternoon, de light come and it be like fireflies in de village. Laksman likes to crawl dere. Watch de light dat come through.

Thomas and Henry build a hut in garden. Like de hut I lives in village. But bigger. De hut be bigger dan Murukananthan house. And very pretty. Like maharajah house. Wit pretty carved wood everywhere and lights.

'Who live in dis house?' I asks Balini *baba*. 'Is it for Missy and her new husband?'

'Silly girl! Dis house is not living in! Dis house for waiters to serve drinks from!'

And she be right. Two day before *sangeet* waiters come. Cooks come. Dey all be fine men. Wear shirt and pant. No sarong. Clean white shirt. Not like Murukananthan. I stands dere. Watching. My Laksman watch too.

'Eh, Gopal,' Balini *baba* says. 'I tink Pilar in love! Like in film show!'

'Love, love,' Gopal laugh. He pretend to be woman. Walk like woman.

'Eh, Balini *baba*,' I says loudly. 'I tink de hijra dey come early . . . de wedding in five days, not now!' Hijra be not man, not woman. Dey comes to bless marriage. Many mens no like hijra.

De waiters laugh now. 'De hijra only come day of wedding. You be confused, Gopal. You come early to practise,' dey laugh. Gopal walks away angry.

Buts I works. I cleans de garden. I chops wood. I likes working in de big house. Laksman likes being in de big house. I can let him play. Dere be no dirt on ground.

De day before *sangeet* a big lorry comes in. Drive close to kitchen. Careful wit de mango trees he goes around. I sits at

kitchen door washing more glasses. I is so tired I unties my
*pallu* and lets my Laksman down. Wash an stack. Wash an
stack.

'What in dere?' Balini *baba* asks, coming out of de kitchen.
She crazy busy wit work.

'More glasses for *sangeet*. And plates,' de driver says.

'But we gots plates and we gots glasses. We got more dan
we needs,' she says.

'But de Sir has ordered more.'

'Well I don'ts have de space for it!'

'*Akka*, I gots lots more to deliver for *sangeet*. I not waste
time wit you!'

'Drop it off at de top of de garden den. I will get Gopal and
Henry to move it after I talks to Big Sir.'

But Gopal and Henry gets angry. 'I not works for you,'
Henry says. 'I not carry heavy glasses! Sir says drops off at
kitchen.' Everybody crazy angry. Dey all too busy wit work for
*sangeet*.

'I be very tired. I works hard,' Gopal says. He chops big
load of firewood ands he hang all lights today.

'I work hard too!' Balini *baba* says. 'And I don'ts have more
space for more glasses and plates.'

'You stupid woman! Dat not my problem,' Gopal says. But
he looks scared.

'You calls me stupid woman! You calls me stupid woman!'
Balini *baba* screams and hit Gopal. Everyone stops and stares
at fight. Balini *baba* grab broom and hit Gopal over de head
again. 'I old enough to be your mother. You mother die, I looks
after you after she die. And you calls me stupid woman!'

I so busy staring at fight I not see lorry keep coming to
kitchen outside.

'*Aiiiiii!* Pilar, looks!' Balini *baba* screams.

I screams. Laksman behind lorry. I cannot move. I tink I die.
My boy die, I die.

Balini *baba* moves. She run like wind. She grabs Laksman

and pushes him away. And de wall of glasses falls on her. In de afternoon. Tiny tiny pieces of glass. Everywhere. Shine. Like precious stones on Madame finger rings. I scream. My boy safe but Balini *baba* be all cut up.

Dey say de doctor put sewing stitches. Like saree blouse. She sew up all over. She too sick to do *sangeet*. Balini *baba* sits in bed in corner and cry.

Sir comes to kitchen. 'Just as well I ordered the extra glasses and plates,' he says. 'Who are you?' he asks me.

'I be Pilar . . .'

'Ahh . . . yes, Murukananthan's wife. Well, you'll be the kitchen and house girl now. Make sure you wash your hands and feet each time you come into the house. And use soap,' he says.

Dat is hows I starts working in de house. My Laksman and me. Just like dat.

Working in de house mean I no go home.

'Koddi, Pilar is to work in the house now,' Sir explains to Marmee, giving her paper money. 'She can go home one day a week. On a Tuesday. That is her day off. But at all other times, she lives and works here. I do not want disease from the town being carried into the house every day.'

I shares a room wit Balini *baba*. Most of de time she sits and cries in pain. I feels sad. De doctor come and give me medicine to give her. 'Put this powder in water,' de young man says. 'It's for the pain.' He wears smart clothes. Western clothes wit cloth string around neck.

'Is dat cloth string around neck like for cow?' I asks Balini *baba*.

She laughs weakly. 'Dat necktie. Foreigner clothes.' Den she asks me to go get de paper dey use to start de cooking fire outside. 'If you work in de house, you must learn.'

Dat nights I wash Balini *baba*'s cuts wit water boiled wit *neem* leaves from de garden mixed wit turmeric. Whiles I wash, she teach me. Showing me pictures from de papers. 'Western men wears pants, shirt and necks tie. Womens wear dress.'

'Girl childrens wear dress and deir mothers wear dress too?'

'Yes,' Balini *baba* says, shaking her head. She be confused too. It be very strange. How peoples know if girl child be old enough to marry if she and mother wear same clothes?

Balini *baba* be right. I must learn. Sir, Madame and Missy have many important friends. Tamil friends. Hindi friends from New Delhi. Foreigner friends. Dey all talks in white peoples' language. It be like putting oil in frypan. Loud like firecrackers and very fast.

But I no listen. I too busy. I house servant now. I even gets new saree. White wit blue lines and little silver leaves. I now takes bed tea for Sir, Madame and Missy. Ands I makes sure Gopal sweeps de house and not sleep under stairs.

I also gets ready for *sangeet*. I makes sure all house is clean. Balini *baba* tells me whats to do and I do it wit Laksman tied to my back. Gopal and I takes Balini *baba* to see what be happening. And she be very happy. 'You works hard, Pilar. You works good. I be so proud of you.'

So proud dat on day of *sangeet* Balini *baba* says to Sir, 'Pilar can helps upstairs. She cans help Mama Leela.'

And dere be lots to do. I goes up in de morning. My Laksman sleep in my *pallu* drinking titty. Missy still sleep in bed. Mama Leela sleeps on floor next to Missy. Missy room big as two village hut. And Missy have bathroom in room. And her clothes room. *Aiii!* Dat be bigger dan one hut. Wit saree of every colour everywhere.

But soon Missy wakes up. She takes tea and peoples come. Dey wash her face. Dey put crushed cucumbers and buffalo curds on her face. Den dey comes to wash her hair. Dey use water dat dey put lotus flower in. I stands at de door and I can smells it. It so sweet make my head spin.

After lunch tings get more busy. More peoples come to do her hair and dey put henna on her hands and feet. Den dey paint her face. De peoples asks me to do jobs for dem. 'Pilar,' dey says, 'get me a cup of tea!' Or 'Pilar, can you ask Gopal to get more ice for my drink?' I runs ups and downs stairs so much I dizzy.

Maybe dat why I no realise I in room wit Missy and Sir. I comes out of Missy's bathroom. I comes out and see Missy in front of mirror. She like goddess. Like Hindi film star. I stands dere like rock when I sees Sir comes in.

'Shanthi, *putta*, you are so beautiful. I am so proud of you,' he cries. 'You don't have to do this. You don't have to marry him.'

'But I have to. I really do,' Missy says.

'But he is half a man,' Sir says. I see tears come from his eyes. 'Shanthi, you only have to say the word and I will cancel this wedding. I will send everything back and I will make your excuses to old Mr Nair. I'll even organise a marriage for his daughter if you will not marry his son.'

'No, Appa.'

'Why no? Why, my *puttar*? Why are you breaking my heart like this?'

'Because I love him.'

'But he is not worthy of you . . .' Sir pleads.

'Appa, please listen to me. I have loved him since I was a little girl.'

'Yes, I remember. You hid in the staircase watching him when you were eight. You were too scared to even speak.'

'I never thought he'd agree to the proposal. But now he has,' Missy says. She smiles.

'Shanthi,' Sir says, looking very sad. He open his mouth and closes it. Opens it and closes it again. Den he tinks and he speaks. Slowly. 'I don't know that he has agreed to this marriage at all. I think this is more his father's doing.'

'I don't care as long as he is mine.'

Sir shakes his head. He be very sad. 'My darling girl. I can save you from this farce until I hand you to the *pusari* tomorrow. Just one word from you, my darling, or even a look, and I will call this off.'

'Appa, you worry too much. All will be well in the end.' Missy smiles again.

Sir leave room. I is in room wit Missy. I turns to go back wit cleaning tings to bathroom when Missy looks up and sees me.

'Ahh, Pilar,' she says. I looks up. 'I gather you heard all that?' I nods my head. 'Then you'll understand why I'll have to make you my personal maid. I cannot have you blabbing all that down in the shanties.'

And dat is hows I become Missy Shanthi's servant. Now I do more more. Just like dat.

Now I know de roads. I even goes into town wit Henry for tings for Madame. Like oil for her head massage. She say she like it new. 'Bring me some fresh oil for my headaches,' she says. I no tell her dat medicine man give me oil from same pot every day.

I walks through town slowly dat morning wit Laksman. Like first day, peoples busy. Cows. Dogs. Bicycles. Cars. Buses. It be early buts I stops at de temple. I never been to big temple before. In my village, dere only be one tree wit Mariamman. I walks in and looks.

'*Thangachichi*, you are here to do a pooja for your son?' de young *pusari* asks me.

He mistake me for a rich woman wit money for pooja. Maybe dat because of my new saree. Madame gives away saree yesterday. 'My daughter is married now, what use do I have for grand sarees,' she says and she opens her cupboard.

Her clothes room as big as Missy bedroom. She gives Mama Leela and her servant Miss Sonali de best sarees. Bright colours like on parrot. Orange. Blue. Green. Yellow. She gives Balini *baba* and me less good saree. Balini *baba* no go out much now dat she look like cut blouse, so gives me her sarees too. And I takes em. So under one arm I carries about fifteen sarees for Koddi and idiot sister-in-law. In my other hand I carries big bag of dosai and biryani. Three day old. From de wedding. Just as well Laksman sleep in my *pallu* tucked in closely cause I no got arms to carry him.

I shakes my head. I explains to *pusari* I comes back wit *vadai* and dosai another time to make pooja for my Laksman to be smart boy. Make him good boy.

Then I goes home.

'You come back have you?' Koddi asks, waking up.

She sleeps next to father-in-law. And father-in-law sleep next to brother-in-law who sleep next to idiot sister-in-law. Next to her Murukananthan little brother. Five peoples. All sleep in one room. Murukananthan, Laksman and I sleep dere too. Now I no understand how.

Koddi sees I gots dosai and sambar. She grabs de bag from my hand and she calls. '*Eii!* Wakes up! Wakes up! All of you. Pilar, she brings food.' Dey all wakes up real quick and eats. Peoples here not fat like in de big house. In de big house dere always be food to eat.

'Eh, Pilar, what's you got dere?' Koddi she asks after a while, pointing to de bag under my arm. I squats in corner of hut wit my Laksman.

'Sarees,' I say. Koddi, she stuff dosai into mouth quick and drinks *thairu* fast and come over. Fast. De milk still dripping corner of her mouth.

Father-in-law eat and burp loud. Den he go outside and do *sani*. Right in front of door. It be very smelly.

I say nuttin. I no want to say anytin. Maybe it good I work in de big house. I no like boy grow up like Murukananthan family.

'All dis food, it come from wedding?' idiot sister-in-law asks. 'I hear dey did not eat much.' She got big eyes and big ears and she go down to well by end of street and gossip all de time.

'No, dere be lots of food. Aloo gobhi. *Vadai*. Dosai. Biryani. Dis just what left,' I says.

'I hear de groom did not even come to *sangeet*,' my father-in-law says, coming in limping.

'Pilar is stupid girl, she knows nuttin,' Koddi says.

'I hear de groom did not tie *mangala sutra* around her neck,' my brother-in-law says now he finish eating his food. He put all his fingers in mouth and suck. 'And he tie string around her waist. Like second wife.'

Sir is de richest man in Kanchipuram. Everyone in town talk about wedding. I works at wedding. I hears all de peoples saying nasty tings about de new Sir. Dat he not good enough for Missy.

'Is dat true? De big Miss from Kanchipuram Silk? She second wife?' idiot sister-in-law asks.

Again I no says anytin.

'Dey say he be very ugly. Burnt like a *vadai*. Dey say you cannot see his eyes and his legs like banana tree. All scaly and ugly,' my father-in-law says.

'Poor Missy,' Marmee says now. 'It cannot bes easy to marry man like dat. If he be so burnt maybe he cannot do man ting.'

'Man can always do man ting,' my brother-in-law laugh. He smile ugly smile.

I pretends I cannot hear. It not my job to talks about Missy, Madame or Sir. And house servant never says what happens in house out of house, Balini *baba* says to me.

But maybe it true. When I wakes up next day after wedding, I takes bed tea to Missy and new Sir. New Sir sleeps on one end of pretty bed, de middle all nice and tidy. Missy sheets thrown back and she gone. I is scared Missy nots in bed so I goes to bathroom.

And dat is where I find Missy. She is crying. Not making noise but tears come from her eyes. I looks at what she is doing. She has saree in hand and she trying to prick her finger wit pin to puts blood on saree. But she be scared.

I carefully takes saree from her. I pricks my finger. I have good blood. Lots of blood. And we puts blood on her saree. Everywhere. We needs more blood so I pricks my finger again. And I puts more blood on de saree.

Den she turns to me and says, 'Pilar, this must be our secret.

And if I find out this has got out, I will tell everyone you stole from me. Do you know what they do to thieves?'

I shakes my head.

'They put thieves in jail. They will take your Laksman from you and they will put you in a pit.'

And it be de saree wit my blood is de saree dat Missy take to see her mother, Dhobi woman and her new sister-in-law. The Dhobi woman wash my blood not Missy blood. But I says nuttin to Murukananthan family. I no want to leave big house. I no wants my Laksman to *sani* in front of house. I wants him to *sani* in toilet like good man. Like smart man.

It be two months now dat I work in big house. Now I knows my job good. Balini *baba* says dat. '*Aii!* Dat Pilar. She good girl. She works hard. See, all Missy tings clean and she does housework too.'

Even Madame say dat. 'I don't know what I'd do without Pilar,' she says. I gives her head massage every day. 'Now my daughter is married, I feel I have no purpose in life. I can't wait for my grandchildren to start coming!' And she start playing wit my Laksman.

Everybody play wit my Laksman. He crawl good now. Madame, she plays wit him day and night. Like he be toy. Even Sir play wit him. He bring him little car and dey sit in big hall and dey plays. All afternoon after Sir comes back from town. He comes home from work tired, so he plays wit my Laksman. 'I used to play like this when Shanthi was a little girl. Do you remember that, Selvi?' he says to Madame.

Madame plays wit Laksman. Sir plays wit Laksman. Balini *baba* she play wit Laksman. Mama Leela she play wit Laksman. Even Gopal and Thomas, dey also plays wit my Laksman. Sometime at night, Laksman crawl and sleep wit Balini *baba*. He likes to play wit her nose-ring and bangles. He not scared of her even if she look like she be cut-up saree blouse. So sometimes now he only come to me when he want titty!

De only peoples not play wit Laksman be Missy and new Sir. Dey be in deir room all day. Not dat it be room. Now dat Missy marry, Sir give her own part of big house. It has three bedrooms, a room for dem to sit and three bathroom. I goes in dere every day to clean. Only dere be nuttin to clean.

De new Sir. He no do much. He sits dere all day. De reason he not come to *sangeet* because he cannot even stand for long. He be burnt bad. One eye he cannot see. Dere be all skin over dat eye. De other eye, he can see. He arms and legs like bark of tree. All burnt and ugly. And some places it still not healed. De doctor come to house one time a day and give Sir medicine.

'Mrs Shanthi, you will have to rub this salve onto his arms and legs every day. It is essential that he rests,' he says.

I no understand what doctor says but I sees. Sir is stiff. Like old dead cow.

Sir no speak to Missy. But she speaks to him all de time. She bring him dis. She bring him dat.

'Darling, look! I've got Thomas to go down to the market and get you fresh rambutans. I remember you saying once that you loved them,' Missy say. 'I got Henry to drive down to Puducherry to get some fresh king coconut for you. I hear it is great for healing burns.'

And she send Thomas all de way to Madras every two weeks. 'Sweetheart, I know you like tea from Sri Lanka. From home. I have had it sent for you especially.'

But he looks at Missy like she be cow or dog. Or like he no see her. Like she be nuttin.

I gets angry. My Missy be very pretty. Her skin be like milk and she be plump like fat chick Guru Rameshwaran keep for eggs for his son. Missy titties like ripe watermelons after monsoon. Murukananthan likes Missy titties. I hears Murukananthan and his brothers before Missy gets married. Dey says Missy be most beautiful woman in Tamil Nadu.

And Missy talks to him, de new Sir. Reads to him. 'I saw you got a letter from your sister today. If your eyes are giving you trouble, I can read it for you.' And if no letters, she reads books for him. Missy reads, and after little while, new Sir, he stands up and walks away. Say nuttin.

No. New Sir, he sits dere. And does nuttin'. Says nuttin'. Another month pass. I still takes down to Dhobi woman Missy red cloth to wash. Madame sees me carry covered bucket. Madame be big worried. She asks me, 'What is in there?' Ands I shows her.

One day Missy go to see friend. She no go out much now she married, she spend all day wit new Sir. In room. But Madame say Missy must go.

'Shanthi, you've known Parvathi since you were in school together, darling. You must go and see her new baby.'

Den Madame calls us. Mama Leela, Miss Sonali, Balini *baba* and me. To her room. She ask me to bring tea and big plate gulab jamun. Mama Leela, Balini *baba* and me, we sits on floor. Balini *baba* still got pain from being cut so Madame gives her a little cushion. Miss Sonali she sits on little chair. Madame, she sits on bed.

'Oh Mama Leela,' Madame cries. 'It's been two months and my daughter has not conceived!'

'Madame, Missy becomes big girl it be ten years. Her bloods nice and red. Dere be nuttin wrong wit my girl,' Mama Leela say grumpily. 'It be dat man.'

'My sister, she be married for four year,' Balini *baba* she says. 'No baby. Her husband in army. She gots many mother-in-law problems. She runs away. She go live wit my brother in Ooty. In de hills. Her husband come back from army. He be very angry and goes to Ooty. Dere dey do man-woman ting. And she gets baby.' Balini *baba* drink her tea carefully.

'Maybe I should suggest to Shanthi that she goes on a little holiday to Ooty with her new husband,' Madame says.

Den Miss Sonali, she speaks. Miss Sonali, she be intelligent woman. She studies until her father dies. She writes and she reads. She writes all de letters and messages for Madame. I wants my Laksman to reads and writes like Miss Sonali.

'Madame,' Miss Sonali she says. 'We live in the City of Temples. Kanchipuram is where the Kamakshi Amman dwells. Why don't we do a big pooja? I know of a great many hardships that have been relieved by her gracious intervention.'

I no understand much of what Miss Sonali says. She use big words.

'You are quite right, Sonali. We should ask the *pusari* to help us with a pooja. Lal and I aren't very religious but I will try anything.'

So dat how Madame, Mama Leela, Miss Sonali, Balini *baba* and I goes to temple. For seven days. Before crow cry in sky. Madame, Balini *baba* and Miss Sonali goes in car wit Henry, Mama Leela and Laksman and I, we walks. Mama Leela she angry Balini *baba* go in car and not her.

'I be older dan her! I be house servant and she be kitchen servant,' Mama Leela she complain.

I no say nuttin. I no say Madame take Balini *baba* in car because people scared to look at her on street now. Mama Leela she very angry – she even angry wit me.

'Pilar, leave Laksman at home. He will be asleep when we get back,' she snaps.

I tries dat morning. I tries putting him away. But he sleep wit tumb in mouth and he play wit end of my saree. I takes my saree away, he wakes. He crawl into me like little dog. So I takes him. I no mind. I can walks now and give him titty. But Laksman, he wake when we gets to temple. Every day. He sit and watch *pooja* like he watch de television in Big Sir house he never put on. Says it takes too much electricity. Dey only watch TV when peoples comes to visit.

I sits dere for seven days and I listens. In de cold light. When de air is clean and dere be no cars or buses. Maybe dat how I starts to love Kamakshi Amman. I listen to de pooja wit Laksman on my lap. My Laksman. He sits and listen too.

And when we comes home, he start to play click-clack wit sticks.

'He is a Saliya, all right,' Sir laugh. 'If he studies with his grandfather, he'll be the best saree weaver in all of Kanchipuram. I'll be glad to sell his sarees for him!'

I no says anytin. I no want my boy click-clack Saliya. I no wants him work day and night to earn enough to eat. He go school and get proper job.

And now I haves dreams. In my dreams, Kamakshi Amman she come and she smile. She tells me my Laksman become big man one day. A rich man. And she smile at me. She takes me on beautiful train ride.

After seven days pooja, we comes home. I goes to see Missy and new Sir wit bed tea. Dey still sleeping. I goes to bathroom and see bucket in corner for Missy red cloth. I covers it quick and runs to de Dhobi woman. I no want to show Madame. She be so sad. She want grandchildren so bad. But how Missy give parents grandchildren when she and new Sir no do man-woman ting? Every morning I goes into deir room wit bed tea. Dey sleeping. She on side of window. He on side of door. Big bed. Middle very tidy. Nuttin happen dere.

t been six weeks since pooja ands I tinks it make new Sir worse. He sit dere everyday now in de dark. He not even go out and sit on verandah. Missy says it because de sun hurt his skin. I no know how Missy know dis. Because new Sir, he never speaks. I never hear new Sir speak.

So Missy she works harder. She makes special special food. Everyday new ting. 'Make sure you put more turmeric in the lentil curry. And his sister wrote to me that he loves pureed avocados with milk.' But new Sir, he no notice. He eats his lunch like cow eat grass and sits dere. Looking out. Den he walks to bed and sits dere.

One morning Missy she comes to kitchen and says, 'Balini *baba*, my husband's sister is coming to visit. Could you set an extra place for her at dinner and set up the best guest room?' Den she turns to me. 'Pilar, could you take special care with the cleaning? I want everything spick and span. And please don't mention to my husband that his sister is coming to visit – I want it to be a surprise.'

So I cleans. While new Sir sits on chair after breakfast wit glass of big water. I makes de bed. I sweeps de floor and I cleans de toilet. I wipes de furniture wit wax Balini *baba* make wit oil from sandalwood tree and ginger lily. It smell so good. Even my Laksman he likes de smell and he grabs de cloth to play. My Laksman he already start to walk now. Even he run. He run fast.

'Go, Laksman,' I says. 'Go play outside on verandah. I haves to clean dis.'

My Laksman he no wants to go out and play. He grabs my cleaning cloth. I pulls it from him. I smack his bottom wit my hand. Only small smack. But my Laksman, he gets angry. He cry. He runs out. Just den, new Sir, he stand to go to bed. My Laksman he run into new Sir. Little boy run into big new Sir.

One minute new Sir be standing dere and de next he be on de ground screaming.

I grabs my Laksman and goes to help de new Sir, but Missy she come in.

'Pilar! What has your son done to my husband?' she cries.

'Nuttin,' I says very scared holding tight my Laksman. 'It be only an accident. He only playing.'

'My husband could have hurt himself badly,' Missy she says helping new Sir up.

I worried. 'He only playing,' I says again.

'How dare you speak back to me!' Missy she shouts and she raise her hand. I turns around quick so my Laksman he not get hit.

I is so surprised when I feel no pain. I know pain of hit. My father, he get angry, he hit.

I evens more surprised when I hears new Sir speak.

'Shanthi, no. Don't hit her. It was hardly her fault,' he says. He standing up straight now and hold Missy hitting hand.

It de first time I ever hear new Sir speak. He speak but he speak funny. His Telugu little strange.

'But that child could have harmed you, my darling,' Missy she say.

'Hardly, Shanthi, he just bumped against a part of my leg that hasn't quite healed,' he explained. 'And don't ever hit any of the servants. I will not tolerate violence of any kind.' New Sir drops her hand like hot chapatti.

'*Ana!*' I hears a voice. And dat is when I notices dere be other lady wit Missy when she come in. I see a tall grand lady. She very dark wit lots of gold jewellery.

Missy she looks at new Sir and den at her sister-in-law and starts to cry. She tinks new Sir he scolds her. She cry and runs away.

I stands dere when new Sir sister come to him. Help him to bed.

'I didn't know you were coming, Gauri,' new Sir says to sister.

'We were planning it as a bit of a surprise for you, Shanthi and I. And now you've ruined it for her.'

'Well, it was hardly my fault. You know I hate violence.'

'All the same, Raju *ana*, you need to be patient. And try being kind. She deserves that at least after all she and her father have done for us.'

Now I know new Sir name. Raju.

'Yes,' Raju Sir says. His voice bitter.

'Have you told her about Nila yet?' his sister asks gently.

'Yes,' he says, quiet now. I see de tears.

Who dis Nila?

'But *ana*, she is dead. You know she is dead. You have to move on,' his sister say now kneeling in front of him.

Den she stop. Raju Sir sister sees that he tired. Face drawn in pain. 'Oh, *ana*,' his sister says. 'What did those Sinhalese people do to you? You are still in pain even after two years.' She look so sad.

Raju Sir sound impatient. 'It was Sinhalese people who saved me, Gauri. If it had not been for the monks from the Paramananda Vihara, I would have died. You know that. They came and doused the flames on my body with their cotton robes. Several of them were burnt and badly beaten, but they managed to get me to hospital. They saved me, Gauri. Do not hate all Sinhalese. Stupidity and cruelty is characteristic of all humanity and does not belong to any one race alone.'

I is glad Raju Sir sister gone. Balini *baba* glad Raju Sir sister gone. Even Missy she be very happy dat her sister-in-law gone. Home. Far away.

'Oh, Pilar,' Missy she says after Thomas drives Missy Gauri to airport in Madras. 'Can you please bring my mother's oil and give me a head massage? I have a headache.'

And I understand why Missy head hurt. My head hurt. All de time Miss Gauri stay here in Kanchipuram she fight. She fight wit Big Sir. She fight wit Missy. She fight wit Raju Sir.

'Mr Govindarajan, you must understand that you are obliged to provide us with a certain amount of work. It was a condition of my brother's marriage to your daughter,' Missy Gauri says to Big Sir.

'But the labour costs are too great,' Big Sir he says.

'But the Sri Lankan rupee is worth less than the Indian rupee!'

'All the same, you spend far too much money running your mill. I had my man look over your accounts. You could be making double the profits if you didn't spend so much on your staff. The cost of the training program alone is prohibitive.'

'That is none of your concern!' Miss Gauri say angrily.

'No, Miss Nair, it is very much my concern. We provided a substantial cash injection into your business. We are your partners now.'

'It is a silent partnership! It is all in the marriage contract – the day-to-day running of the mill is my affair.'

'I am not going to waste my money and send commissions to be woven when I can do it here for less than half the cost!'

Missy Gauri she fight wit Missy Shanthi too.

'Really, *thangachichi*, you should let my brother go to the doctor by himself. You baby him too much. He was far more independent in Sri Lanka.'

'But the doctors here say that he should rest.'

'Well, we had him seen by doctors from Australia and they said he should be exercising. They said we should not pander to him,' Missy Gauri say. 'And by babying him, you are making him worse, not better. Fine kind of wife you are, Shanthi, if you don't want your husband to get better.'

Missy she wants to argue. I know. I sees it in her mouth. Tight like a cow's bottom. But Gopal and I, we serves food. We says nuttin.

But de big fight! Oh, de big fight be between Raju Sir and Missy Gauri.

Missy Gauri she no let me clean room anymore.

'He is quite capable of making his own bed, Pilar. Make him do it!'

And she make him walk. To de dining room. Three times a day.

'What is this?' Missy Gauri she cry. 'He is not an invalid. He can come out and have his meals with us like a normal human being!'

'There is mail here for you, Raju,' Big Sir he says, handing over some letters. Only Missy Gauri she grabs it.

'Oooo, there is a letter for you from Guru Sindhu,' Missy Gauri says. 'I wonder what he says. He told me he was going back up to the hill country before I left.'

'Give me the letter, Gauri,' Raju Sir he snaps. He stop eating idali and sambar.

'You'll just have to get it from me,' she says and runs out into de garden.

Raju Sir he run after her. Like sick dog. He cannot run fast. He asks her to give letter but she won't.

'You are a horrible woman, no wonder no one will marry you!' Raju Sir say angrily.

Missy Gauri she no care. She laugh. She run. Dance around sick brother. Every morning for a week Missy Gauri do dis. She not run far, though. Just a little bit to makes Sir walk bit more.

But my Laksman, he laugh. He loves to watch Raju Sir and Missy Gauri. He laugh and claps hands. Balini *baba* takes him out to watch whiles I washes de clothes.

Afternoon before Missy Gauri leave, big truck come. I is careful dis time. I ties my Laksman in my *pallu* nice and tight. He no go near no truck. Miss Gauri she asks Gopal and me to clears de hut dey made for de *sangeet*. Gopal little angry. He, Henry and Thomas, dey go dere in de afternoon some times and sleeps.

But we does what she says. Den she gets Henry, Thomas and Gopal to takes stuff from truck to hut. Boxes and boxes and boxes. And she locks de door. Den she turns to us and says, 'None of you should go in there. Get nothing from in there for Raju Sir and don't help him move anything in there.'

So morning Missy Gauri go back home she and Raju Sir have fight. Biggest fight.

'What? You've done what?' Raju Sir yells.

'We needed more space, so I cleared out your bungalow. I have brought everything and it's all in the hut in the garden.'

'Why not bring it into the main house back at the mill? You did not need to have it sent over here!'

'*Ana*, this is your home now. Appa asked for all your paintings to be returned from London,' she said. Her voice soft.

'Are you insane? The paintings are priceless. You've brought them over here and left them in that damp hut in the garden? Why are you doing this to me?' Raju Sir says angry.

'To save them, you have to go out there yourself,' she say. 'I have left instructions that no one is to help you. You must go and save all the paintings yourself. And the key to the hut is on the lintel above the door.'

Brother and sister no speak anymore.

Murukananthan he come home. He surprise me. I is dere in de big house wit my Laksman, Balini *baba* and Gopal. We stands in de back of house watching. We watch Raju Sir. Missy there too.

'Darling,' Missy says to Raju Sir every day. 'You don't have to do this. I can get Henry and Thomas to bring your things in from the hut.'

Sir he not answer back. He just walk. He no even see Missy. Like she no speak. He walk one day, one step. More Sir no speak, more Missy she try. She bring sticks to help Raju Sir walk and he throw dem away. She bring chair wit wheels but he snap at her like mad dog.

I so busy watching Raju Sir I no see Murukananthan come through gate. He come and grabs me. By de arm. I is so scared I scream. I no know who he is. I push my Laksman away so he be safe wit Balini *baba*. It take me minute to realise who he be.

'Eh!' I says to Murukananthan. 'When you come back?'

Murukananthan look at me strange, like I be someone else.

'Why you no come home?' Murukananthan he ask me. 'Tuesday you day off, why you not come home?' Den he drags me home. Me and Laksman. My Laksman so scared, he scream too. He scared because he no know his father. I no tell him dat I spends my Tuesday in Kamakshi Amman temple. Dat I sits dere ands I pray.

'Eh! Pilar, you comes home now?' Marmee say. 'She no come home since after Missy wedding.'

251

'Pilar, she be too good for us,' idiot sister-in-law laugh. She wit child now. Not long, though. Small stomach.

Marcel and brother-in-law work now. Marcel he walk wit small limp. Brother-in-law arm not straight. He cannot bend arm to drink tea. But dey work now. Click-clack. Click-clack. Dey makes saree all day. All night.

'So, is Missy wit child yet?' idiot sister-in-law asks.

I says nuttin.

'If she is, she will surely have dat special scan. Is she? Has been to the hospital?'

'She goes to hospital wit Raju Sir every second day,' I says. It be truth. I no lie. I believes in God.

'She must be wit child now. She must have had de scan. Everybody has scan now,' sister-in-law say.

'What dis scan ting?' Murukananthan asks. Murukananthan and his brother dey eat *vadai*. No plate. Nuttin. From de banana leaf on floor.

'I tolds you de other day,' sister-in-law says. 'I goes to hospital to have baby dis time,' she says proudly to me. 'No idiot midwife come. Dey say I can haves scan next week. Dey can say if baby be boy or girl.'

'If girl, you kills baby,' Koddi she says. 'Dat what dey do now. Dat what dey do wit Agilan wife. Now Agilan have three son, no daughters.'

'Sure Missy will kill if it be baby girl,' idiot sister-in-law says.

'Dis scan ting, you needs paper money for dat?' I asks.

'Yes, twenty-five rupee. And twenty-five rupee to kill baby if it be girl,' Koddi say.

I know how dey gets dat money. From me. I works in big house so dey can kills baby girl.

Dat night Murukananthan he take me. Before even Koddi and Marcel fall asleep. I hear Koddi fart and Marcel complain dat his leg hurt. Laksman he still drink from titty. But Murukananthan he push my saree. He inside. Den out. In. Out. In. Out.

I goes to work next morning. De first ting I do when I gets to home is I wash. I wash everytin. I wash myself. I wash my Laksman. I use soap. We be clean.

But my Murukananthan, he come. He come every night. After I takes Sir and Madame bed tea. He stand at kitchen door. I gives my Laksman to Balini *baba* and I follows him. He no take me far. Maybe five or six step from kitchen. Den he push me to ground. Push my saree up. He do his business. He no speak. He no say anytin. Den he leaves.

Gopal, Henry and Thomas dey laugh. I hears dem. Dey stand by kitchen door and dey laugh.

'Get away wit you,' Balini *baba* she say, holding my Laksman. But Balini *baba* she cannot chase three mens. Dey laugh. Dey laugh at Balini *baba* too.

After I runs to bathroom, I wash. I puts my fingers inside me and I wash. And I cries. I no understand why I cries. Dis is how dey do man-woman ting in village. Behind trees. Near de cow shed. In de fields. I know Murukananthan gone back to work on railway when he stop coming. After seven days.

Missy she gets her period again. Madame she be very sad. She cries. 'Why, why can't my daughter conceive a child?'

If I have daughter I no want her to man-woman ting. Man-woman ting ugly. I no understand how ugly man-woman ting can make beautiful baby. Maybe dat be god's joke. Make you do ugly ting to get beautiful ting.

n de big house, no one go out to buy anytin. Everytin come to house. Every day vegetable seller come to house wit vegetables. De cowherd come wit two young cow and takes milk fresh and give it to Balini *baba* for de bed teas. Three times a week de dry-goods man come. We don't know he come, but he check we got enough rice, *atta* flour for chapatti and oil. De big pots in de kitchen always full. Merchant come, merchant go. No one care.

Laksman and I be living in big house four month now so I very surprised when Gopal come running into kitchen. I just come back from giving bed teas. He so happy I see de only teeth left in mouth shaking. Like *thairu* not properly set in pot.

'Balini *baba*! Mama Leela! Pilar! He come! He come!'

'Idiot! Who come?' Balini *baba* she ask, taking tea tray and giving me dosai to eat.

'Mustafa Mohamadeen! Mustafa Mohamadeen!' Gopal he say.

'Oh my,' Balini *baba* say. And she run to her room to checks her moneybag. 'I think I have ten rupee left. Maybe I buy sometin.' Balini *baba* very happy. She no go to shops much now dat she got cut up.

'I have been wanting to buy a new cross for my wife,' Henry say. Henry he pray to dead man on cross.

'Who Mustafa Mohamadeen?' I asks Balini *baba*.

'You no know Mustafa Mohamadeen,' Henry he laugh. 'Mustafa Mohamadeen only be greatest trader south of Andhra

Pradesh. He travel de seas and all over India to bring best tings. Good tings!'

Just as sun rises, Mustafa Mohamadeen come. He come wit fifteen bullock carts. It take Henry and Thomas together to open both sides of big gate. Normally only one side of big gate open so Sir can come and go from work.

By de time Madame, Missy and Raju Sir finish breakfast, Mustafa Mohamadeen set up big tent. Like wedding tent. All colourful. Red. Blue. Green. Yellow. Everybody from de houses around come. Not many peoples, though. Only few peoples live in big houses. Across river, many peoples live in small houses.

Madame and Missy dey go first. Raju Sir, he walk now. Only he walk to de hut in de garden every day and sits dere. He close door and sit dere. He walk past big tent like it not be dere.

'Mrs Govindarajan and young Mrs Nair, what a pleasure it is indeed to be serving you today,' Mustafa Mohamadeen he says wit big bow. 'But I am heartbroken, muchly heartbroken, to know that young Miss Shanthi here got married. To a man from Sri Lanka. There is nothing to hope for in Tamil Nadu anymore. Nothing!'

Missy she giggles.

'How can I interest a young bride who has everything?' he says. 'How about perfume? I have perfume from Africa, Persia and even from our own Himalayas. They say that African peony rose combined with Himalayan musk makes a man fall more in love with his wife than all the poetry in India!'

So Missy she open bottle after bottle and she smells what in dere. If she like de smell, den she rubs it on inside wrist. She buy maybe ten bottles. All glass. Different colours.

'And what about you, Madame? How can I please such a grand lady? I have just come from Rajasthan and I happened to procure some divine sculptures – perhaps you would like to see them?' So Madame she buy new statue of god Ganesh and Kamakshi Devi. I no understand why, she never go to shrine room anyway.

After Madame and Missy and de other madams dey leave, it be our turn. De servants. Gopal he rush in. He almost push Balini *baba* over. He buy sweets, gulab jamun and sugar almonds.

'Eh, Gopal,' Balini *baba* says. 'You want to lose more teeth, you idiot?'

But Gopal he no listen. He be real idiot.

Henry and Thomas dey buy new shirt, little pendant wit dead man on cross and new pants.

Even Mr Krishnapillay and Miss Sonali dey buy tings. Miss Sonali buy bangles and Mr Krishnapillay he look at box in corner.

'Here,' Mustafa Mohamadeen says, coming forward. I no see him properly before. He got one eye blue. Other one eye black. Like cat. Only if he be cat he be killed for being evil. 'It is a cassette recorder. It is the latest thing from the United States. They say this latest technology will last one thousand years. See, you put these tapes in and play.'

And de tent filled wit music. Hindi music from film. Gopal, Balini *baba* and Henry dey starts to dance.

But my Laksman and I just looks. We looks at dis. We looks at dat. Dere be lots to look at.

'How about a toy for the young boy?' Mustafa Mohamadeen asks.

I shakes my head. I is scared to look at one blue eye one black eye.

'Why? Why not, young *amman*? Buy the fine young boy a toy. Here, how about this wind-up monkey!'

I sees my Laksman look at toy. He likes it. Monkey gots cymbals and when you winds it up, it dance and plays. My Laksman smile and laugh. When he smile, he got dimple in cheek and his eye shine like lights.

'No,' I says and I turns to leave. I works hard but Big Sir give paper money to Koddi.

'You got food. You got clothes. What you need paper money for?' Koddi she says.

Laksman he scream. He stretch his fat hands out and he wants de monkey. He scream and he scream. I cannot carry him. He twist dis way and he twist dat way. He be big boy. He be strong boy. I somehow takes him outside, but he scream ands screams. I is sure you can hear scream down in Kanchipuram.

I takes him to kitchen to make quiet. But no. He want to go back to tent. He scream more and runs. I chase after him. I grabs him. Only my Laksman he scream more. Like I killing him. Gopal, Balini *baba* and everybodys comes to de kitchen. Dey stands dere and stare. Stare at my Laksman scream and fight his *amman* like crazy dog. He lie on ground and he kick me, bite me.

'What's going on?' a loud voice calls. We looks up to see. It be Raju Sir.

'It be Laksman,' Gopal say. 'He wants toy monkey but Pilar no got money for it.'

I looks away. I so sad.

He looks at Laksman for a moment. Den he looks at me. 'Come along,' Raju Sir say. He picks up my Laksman. Laksman he stop crying. He hug Raju Sir like he be God. Dere be pain on Raju Sir face but he walks wit Laksman to Mustafa Mohamadeen tent.

'This young man would like that wind-up monkey,' Raju Sir say to Mustafa Mohamadeen.

While Mustafa Mohamadeen wrap up monkey, Raju Sir play wit my Laksman. He play akar bakar bombay bo. My Laksman laugh and laugh. He laugh so much and giggle dat he knock over sometin.

'What is this?' Raju Sir ask from Mustafa Mohamadeen, picking up bundles of whitest of white thread.

'A fine Saliya, sir, like you would recognise it as silk,' Mustafa Mohamadeen he says.

'But there is something different about it. It is shinier than normal silk. Why is that?'

'It is silk that has been thrown without killing the silk moth.'

'How can that be possible?'

'I am astounded as you are but I got it from a young man in Sri Lanka.'

'But there isn't a sericulture industry there.'

'Indeed sir but this young man managed to throw some of the finest silk I have ever seen. Look at the quality of this. The silk is so supple and fine I can't bear to touch it.'

Raju Sir puts my Laksman down and he takes de silk outside de tent. Looks at it in de sun. Touches it. Feels it. Holds it to his face. And when he holds it to his face, de sun shine on it. I really see Raju Sir for de first time. Not in de shadows. I sees half his face not burnt. Dat side he be very handsome.

'How much for the silk?' Raju Sir he ask.

Mustafa Mohamadeen not stupid man. He see Raju Sir really like silk. 'Ten thousand rupees,' he say.

Everybody gasp. Balini *baba* she gasp. Gopal he gasp. Thomas and Henry gasp. Even Mr Krishnapillay he gasp. Dat enough money to buy house. To buy cow business. To buy God! I never even heard dat much money in my life!

'Krishnapillay, could you please bring my chequebook from my study?' Raju Sir he calls out.

'Sir usually settles with Mustafa Mohamadeen by the end of the month . . .'

'My father-in-law does not need to pay my way,' Raju Sir snaps. And for de first time we tinks Raju Sir not statue. He be real man.

Dat night de servants gots party. After de family sleep. Not real fancy party like for Sir or Madame. But our own party. Balini *baba* she buy two bottle drink from Mustafa Mohamadeen and she make Gopal share his big box of sweets. 'You eat more sweeties, more worms grown in belly,' she say.

Henry he close de door between house and kitchen and we

push big cooking table to corner. We sits on de little stools and we talks. Even Mr Krishnapillay come down. We be happy Mr Krishnapillay he come because he bring cassette recorder. He puts on music.

Laksman he sleep. He be tired. He spend afternoon playing wit monkey by de hut in garden. Raju Sir he leave door open so he can looks at Laksman while he play. 'You get on with your work, Pilar,' he says. 'I'll keep an eye on him.'

I sits dere and I listens to others talk. 'I worked for family fifty years now,' Mama Leela she say. 'I come when Big Sir be little baby. Even den he eat too much. One day he eat five aloo prata. He be sick,' she laugh.

'When you come?' I ask Balini *baba*.

Balini *baba* she look sad. 'In 1946, Big Sir father he find me on road from Karachi. He bring me here. I work for family from age five. Mama Leela look after me like mother.'

'You no get married? You no have children?'

'I is married. I married old gardener. But he dies. He no gives me children.'

I so sad. Poor Balini *baba* has no babies.

Den Mr Krishnapillay asks me question. 'Where you come from, Pilar?'

I shrugs. I no know.

'Pilar be stupid girl from village,' Gopal he laugh. But Balini *baba* she hit him across de ears.

'Pilar go from being garden-kitchen servant to house servant to Missy servant in one week. Pilar she be smart. She know not to talk too much. Not like you, Gopal! Gopal be empty pot make big noise!' she says.

'Pilar, have you ever gone to school?' Mr Krishnapillay he ask.

'No,' I says. 'I no understand letters.'

'But you are a smart girl,' Balini *baba* she says. 'More dan just village girl.'

I looks away and mumble, 'I not smart.'

'Eh! Pilar not smart? You looks after house during *sangeet*. You looks after Missy. And Missy not easy to look after.'

Mama Leela nod lots.

'Missy she be very fussy. She like bath cleaned one way. She like tea another. Many house servants no like work for Missy because she so fussy and angry. If she no like you, you tink she lets you give her head massage? No, Pilar, you smart woman. I sees dat idiot you marry, Murukananthan, he be too stupid to be Saliya. Dat why he work on railways. How Laksman smart boy if you not smart wit Murukananthan stupid?'

Gopal who live near Murukananthan all his life tell stories. Stupid Murukananthan stories. Like time he drink water from drain because his brother told him to. 'Dey say he never marry. But he marries you, Pilar. And he gets good dowry.'

'But a good dowry is all a poor man can dream of,' Mr Krishnapillay he says. He rarely speak so we alls surprised.

'How is de marriage brokering going?' Mama Leela she asks.

'Not so well. I have only 5000 rupee in savings. Even a poor man won't give his daughter to someone with so little.'

'I want big dowry too,' Gopal he say. 'I wants to own my own sweetshop some day.'

'Idiot, no father give dowry for toothless man to lose more teeth,' Balini *baba* says and slap Gopal across ears again.

Gopal he gets angry. He stands up. Retie sarong.

'You see,' he says. 'Just you see, I be big sweetshop owner one day.' Den he goes away to sleep.

Henry and de others laugh.

'What you wants to do wit dowry?' I asks Mr Krishnapillay. I helps Balini *baba* cleans de kitchen.

'I went to university, you know,' he says sadly. 'But I cannot find a job. They don't hire Saliyas into Brahmin businesses. So I want to start a small tuition school. Help children with their education. But I need money for that. What do you want to do?' he ask me.

I no know what to say. I wait for moment. Den he ask me again.

I looks at my Laksman. He sleep on floor. Balini *baba* she makes him a little mattress wit old sarees.

'Mother,' I says. 'I wants to be de best mother.'

'If I have my mother's love, I need nothing else,' Mr Krishnapillay he say in Hindi. But I understand. I speak Telugu but I knows dat in Hindi. Dat be a great truth.

My grandfather be Saliya. My father be Saliya. My mother be Saliya. My *marmee* be Saliya. My *marcel* be Saliya. I know Saliya job. I cans weave saree too. No big ting. It not big job. Just get thread, put in loom and weave. I does it when I little girl.

But dere be differences in Saliya. When I comes to Kanchi-puram I understands. My grandfather different to Marcel. My grandfather only make one type of saree. Saree for village woman. Woman who work field. Poor woman. Rough. No fine cotton. He make maybe two or three designs. How he make saree he keep in head. No picture. No nuttin.

Marcel he take one design from Big Sir every three month and weave it. He puts it on weaving hut wall. Only one design. And he makes it one hundred times. Same design. He no tink about it. He do it. Same wit brother-in-law. Dey same same saree over and over. No tink.

Raju Sir he be different. He no start straightaway. He tink long time. He sits in chair and tink. I know he tink cause he feel de silk in one hand. He close his eyes but his finger dey feel de silk.

Den he starts opening boxes. He look for sometin real hard. Here, dere, everywhere. When he finds it, he sits down. It be a suitcase. And he bring out what he find. Big boards. It got pictures of saree on it. Every little ting. He puts de board up on wall. He looks at it. He look at silk. Den he sits and he tinks.

How I know all dis? Because my Laksman he love Raju Sir now. Every time I put down to do work, he run to hut in garden. Now I spend half my time running to hut to grabs my boy. And it be dangerous. Raju Sir tings everywhere. I no want my boy break anytin.

'Oh, don't worry about him, Pilar,' Raju Sir he says and he puts drawings high on wall. And when he take a rest from opening boxes, he play wit Laksman. Not like Madame or Big Sir play wit Laksman. He teach him tings.

'See, *putta*, it is always a good idea to pick up the edge of your nappy and hold it if you are running around,' he tells my Laksman wit a laugh when he trip over.

I comes back from cleaning de windows in Madame and Sir room. It be big job. I cleans while Gopal he holds my legs. Henry he used to do it but den he become too fat. Only Pilar tin enough now. So I does it. Only I haves to hit Gopal wit broom several time. He likes to feel my legs. So ever time he get past my ankle, I hits him on head. Many times. When I finish I find Raju Sir has my Laksman on knees and he reads him picture book.

'Laksman, this was my *hodiya*. My first book of letters,' he says. 'I know these aren't Telugu letters,' he explains when he sees me stand dere like I just steps in cow dung. 'But I have got Henry to go and get the equivalent in Telugu. And a few more books and toys.'

So while I work, Laksman now he sits and play wit Raju Sir. He come to me when he need titty. He still my boy.

But I is still very careful. When Raju Sir makes Henry go into town and buy new loom, I is dere when he sets it up. I no let my baby boy near heavy loom. I know many accidents happen near loom. Many peoples head break when heavy wood falls on dem.

Only Madame she gets angry. 'Pilar! Pilar! Where are you? It is hot and I need a head massage!'

Again, Madame she calls me.

'Pilar! Pilar! Where are you, girl? I don't pay you to stand and watch in the garden!'

I know Missy be dere. I can smells her. Everybody smells her now. Every day different different smell. She come out and she watch Raju Sir. She stand below mango tree and she watch. She watch him like tiger wanting juicy goat. But Raju Sir he no see her. He treat her like smelly dead cow.

'Pilar! Pilar! Where are you, girl?' Madame she calls. Madame she gots really high voice. Like call of monkey. It give you headache. Dat why I tink she get so many headache. Her own voice.

I puts down my boy but he runs straight into hut. I runs in after because dere be nails and saw and dangerous tings in hut. Setting up loom not easy. It take Raju Sir, Gopal, Henry and carpenter from Kanchipuram.

'Pilar! Pilar! Come here right now!' Madame calls again. Dis time only louder.

'Pilar, give him to me,' Missy she says finally. I tink she getting headache too.

I gives my Laksman to Missy. My boy he like Missy saree. It be bright and colourful, not like Pilar saree. Pilar saree always white. Big Sir say servants must always wear white saree like widow so dat way we knows when we be dirty. Den we knows when we needs to change saree. Big Sir really scared of dirt. So my Laksman he play wit Missy saree and Missy gold earrings and Missy necklace. And when he tired, he fall asleep on Missy neck smelling her perfume.

After dat, all de time when I needs to do work, I leave my Laksman wit Missy. Raju Sir need to hard work and cannot have little boy playing nearby. And Missy she start to like my Laksman too. She play akar bakar bombay bo wit Laksman. My Laksman handsome boy. He be smart boy. Everybody love him.

It take dem three days to set up loom. It be big loom. And new. Oh so pretty. Not like Marcel loom in Kanchipuram or my grandfather loom. It has bright, shiny wood and de loop for string brand-new. Not old wire like wit Marcel.

When dey finish setting up loom, Raju Sir he say it need to be dedicated.

I is so excited. I know loom dedication. It when we ask Mariamman to help us Saliya. I know, my grandfather do it once a year. It be big pooja wit every ting.

So Raju Sir, he asks Gopal to go into town and gets lotus. But dere be no lotus. Gopal he gets jasmine. Bags and bags of jasmine. And we makes oil lamps. Hundred of oil lamps. We puts it around shrine in garden like for Navaratri.

Laksman he love dis. He love de flowers. He love de incense. He love rice cooked in coconut milk like Raju Sir ask Balini *baba* to make. But I no give him rice. It not be twelve month since he born and I no take him to temple to have rice pooja yet.

But Madame she be very busy dat day. She gots friends coming and Sir give big party. 'Pilar, I want you to polish the floors and clean all the bathrooms. You don't need to get involved with Raju's silliness. If he wants to weave a saree he can ask one of a million weavers. And he certainly does not need to do a loom dedication like a silly village Saliya.'

Laksman he no want to come wit me into house to polish floors and clean bathroom. He want to be outside to see pooja. I even make him little dhoti from old saree Balini *baba* give me.

So again I leaves my boy wit Missy. But I feels sad. When I turns back to look, I see him on Missy hip. He grab Missy necklace and put his head on her neck. When Raju Sir light oil lamp to pray to God, Missy go near wit my Laksman. Dey look like family.

Murukananthan he come back. Dis time I finds out before he come. Gopal he tells me. 'Eh! Pilar, your *poorchen* he come back!'

'How you know dis?'

'I sees Murukananthan down in Kanchipuram. He say his wife make good paper money so he no work no more.'

I no wants Murukananthan to come to big house. So Tuesday just before crow cries I leaves de house. I asks Balini *baba* and I takes wit me roti, dosai, idali and sambar. I takes extra. Laksman he come too.

I goes in early. I change out of my big house saree and I puts on my shanty saree. I puts breakfast out on table like at Big Sir and Madame house. I puts it out before everyone even awake. But dey wakes. Wakes fast. And dey push me. To gets to food. Dey eats it like dey no see food for weeks. Maybe months.

'Where you baby?' I ask idiot sister-in-law. Dere be no tummy now.

'It be girl,' she says wit smile. 'Dey takes her out. I no want to be girl mother. Now I can only be boy mother.'

Marmee smile proudly too. 'Your sister-in-law smart girl. She bring luck to family.'

I says nuttin. For weeks after her last baby dies, Marmee scream dat idiot sister-in-law bad luck. She bring *dhosai* to house. Now she kills baby girl, she bring good luck? And what about mother who go mad when baby die? How come mother go mad for baby boy but not baby girl?

After Murukananthan finish eating, I goes near him.

'What?' he ask. 'What you want?'

'Gopal he tells me you no work no more. Is dat true?' I asks him.

'Dat none of your business, woman,' he says and he walk out. He no come back.

I spends de day in Murukananthan parents' house. I cleans here. I cleans dere. Marmee sits dere and she complain.

'I is old. I cannot do hard work anymore,' she says.

But when I tries to do cooking, when I tries to make chapatti, she laugh at me. 'No! No stupid village girl do dis. Go! Go away,' she say and hit me wit broom.

Idiot sister-in-law, she gossip. She go to tap for water and she come back and she gossip. 'Dat Meena Devi, she gots baby girl. Her *marmee* so angry she break pot on Meena Devi head and throws baby into cooking fire,' she say.

'Why she not have scan ting?' my *marmee* she ask.

'Dey cans only take baby out if less dan three month old. I heard dat Rachita baby dey takes out when she be four month and de baby she cry.'

'At least it not full baby. De police now dey very careful. Dey look in river and dey look in rubbish bin. Dat why Meena Devi *marmee* put baby in cooking fire. Cannot catch.'

Murukananthan he come back just before dinner. 'Pilar, you come wit me!' he says.

'Why?' I asks him. It be dinnertime and my Laksman he want titty soon.

'Why? Woman you no ask why. You just come,' he says and he drag me out by hair. I have no time to take Laksman.

He drag me by hair all de way to Kanchipuram town. Until we gets to Muslim paper money lenders.

'Dis be her,' he say. 'Dis be my wife.'

'You work at big house?' dis man ask me.

I nods. I is too scared to speak.

'What you do?'

'I works for Missy. I cleans her rooms and I do little bit kitchen work.'

'So you no lie, Murukananthan. Many people dey lie. Dey say deir wife got good job only dey don't. Dey cannot pay interest on money I lends dem. You pay me 100 rupee a month.'

Murukananthan and I, we walks back.

'Murukananthan,' I asks. 'It true den, you no work in railways? Why you borrows money?'

'You make good paper money,' he say gruffly. Den he walks fast. So fast I run after him.

I gets to house and I goes in. Dere I see Marmee. She give my Laksman dosai and sambar from morning for dinner.

'*Eiii!*' I cries. 'I no give him food yets. I no done rice pooja for gods for my Laksman.'

'He cry he hungry, I gives him food,' Marmee she yells. 'And rice pooja only for stupid village babies. Not Kanchipuram babies.'

Next morning, I rises early. I is very tired. Laksman no sleep good. He wakes up all de time crying. I leaves early. I takes my crying Laksman to big house. I leave him wit Balini *baba* while I wash and takes de bed tea.

I comes back and I find Balini *baba* covered in vomit. My Laksman he vomit.

He vomit all morning.

By time for morning tea, Missy she come looking for my Laksman. See Missy she be smart woman. She understand dat Raju Sir no look at her like dog if she play wit my Laksman.

'What? What is wrong with the baby?' she cries. And my Laksman vomit on her.

She go running inside house. I is so scared she go get Big Sir and he throw us out. But no. She bring Raju Sir.

'We need to get him to hospital!' he says when he see my boy no open eyes and he ask Henry to get car ready.

Raju Sir takes my Laksman to hospital. No poor peoples hospital but rich peoples hospital. Dey puts needle in my boy arm and dey make him stop vomiting. Missy and Raju Sir save my boy. Dey looks after my boy like *appa* and *amman*.

We starts preparing for Sharada Navaratri two month before. We must cleans de whole house, de whole garden and everytin. We wash, we clean and we wash more. At nights I falls onto my mat and I sleeps. My whole body it aches.

Now while I works Missy and Raju Sir looks after Laksman. I no complain. My boy be so sick I no got time to looks after my boy. I no works I no able to pay money for hospital. But Raju Sir and Missy dey say dey no want money. 'Don't be silly, Pilar, we are hardly going to take any money from you.'

So I works more hard. I wants dem to realise I thanks dem for it. I thanks dem for my boy life. Now I understand how idiot sister-in-law go crazy when baby dies.

And my Laksman still very sick, de doctors tells we must feeds my boy rice porridge. It stop de water *sani*. Titty milk no good. De doctor tells me to dry-fry rice and to grinds it. Only my Laksman no like rice porridge. He spit it out. He throws it against wall. He cry. He cry. It take me one hour to gives him one spoon. Whiles I have to do work I no gots time to feed my boy.

So Missy she takes over. She sits dere in de hut while Raju Sir he starts weaving saree. My Laksman he likes to watch Raju Sir weave saree. Up. Down. In. Out. He looks at silk. He play wit little bit of silk. And when he not tinking, Missy she put rice porridge in mouth. He no understand but soon his tummy full.

269

Raju Sir and Missy dey laughs at my Laksman. 'Oh look, Raju,' Missy she say. 'Look at his curls. Aren't they adorable. And he is so smart. He can repeat the alphabet. Here, listen,' she says and dey says de words together.

'And he is so affectionate, too. Look,' Raju Sir he say and my Laksman kiss him on burnt side of face. My Laksman not scared of Raju Sir. I see other babies. Like Missy schoolfriend babies. Dey scared of Raju Sir. Dey looks at him and dey cry. Dey point at him and dey cry. Or runs away. But not my Laksman. My Laksman brave boy.

Sometimes Raju Sir start crying when he weaves saree. Dere be paintings hung up in de hut now. Beautiful paintings of a beautiful woman. He looks at paintings and he cry. He cry and he weave, like he put sadness for losing wife into saree. Only Laksman can make him stop crying. My boy go to Raju Sir, touch his face and stop him crying. Kiss him.

No, Raju Sir not like Murukananthan.

Murukananthan no even come to hospital while Laksman sick. He no care. He busy. He and his brother dey start business. Dey sells saree in Kanchipuram now.

But Murukananthan he come when he wants to do dat ting. First time he come after Laksman in hospital he screams at me. 'Woman, you gots your blood. Why you not tell me? I have *pooja* to do. For de new business. How I go wit your bloods!' he curse me. It be first time I gets my blood since I have Laksman. 'Its de titty milk,' Mama Leela she tells me. 'When you gives titty milk, you no gets blood.'

Murukananthan he come again. When it be slow in his saree shop he come. Which is all de time. De others dey no laugh no more. Like dey see monkey do trick so many times it no trick no more. Maybe Balini *baba* or Mama Leela say sometin to Missy because Missy one day gives me de key. Key to Raju Sir hut.

'Just lock the door after, Pilar,' she say.

Not dat she or Raju Sir or my Laksman ever see

Murukananthan. Murukananthan never even look at his son. Never play wit him. Never see handsome boy. No understand he be smart boy. He no bring Sharada Navaratri presents for Laksman. Even Henry and Thomas who pray to dead man on cross buy presents for children. Boxes of sweets or wind-up toy.

All childrens even in Kanchipuram have toys. I know dis because I go to town to takes Marmee and Marcel gifts from Big Sir and Madame. I keeps Laksman close on my hip now. I no even put him down in filthy house. Not dat Marmee or Marcel care. Dey takes gifts and turn away. Like I no dere. Like I be cow dung.

I goes home to Big House early. I is so sad. I no can buy Laksman any bright toys or balloons he see in town when we goes back. Town lit up like party. Stalls everywhere. People everywhere. *Appas* and *ammans* dey buys deir children tings. Toys for festival. Only my Laksman he cries and he cries. He looks at tings and he wants dem. He reach out wit his fat fists.

'Amman,' he cry. He just want to see. But I know if he see, he want. 'No, Laksman,' I says. 'Mama no gots paper money.' I no got money to buy my boy nuttin. I no gots money buy him medicine. I no got money to buy him clothes. I no gots money.

So my Laksman he tears my hair. He pull at my saree. He bites me. By time we makes it to big house it look like Murukananthan he take bad coconut *arrack* and hit me.

Only my Laksman he be lucky boy. He be lucky like his name.

'Tidy yourself up,' Balini *baba* she say wit excitement. Dey do sometin while Laksman and I go to town.

When I goes into house, I be like Laksman. So surprised. So happy. Everywhere tings. Everywhere toys.

'Oh, it is lovely to have a child in the house again,' Madame she cries and she picks up my boy.

'Look, Laksman, look,' Big Sir he say. Dey buy him a rocking horse. Wit pretty face. 'We had it sent for you all the way from Rajasthan,' he say.

And Missy she buy him clothes. Little kurta and sarong. I tink he look like little Sir when he dressed so fancy.

But de best present. De best present it come from Raju Sir.

'Come here, *puttar*,' Raju Sir he says. And he gives my boy books. I so happy. My boy be educated man. Smart man. Not stupid man like his father.

Next morning I wakes up and I goes to drain and I vomits. I no get bloods again. I be wit baby. I tink it very sad dat Muru-kananthan be father again when he no know how to be father and Raju Sir no be father when he be good father.

'Dat Gopal he up to sometin,' Balini *baba* she say. She help me wash dishes after big Sharada Navaratri celebration. We celebrate nine days. Big Sir, Madame, Missy and Raju Sir dey celebrate. Peoples comes to house. Peoples have tea, drinks, exchange presents and dey makes mess. We cleans.

'Why you says dat?'

'He always asking you question now. He always go up to clean Mr Krishnapillay office,' Balini *baba* says.

'Maybe he wants to learn letters and numbers. He really want to open sweet business. He ask me how Murukananthan gets money for saree business. I tells him Murukananthan gets money from Muslim moneylender in Kanchipuram.'

'So dat why Gopal he go into Kanchipuram all de time now. To borrows money!' Balini *baba* she says.

I shrugs. It not my business. My Laksman my business. I goes to look for him. I leaves him wit Missy before when I goes to clean de bedrooms.

I finds dem in garden hut. Raju Sir he almost finish weaving saree. I sees it now. He bring de loom out into garden so he can sees better when he weave.

De saree he weave, it be beautiful. It not white saree like for widows. It not gold saree like for bride. It be sometin in between.

'She made this look so effortless,' he muttered.

'Nila?' Missy she ask. Missy gots my Laksman on her knee. Dey plays wit little wooden blocks.

Raju Sir he looks up. He sees Laksman playing nearby and he smiles.

'Yes, Nila. She was a wonderful saree maker. Gifted.'

'And this was one of her designs.'

'Yes, she won the design prize with this,' he says.

My Laksman he walk over to Raju Sir now he says something. He points to de board wit de pictures.

'Yes, *putta*, she was a wonderful designer. Look at the line and form of her designs. Magic.'

Den my Laksman go to play wit de saree. Raju Sir he quick. He picks it up before Laksman can put muddy fingers on it.

'Oh no, I won't let you get your hands on this just yet,' he laughs. 'But I agree with you, it's pretty irresistible. Look,' he says. 'Look at how Nila designed it so that you can see the play of colours through the fabric. Wait till you see the *pallu* she designed. It is beyond beautiful. A peacock. And I found the perfect peacock blue for its plumes.'

And it be true. Raju Sir he goes into town wit Henry and he buy dis. He buy dat. All for saree. He work on saree and Missy and Laksman dey plays next to him. Slowly Raju Sir let Missy help him even. Teach her to weave. A few days later he and Missy take car, dey say dey go into Madras.

'Pilar, can we take Laksman with us?' Missy she ask. 'I was hoping I could take him to the zoo in Madras after Raju goes to the gem merchant. He wants to buy real sapphires and rubies to decorate the saree.'

How I say no? How I say she cannot take my boy see tigers and lions? I want my boy see good ting. I jealous buts I let him go. But I is happy. He cry and cling to me until Missy takes him and gets into car. I still his *amman*.

I is even more happy Laksman not home. I very happy Laksman he never see. He never see what happen to Gopal.

Gopal he go home one week ago and he no come back. So Big Sir he get Henry to go into town to looks. And Henry he comes back say Gopal no come no more. Dat he own sweetshop in town. But laters we see Mr Krishnapillay. He come running out of room. He crying. He orders Henry to come. Take him to see Sir in Sir office in city. Dey come back.

'Thomas, I want you to go into town and fetch Gopal,' Big Sir he says. 'Tell him I have money to give him. Congratulate him for starting his business.'

I sits down wit Balini *baba* to make mango pickle. We gots so much mango from mango trees now. We sits behind kitchen wit knife and we cuts de mango and puts it in chilli water wit vinegar. In hot month we leaves it outside tills it ready and we have it wit dosai in cold month.

Dat when Gopal he come. He come to kitchen. 'You two servant girls. I businessman now. Looks, I got new shirt,' he brag. So Balini *baba* and I we looks at shirt. He tells us about how he start business. How he must go back to town soon because dey bring more sweets to sell.

He sound so proud. He sound so happy.

So we alls listen to him, Balini *baba*, me, Mama Leela and even Henry. We no realise dat Big Sir he come. He bring leather belt. Belt he use to put up his pants. He big man. He use big belt. We all scream when Big Sir he raise him arm and brings belt down. He hits Gopal.

'Gopal, you idiot!' Big Sir he shouts. 'Did you think we would not find out? Did you think Krishnapillay would not look at the envelope he kept his money in? How dare you! How dare you thieve from Krishnapillay!'

Den we understands. Dat Gopal he starts his sweetshop wit Mr Krishnapillay money.

Balini *baba* tries to save Gopal but Big Sir, he make Henry and Thomas take her away. They holds her in corner wit me and Mama Leela. We alls screams and cries.

Big Sir he hit Gopal until Gopal covered wit blood. His face. His body. His everytin.Gopal he do nuttin. He be too scared.

Den two policeman come in police car. Dey puts Gopal in back. And dey takes him.

'Let that be a lesson to all of you. Harbandas Lal Govinda-rajan does not tolerate thieves!' Big Sir he says.

Den he go inside and have big milk tea. We finds out later dat Gopal he dies. In jail. All wounds get pus. He gets fever and dies. He poor man. And thief. No one cares.

t take my father, grandfather and *marcel* only two, three weeks to make one saree. But Raju Sir it take nearly two, three month. First he weave saree but he leave de top and bottom borders undone.

I sees what he do next. He make lace. Beautiful lace. It take him hours. Days. Weeks. Slowly. Along bottom. And on top. Like saree float between foam. I also sees tricky ting he does. I goes in to give my Laksman rice porridge and I sees Raju Sir he puts little silver balls into lace. It hold lace down. Beautiful. When lady wears dis saree I tinks she look like she walk on white lake.

Den he decorate saree. He takes needle and thread and he make picture of peacock. So beautiful you tink real peacock on saree. And he puts precious gemstones on saree. In eyes he use little little rubies. Red. On body he use real sapphires.

'Raju, you'll need to start bringing the saree into the house at night,' Missy she says. 'It is precious enough with all the gold thread and gem stones you've used on it.'

Big Sir he come and look at it one day. He look at his son-in-law for long time. 'I never knew,' he says to Raju. 'Your first . . . er . . . wife . . . she was very talented.'

'This is the calibre of work you can expect from the mill in Sri Lanka,' Raju Sir he say. 'We don't produce a great deal at my saree mill but what we produce is beautiful. It is of the highest quality and they are sarees that last a lifetime.'

'And you can guarantee quality? You can guarantee high standards all the time?' Big Sir he asks.

'I wasn't even the best saree maker at the mill. There are people one thousand times better than me.'

Dat night Big Sir he puts big lock on hut gate. Raju Sir he no care. He no afraid of thieves. 'Forcing people to live in poverty is what makes thieves of them. If we had encouraged Gopal to talk of his dreams and helped him reach them, he would be alive today,' he says sadly.

Missy and Laksman dey play and learns while Raju Sir work. Dey sits dere like family. Every morning my Laksman leave my mat to go wit Missy to pray to Ma Savitri – Raju Sir say she is same as Mariamman. Dey lights holy light together. Den dey eats breakfast. Now my Laksman he eat wit Sir, Madame, Missy and Raju Sir.

At first I is scared. It no good servant baby sit wit master. I says dis to Missy.

'But Pilar, we're all Saliyas, aren't we?' she ask.

Big Sir he raise bushy eyebrow at dat. 'You are sounding more and more like your husband, Shanthi.'

Two days later Raju Sir go to office in Kanchipuram in afternoon. He interest in business now. Missy she happy, Big Sir too. Dat afternoon be my appointment to see doctor in hospital for baby. Raju Sir take me to Kanchipuram wit him.

Murukananthan he no come much now I gots baby in belly. His business bad all de time. 'Women dey no buys saree,' he complain. 'I need good luck,' he says. 'You only have baby boy. You go and have dis scan ting.' I no tell him nobody buy his saree because he only have ugly saree in his shop.

I is scared. I no want to do scan ting. Even if baby girl I wants it. I wants to say what if my baby girl like Laksman. Wit big beautiful smile and big eyes. Everybody love my Laksman. May dey love my baby girl. But I no says dis.

Raju Sir he take me in car to hospital and drop me off at gate where he see Murukananthan. Murukananthan he no talk to me. He drunk. I can smells de *arrack* on breath. Henry say he always see Murukananthan drinking in Kanchipuram and visiting *devadasi*. 'Pilar wit baby – man gots to do man ting,' he says to Henry.

First we see midwife. She look at me. Looks at my teeth. Den she asks me questions. Private questions. I cannot answer. But she make me. She takes bloods den. Dis so different to when I has my Laksman. When I has Laksman, Shrugravethi Devi from next street she come when I gets pain. She helps me. She and Marmee holds my legs apart when Laksman he born. Dere be no question. No taking bloods.

Den we sees doctor. He young man. I so scared man touch my belly. I tries to move away but Murukananthan he hold me dere. He hold me down and doctor puts cold ting on belly.

'She stupid girl from village,' Murukananthan he say to doctor.

But it take doctor only little time.

'It's a girl,' he says. 'When do you want me to take her out? You'll need twenty-five rupees for that.'

'Next month,' Murukananthan he says. 'I no gots money dis month.'

'As long as it's before she is four months along,' de doctor he says. He no interested. He no care he going to kill my baby girl. Murukananthan he leave me at hospital gate. He no care now I gots baby girl in belly. I walks to de big house crying. I cries all de way. I love my babies. Babies make me mother. Mother make me alive.

One time a month dey show a film on television. And Big Sir gots television. First time I sees television in Big Sir house I is scared. 'What dis evil ting,' I asks Balini *baba*.

'You no see film?'

'No, I no leaves Murukananthan street until I comes here. He bring me to his parent house and leaves me dere. I no go out. I no do nuttin.'

Balini *baba* den tells me about films. I only see TV. I no go to films. No paper money.

Not dat Big Sir lets us watch TV. Not even his family. He say it use too much electricity. But film night it be different. Film night Madame, Missy, Big Sir and even Raju Sir dey comes out and watch. In de big room wit chairs. Neighbours dey come too. Dey sits on chairs. 'Rich people no go to film theatres to watch film. Too common,' Balini *baba* she explains.

'But dey have TV in house, *nah*?' I asks. I knows dis because I sometimes go next door to get curry leaves and I sees TV in dat house. And dere Sir and Madame dey watch it all de time.

'Yes, Pilar, but dis way dey gets to watch it together. Have chai after and masala dosai.'

We servants sits on mats outside in garden and looks in. When it rains, we used to have to go back to servant house and not watch. Den Raju Sir he says sometin to Missy and Missy say sometin to Big Sir. Now we is allowed to sit in front of kitchen door wit mats and watch.

Not dat I cares. For days now all I does is cries. After I finish works I sits on my mat and cries. 'How I lives after dey kills my baby?' I asks Balini *baba*.

Balini *baba* cries too. She gots no answer. 'Stupid shanty people! Without girl how deir son marry? Dey all becomes hijra.' But dat evening Balini *baba* she comes and gets me. 'Come, Pilar, come. You cry it no do you good. Come watch film wit us.'

I goes in and sits down. Henry, Balini *baba* and Thomas dey gets extra mat for me and little pillow because of baby. It only when I sits down wit Laksman in my arms dat I see. On de far wall like a golden rain falling from sky. Raju Sir put saree on wall. Like picture.

'When dat happen?' I asks Balini *baba*.

'He finish saree yesterday. Henry and Thomas puts it up dis afternoon while you cries.'

From top to bottom de saree it be beautiful. Like waterfall wit peacock at bottom.

Neighbours den dey come. Doctor from next door. Even de Sir who work in Kamakshi Amman temple in Kanchipuram come. Dey looks at saree.

'Oh my goodness,' de doctor he say. 'You are a real artist, Raju Nair. A real artist.'

'Wait till you see the paintings. They came from London the other week,' Missy she says. 'Laksman adores them. Come, they are hung in our sitting room.' She takes de guests to her part of house, but dey soon hurries back because film about to start. Dey look at Raju Sir like dey scared of him.

'We are in for a treat,' de doctor he says. 'The film tonight is called *Mother India*.'

'An Indian classic,' Big Sir he says.

'Remember, Lal, you took me to see it on our honeymoon?' Madame she smile. 'Back then only quality people could afford to go to cinemas.'

I cries through all film. It so sad. Sad story of Radha and

her life. Her husband his arms crush. He leave her. Den her baby get killed in flood. I cries. And I cries. And when she kills her son, I cries so much dat Madame must stand up and say, 'Oh please excuse my servant Pilar, she is pregnant.'

But I still dere when film finish. I dere when de Sir who work for temple speak to Raju Sir and Missy.

'As you know, it will be Shree Panchami in the next few months. We usually do a pageant from the temple to the river. The main Kamakshi Devi idol is dressed in a new saree and paraded through the city to herald spring. I would be more than honoured to give you 75,000 rupees for that saree,' he says to Raju Sir.

'No,' Raju Sir he says.

'How about 80,000 rupees?'

'That saree is not for sale.'

'But you are a Saliya. You understand that this is a gift to the goddess. Your patron goddess. It is your duty to give it to her,' de temple Sir now he says.

'I want you to understand this, and I will only say it one more time. That saree is not for sale,' Raju Sir he says and walks away.

'Well! Well! I have never heard of anything more ridiculous! Lal! Have a chat with your son-in-law. I could go to the temple trustees and even secure a lakh for that saree.'

I is very surprised when I hears Missy speak. 'As my husband said, that saree is not for sale. Please do not ask for it again,' Missy she say and walk to follow Raju Sir.

'Are you Pilar?' a beautiful lady asks me. I nods. I be standing outside Kamakshi Amman temple. It be early morning and I gone for my prayers. I has left my Laksman wit Raju Sir and Missy. Sometime he fall asleep wit Missy now.

'Come,' the beautiful lady says. I follow her. We goes inside and we prays. She take me close pooja table to gods. Close like rich peoples. No one argue wit her. She can go as close as she want. She take de lamp from *pusari*. Dat is not right. Only mens can hold holy light.

She laughs at me. 'Yes, Pilar, I can hear your thoughts,' she says. 'That boys are lucky and girls are not is nonsense made up by men. As is this nonsense that only men can hold the holy fire.'

Dat when I notice de beautiful lady looks like de statue behind her. And dat statue look like Nargis, de lady who is Radha in de film last night. 'Yes, the likeness is astonishing, isn't it?' she smiles. Den she ask me to follow her.

I follow her. She slow down a little. I cannot walk fast as her wit baby in my belly. We come back to big house. Big Sir house. Only it be different. Dere be sometin different and I don't understand.

'Don't be scared, Pilar,' de beautiful lady she says. She walks through front door. I tries to go back and go through back door, but she pulls me wit her. 'You follow me,' she says. Ands I do.

Dere be no one in de house. It be empty. Very strange. House should be busy dis time of morning. Even if it too early and everyone still sleep. Henry and Thomas should be sleeping by stairs. Dat what dey do. Dey sleep by stairs to protect family from thieves.

But dey nots dere. Balini *baba* not dere. Mama Leela not dere. And dere be no Thomas or Henry or Mr Krishnapillay. Ands evens more strange, dere be picture of Big Sir on dining table. And in front, dere be his pants. I picks up his pants. I looks for his belt. It not be dere. I tinks dere going to be big trouble if Sir cannot find belt for going to work in little while.

Dat when Big Sir money wallet falls out. It be full of paper money. I don't dare touch it.

'Pick it up,' de beautiful lady says to me. I cannot say no. She is Radha.

She come over and she show me how much paper money to take. Three pieces from de end. 'That is all you should need, Pilar,' she says.

Den she walk into big room. She slowly go up de stairs around big room and take de saree dat Raju Sir make from de wall. It hang from top of staircase to floor. 'Help me fold this,' she says. I is scared. I no want to be thief. I no want Big Sir to hit me wit belt. But I helps her.

She asks me to follow her more. I is very scared now.

She take me to de railway station across from river. She show me how to buy ticket. 'We must catch the train that is at quarter past five in the morning,' she says. And she show me where to catch train. She climbs on train wit me. And we rides. And we rides. And we rides. I is tired. I puts my head on her shoulder to sleep. Dat when I feel my baby move.

'Yes, she is precious,' Radha she says to me. Den we in town I no know. 'Just get off at the last stop,' she says.

She show me how to go to a shop. It be early evening now. She tells me to show dem de saree. I do and dey give me money. More paper money dan I know what I does wit it.

'Without this money you cannot enter the ashram for life or keep your daughter safe. Put it in your *pallu*,' she says. 'Tie it nice and tight.'

'Come,' she says and she show me how to take another train. 'Make sure you catch the train that leaves at six-thirty in the evening. Promise me you won't miss it.'

Dis time we no ride so long. She show me sometin out de window. 'Remember that tree, Pilar – it is very important. You must get off the train as soon as you pass that *kikar* tree.'

It be difficult to get off train because it very busy and noisy. Lots of peoples. Peoples pushing me here and dere. I is scared I nearly not gets off train. But I do. I turn around and Radha not dere. I so scared I no know what to do. My heart start to go fast. I no know whats to do.

Dat when someone tap me on shoulder. It be another young woman. She wear white saree and she look so beautiful. Maybe more beautiful dan Radha. She show me sometin. It be a little peacock. It be so small it fit into her hands. I gives her de money in my *pallu* and she gives me de peacock.

'Do not be afraid. Everything will be all right now,' she says. And I follows her. I follow her out to de road and into a temple.

Dis temple is big. So big it go up into sky! And so beautiful. It be all white and dere be peoples dressed in white everywhere. It next to a green river. So big. So beautiful. Like long green and gold lake. I take a step into de temple, de floor be very cold I tinks.

And dat when I wakes up. I still in Big Sir house. Balini *baba* she be next to me. Laksman he sleep next to me. And for first time I feels my baby move. Dat when I realise it all be a dream. A beautiful dream because my baby girl safe. But very sad dream too because I no have my Laksman wit me.

De hot season it coming now. It get very hot during day. So everytin it start early now. We wakes up just after de crows go to mountains to rest. We must makes everytin ready before Big Sir, Madame, Missy and Raju Sir dey wake up. Because even dey wake early because of heat. Heat very hard when you have baby in belly.

De heat it more hard because Gopal not wit us no more. No one to do de big cleaning jobs. See it be Gopal job to gets up dere and cleans de ceiling fans. Dey be so dirty now. Thick dust like slime on shanty house drain. And whens we puts ceiling fan on it throw dirt everywhere.

'For god's sake switch that fan off,' Madame she cry one day when we puts it on in de living room and dirt fall off into her cold lassi. She very embarrassed. Her friends Mrs Sharma and Mrs Patel come to take morning tea.

'It is so difficult to find good help these days,' Madame she complain.

Mrs Sharma and Mrs Patel dey complain about deir servants too. Dat dey lazy and dat dey breaks tings. Dey never talks about how Mrs Sharma hit her servant for eating too much. Everyone on street know Mrs Sharma very stingy. Mrs Patel, her house always a mess because she gossip all de time. She go from house to house to gossip. But dey leaves very quick. It be too hot in big house.

One day Venay make paneer dhal wit chillies. Big Sir he like paneer dhal wit chillies. He come home for lunch and he take off shirt sit down at table.

'Lal, please put your shirt back on,' Madame she says. 'It is uncivilised to have lunch bare chested!'

'Leave me alone!' he growls. 'What is uncivilised is not having ceiling fans work. Selvi, why haven't you got the servants to clean them yet?'

'Which servant, Lal? Which one? Since Gopal died there is no one to do the heavy cleaning.'

'What about Pilar?' he asks rudely, cutting Madame off, pointing to me. 'She is a hard worker!'

'I can hardly ask a pregnant woman to climb a ladder, can I?'

Big Sir he look me up and down and den ignores me.

'What about Thomas or Henry?' he demands.

Madame she lowers her voice. 'You know they are Catholics and the priest here is quite against electricity . . .'

Raju Sir he stand up. He well now and walk good but he still very stiff. 'I'll clean it after lunch,' he says.

'Raju, don't be silly,' Missy she says and pulls him down to his chair. 'Get Venay or Gunay to do it, Amman. Actually, I will get them to do it this afternoon.'

'Venay and Gunay are cooks. I do not want them coming into the house,' Big Sir he snaps. 'I don't want them trekking their dirt in here,' he says wiping his neck wit his handkerchief. 'This heat is intolerable! Pilar,' he says to me. 'Get more hot chillies from the kitchen. Maybe I can sweat myself cool.'

And I do. I brings red hot chillies. Vernay mixes vinegar wit de chillies. Big Sir he mixes it wit his rice and eats.

'Lal,' Madame she scolds. 'You'll get an ulcer from all that chilli!'

Only Sir he go red. 'Water! Water!' he calls. I runs and get him water which he drink fast. It splash all over face. 'Goddammit!' Big Sir roars. 'I am going to clean this damn fan even if I have to do it myself!'

Missy, Raju Sir and Madame dey finishes deir lunch. Dey shakes deir head and den dey goes to deir rooms. Every one sleeps in de afternoon in de hot season.

Henry bring de big ladder into de house. He sets it up and Big Sir he climb wit big dusting cloth he takes from Balini *baba*. 'I am going to do it right,' he says. Only he not big enough. He no reach de ceiling fan. 'Damn thing,' he says. 'If only I could tip the blades so I can clean the sides.'

We never understand what Big Sir tinking when he do what he does next. But he takes off belt from his pants and he try to catch blade of ceiling fan. To pull it down.

'*Eii!*' Balini *baba* she scream when she sees dis. See Big Sir pants fall down.

'Shut up, you stupid woman!' Big Sir shout, only he lets go of de ladder.

Den he falls. We alls screams.

Everybody crazy now Big Sir in hospital. It same hospital Raju Sir and Missy take Laksman to. Madame she stay wit Big Sir. She sleep on little bed ands I have to go in every morning to rub oil into her back.

'Pilar,' she says, 'you have no idea how I am suffering for my husband. No idea.'

I no tells her when I is here wit my Laksman dey no give me bed. I sleep on floor mat.

Missy she comes and spend day wit her *amman*. Spend day dere and come home at night.

'I have to be there for my parents,' she cry. And Missy she cry all de time. She scared her *appa* die.

Big Sir get angry about dis. 'You silly women,' he say loudly. 'Stop crying. It is only a dislocated shoulder! The only reason I am letting the quack keep me in here is because of the air conditioning!'

He also like dat everybody in hospital clean. Dey wash deir hands. Dey puts deir hair in net. And dey wear mask. So he lies to de doctor. 'Doctorji,' Big Sir he says. 'I think I need a few more days of rest here. I can never get any at home. I am forever doing this and that.'

Dat be lie. Big Sir do nuttin in house. And now Raju Sir work in office, Big Sir want to take holiday. Take break.

Missy and Madame dey no complain either. Dey likes being in hospital. Dey likes fuss. When dey be in hospital wit Big Sir, lots of people come to visit. Deir neighbours, deir relatives, everybody. Balini *baba* and I be dere all de time. We makes tea and we give out biscuits to visitors. Like big party. So Laksman be in hospital wit me.

Dat when I realise some people tink Laksman be Missy and Raju Sir baby.

'He looks just like you, Shanthi,' an old aunty say. 'You must have got pregnant straightaway child to have such a big baby.' Missy she not correct her. Maybe dat because sometime Missy she act like Laksman *amman*. One day twenty peoples come to visit Big Sir and Laksman he start to cry. De aunties and uncles dey pinch Laksman face and calls him cute boy. One uncles toss him in air and say he fat *putta* like his *athappa*.

I tinks Big Sir nearly chokes on his chai dat someone confuse servant baby wit his grandson.

Dat when Missy take him out. To play wit children elsewhere in hospital.

'Don't worry, Pilar,' she says. 'I'll only take him to where children with broken limbs are. They have a TV in there.'

I so busy making tea, washing cups, dat I no notice it nearly dark. Time to go home wit Balini *baba*. I goes in search of my Laksman. I looks through broken limb children but my boy not dere. I look in ward where dere be babies, my Laksman and Missy not dere.

I finds dem in lady ward. Where all de sick madames and missies are. Missy find her old schoolfriend. De one Madame sends Missy to visit when Balini *baba*, Mama Leela, Miss Sonali and me we drinks chai and eat gulab jamun to talks about what wrong wit Missy and Raju Sir.

I walks in. My Laksman asleep on Missy shoulder. His hand in her saree blouse and his head in her neck. Missy she sit dere and she talks to her friend. Holding her hand while she pats my Laksman wit de other. Her friend crying.

'I had no choice, Shanthi,' Missy Parvathi she cries.

'It will be all right,' Missy she says.

'No, it won't,' Missy Parvathi she cry. 'I can't have any

more children. The doctor told me that. Vinod is sure to take me home and dump me with my parents!'

'Don't be silly! He adores you!'

'We already have two girls and the in-laws are obsessed with having a grandson. That is the only reason I agreed to it. Even at this late stage.'

'Was it painful?' Missy ask in a quiet voice.

'Yes,' Missy friend now sobs. 'It was awful! They said I didn't need a general anaesthetic, so I saw everything. I wanted them to stop but the doctor had already started.'

'I am so sorry . . .' Missy she say. She now gots tears.

'They killed her first, you know. They killed her. They injected her heart with poison. And I saw her. When they sucked her out of me into a glass bottle, I saw her. I saw her hands. And her feet. They were so perfect.' Missy friend cry like crazy now. She all alone. She cry for her dead baby.

Now Missy she sob too. My Laksman he wake up. He look at Missy and touch her face. Make her stop crying. Dat when I know. Dat when I know whats I must do. My son got *amman*. My daughter need life. But I no know hows to do it. I no thief. I no wants Big Sir to kills me. But maybe it better Big Sir catch me and puts me in jail dan dey takes my baby out and kills me.

De message it come just before midnight. Gopal his brother brings it. 'You *marmee* say come quick. Come to poor peoples hospital.' I leaves my Laksman wit Missy. 'Take care of my baby,' I says to her and I runs. I runs. I runs wit Gopal brother. De poor people hospital on other side town. It longs way. I no breath when I gets dere.

Marmee dere. Marcel dere. Brother-in-law dere. Idiot sister-in-law dere.

'Where is my Murukananthan?' I ask. Before dey can answer de doctorji he come. He ask who Murukananthan wife be and I says me. Dey takes me. Murukananthan not dead yet. He drink poison. De doctor say it take hours or maybe even days to die.

I sits next to Murukananthan. I cry. I is scared now.

Marmee she come after a while. De doctorji explains to her and Marcel. Dey both scream. Dey scream at Murukananthan. 'Please, *putta*! Please no die! We gets you new wife!' dey scream.

I hear brother-in-law talk to Gopal brother. 'He no pay de moneylenders he borrow for shop. He start drinking down in town. Dey come after Pilar now for money. She work. She gots money!'

I scream more inside my head. But den Murukananthan he wake for little bit. He open eyes and he vomit. Black poison. And his face it swellt. Like dead animal. So it be just before crow start to cry dat he die. Doctorji come and explain dat Murukananthan gone to God.

292

Marmee she start screaming. She go crazy. First she lies on ground and she scream. Den Marmee she stands up. And she slaps me. Hard across ear. And she hits me and hits me. I lifts my hand to stop Marmee. She old but strong and her arm bony. She hit me more.

'What? What?' I cries.

'My boy! My boy!' she cries. 'He dies! He kill himself! You gets baby girl in belly and he kills himself!' Marmee she scream. She tries to kick me in belly but I steps away. 'Filthy widow! Get out of my sight!'

Marcel and brother-in-law dey come to me. 'Get out,' my brother-in-law shout. 'Unlucky woman! Get out! You are *dhosai*. You bring *dhosai*!' Dey push me. Dey push me straight out of hospital door into street. I falls. I falls into drain. 'Go,' dey say. 'Go back to village! Your sister-in-law takes job! Big Sir no keep *dhosai* widow like you in house.'

I looks at dem. I no know what to tink. I no tink. I stupid girl from village. What I know? I walk to temple. I sits dere and I pray. I pray for long time. Maybe God will help me. I pray so hard maybe dat why I hears my name when de *pusari* toll de bell. 'Pilar . . . Pilar . . .'

I look up. I see Radha. She walk. She look at me and she ask me to follow her. I follow her. Back to Big Sir house. It be exactly like my dream. Only when I gets to house, Radha not dere. I walk in and dere be no one at house. De house be empty. No Balini *baba*. No Henry or Thomas or de cooks. I go upstairs. I cannot find Missy, Raju Sir or Madame.

Den I go downstairs. I see dat dey put Big Sir picture on dining table. His pants on floor like de day he fall from ladder. So I go out de house and I knock on neighbour door.

'What happens?' I ask de servants in other house.

'What happen to you?' dey ask first. 'You look like you see ghost.'

'Nuttin. But where my Laksman? Where Missy?'

'Didn't you hear? Just after midnight they got a telephone call that Mr Govindarajan got sick and died.'

I go back into house. I do like my dream. I takes enough money for train and I takes de saree from de wall. I walk down to train station and I takes train. I no understand how dis happen but it happens. And I know my baby safe and my Laksman he be safe too. Maybe dis be Radha plan.

# The Second Drape

Mysore, Karnataka, India, 1989

'Arrrggghh!'
       'Eiiii! Eiii! Eii! Eii!'
       'Oooh oooh oooh!'
Sarojini thought she'd heard every sound under the sun during the throes of passion. There were those who screamed. Those who cried. And even those who resorted to animal sounds as they reached the pinnacle of their ecstasy; woofing like a dog or grunting like a pig. But never before had she heard anyone call out for their mother as they spilled themselves inside her.

'Surely that has got to be wrong?' she grumbled to her housemate Kalpana. 'Why would anyone think of their mother right at that moment?'

'Surely the one thing you should know by now is that there is no right or wrong when it comes to sex,' Kalpana observed acerbically as she came over to squat by the drain to brush her teeth. 'Was it the business man from Bangalore?'

'No, the teacher from Puducherry. His wife is in hospital here in Mysore.'

'Hmm . . . such a handsome young man. Who would have thought it?'

'That he is not having sex from his wife? The woman has a heart condition!'

'No!' Kalpana said before spitting noisily into the drain. 'That he would have hang-ups about his mother. I think there is a name for that disease . . .' she said, tapping her head with the end of her toothbrush to recall the name of the condition.

Sarojini rolled her eyes. For quite some time now Kalpana had been seeing the Chief Psychiatrist at the Mysore University Hospital and so she fancied herself one, too. She was forever trying to pick apart people's conversations now and give them mind diseases.

'That Poornima – she has this crazy person disease . . . Nar – something. Who can remember these fancy *ferenge* words . . . but I can describe it. It's named after a Greek god who saw a reflection of himself in a water hole and fell in love with it and fell into the water and died!'

'She is but sixteen. If you don't love yourself, then you never will,' Sarojini replied exasperatedly.

To which Kalpana just sniffed. She liked to think of herself as a perfect embodiment of *devadasi*. A detached provider of a service that necessitated the same degree of dedication and education as required by a doctor or teacher. 'The *karma sutra* has 1250 verses and comes in thirty-six bound volumes. I doubt any green horn village school teacher has read half as much.'

'Neither have you,' Sarojini muttered to herself as she followed Kalpana into their small home as she kept muttering names of disease. 'Was it schizophrenia? Or was it hypomania . . .'

The women separated into their own rooms in the little hallway that led from the little sitting room all the way through the tiny kitchenette. Although their living arrangement was a relationship of convenience that had started some years previously it had developed into something of a haphazard friendship. And when they returned to the hallway almost twenty minutes later, they were as equally elegantly turned out.

'Should we tell Mrs Teacherji when we'll be back?' Sarojini enquired as they walked out into the bright sun of the day.

'She does not care,' Kalpana muttered, casting a derisive look over to the verandah where the widow sat reading her morning paper. 'Low caste cow.'

Sarojini wished to disagree yet she could not help but accept the truth of Kalpana's words. Mrs Teacherji at best tolerated them but the retired schoolteacher's annexed home was a godsend. Situated in one of the respectable parts of Mysore and backing onto a narrow canal that had another dead end street backing onto it on the other side, the location alone enabled them to ply their trade with little harassment.

'Just go past the cinemas to the TK Water tank road. Go to the very end. You can take a large step over the canal and you will be at the girls' house,' Mamaji would tell the clients she sent the girls' way. 'It is all very respectable.'

Sarojini and Kalpana did not take the short cut across the canal that morning; instead walking the long way to Maruthi Temple Road to catch the bus across to Fort Mohalla.

Yet even among the midmorning human crush in Mysore, they somehow stood out. Or even apart. Young women chose not to stand too close to them on the bus. A young mother took her school-aged son to sit as far away as possible, pointing out various billboards along the highway, determined to distract him. Men could not help but let their eyes stray lecherously towards them.

Perhaps it was the glamour of their sarees that set them apart. Few women would wear such costly sarees on a bus. Or it could have been the snatches of their conversation that fellow travellers could hear if they strained hard over the din of the traffic.

'I've never heard a man call for his mother before, when he's about to . . . you know. You really don't think that's strange?' Sarojini asked her friend.

'I once had a man demand I make love to him while he wore his wife's saree,' Kalpana told her.

'What about making love on temple grounds? That is strange, is it not?'

'No stranger than a man insisting he watch you pee in front of him,' Kalpana said. 'Or taking a man's member in your mouth while his pet dog looks on . . .'

Sarojini bowed her head in acquiescence. That was strange.

They alighted at their stop and made their way through the older part of town, where palatial houses with large lush gardens soaked up the interminable summer heat.

'I still think it is strange that he called for his mother,' Sarojini insisted as they opened the gate to the most run-down of the old places.

In her heyday Moona Mahal had been a grand lady, her white balconies garlanded with bright lanterns and the constant hum of music from the sitar and tabla players who had been permanent residents here at the time. It was rumoured that even Nalvadi Krishna Raja Wadiyar, the last great maharajah of Mysore, had been a regular visitor, bringing sahibs to watch the nightly dance and music shows.

'No stranger than a man wanting to suckle at your breast like a baby while he fucks you,' Kalpana pointed out. 'Surely the one thing you should know by now is that there is no right or wrong when it comes to sex,' she said, then waved as she spotted a friend. 'Rekha!' she called. 'Sarojini is complaining about an *arari* who called out for his mother while he was doing it!'

Rekha covered her eyes in frustration. '*Aiii!* Don't get me started! Last week I had to deal with a man who wanted to do it outside. In the middle of the day. In this heat. Just look, will you! Just look at the sunburn on my back,' she cried, turning around and lifting her blouse to show them. 'This is after three days and my ayah applying papaya three times a day.'

Sarojini and Kalpana made sympathetic noises as they went around the side of the house to the verandah out the back, where they joined a large group of women similarly dressed in bright colours and beautiful fabrics. This was the ritual gathering every Monday of the *devadasi* in Mysore. These were not prostitutes one might find on a street corner, but handmaidens of the gods.

'You say it was his mother's name he called?' Rekha asked Sarojini. 'That's not so strange. Not like Kumar Ramachandran.'

Ramachandran was a rich Mysorese businessman and cricket fan who would call out for the great batsman Sunil Gavaskar in his moment of ecstasy. All the *devadasi* in Mysore knew him.

The ancient *pusari* sounded the chimes indicating that the pooja was about to start and an elderly *gharwali mamaji* floated to the central dais holding a large statue of the goddess Yellamma.

Sarojini pulled a face at Kalpana, unhappy at being so teased.

'Well, what do you want to hear when men are making love to you?' Kalpana whispered. 'Words of love?'

'We trade in love, Sarojini, but we do not love,' Rekha seconded softly.

'I didn't say I wanted to hear words of love!' Sarojini protested in a hot undertone.

'What then? What do you want to hear? That you are beautiful!' Kalpana replied. 'Oh! And the name of that mind disease! I remember it! It is called Oedipus complex!'

By now the pooja had begun in earnest so Sarojini and her friends were subjected to disapproving glares from more than just Mamaji. Some of the older *devadasi* turned huffily and stared down their noses.

'Well? What did you want to hear?' Kalpana whispered.

'My name,' Sarojini said softly, closing her eyes in prayer. 'Even if it is just once in my life, I would like one of my lovers to call me by my name when he comes inside me.'

'If I had as much sex as Mrs Vinaygam thinks I do, I would hardly be able to stand, *nah*!' Kalpana stomped into their little kitchen carrying a steel pail full of milk and slammed it onto the bench for effect.

'*Achaa* . . . what did she say now?' Sarojini asked. She was making chai in the little kitchenette in her housecoat.

'Oh . . . nothing much . . . that her back was sore from doing all the housework and carrying home all her papers from school to mark. Made a snide comment that it was easy for some because all they ever did was lie on their back to earn a living.'

'Ignore her. You know she has been in a foul mood since her husband went abroad to work.'

'But why is she carrying on like a *banderi* on heat? So irritable and nasty?'

Sarojini shrugged. She thought it was Kalpana acting like a monkey on heat, hissing and spitting. Perhaps she wasn't feeling well. So Sarojini made her friend a strong cup of chai. One well laced with *ashwagandha* to calm the mind and heat the body.

Dawn had not even lit the morning sky when the two women made their way across to the Maruti temple to do *abishekam*. They brought fresh milk for Lord Hanuman – the reason Kalpana had risked the markets so early in the morning.

When they got to the temple, they did not waste any time, darting into the little anteroom adjoining the main shrine to

302

change with the three other girls already there. Experienced and talented, it only took them an hour to do their make-up and drape their elaborate red and gold sarees.

The make-up was dramatic – heavy lines on the eyes and bright colours on the lips and cheeks. The paints were iridescent against Sarojini's pale skin, so uncommon in Karnataka. She then oiled her long black hair using a mixture of ginger lily and *neem* oil to give it shine before plaiting it into a thick rope. Next she hid tiny silver weights at the end of her plait, so it would swing sinuously as she danced, and threaded garlands of jasmine across her crown and along the length of her braid.

Draping a saree for dance was very different to draping a saree for wear. A woman needed to have her legs free so that she could do the squats and hold the classical *karanas* as required by Bharatanatyam. To preserve her modesty, Sarojini wore tight leggings instead of an underskirt and used heavy gold chains to hold the elaborate crests of pleats in place on her waist before pulling on the heavy ankle bells.

The drummers were already tuning their instruments in the courtyard beyond when Sarojini saw that Kalpana was still visibly shaking. 'Breathe, calm your mind,' she counselled quietly. '*Om nam Shivaye . . .*' She reached forward to give her friend's hand a quick reassuring squeeze, only to find it cold and clammy. 'Are you unwell, Kalpana? I'm sure the *pusari* wouldn't mind if you were to sit out.'

'Don't be silly, Saro. How can I not dance after all that *ashwagandha* you put in my chai. I feel like I am on fire!'

'As you should be, Kalpana. Bharatanatyam is the fire dance,' Sarojini said softly as they moved into Alarippu, the first movement, invoking the gods and thanking the audience for their participation.

Though no one in the audience noticed, Kalpana wasn't in form. She didn't quite hold her poses, the *karanas,* for as long as she should have, and her *hastas*, the expressive hand movements, lacked their normal grace and crispness as the dancers proceeded into the main shrine.

'What is going on, Kalpana?' Sarojini whispered in the few moments before they launched into the dances of the Kautuvam.

'She said she'll be here,' Kalpana whispered back.

'Who? Mrs Vinaygam? Why are you letting her upset you so much?'

But before Kalpana could respond, the cymbals started and they had to move into the *karanas* for the Kautuvam. It was strange that Kalpana was so shaken by a neighbourhood gossip. Being a *devadasi* required a certain thickness of skin, for the public adored and reviled them in equal parts.

'They need us,' Mamaji would explain to the young girls she selected at the Yellamma dedication ceremony. 'We are the servants of God. But do not expect them to like us.'

'Why, Mamaji?' a shy young Sarojini had asked.

'We, the *devadasi*, were once great. Kings and rich temples paid handsomely to protect us. They cherished us. We were the guardians of literature, poetry, music and dance. But then the *ferenges* came. They called it "civilising" the heathens. Our people, devout Hindus, wanting to be more chaste and pure than Christians, called us sluts and threw us out of our temples. They made us into whores!' Mamaji's soft brown eyes had clouded.

Sarojini didn't have much time to think as the Jatiswaram started. The complex footwork and *hastas* required concentration. They were supposed to be telling the story of the god Hanuman, not worry about some silly woman and her opinions.

The great Lord Hanuman was an incarnation of the Lord Shiva. Their dance described his youth and lifetime, his strength, and the boon granted to him by Brahma, his mighty feats of war and the peace he brought the land. They would stop just short of the epic battle of the Ramayana. That story would be left for the joyful celebration of Deepavali, just around the corner, when Hanuman defeated the evil king Ravana and brought light to the world.

But things started to unravel far sooner than that for the temple dancers. As soon as the girls had started to dance the celebration of the birth of Hanuman, Kalpana completely lost concentration. She forgot her footwork and only made the most cursory effort at holding *karanas*. So much so that by tacit agreement with the other dancers, Sarojini took the lead, holding her *karana* for a fraction of a second longer than required, allowing Kalpana to move to the back. She felt the great Lord Hanuman's power shift within her, bringing forth blessings to everyone attending, but she was annoyed. It was not easy to take the lead halfway through a performance. To act as a conduit for the gods required preparation and concentration, and she did not wish to disappoint them.

'What was that all about?' Sarojini demanded as soon as they got into the change room.

'She thinks after all that I have energy for sex!' Kalpana complained. 'My feet hurt. My back hurts. This awful make-up makes my skin break out and all she can think about is that my job is easy!'

Sarojini wanted to give Kalpana a piece of her mind, but the tears already in her friend's eyes stayed her tongue. She helped her housemate pack her heavy costume bag and guided her to the door.

But just as the girls stepped into the muggy light of the overcast day, she saw him. Well rather, they both saw him. Abhay Promod. Mrs Vinaygam's much younger brother. A captain in the Indian Armed Forces. Resplendent in his green uniform, his chest covered with decorations from his time subduing the troubled border with Pakistan. Tall. Straight. And very handsome.

'Did you know?'

'Yes, she mentioned that her brother was in Mysore. And that she'd arranged a marriage for him with a respectable girl with a large dowry,' Kalpana said, her voice catching on the last word.

'We cannot trade in love and not feel love ourselves,' Sarojini said gently as they made their way through the back of the temple, leaving the front clear for Abhay and his family. His mother and father were beaming and there were tears and smiles all round; clearly it was not appropriate for whores to intrude just at that time. No matter that Kalpana and Abhay had grown up together.

Sarojini was finding it hard to make ends meet. She sat on her bed counting notes and scribbling in a small brown notebook; her outgoings just about tallied with her expenditure and she wasn't saving anything. With Deepavali coming up, she just could not see how the meagre sum in her possession could be stretched to do all it was supposed to. She'd gone to the temple bursar to collect her payment for dancing that week and found the money he gave her a little lacking.

'But sir, I took the lead in the dance the other day and that pays seventy-five rupees more,' she'd protested.

'No, Kalpana Pillay did the lead,' the bursar insisted.

'No, I did. She stepped back a third of the way through!'

'But she is from a Brahmin family,' the man said and firmly closed the window to the office.

Then her landlady had confronted her as she came home. '*Achaa* . . . the bills keep going up and up and there's always talk of them cutting the pension,' she said angrily, waving a bony finger all bent and misshapen from arthritis. 'And you know . . . they aren't happy that I keep you girls here. The neighbours. Mrs Chelvam is a good, virtuous woman, never mind that she is Christian. She worries, you know . . .'

Sarojini only sighed, but Kalpana was offended. 'She worries? About what? That being a *devadasi* is catching? That her daughter can catch it by passing us on the street?' she growled irritably. But Kalpana didn't have the same worries Sarojini did.

Kalpana had been dedicated to the god Hanuman by her highborn Brahmin parents as a vow. Her father had been in a serious car accident and had been in coma when her mother had visited a *jogti* at the temple. 'Tell me,' Kalpana's mother had pleaded. 'Will my husband survive? I have four children. What will become of us?'

'A blood sacrifice must be made . . .' the *jogti* had said, spittle frothing from her mouth, her eyes rolling back into her head. But it had been the stench emanating from the woman's matted hair that had made Kalpana feel ill as she peeked out from behind her mother's saree. She had wanted to run out of the temple.

'I knew,' Kalpana reminisced. 'My heart fell to my feet and I felt faint.'

'That girl! Hanuman must have that girl!' the *jogti* had declared.

'And I have never understood that. God Hanuman was celibate all his life, according to the Puranas!' Kalpana said, scratching her head. 'But that was that. My *devarige biduvadu* happened the very next day. It was a Friday and a full moon during the month of November. I stood there in the middle of the *jogati-patta* as they lit the four fires around me and I wanted to scream – which was when I saw Abhay. He'd found out somehow and came running into the temple . . . it took four *pusaris* to stop him from getting to me.'

'But you could have said no – nothing is set in stone until the priest ties the beads,' Sarojini insisted.

'How could I not do it, Saro? My father woke up that morning and his first words were *Tai Hanuman Udho Udho* . . . he gave praise to the Lord Hanuman who saved him,' Kalpana said, fingering the brand of Hanuman on her left breast.

Kalpana's parents were still wracked with guilt at what they had done to their only daughter, so they happily covered her costs of living and provided her with an allowance. Her mother had been near hysterical at her *pattam* and had to be sedated at the feast afterward as the wealthy businessman led her young daughter away.

'Calm, *anujate*, calm,' Mamaji had said, holding the heart-broken mother in her arms. 'She is the same age as you when you got married! It will be no different!'

Unlike most *gharwalis*, Mamaji would not let girls under her care undertake their *pattam* until they were at least seventeen. 'A child of twelve or thirteen is not capable of handling a man's passion! What nonsense is this!' Mamaji would roar at the *araris* if they spied a young girl at her house and asked for her. 'I give out no children. If you wish to mate with a child, then mate with a frog. You may get more pleasure from that!'

Like all *pattam* ceremonies held under Mamaji's auspices, Sarojini's own had been a grand affair. Sponsored, of course, by Harindra, the man who'd found her as a young child playing in her uncle's garden in the rural village some five hundred miles from Mysore. For the second time in her life, Sarojini had been dressed as bride, the first having been at the *devarige biduvadu* that Harindra had also sponsored.

She'd come out bedecked in a bright yellow saree, a saree he'd chosen for her. He'd even chosen the heavy jewellery that covered her neck, arms and ears. In front of the feast laid out on a long table, she'd actually felt like a bride, though there had been no sacred flames or any wedding guests. Just her mother and her uncle, who spent the whole time looking at the trays of money, rolls of hundred rupee notes bound with rubber bands, more money than they had seen in a lifetime. Money that they would share with Mamaji.

There had been no vows, no promises of devotion for seven lifetimes as required by the Vedic texts. The priest only reminded her of her duties. 'Remember that you cannot claim the right to be the wife of any man. You must fast on Tuesdays and Fridays. If you are hungry, you may not ask for food.

If anybody abuses you, you may not retaliate. And chant *Udho Yellamma* as many times a day as you can!'

Sarojini and Harindra had then retired into the little bungalow behind Mamaji's mansion. Though she could recall little about the events of that night, she remembered feeling as if she was on fire and Harindra's middle-aged *poolu* deep inside her young body the only cure. Only later she found out that Mamaji had laced her chai for days before with extracts of *shatavari, ashwagandha, gokshura* and *bala* – enough aphrodisiacs to send a corpse into a passionate frenzy.

In the months that followed, Harindra – Sir, as he'd insisted she call him – had been the most attentive lover. He'd set her up in a little annexed house, complete with an ayah to do the cooking and cleaning. He'd come during his lunchbreak from his senior government job and Sarojini would wait for him bathed and dressed. 'Dress in yellow, my sweet little sunflower, dress in yellow,' he would insist. It took a while for Sarojini to notice that he'd started to visit her only every second day. He was a busy public servant, after all, the deputy head of the Karnataka agriculture department. He toured the state regularly looking at its farms, which was how he'd spotted her in the first place. Sarojini was as heartbroken as any young woman could be when her landlord informed her that her rent had only been paid for another month and she would have to find alternative accommodation.

She had shared with the sharp-tongued girl from Calcutta for a while, another of Mamaji's *devadasi*. But the Bengali girl was not only a slattern but highly strung as well. She had a regular and exceedingly wealthy client and never thought of tidying up unless he was about to visit, mouldy underwear strewn everywhere and filthy teacups. And when he was with her, she'd fight with him. Loudly and using obscene language! Sarojini's middle-class patrons found it very off-putting.

She then spent several months flitting from one household to another. It was difficult for a *devadasi* to find regular accommodation, and the only places she could find were smelly unhygienic rooms down by the slums.

'I can't do it! I can't do it with little children looking at me through the window!' one of her lovers had roared, completely distracted by the string of spellbound young urchins peeking through Sarojini's grimy window, and rose from her bed to chase them away. Needless to say, she never saw him again.

Now she lived with Kalpana, renting a little annexe tacked onto a retired schoolteacher's home. Yet she was never too sure from one month to the next that they'd be allowed to stay – or that she'd be able to afford the rent.

So she was desperately looking for a protector. Someone who would foot the bills for her while providing a bit more to help her support her desperately poor family. The problem was that rich men didn't want to support a *devadasi* anymore. It did not have the high social status it used to have, when it was seen as a sign of affluence and influence. They preferred cars now.

Sarojini stretched out on her bed, facedown, and pummelled her fists with frustration.

'Come now, Saro,' Kalpana said, coming into the room and perching on the bed. 'You'll find someone.'

'Is Abhay here?'

'Yes. He's in the living room. He says that he'll never consent to the marriage his sister has arranged.' Kalpana and Abhay had grown up together. Had it not been for Kalpana's dedication, they would be married by now. 'Come, Saro. Let's go out for some dinner. The bazaar is on in town tonight.'

'No, Kalpana, no, I am not in the mood!'

'Don't be silly! Please come.'

'I have a headache,' Sarojini lied.

'Please, Saro . . . it is just that Abhay has brought a friend home for Deepavali, and I don't want them talking about the army all night,' Kalpana pleaded. 'I want some time to talk to Abhay for myself.'

Which is why Sarojini went out that night, not knowing that it would be the night her whole world would change forever. Years later she would wonder what her life would have been like had she stayed on that bed and cried instead.

Mysore was a busy city at the best of times, but it became a madhouse near Deepavali. Abhay and his friend Rakesh had fetched the two girls and now they wended their way through the bazaar together, dodging the crowds. 'You'd think they'd never heard of Deepavali before!' Abhay commented. 'It comes every year!' he called out to a little lady who almost bowled him over as she hurried along, carrying a large bag of shopping.

Kalpana shushed him. 'She probably has six children, twenty in-laws and forty more relatives to cook for. Remember how my mother started preparing for Deepavali months ahead of time? The unending cleaning?'

'How could I forget? Aunty Pimmi always called me when she needed someone to clean the cobwebs. Just because I was the tallest boy in the neighbourhood!' Abhay mimicked Kalpana's mother's high-pitched squeal. 'You stupid boy! Come here! Come here now! Do you think God does not know? Do you think he'd never find out that your house is not clean? Shame on you!' Kalpana doubled over with laughter. 'She couldn't twist my ear, remember?' Abhay said. 'I was too tall for her. So she hit me with the broom instead. But your mother does make the best gulab jamun south of Delhi.'

'She was from New Delhi. She grew up just outside Dera Mandi.'

'Which explains your skin, Kalpana,' Abhay said softly, caressing her upper arm under the guise of helping her across a drain as they crossed the street to the restaurant. 'So fair. So soft. So beautiful. Like the snow-tipped mountains of Kashmir.'

Only their moment of tenderness was interrupted by the harsh glare of neon as they entered the restaurant. The waiters greeted them by the door, bustled them speedily into their stall, slapped down stainless steel plates covered with banana leaves and filled their glasses with lassi before they could even blink.

'We'll have the standard meal,' Abhay declared. 'Rice with curry and *paayasam*.' A waiter started filling little bowls with sickly sweet porridge to start the meal and Abhay sighed happily. 'I miss home,' he said. 'They only eat sweets at the end of a meal in the north. And I never have any space left.'

'*Achaa* . . . I never knew that,' Kalpana said. 'They eat their sweets after a meal? How strange!'

'Yes, *muddu*,' Abhay smiled indulgently. Kalpana was glowing, a sweet little smile twisting her lips, her eyes bright with joy.

Sarojini and Rakesh were not quite so pleased with each other's company.

It had all started wonderfully. Rakesh had been very friendly, eager almost, when Sarojini had come out of her room to meet them.

'You're Sarojini? Kalpana's housemate?'

'Yes, I am? How do you know?' Sarojini had asked, confused.

'He has seen a photo of you with Kalpana at her brother's wedding,' Abhay confessed, shamefaced.

'Which one?' Kalpana asked.

'The one of you both tying beads to your sister-in-law's *thali*.'

'How did you get it?'

'I stole it when your parents brought the album over to show my parents during the wedding visit.'

'And you are a dancer, Sarojini? Like Kalpana?' Rakesh had asked.

'Yes, we studied under the same master. We do most of our performances together.'

'Kalpana is the lead dancer, though – she does most of the complex parts and stories,' Abhay had interjected proudly, beaming at Kalpana.

'But Sarojini is more talented,' Kalpana insisted. 'Why, just on Tuesday she took over from me when I wasn't feeling well!'

'So do you train for long? I know dancers train from when they are children for Odissi,' Rakesh said.

'You are from Orissa?' Sarojini had asked in stilted Hindi. Mamajee insisted that all her girls learn the *lingua franca* of the land.

'Can't you tell? I have been told my Oriya accent makes my Hindi almost incomprehensible.'

'Well, we are in the same boat then! I have heard the same about my Kannada accent!' Sarojini had laughed before she attempted to make small talk, discussing some light federal politics and the antics of film stars. That was another one of Mamajee's edicts – that they had to stay abreast of world issues.

And Rakesh responded like any man who'd been without female company for four months and confined in the harsh environment of the Hindu Kush. With enthusiasm and sheer pleasure. For about a quarter of an hour, their conversation tripped along. They discovered that they both adored Madhuri Dixit and could only barely tolerate the Bharatiya Janata Party. 'India must be for all Indians. Not just Hindus! What is this Hindus first nonsense?' Rakesh had declared, at which Sarojini nodded.

They had stepped out as soon as Abhay pointed out that they would be stuck in the interminable traffic if they didn't make a move. And that was the moment when things changed.

'Sarojini,' Mrs Teacherji called out, irritable from the verandah. 'I hope you are not going out!'

'I am indeed,' Sarojini called out in a pleasant voice.

'Isn't tonight Mr Murkesh's night?'

'He's gone to Bangalore to visit his sister,' Sarojini said through gritted teeth at the old busybody.

But the damage was done. Rakesh had taken in a sharp breath of distaste. His face contorting into a moue, as if he'd stepped on a pile of fresh cow dung. '*Devadasi*,' he hissed under his breath.

Not that Kalpana or Abhay noticed. They had already got to Abhay's old banged up ex-army jeep. But Abhay did comment when they got into the car. 'Are you okay, Rakesh?'

Raskesh mumbled something and determinedly looked out the window. But he could not avoid looking at or interacting with Sarojini or the others throughout dinner.

'What would *you* know of poetry?' Rakesh smirked derisively.

'*Haa* . . . who exactly knows poetry then? The Dalits? Or the Kumhas? Certainly not the Brahmins or the Kshatriya! Thousands of years in-breeding means they are stupid!' Sarojini hissed looking over to Brahmin Kalpana and Abhay, who were both wearing idiot expressions of adoration on their faces.

'Oh, the *devadasi* then? Really? Whores?'

'Handmaidens of God! Or did you fail *bahasa*? And Asha Bhosle and Lata Mangeshkar come from *devadasi* lineage. As does Mogubai Kurdikar!'

'Three has-been singers? That is your proof?'

Sarojini gritted her teeth, and without forgetting a single word, recited the poem *Adikar* by Mahadevi Varma. Through her voice, she conveyed the joy, the inspiration and the hope that was inherent in the verses. When Rakesh looked non-plussed Sarojini tried a different tack, reciting the Hindu epic *Brahma, Vishnu and Shiva* by Rabindranath Tagore, the great nineteenth century Indian poet.

'So, you can memorise a few words – any *banderi* could do that!'

Sarojini bit her tongue; there was no talking to this man! And not that she could do anything about it. Kalpana and Abhay were sitting flush against the wall with their heads close together in deep conversation. So it happened that while

Kalpana and Abhay had a delightful evening full of conversation, great food and conviviality, Sarojini and Rakesh barely managed to stomach the rich curries in icy hostile silence.

'As always, it was just delightful to take you girls out for a meal,' Abhay complimented grandiosely as he pulled up in front of Mrs Teacherji's house. 'Eh, Captain? Wasn't it lovely to go out with couple of charming young ladies?' he continued obliviously. 'I forgot to tell you *cheluvi*. Captain here saved my life! Pulled me out of the way of some sniper fire! That is why I invited him to spend Deepavali with my family here in Mysore!'

'*Aii*! I didn't know you'd been in danger!' Kalpana squealed. 'I must go to the temple tomorrow morning and thank Lord Hanuman for protecting you!'

'What do I have to be worried about when I have the great God's handmaiden in my heart all the time?' Abhay asked softly. Which was when Sarojini thought it was time to alight from the vehicle. It should have been Rakesh's cue to alight, too, to give the couple some privacy, but he didn't.

All the same, Kalpana came out a few minutes later humming a cheerful tune. 'Wasn't it a wonderful night? Magical?' she asked Sarojini, grabbing her friend's hand as they opened the door. 'I cannot imagine any one I could love more or better than Abhay. He is a man. A real man. So kind, so generous, so thoughtful!'

And as the girls parted company at the corridor all Sarojini could think of was how much she despised Abhay's friend Rakesh. How narrow-minded and bigoted he was! How people like him made their already precarious lives even more uncertain.

One never missed a summons from Mamaji, no matter what. Appointments with *araris* were rescheduled and alternative arrangements made for other *devadasi* to take over for performances. Sarojini dressed with care for the meeting, wearing a saree in a bright blue brocade. She had already washed and oiled her hair and now she twisted it into a bun, winding a garland of fresh jasmine around the heavy bundle of tresses. She dusted her face with some coloured talcum as well, using dark *kajal* to line her eyes.

'Mamaji is in the top room,' Poornima said. She was a girl of about seven who'd been living with Mamaji for about a month now. She was carrying a plate covered with a banana leaf. She'd been to the dining room to have lessons in dining etiquette. Desperately poor rural girls such as herself and Poornima needed to be taught everything when they arrived in Moona Mahal – from the proper use of lavatories to speaking properly and even how to eat!

'It is difficult to teach these children not to fall on their food after years of starvation but no man likes to see a woman stuff her face like a pig!' Mamaji would declare.

Mamaji spent the months of March and April and November and December being driven around Karnataka looking for newly dedicated young girls. She would assess them for charm, beauty, agility and their ability to sing or dance before offering for them.

'I would like to take all the girls . . . but there is only so much I can do,' she would sigh, looking at her lone gold bangle. Once upon a time, bejewelled bangles and bracelets had adorned her arms from wrist to elbow, but now Moona Mahal was mortgaged to the hilt and there was no one to continue the girls' education once she was gone, no one to teach them the beautiful rituals of the Hindu tradition.

Sarojini cautiously climbed the rickety stairs to the topmost room and stood nervously waiting to be noticed. It was a typical Mysorese retreat, a covered rooftop courtyard where the elderly *gharwali* lay on her divan, fanning herself gently, around her an oasis of potted plants – heliconias, anthuriums and even orchids.

The elderly lady cracked open an aged eye to look at Sarojini and sighed. She'd had such high hopes for this girl. 'Come, daughter, come,' she beckoned.

Sarojini knelt before her. 'Mamaji,' she murmured, bowing to touch the floor with her forehead.

'How are you child? I haven't spoken to you properly for months now . . . When was the last time? I think it may have been just after you left the rented room in Gayathripuram.'

'Even before that. When I was staying near the school . . .'

'Ahh . . . yes, that little back room you shared with Rekha . . . when was that?'

'Two years ago.'

'Hmmm . . .' the old lady said, sitting up a little higher on her divan. She gestured to the ornate tea things on the side, so Sarojini poured them both a cup. 'Now, child, surely it is time to find a long-term prospect and settle down. Have a child or two. It is perfectly permissible for us to have children, you know. Are you taking your *pippalyadi yoga* and *japa* concoction?'

'Every day, Mamaji. Two cups before breakfast.'

'You must stop. It may take you a month or two to conceive. A family is what you need. You will stop dancing in the next few years, let the younger girls take over.'

Sarojini was silent.

'So? Have you found a proper *arari*? A nice businessman or a wealthy lawyer? Someone who'll take pleasure in having a beautiful woman like you to bed, and perform for him privately?'

Sarojini shook her head sadly.

'And neither will you, if you continue to behave like a shrew . . . Oh, Sarojini,' Mamaji chastised. 'Did you think I would not hear about it?'

Sarojini sighed. She'd attended the Deepavali celebration at Kalpana's parents' house several days before the new moon. She would soon be leaving for her own home in the rural district of Uddur, where she would join her own family for the festival of lights celebrations during the darkest phase of the moon.

She had sat down to sing at Aunty Pimmi's request, after all the oil lamps had been lit in the courtyard. The sitar player and the tabla drummer sat next to her as Sarojini did a few vocal exercises. Rakesh had sauntered in not long after and sat down next to an elderly uncle. '*Devadasi* may sing and dance but they are prostitutes,' he had muttered, loud enough for Sarojini to hear him. 'Selling themselves to the highest bidder.'

Several people shifted uncomfortably.

'Poor girls being forced into it by their ignorant parents,' Rakesh said. 'Surely the police should put a stop to it. Lock up the priests! Lock up the *gharwalis*! Lock up the parents! That's what I say.'

There were strained smiles all around. Kalpana's father stood up and left the courtyard. It was Deepavali, and it would be bad luck to cause a commotion.

'Call themselves singers and dancers! What nonsense!' Rakesh continued.

That was when Sarojini opened her mouth and let the music soar over the people gathered. She sang effortlessly, from her heart. She sang of the joy of the celestial couple, Rama and Sita, as they returned to Ayodhya, where the city dwellers had lit simple clay lamps to guide their lord and lady back to their homeland.

Sarojini did not need to look at the people in the court-yard to know that they were captivated by her voice. Some sat still as stone, while others blinked away tears as she moved smoothly into her second, third, fourth and fifth raga. As she let out the final note into the air and closed her mouth, there was a moment of silence, then thunderous applause – but as the rapturous clapping and cheering died down, she heard Rakesh's voice again, louder now.

'I've heard they spread disease.'

'Not that you'd know. Only a frog would sleep with you!' she'd snapped.

No one had uttered a word of protest when she and Kalpana had been insulted, but now there was a hiss of outrage from the other guests. 'The cheek of the whore! Insulting a man from the Indian Army! Low caste slut!'

Mamaji had been right, all those years ago – it was a *deva-dasi*'s fate to be both adored and reviled.

For Aunty Pimmi's sake, Sarojini spent the rest of the evening making polite conversation, smiling and laughing as though nothing were wrong, but she was furious. She was careful to stay far away from Rakesh, not trusting herself to keep her temper. She stayed away from Mrs Vinaygam too, just to be sure.

Kalpana was quiet on their journey home that night in the old taxi that had been ordered for them. Sarojini thought she was going to apologise for the way Abhay's guest had treated her, but Kalpana had something else on her mind altogether.

'Abhay has been posted here to the barracks in Karnataka,' she said. 'He wants me to live with him in his quarters.'

'While he is posted here?'

'No . . . forever. He's been made lieutenant, so he says he has the money for us to start a family instead of having to depend on his parents. Have a home of our own.'

'What about his family? His sister? They will not be happy.'

'That is their problem, as Abhay said.'

'But what about your dancing? You are one of the best dancers in Mysore!' Sarojini protested weakly.

'I would have to give up dancing after the babies come anyway,' Kalpana whispered, turning to Sarojini with stars in her eyes. 'Oh, Saro, he wants to be with me. He wants to have children with me. He doesn't care that I may have had ten men or even a hundred men!'

'So, you will cut your beads, then?'

'Oh no! I will never cut my beads. We'll just live together as husband and wife without being married. The army does not ask for a marriage certificate to prove these things.'

'Kalpana, I am so happy for you,' Sarojini told her friend, but she couldn't help worrying. When Kalpana moved in with Abhay, Sarojini could not imagine being able to pay her rent. Her family in the country would suffer too. The money from her *pattam* had long ago been spent on food and farming equipment.

So when Mamaji broached the subject of an introduction, Sarojini knew she was in no position to refuse – particularly when Mamaji made it clear that this would be the last man she'd formally introduce her to. Several people had contacted her after the Pillay family's Deepavali celebration to express their displeasure at Sarojini's behaviour, and Mamaji's patience was not unlimited.

'I am not going to say that he is wealthy. He is not. He is a Sri Lankan Saliya and he works as one too. Weaving for a living,' Mamaji said. 'I am not even going to say that he'll be an attentive lover, Sarojini. He works in Kanchipuram most of the time, but he'll spend two weeks at a time here in Mysore. He has some friends here. And it is far away enough from both Sri Lanka and Tamil Nadu that he can be himself here.'

'What do you mean? Why can't he be himself around his own home?'

Mamaji looked uncomfortable. 'Sarojini, I could have introduced him to several girls. Aradhana is at a loose end as much as you are. But I thought of you. Not because you are more experienced than she is, but because you are a dancer. And a singer. You understand . . .'

'Understand what, Mamaji?' Sarojini asked.

'That there may be more to a person than meets the eye.' Mamaji reached forward for the little bell by the tea tray and rang it decisively.

There was a rustle by the stairs and Sarojini turned to look. No matter how desperate her circumstances, no matter what her situation, she could not help but feel a deep revulsion at the sight of the dwarf who limped towards her.

Sarojini usually said that she came from Gokak if anyone asked where she hailed from. But that was not strictly correct. Gokak was the nearest city of any repute to the hamlet where she was born. The hamlet itself was another ten miles or so from Hulloli, which was a bus ride north of Gokak. Sarojini wasn't even sure that the peasants had got around to giving it a name. She described it as the collection of huts near the grove of stunted coconut trees to the tuktuk drivers she collared in Hulloli to get her home.

Not that she had to haggle over fares that day. Her little money purse tucked carefully into her saree blouse was full to bursting with rupees. Mamaji had said that the *arari* wasn't wealthy, but he certainly was generous with what he had. In fact, Sarojini could hardly heft her battered old suitcase from the bus and the tuktuk driver had groaned audibly as he tucked it under her feet and revved the four-stroke engine. 'Your family will have a good Deepavali,' he'd muttered enviously.

And indeed they would. Sarojini had a new saree or lungi for each member of her family. She even had a kilo each of burfi, laddoo, kaai kani halwa and tins of gulab jamun. She had to hang onto the parcels for dear life as the three-wheel driver careered around the narrow rural roads, miraculously avoiding ditches, cows and goats with expertise. Her nieces and nephews would enjoy the celebrations that evening, their little fingers greedily stuffing food into their mouths until their bellies stuck out like balloons against their stick-thin frames, hunger sated for at least one night of the year.

Yet even the joy of seeing her brothers and mother so well looked after could not stem the squirmy feeling in the pit of Sarojini's stomach at the thought of being with Karuna again. It wasn't as if she'd never been with ugly or old men before, it was just . . . he was a dwarf. Once he took off his sandals, he barely reached her bust, his stubby arms and legs at odds with his stocky chest and large head.

'Please don't call me Sindhu,' he'd begged that afternoon. 'That's what my students call me.'

'But I thought you were a weaver, a Saliya saree maker, not a teacher,' she'd quizzed him, turning around to start unpinning her saree so she didn't have to look at him.

'I am, but I spend most of my time teaching these days,' Karuna whispered, coming close. 'Please, let me undress you,' he'd asked. It had taken all of Sarojini's willpower to not push the man and run away.

Yet what happened next surprised Sarojini into silence. He took her by the hand and led her to her bed, pushing her to sit down so that they were the same height before he kissed her. On the lips. Sarojini hadn't been kissed since the first time Harindra had taken her. And certainly not with such a desire to taste, to savour and even to understand.

He undressed her slowly, easing her skin-tight saree blouse from her arms, kissing the nipples of her breasts. 'It has been so long . . . so long . . .' he kept saying over and over again.

Perhaps for the first time, Sarojini met a man who looked to her pleasure before seeing to his own. His gnarled, callused hands were tender and soft as they caressed her breasts and touched her between her legs, massaging, teasing and arousing until he was rewarded with the wetness that had been his quest.

But as he entered her, she could not help but open her eyes and look at him, albeit briefly, and whatever arousal she'd felt disappeared instantly. He was a singularly unattractive man, his large head and prominent jaw so at odds with his small body. So Sarojini closed her eyes to think of a more attractive man, her mind riffling through a list of Hindi film stars – Amitabh Bachchan, Anil Kapoor and even Jeetendra – yet none would stay, their handsome faces and muscular bodies fleeting through her mind. It had never happened to her before, and she started to worry. Without this man, she would end up on the streets working as a common prostitute. She would have to feign pleasure to keep him interested.

Karuna paused a moment, as if to ask what was wrong. She lent forward to kiss him, only to have the image of Rakesh flood into her mind. Thinking about the boorish army Major sent an electric thrill through her, and she kissed the dwarf again, anger tingeing her arousal.

When it was all over and done, Karuna hadn't raced out of her narrow hard bed, as most *araris* did. He held her close, kissing her hair, stroking her back. Yet as she lay in his arms, or rather as he lay cuddled up in her arms like a puppy, she could not think of the man she was with but rather the man she'd never consent to be with no matter what!

She was still thinking of Rakesh now when the tuktuk driver pulled up by the grove of stunted coconut trees. It was well past the midday meal and everyone was still out working the fields. Sugar cane was the mainstay her brothers produced, along with *jowar* and betel leaves. In the distance she thought she could see her diminutive sisters-in-law with their children helping fertilise and tend to the crops. She went into the little mud hut, just three rooms with a communal eating space, and breathed in deeply the smells of home – the fragrance of the wood fire from the lean-to kitchen and the sickly sweet fragrance of the decaying bunch of bananas hanging on the verandah.

'You home,' her mother observed crisply coming through the back door. 'I no think you come till evening.'

'I was lucky, Amman,' Sarojini replied. It'd been a year since she'd last seen her mother, but the woman looked as if she'd aged another decade. 'I caught the first train at four am, and there was a bus to Hulloli just as I got off.'

'Hmmm . . .' her mother said as she bustled about helping Sarojini unpack, putting the food out and covering the plates with banana leaves. 'You help me cut betel leaves. I give betel leaves, he give me oil for tonight.'

'Why, Amman? Doesn't Uncle Uday buy oil for all of us?'

'Not this year,' her mother grunted in a voice that brooked no further discussion.

So Sarojini went to the well to wash away the dirt and grime of the road before changing into a simple village saree. Silks and brocades were of no use here. Simple sturdy cotton sarees that did not much show dirt were needed. As the sun set, Sarojini and her mother made their way to the general store some three miles away, two large baskets of betel leaves balanced on their heads.

'You come back, have you?' the shopkeeper asked Sarojini irritably, pointedly placing the oil for the lamps in a bottle on the ground. Sarojini gritted her teeth and ignored him. There was no need for that kind of behaviour. Her family were Shudras, not Dalits. He would not be obliged to undergo any ritual ablutions for having touched her or her mother. Notwithstanding, he'd been one of the many men who'd lined up to offer for her after her first *pattam*, only to be turned away by Mamaji. 'The *devadasi* are the property of the village,' the surly shopkeeper had complained. 'There are enough whores in Mysore already. Why take village girls?'

The two women then walked home at dusk, a magical time

for Sarojini as she breathed in the clean, fresh country air, but the peace lasted only until they arrived home.

'Eh! You use all de eggplant! All of dem?' Sarojini's mother shouted at her youngest daughter-in-law, a girl who was only seventeen but already a mother of three. 'Why you do dat? You waste so much! Your dowry all gone and still you waste money!' Then she scolded Sarojini's older sister-in-law. She'd dressed her two children a bit too early and they'd managed to smear dirt on themselves. 'Filthy children. Like deir mother!'

Sarojini's mother bustled about, getting everything ready for the Deepavali celebration, haranguing them all and barking orders. 'Too much batter for dosai! Not crisp enough! No, no, no! Don't use salt in the sambar. It be bad luck!'

She stopped only when the youngest sister-in-law's brother, a prosperous labourer who worked at the cement factory, rode up and gave her a few rupees to celebrate the festival. 'Here, *anujate*,' the earnest young man yet without a family said. 'Spend it on the children.' As soon as he'd left, Sarojini's mother took it. 'What you need money for? Your children no go to school!'

'What do you mean, the children aren't going to school?' Sarojini demanded. 'I send money for their books and uniforms!'

'They be needed out in the fields,' her brother said, not looking at her.

'But the government says that all children must go to school! It is the law!'

'Why?' her brother growled back. 'They make children go to school for what? So they work fields! Dey no need schools for dat!'

'No, but with an education they have a future! Maybe your boy will get a job in Gokak,' Sarojini pointed out. 'Look at Aravind!' she said. Aravind was their only cousin who was educated. 'He even went to college!'

There was silence.

'Aravind he die six months ago,' her sister-in-law said gently, speaking for the first time. 'He drink fertiliser and he die.'

'He gets education but no one give him job. Dey say if Shudras work in shop or office dey spend more time cleaning it!' her brother cried.

Sleep did not come easy to Sarojini that night despite her exhaustion. Aravind had been her childhood friend, playing with grasshoppers and crickets with her in the long grass. As she finally fell asleep to the snores of her brothers and their families, she could not be but thankful for her good fortune. Her life was not easy, but as a *devadasi* she had been freed from the daily oppressions of being a village wife and escaped the brutal stigmatisation of her caste.

'Who's there?' Sarojini asked in a terrified voice. 'I have a cricket bat,' she said, groping in the dark for the willow-wood bat Karuna had left by the entrance.

'But I can't bowl a cricket ball,' came the dry response from deep inside the narrow home.

'Oh, it's you!' Sarojini said, sagging beside the wall in relief. 'I thought you were coming tomorrow.'

'No, I was able to leave Kanchipuram early,' Karuna said, coming out of the little sitting room they'd fashioned out of Kalpana's old bedroom. 'Oh my dear girl!' he said, dragging her by the hand back into the sitting area and taking her heavy bags from her shoulders, 'you look exhausted!'

'Yes, ten performances in eight days,' Sarojini sighed as she collapsed on the little divan. It was festival season in Mysore and she'd been touring the countryside dancing and singing.

But now she had a home to come back to. A real home. Something she'd never really had since the age of eight. Karuna had taken over the lease to her annex completely once Kalpana had left and insisted on decorating it with coloured curtains, comfortable furniture and pot plants.

'You don't have to work so hard, you know,' he said that evening, gently slipping her sandals off her feet. 'I can quite happily support you.'

'But I love to dance, Karuna. And sing. It gives me something to do while you are ... you know ... not here.' It had been three months since the start of their liaison and things were going very well. 'And how's everything in Kanchipuram? Will you start teaching there as well?'

'Ah no, my dear, no. My home is in Sri Lanka. You must come with me one day. I only come here to help Raju with his business,' Karuna said, limping away to the kitchen.

'And what about his son? Little Laksman? Is he well?'

'A cheeky little monkey! You know what he said to me? He asked me how can I be a grown-up, when I am so small. Treats me like I am one of his friends because I am not much bigger than him,' Karuna replied with a laugh as he came back into the room with a cup of tea for her.

'When did you come in?'

'A little after midday. Your landlady let me in.'

'She likes you,' Sarojini teased him. 'She is always asking me when you are coming back. She was muttering about getting a new saree the other day. Maybe you can take her shopping again!'

'No, my dear, I don't think so. I haven't quite recovered from our last outing. When she asked me to accompany her to the train station, I had no idea that she wanted to have dinner with me, nor did I need her to tell me she had three lakhs in savings! She said it should be sufficient dowry for a man like me to take a widow like her.'

'She is in love with you.'

'But you are all the woman I need,' he replied.

Sarojini looked away. She was not quite sure how she felt about Karuna, despite his many kindnesses. After Kalpana had left, Karuna provided her not only with money to cover her rent but enough of an allowance for her to regularly send money back to her family in Gokak. Which she did, with a stern missive informing her family that her continued financial support was contingent on them sending her nieces and nephews to school.

'Come now,' Karuna said, interrupting her thoughts. 'You are tired. Let's go to bed.'

They did not sleep immediately, but lay in bed talking by the glow of a single dim light globe. Sarojini found Karuna's life in Sri Lanka fascinating and was always asking questions about it.

'So you are still living in Panadura? Despite the fact that the Sinhalese burnt the factory down? Don't you hate them?'

'I am Sinhalese. The actions of a few idiots don't represent the many.'

'But why did they burn the factory?'

'Anger, I suppose. Raju had run foul of some thugs nearby and they took their revenge. The old *chettie* died six months before the troubles in eighty-three and Gauri fled to England.'

'Did they ever find the men who burnt Raju?'

Sindhu looked at Sarojini and gave a sad, cynical smile. 'No. Justice is very selective in Sri Lanka. As it is here, in India. You need to be the right person at the right place and time. The thug who did it, Manoj Mendis, has become respectable now. He worked for a politician as a standover man for a while and then he took over a Tamil floor wax business after the riots. The owners ran for their lives and Manoj walked in and took over.'

'But Raju is happily married now to Shanthi in Kanchipuram,' Sarojini sighed. It all seemed like a fairytale to her – a tragic story, but with a beautiful and satisfying ending.

Karuna looked at her in the dark. 'I don't know that they are happily married, Sarojini. I know they both love Laksman very much and they'd do anything to keep him happy.'

'A child is a blessing, the greatest gift anyone could ever be given,' Sarojini replied. 'Did I tell you I saw Kalpana the other day?'

'How? I thought she was in Uddur?'

'Yes, well, the barracks are near Uddur . . .'

'They are living together? Did they get married?'

'Oh no! Kalpana would never cut her red beads. It would unravel the vow that keeps her father safe, and there are stories,

Karuna. Horrible stories of what has happened to women who walk away and cut their beads.'

Karuna looked sceptical. Sarojini knew he was a devotee of the goddess Saraswati, who seemed a great deal more benevolent a deity than Yellamma.

'You were in Uddur, then?' he asked.

'Yes, for a performance. She'd come with several other army wives to do a Hanuman pooja. She came to see me while I was changing. She's pregnant, Karuna. She and Abhay are over the moon. She only just found out. And because it's been several months since she's stopped being a *devadasi*, Abhay's sister cannot claim that the baby is a bastard!'

Karuna grinned. 'We must do something for her. I'll weave her a layette myself. Lots of clean white cotton cloth for nappies and I'll even show you how to embroider a few baby shirts.'

'You sew?'

'I am a master saree maker, my dear. I can weave, sew, embroider, dye cloth, make lace and design!'

He noticed then that Sarojini had fallen quiet, and even in the dim light he could see something was troubling her.

'What is it, my darling? What's the matter?'

'Oh, nothing. I was just thinking . . . Well, I was thinking it's a pity that . . .'

'That I am a dwarf . . .' Karuna said wryly.

'I didn't say that!' she cried. 'It's just that . . . it's just that . . .'

'It's just that you can never have with me what Kalpana has with Abhay. My dear girl, I can give you affection. I can give you money – as much as I have. I can give you comfort. But I cannot give you a child. I can never be a father. Being a dwarf is in my blood. I will never do that to another living soul, make them live the cursed existence I have,' he said softly in the darkness.

'I hear your new *arari* is a dwarf!' Rekha giggled. It was yet another Monday morning at Moona Mahal but the morning pooja had finished and the ladies were milling about enjoying cups of chai and munching on sweet ginger biscuits.

'My mother said she saw you down by the Devaraja markets. She wasn't quite sure if he was your son or your slave!' she continued nastily.

'Oh, the time of keeping dwarves as slaves has quite gone in the past . . .' the sharp-tongued Bengali Sujata added. 'Maybe he's her houseboy!'

Sarojini glanced across the floor to where Mamaji sat, surrounded by older *devadasi* who worked in the temples.

'It is the very opposite of needing to use a ladder, *nah*?' Rekha giggled.

'Is his *poolu* as small as him? Surely it'd be like not having anything down there at all!' Rekha said.

'So what exactly is he paying you for? If you ask me, you are on the winning side of this deal. You get his money and . . . he gets nothing!' Aradhana hooted with laughter.

'It's not like that!' Sarojini snapped and walked away.

She found herself making her way down to the little ornamental lake in the corner of the property. It'd been a favourite haunt of hers when she'd been a resident at Moona Mahal. This was where she used to go to dry her tears after brutal dance masters insisted she practise until her feet bled, or when her voice was hoarse from singing.

Life with Karuna was more difficult in some ways than Sarojini had expected. 'Come now,' she had insisted a few days ago. 'We have been stuck in this little annex for three days. Let's go out.'

'I am more than happy to go out, my dear,' he'd replied. 'But I thought we'd spent a great deal of time in the garden yesterday already!'

'I'm not talking about the garden, silly!' Sarojini had laughed, watching the little man pull on a singlet before donning his lungi. 'I am talking about the market! We need to get some fresh fruit and vegetables.'

'Why don't you go?' He gave her a hundred rupees. 'If you can, please get some fresh sugar cane. There is lime in the garden and I thought I could make you some fresh juice this afternoon.'

Sarojini had rolled her eyes. Under Karuna's care, the little garden outside the annex was looking lush and beautiful. In the week or so he spent with Sarojini each month, Karuna spent hours weeding, pruning and tending it. 'I know I am not beautiful, Saro,' he'd confessed. 'But I cannot survive without having beauty around me.'

'Come with me, Karuna,' she insisted. 'You are so much better at choosing fresh vegetables than I.'

She understood his reluctance as soon as they stepped out of the gate and onto the street. Sarojini had always attracted a fair amount of attention, even when she was dressed in a simple blue saree. Maybe it was her fair skin, so uncommon in the south of India, or even her natural dancer's grace; people were aware when she was in their midst. Eyes of both men and women would trail her through crowds. When she was followed by a dwarf, though, it all became too much. There were whispers and comments. Some people pointed. More than one street-side thug called out helpful hints about what a small man could do with Sarojini. Even the traders at the market had been rude, speaking only to her rather than the man who carried the purse.

'Six rupees for four banana leaves! That is insane!' Karuna had grumbled at a vendor.

'Away with you, you filthy dwarf!' the vendor had roared back.

It had confused Sarojini no end. She bargained more rigorously than Karuna ever did and knew that many of the sellers would usually be offended if deprived of the chance to haggle.

'What? What do you want? Are you here to cheat us?' more than one vendor had demanded as Sarojini and Karuna stopped to inspect their stalls. 'Those little fingers filch things faster than a monkey!'

They had abandoned the market after no more than a quarter of an hour, fleeing home without any fruit or vegetables to speak of. Sarojini had had to brave the night markets later to buy them a simple dinner of dosai and sambar.

'How do you do it?' she'd asked Karuna that evening.

'My dear, I have been a dwarf all my life. It is what I am used to.'

'But why do you put up with all the abuse?'

'Because I don't have a choice. I wanted something more for myself than being a village dwarf and working with other village dwarves. I found I had a gift for weaving early on and I was very lucky that old Mr Nair, Raju's father, took me on as an apprentice. I now have a life that is beyond anything most other dwarves reach. I have my own home. I can travel. But if I want to go out into the world, I have to put up with the abuse.'

Standing by the shore of the little lake, Sarojini heard the rustle of sarees in the distance, indicating that the *devadasi* had started to leave Moona Mahal. Like migratory birds, the brightly dressed women would be leaving in droves, going back to their little rooms and houses where they would start to ply their trade in the afternoon. She waited for a while to be sure they had all gone. She'd given in to a fit of tears thinking over the horrible things the other *devadasi* and the people in the market had said, and she didn't want anyone to know it.

The thing was that she didn't know what she thought about Karuna herself. Her feelings of revulsion had long ceased, but she knew that life with him would be difficult. She could not bear to see him reviled and abused. The only world she could share with Karuna would be the one in their home. Yet Sarojini was young enough and passionate enough to want more.

She stood and made her way through the gardens, so focused on escaping without being seen or teased by the other *devadasi* that she didn't notice the frail Mamaji until the old woman pounced on her, putting a firm hand on her shoulder as she was about to sneak out the back gate.

'Everybody has a right to love, child,' the old *gharwali* insisted with a fierce fire burning in her eyes. 'Everyone has the right to be touched. Everyone has the right to feel the life-making fire that is sex. Denying anyone that is what is wrong!'

'Close your eyes. And if you peek, you don't get it!' he commanded in a stern voice. Karuna had arrived unexpectedly early from Kanchipuram again that month. A whole three days in advance in fact. And he'd brought something for her.

'I am not a child!' Sarojini protested, poking out a pink tongue.

'Oh, really? How have you managed to damage that heliconia plant, then? And don't get me started on the state of your kitchen. I have only been away a fortnight, and look at it!'

'All right! All right! I'll close my eyes,' Sarojini grumbled. 'What now?'

'Hold out your hands . . .'

'No snakes?' Sarojini queried, quickly opening her eyes again.

'My dear, would I give you any snakes?'

'My cousin Aravind used to always do that.'

'The one who died?'

'Yes . . . He'd tell me to close my eyes and stick out my hands and he'd put baby king cobras, green lizards and spiders on them! My uncle said it was his destiny to become a snake-charmer!'

'So why did he go to school, then?'

'With the money they got from my *pattam* they thought that he could finish college. But my uncle hadn't thought of him not being able to find a job. It's such a pity – if only he'd become a snake-charmer, he'd still be alive today.'

'If *onlys* were flowers, the world would be filled with rose petals,' Karuna replied sadly. 'Come now, close your eyes and hold out your hands.'

Sarojini never expected to feel what she did next. It was something soft, small and mewling. 'Oh! Oh!' she cried, lifting the little kitten to her neck to caress it. It was grey with the brightest green eyes.

'Laksman's cat gave birth to yet another set of kittens. Shanthi was threatening to drown the whole lot of them, so I took one for you and gave the rest away to the workers at the mill,' Karuna said dryly. 'This way you'll have some companionship while I am not here. Are you sure you don't want your mother to come live with you for a little while? I am more than happy to pay for her rail ticket and the additional expenses.'

'No, Karuna. She is best on the farm, although I am sure my sisters-in-law would appreciate the holiday from her company.'

'Is she a traditional Indian mother-in-law?'

'I suppose. She doesn't know how to be anything else. She was tortured by her mother-in-law, so it is her turn now to torture her daughters-in-law. Every generation of wives, waiting for the husband's mother to die.'

'And the same applies for sons-in-law. I sometimes struggle to understand how Raju puts up with Shanthi's mother.'

'Why?' Sarojini asked curiously, following Karuna into the kitchen. She helped him with the ingredients for his special potato dish, peeling the potatoes, chopping the onions and shredding the curry leaves. The little spicy balls of boiled potato dunked in batter and deep-fried were simply divine with a yoghurt dipping sauce.

'She blames him for not giving her a blood grandchild. Not that either Raju or Shanthi could love Laksman one jot more if he were their own flesh and blood, but he is not their real child.'

'Is Raju incapable of fathering a child?'

Karuna sighed and looked at Sarojini as he mixed the spices. 'I trust you will never repeat this, my dear. Not to anyone. And especially not to Raju and Shanthi, should you meet them someday. I haven't told anyone – not even Gauri. But Raju did father a child with his first wife, Nila. A little girl. I only found out very recently.'

'But you told me Nila died in a crash on her way to the hill country,' Sarojini protested.

'That is what we were led to believe when Raju tried to find her, but I went to a ball up in the high country not long ago. There I met an old lady . . .'

'It's such a pity that girl who used to work for you is in the lunatic asylum in Nuwara Eliya,' the old lady had said sadly to the weaving master. 'I gave *dhanay* there and I saw her. She was such a kind girl!'

'Which girl?' Karuna had asked curiously.

'I think her name was Seela . . . no . . . could it be Anjula . . . oh, something ending with *la*. Sold me five sarees. Not very pretty, though. Dumpy like an oil cake,' the old lady said.

Karuna's heart had jumped to his throat. 'Are you sure? Are you sure she used to work for us?'

'Of course I am sure, man! I may be old but I am not senile!' the woman had huffed. 'I know the very girl who sold me five sarees and I know it was her I saw tethered to the wall in the asylum.'

'I was sure she meant Nila,' Karuna told Sarojini, 'so I went up to the asylum the very next day to have a look. Someone had taken her out just three days previously. But I was able to get most of the story from the matron who'd cared for her—'

He was cut off by a sharp rap at the door. It was already well into the evening and too late for visitors.

'Who is it?' Karuna called out, automatically standing in front of Sarojini.

'Abhay,' came the voice beyond the door.

'What? What is it, *ana*?' Sarojini demanded, hurrying to open it.

'Saro!' the army captain cried joyfully. 'I have a son!'

Pranay was an easy kitten – a delightful bundle of fur who gave no trouble and learned to do his business outside within days. And he was a very placid cat, too, happy to go into his basket and be carted all the way to Uddur a couple of times week so that Sarojini could help Kalpana with the baby.

Abhay had gone against his parent's wishes in starting a relationship with Kalpana, so he could not, as custom would dictate, demand that his mother come and help Kalpana with the baby.

Aunty Pimmi also had responsibilities. Kalpana's older brother's wife had given birth to a child several days before Kalpana and she was needed at home to help with that baby. 'If I could split myself in half and be in two places at the same time, I would!' she cried.

'Don't worry, Aunty. Kalpana has another family she can rely on,' Sarojini had said calmly before getting in touch with her *devadasi* sisters. When Sarojini had to go into town for dances or other performances, Aradhana, Rekha or even Sujata would come. And when Karuna came into town, he would stay at a little bedsit just outside the army base, so that Sarojini could visit him surreptitiously at night.

'This is so unusual for me! I never have to sneak to see a man. A man usually has to sneak around to see me!' Sarojini giggled.

'I usually don't have to sneak,' Karuna confessed. 'No one

sees beyond the fact that I am a dwarf to have any interest in what I do!'

But the sneaking around and subterfuge were essential on the army base. Kalpana was petrified that if anyone found out she'd been a *devadasi*, not only would she and her baby be ostracised but any hopes Abhay had of progressing in his army career would be cut off.

Abhay did not seem to agree with her. 'The Indian army is well used to scandal,' he chided. 'Everyone knows the brigadier sleeps with anyone who is willing – and there was even a book running on whether Major Bagum's third son is actually his or the child of the tuktuk driver who works at the market!'

'All the same, it is what it is,' Sarojini replied, taking care to hide the red beads on her *thali*. 'It's better to be safe than sorry.'

'You are sounding more and more like Mamaji, you know!' Kalpana told her playfully. 'Turn the other cheek! Don't fight! Don't make trouble! Are you planning on taking over from her to become the *gharwali* of Moona Mahal?'

They were careful not to discuss this subject in front of Major Rakesh, who often visited to see Abhay and the new baby. Sarojini had not been pleased to see him, and had wondered at first if she could remain in the cramped little house in his company, but he had been surprisingly pleasant, even courteous, and had not said anything to give her offence. The turnaround was puzzling, but she could not complain. He had been a great help while Kalpana had been in hospital, ferrying people around in his army jeep.

He'd also protected Kalpana, always in attendance when the more virulently gossipy army wives chose to drop in and visit the newcomer.

'So, why isn't Captain Promod's family here helping? Especially since they live right here in Mysore,' Sonia Bishwari had observed icily.

'It's just that my sister-in-law is busy as a teacher and Abhay's mother is really busy too helping her,' Kalpana hedged.

'But it is highly inappropriate! It's as if his parents did not approve of you!'

Rakesh stepped in. 'Mrs Bishwari . . . how is the major doing these days? Still doing a great deal of travel to Hyderabad to visit his sick mother?'

Even now Sarojini felt grateful to him for intervening to save her friend. She thought of it again as she stood in the kitchen of the little army house and took out a large steel bowl, starting to put together the ingredients for Mysore *pak*. That weekend, Kalpana and Abhay's little baby boy would leave the house for the first time to visit the temple and be given his name. Sarojini was making food and sweets for the celebration that followed.

She took out besan flour, jaggery, milk powder, ghee and semolina, and became so caught up in her task – mixing the ingredients, kneading the dough, spreading it with coconut oil and evening it out with a banana leaf – that she didn't hear Rakesh come in, and when he placed a few dishes in the bucket for washing she almost jumped out of her skin.

'Oh! What are you doing here?'

Rakesh pointed to the plates in the bucket, then looked at the small trays of food she had already made, unimpressed. 'Abhay is a rich man,' he said. 'You can afford to make more sweets for the baby's first going out ceremony than just some Mysore pak and a few gulab jamun. The family will expect more.'

'There aren't many coming,' Sarojini told him. 'Just Kalpana's mother, father and brothers. Her uncles and aunts have declined the invitation.'

'His family aren't coming?'

'Of course not. His sister sent a note asking Abhay to check that the baby had three birthmarks on his back. Apparently all baby boys born into their family have them.'

Rakesh snorted in frustration. 'She is a nasty one. Always reminds me of a *banderi*, hissing and spitting! This is a big occasion. It is important that as many people come to celebrate the little one's birth as possible!'

Sarojini shrugged. What could she do?

'And I suppose your *devadasi* sisters aren't coming either. They won't celebrate the birth of a male child, will they!' Rakesh sneered.

Sarojini looked up curiously at him. Yes, the *devadasi* never celebrated the birth of a male child. They were perhaps the only people in India who did not light firecrackers and boil fresh cow's milk at the birth of a boy. Yet there was much fanfare and joy at the birth of a girl. There were celebrations. There were ceremonies. There were official announcements and gifts for the girl's mother. No *devadasi* girl child was ever drowned in a bucket or fed to the crocodiles.

'You know a lot about the sisterhood for an army major,' Sarojini countered, looking Rakesh in the eye.

'That is probably because my *devadasi* lineage spans five generations. You were made one, but I was born one. My mother was a *devadasi*.'

Sarojini saw Kalpana and Abhay surrounded by a veritable bevy of well-wishers before she darted out through the side door of the mess hall. What had been planned as a small celebration had taken on a life of its own. It was supposed to have been a simple get-together for the dozen or so people coming to the temple, but now it was a full-scale social event for everyone who was anyone at the army base. Officers in full military regalia were throwing back tumblers of Red Label Johnnie Walker whisky, while their wives, bedecked in a maharajah's fortune in gold, passed little Keshto around like a pudding.

Yes, even Sarojini had to concede that Rakesh was not as mean-spirited as she'd thought him to be. He had organised the function and paid for the party from his own pocket. 'Keshto is the closest thing I have to a nephew! If I don't spend for him, who will? And this little boy has all the signs of becoming a great major general! Oh yes you do! Oh yes you do,' he'd cooed at the little boy.

Kalpana's family were also beaming with joy. It was clear that Kalpana was the very epitome of a well-raised, sophisticated and dutiful army wife, smiling sweetly at everyone and ensuring that no one was left out of the conversation, or without a drink. She was finally being treated with the respect and adoration that she'd been born to.

The other *devadasi* in attendance blended in. They did not stand out from the crowd of richly dressed army wives. Hovering in the background, they helped Kalpana with the food and behaved like sisters to their dear friend.

But where was Karuna, Sarojini wondered, looking anxiously around the room. She'd sent him a message that the celebration had shifted to the mess hall. She'd even told Kalpana's house servant to pass the message on. Maybe Karuna hadn't received it, she worried, and thought it best to walk down to the guardhouse and leave another message there.

'Where are you going?' Rakesh demanded as Sarojini darted out of the mess hall. 'And in this heat?

'To leave a message for my *arari* down by the guardhouse,' she replied, looking up at the tall Captain and squinting against the sunlight. In his army regimentals, Sarojini had to admit that he cut a dashing figure. His features were lean and harsh and the broad shoulders that topped his muscular frame made him a favourite among the flirtier army wives.

'The dwarf? Is he coming?'

Sarojini nodded.

'Come, I'll take you down to the guardhouse. You'll get a heat stroke in this sun if you walk down,' he insisted, pulling out the keys to his jeep.

Down at the guardhouse, Rakesh instructed the military policeman to contact him directly at the mess hall when Karuna appeared, and gave the specific instruction that the man should be transported to the mess hall directly by one of the many army vehicles nearby.

When they returned to the mess hall, all the car parks had been taken. 'Of course, the officers who were on duty last night will have just arrived,' Rakesh cursed under his breath. He kept driving further and further away in search of a place to park. In the end they found a spot by a clump of trees almost as far away from the mess hall as the guardhouse.

They walked in silence for a bit before curiosity overcame Sarojini. 'Is your mother still alive?'

'No. She died of syphilis when I was about twelve.'

'Oh. Who looked after you?'

'I lived in and out of a few orphanages. I always did well at school, so I chose to join the army when I was seventeen and entered Dehradun,' he replied flatly. 'Because my father was a highborn Kshatriya, the recruiting officer did not bother asking me who my mother was.'

'Your father didn't support you? He didn't see you as a child?'

'No. He had a wife and two children. But he came with me to my army recruitment interview. Which was really a lot more than I could have asked for.'

'Was she a dancer?' Sarojini asked. 'Your mother?'

'She was the greatest Odissi dancer in Orissa. Her body was more fluid than the Mahanadi that flowed through Cuttack. Looking at her *tribhanga* pose you'd think you were in front of the goddess herself.'

'Ah, Sarojini, there you are!' Karuna called from the door of the mess hall. He'd just arrived, bouncing happily along in an army jeep. 'I was detained in Kanchipuram, my dear. I am so sorry for being late.'

The rest of the afternoon passed along in a blur. Apart from helping Kalpana look after her guests, Sarojini was called upon by Aunty Pimmi to sing. 'Come, child, come. Please sing us a song or two.'

And she did, starting with a simple lullaby telling Keshto that no one would love him more than his own mother. That his parents would lay their lives down for him. That he was more important to them than India, than God and the very universe. That he was their universe now. Sarojini sang with no accompaniment. There was no sitar nor tabla. She didn't need it. Sarojini sang from her heart and every note was pure and perfect.

She sang one more song, then two. The guests had asked for more and more, and would not let her stop. By the time she'd finished, she'd sung for an hour and a half straight.

'You are wonderful,' Karuna whispered to her, coming close. 'You are a delight to see and a treasure to possess.'

Everyone came up to congratulate her on her performance.

'We have Captain Rakesh to thank for this. He insisted that the entire officer corps come to this event. And had we been relaxing in our bungalows as we normally do on a Sunday, we would never have heard your beautiful voice,' the brigadier of the base boomed, wiping tears from his eyes. 'My mother used to sing me that lullaby. There is indeed no greater love than that of a mother!'

The exodus started not long after. People made sure to take leave of both the family and Sarojini as they left, and Karuna joined the throng. 'My dear Saro, I am afraid I have to go back to Kanchipuram,' he explained.

'But you just got here!' Sarojini protested.

'Yes, but Raju is having problems and I must help him. He has started a saree mill like the one he had in Sri Lanka and the other saree merchants are up in arms that he is paying Saliyas too much for their work.'

'But Saliyas are some of the poorest people. Not much better off than us Shudras!'

'Exactly, my dear, exactly! A man may spend a lifetime weaving silk but never be able to afford to give his wife a silk saree,' he said. 'But now I really must go.' Handing over a gift to Abhay and Kalpana, he left, rushing back into Mysore to catch the late train east.

Sarojini started to help Aunty Pimmi tidy up, placing the bottles of whisky in a large bin. 'Aunty Pimmi,' Sarojini said, noting the lines of exhaustion on the older lady's face, 'why don't you take Uncle Rai home. I can finish up. I am spending the night here with Kalpana.'

'Are you sure, child? You have helped us a great deal already today.'

'I am quite sure, Aunty Pimmi. Please go. It is a long drive back to Mysore and you have more grandchildren to tend to at home.'

'Thank you, my dear, thank you,' she said, but before she left she pressed into Sarojini's hand two hundred rupees that Sarojini tried desperately to return.

'I sang because I wanted to sing for Keshto,' she insisted.

'No, dear, you take it. I understand how you girls need to earn your money. If you save enough money from your singing and dancing, you can finally leave that awful dwarf!'

'But he's not awful!' Sarojini cried.

'Oh, my dear, he is. He truly is!' Aunty Pimmi insisted, adding another twenty rupees as she left. 'Save your money and start a little business. Become a singing teacher.'

'She does not understand, does she,' Rakesh observed, coming in as Aunty Pimmi went out. He'd been stacking some chairs away in a little anteroom and had probably overheard the whole conversation.

'Understand what?'

'That you love being a *devadasi*,' Rakesh said bitterly. He had been so kind and considerate that evening that it had been almost enough to make her change her mind about him, but it seemed she had been right after all.

'I am not your mother!' she said. 'Don't take your anger out on me!'

'What are you talking about?'

'Your hatred of your mother has nothing to do with me, even if I am a *devadasi* too.'

'You silly little fool! I love you!' Rakesh declared. 'Abhay spent his entire time in Kashmir looking at that stupid folded photo of Kalpana. Sitting across from him, I spent the entire time looking at you! I fell in love with you and came to Mysore for you, Sarojini. No one but you!'

'Never talk to him about work,' the wife of the lieutenant colonel advised. Although she was a busy mother of three, Mrs Meena Singh was the official hostess to all the new incoming officers' wives at the barracks, serving tea and dispensing advice and vicious gossip all in the same breath.

'So what do you and your husband talk about?' Sunila, the wife of an up-and-coming captain, asked.

'After twelve years of marriage? We talk about how we are going to pay the bills!' Meena Singh laughed. 'Enjoy your newlywed days. They don't last for long. Especially not in the army!' She turned to Sarojini. 'So, young lady, how are you settling in?'

'It's a bit cold,' Sarojini confessed with a shiver. It had been several months since she and Rakesh moved to Lucknow, yet this was only the second or third officers' wives' function she'd attended.

'You'll get used to it – and by the time you get used to it, it'll be time to move again!' the lady laughed. 'We were once stationed in Rajasthan, and I had just got the hang of sweeping the floors to get the sand out of the house when we were moved to Kashmir! From the deserts to the snow!'

Sarojini smiled, helping herself to a sweet biscuit. She was happy. Never in her wildest dreams could she have imagined her life would have turned out like this. Hot on the heels of Rakesh's surprise declaration of love had come his transfer to Lucknow.

'Come with me,' he'd pleaded. 'We'll start our life in a new city. New city. New life.'

'But my family – how will I support my family if I don't work?'

'Silly girl! I'll support them, of course! I don't have any family of my own so it would be my pleasure to share what I have with them. We won't be any poorer for giving them a thousand rupees a month.'

So they had gone to Gokak on their way to Lucknow, catching the train there and spending a few hours with Sarojini's awestruck family. They had never seen an army man and Rakesh had all the debonair charm of a Bollywood film star as he came in and cheerily handed over gifts of money and food.

But now it was Sarojini who felt uncomfortable, at the little afternoon get-together of army wives. Not because she was less well dressed than the others, less educated than them or even because she was a lower caste than them, but because she had to constantly bite her tongue.

As at any gathering of young newly married women, the conversation invariably turned towards their husbands.

There was Babitha only a girl of eighteen, who was married to a major twice her age and desolate with homesickness.

'Army wives just have to bear up!' Meena Singh told her, in a voice not too dissimilar to that of a drill sergeant. 'Our husbands put their lives at risk for our Mother India, and all you can do is cry! Shame on you, girl!'

All Sarojini wanted to do was to enclose the young girl in her arms and comfort her, to tell her that the pain would subside soon, that she would find new friends and interests, and if nothing else, having a family of her own would somehow cure the ache.

Then there was Sukitha, who was a mess after her third miscarriage in as many months. 'Just keep trying!' the older lady advised. 'Bear up and your next pregnancy will be fine!'

Sarojini had had to take a rather large sip of her scalding tea to stop herself from blurting out that perhaps it were best if the young woman took a *pippalyadi yoga* and *japa* concoction for a few months before trying again. To let her body recover.

She had almost had to leave the room and make excuses for an early exit when Nagina, a young Punjabi girl, confessed that she was finding marital relations with her husband terribly painful and unpleasant.

'It is not supposed to be pleasant!' Meena snapped. 'It is supposed to be for making children and nothing more!'

'So you don't enjoy it either?' Nagina asked.

Sarojini looked around and there was a sea of nodding faces.

'How can anyone enjoy anything so painful? It is disgusting!' Babitha cried. 'And he has to do it every night. Every night without fail. Even if I am feeling sick he does it!'

'He even does it when I have my period,' Nagina confessed. 'While I am bleeding and in pain.'

'Bear up, girls! Bear up!' Meena commanded, unpinning her saree fall and flinging it determinedly over her shoulder. 'I haven't had a break from it in fifteen years, but you don't hear me complaining. We are army wives. We are the backbone of India's defence force. We can put up with a little discomfort for the protection of India.'

Sarojini wanted to tell them they were wrong. So wrong. How could these girls take advice from a woman who'd only ever slept with one man?

Marital relations did not have to be something to be 'put up' with. As a *devadasi* Sarojini had learned to enjoy sex. Mamaji had taken great pains to instil in them that what happened between a man and a woman was supposed to be pleasurable.

'A woman who has never felt joy in bed is a half-woman. She knows not what it is to feel loved. Truly loved,' Mamaji had insisted. 'Sex is a high blessing, child. It is the greatest ecstacy your body can feel.'

Still, as Sarojini walked along the busy army laneway to the little quarters that she and Rakesh shared, she could not help but be thankful. Thankful for never having to fear poverty again. For not having to work for a living, not dancing until her feet and back hurt and certainly not singing until her throat was sore.

Sarojini let herself into her little house and sat in silence in the evening light for a moment. Darkness came earlier to Lucknow than it did to Mysore. It was just gone five in the afternoon, but she could already hear the crows crying as they finished the last of their daylight meal and headed to the hills. Pranay the cat was softly snoring in the corner.

They lived in one of a string of prefabricated huts that offered little privacy. Nagina had not needed to reveal that she had intercourse with her husband every night. Living two doors down, Rakesh and Sarojini heard the young girl's protests, and her husband shouting and swearing as he forced himself on her. There were no plants or pretty wall hangings to cover the bare walls and muffle the noise, either. Rakesh was a military man and had no time for such frippery. 'Shouldn't we save that money and send it to your family? And what's the point, we'll be moving soon to somewhere else anyway.'

But Sarojini could not or would not dwell on the uncomfortable feeling in her heart. She had achieved the dream. She wasn't quite sure if she was in love with Rakesh, but he was in love with her. And for someone who had never experienced love, that was enough.

Rakesh liked his food plain. 'I am a simple man,' he insisted. 'Just plain roti and a single curry. No need to waste money on too many vegetables. Just put the vegetables in with the meat and make a mulligatawny out of it. We need to save money to send to your family,' he'd remind her.

Not that Sarojini ate much anyway. She only had the idali or rice left over from dinner for breakfast, made do with tea at lunch and shared something with Rakesh at dinner. 'Careful, darling, you aren't dancing anymore,' Rakesh advised. 'I see so many new army wives stack it on. All you girls ever do is go from house to house having tea parties!'

Sarojini had not said anything. Rakesh had just come back from doing a gruelling week-long patrol along the Nepalese border, finding Maoist rebels and ousting them. She could see from his face that he was exhausted. He'd come home and fallen asleep in his fatigues for six hours before waking up just a few minutes before.

'So, are you excited about the Brigadier's ball?' Rakesh asked, sitting down heavily. He looked expectantly towards the kitchen, so Sarojini jumped up to make him a cup of chai.

'Yes, all the wives are going into town next week to buy sarees and shoes!' she called from the kitchen. 'I'm rather looking forward to it. I thought that maybe I could go in and visit the Hanuman temple in Aliganj and do a pooja for you before you go out on your next patrol.'

She came back and handed him his chai.

'Why would you do that?' Rakesh grumped, taking a deep sip. 'Too much sugar,' he said, pushing it back into Sarojini's hand. 'I used to live on a kilo of sugar for six months!'

'What do you mean, why? I want you to be protected by the Lord Hanuman, that's why!'

'Little girl, why do I need Lord Hanuman when I have my machine gun?'

'But don't all the other wives do poojas? The army wives in Mysore certainly did.'

'Not all. Only silly superstitious ones! You need to seek out the educated ones. The ones who have been to college. Make friends with them. They certainly don't go to temple and do poojas for every little thing. And you making friends with the right wives is very important to me. They can help me along in my career.'

'Of course, darling,' Sarojini agreed. 'That is why I have been going to the afternoon teas and lunches.'

'If you didn't do the teas and lunches, you'd have nothing else to do anyway,' Rakesh said.

'Actually, Rakesh, I have been thinking about that . . . would you mind terribly if I wanted to do something more productive with my time?'

'Like what? You aren't educated. Your *gharwali* didn't send you to school, did she?'

'No, but she ensured we all were taught to read and write, and that we were well educated in mathematics and science, geography, history and politics.'

'So you are an educated woman now, are you?' Rakesh mocked.

'Rakesh, that is not what I said and you know it,' Sarojini protested. 'But I was thinking I would like to teach.'

'Teach what, exactly? Do you want to teach the middle-class army wives how to be a *devadasi*?'

Sarojini looked away to hide her irritation. Rakesh wasn't the most sensitive of men. Especially not after a long patrol.

'Come here,' he said softly. 'I know what you can teach. You can teach me how to fuck you like the other day. I could not stop thinking about it. The whole time I was out trying to catch rebels, all I could think about was fucking you.'

She could not deny him. Within minutes, her saree had come off and before long Rakesh was ramming her against the hard cement walls, his hand over her mouth to muffle her groans of pleasure, her legs wrapped around his lean waist and hips.

'I never understood why some men desire virgins,' he said in her ear. 'Women like you are much better. You know how to pleasure a man. You know how it is done.'

Afterwards, they lay on the bed, slightly apart. Rakesh insisted on lying flat on his back to work out some of the kinks in his spine after days on patrol. Not that Sarojini really minded – he hadn't had time to have a proper shower yet.

'Rakesh, I was thinking that I could teach some of the children – the girls – how to sing and dance,' Sarojini said softly.

'Why?'

'Because it'll give me something to do while you are out on patrol.'

'Have you thought of how you'd answer if someone wanted to know how you learned to dance? Everybody knows that the best dancers are *devadasi*. No. It is best if you do nothing,' Rakesh insisted.

Sarojini had to blink away tears. 'So what would you like me to do?' she asked.

'Do as the other wives do. Go to each other's house and have tea! Aren't you girls supposed to be organising this ball at the moment?'

Lucknow was a very different city to Mysore. The lush, open tropical gardens so prevalent in Karnataka were not at all like the more formal Moghul-styled parks of Uttar Pradesh. Even the Hindu temples were more sedate than their southern counterparts – there were no towering pyramids of statuettes, nor did the ceremonies have the same high drama – but the difference could not have been more pronounced than in the saree bazaars, Sarojini thought, as she was ushered into a large showroom with the other army wives.

In the south, the bazaars were a riotous melee of colours, smells and sounds, as women jostled to find the best sarees, fighting for the attention of the harangued sales people and haggling for the best price. It was nothing at all like this stiff and very formal ceremony. Here they were asked to sit down on large woven mats and offered cups of tea and biscuits before an array of sarees was paraded in front of them and then spread on the floor for inspection. There was no pushing, no shoving and certainly no fighting.

Mindful of Rakesh's instructions, Sarojini did not put herself forward, sitting in the corner and observing it all from a distance. She was terrified of speaking at all. 'One wrong move and we are both done for,' Rakesh had said. 'Imagine if they found out what you did?'

So the shopping expedition started very slowly. No one wanted to hazard an opinion or make a suggestion. Fresh out of college or school, none of them had had the time to develop their taste and had relied on their mothers or aunts to buy their sarees for them.

'What do you think?' Mrs Meena Singh asked finally, holding up a saree of a particularly heavy weave that would make her look like a chicken trussed up to go into a tandoor oven. 'Do you think this suits me?'

'What about this?' Babitha asked, pointing out a saree so gossamer it would be the scandal of the evening.

'I think I'll get this,' Nagina said, holding up a tasselled orange saree more suited to a grandmother than a young woman.

Sarojini could no longer hold her tongue. She turned to Meena Singh and smiled. 'Don't you think a lighter brocade would be more suitable?' she asked, careful to keep her tone light.

'Why do you say that?' Meena demanded.

'Because it would suit your frame better. A light brocade will still hold you in while not bulking you out,' Sarojini explained. She'd been taught to dress by some of the most elegantly turned-out women in India. Women who took pride in their attractiveness and knew how to be beautiful.

'And I think this blue saree best suits you, Babitha,' she said, whisking the sheer gossamer away and pulling out a Benares silk instead. 'The deep blue will bring your eyes out. And Nagina, it's best you steer clear of orange. The only women who can wear orange well are those who've just been cured of TB!'

'Oh, you know so much about sarees!' Babitha cried. 'It must be wonderful to be married so late. At least you've had time to figure out what you like and don't like!'

Sarojini could not help but smile. Yes, at twenty-four, she was the oldest of the new army wives. That smile burst a little dam within Sarojini, and she decided to take charge. 'Come now, girls, let's try these sarees. It's pointless seeing them on the floor if you don't know how they'll drape on your body.'

'Here?' Babitha squeaked.

'Yes, here. Nothing immodest. Just stand up and we'll see how the sarees will drape on you. Just over what you are wearing now.'

Then Sarojini got to work.

'Drape your saree like this,' she instructed more than one lady. 'A saree is supposed to shape you and hold you. You make your saree – not the other way around!'

'You are not old enough to wear that purple saree. Twenty years from now, yes. But not now!' she commanded another.

Sarojini had the confidence that came from wearing sarees from a very young age. She hadn't had to wait till she had married or finished college to shift from dress to saree.

'Now for you, Mrs Sunila – let's find a saree for you,' Sarojini said. Sunila was a quiet girl from Calcutta, and like many people from the east of India, she had a complexion and facial features that were almost oriental. Sharp eyes and a golden hue to her skin. She was also tall and willowy, with the frame and build of the Moghuls who'd invaded India many centuries previously – which made it very difficult to find the right saree for her.

'What about this one?' the nawab suggested, coming forward. He'd really enjoyed having the army wives in his store and the young lady from Karnataka had style and flair. He held out a saree made of chiffon, deep red at the top and fading away to a pale pink at the hem. Its beauty came not from any embellishment, but from this subtle gradation of colour alone. It was unusual and dramatic, the perfect foil for the girl from Calcutta.

'Oh, it is perfect! Perfect!' Sarojini cried, leaning forward to look at it, but as she did so something even more interesting caught her eye. 'What is that?' she asked, pointing to a saree on a model in the shop window that had been pushed aside to make way for the latest fashions.

'Oh that!' the nawab said. 'I bought that saree from a young pregnant woman some years ago. She needed money to enter an ashram somewhere in Dehradun. I don't know what came over me, but I gave her 75,000 rupees for it.'

There was gasp of horror. No one had heard of anyone paying that much for a single saree!

The nawab brought the saree out eagerly and unfolded it on the floor for his awestruck audience. He'd long since relinquished the dream of ever selling it – no one could afford it. But he still enjoyed showing the saree to his customers. 'It is a bride's saree. But it is neither gold nor white. The silk is so pure I have never seen anything like it. See, those are real sapphires along the hem, and gold thread makes up the peacock's feathers!'

Sarojini reached out an admiring hand and stroked the silk. She owned many fine sarees, but this silk was softer and more supple than any she had ever known.

'She was with my father for only two years. She thought she had found a wealthier protector and left my father for him,' Rakesh confessed.

They were seated on a bench in the little park behind the army barracks where there was a short cut into town. A few officers rushed past, waving cheerily to them, off to get the evening meal or a few groceries.

'When did she get syphilis?'

'When I was about ten. We didn't have money for medication, so in about a year she became quite unwell. It was horrible, Saro – her face and body were covered with blisters. I had to wash her and clean her for months . . .'

Sarojini looked away in sadness. What could she say? Sickness and disease were realities for *devadasi*, just as bullets were for soldiers.

Several more officers went rushing by into town. It was Friday, and clear that their wives didn't want to cook the evening meal after a long week. Everybody would be enjoying korma and *parathas* tonight.

'So what have you been doing with yourself?' Rakesh asked, stretching back.

'Nothing much – just doing some gardening and keeping the place tidy.'

'Yes, the lieutenant colonel said that he'd noticed the flowers in our front yard. Where did you get those from?'

'I found the plants thrown out in town.'

'You're scavenging in town now? What if you were seen?'

'No, Rakesh, I wasn't scavenging in town. I went into town and the flower seller was throwing the old plants out, so I took them, cared for them and now they are healthy plants!' Sarojini replied crossly.

'Hmmm . . .'Rakesh grunted. 'Why did you go into town?'

'To buy vegetables and groceries.'

'Why can't you make do with the vegetables and groceries at the army store?'

'Because it is twice as expensive as what I can find outside.'

'But you know I don't like you going into town. It's full of dacoits and you could get hurt.'

'Rakesh, I lived in Mysore all my life. I certainly did not have a chaperone!'

'Then go out with another army wife!'

'But Rakesh!'

'Next time you go into town, do so with one of the senior army wives.'

They were just standing up to return home when they happened to see Lieutenant Colonel Singh coming back from town.

'Off for a walk with your missus are you, Major Vinod? Good, good. Just went shopping in town myself!' the lieutenant colonel said, holding up several string bags bulging with groceries. 'Half the price of groceries in the store!' he added, settling the bags down for a moment. 'I must say, Major, you are a lucky man!'

'Why, sir?' Rakesh asked with a smile.

'Yours must have been the only wife who came back from that shopping trip into town with no saree! Whenever two or more women shop together they waste ten times more money! My Meena came home with six sarees! Can you believe that?'

Sarojini didn't say anything. She hadn't bought anything at the saree bazaar because she had not had any money. She'd asked Rakesh the night before and even the morning of the shopping trip, but he'd forgotten. She'd had to use the little money she had left over from her days in Karnataka when they'd stopped for a soft drink. Rakesh was so frugal with their housekeeping expenses it was just as well that Sarojini knew how to stretch a budget.

'Thank you, sir,' Rakesh replied, more than a little obsequiously.

'Now, Mrs Vinod, you will be coming to dinner with us next Friday night, won't you?'

'I thought it was officers only,' Rakesh said.

'Oh, no, no . . . the brigadier visited me the other day after Meena and Sarojini came home from shopping and he was quite taken with your wife!'

'Why?' Rakesh demanded.

'Oh, you silly boy! He is a happily married man with grandchildren. It's just that we all heard your beautiful wife hum a few tunes as she helped Meena with the sarees and we thought maybe she could sing for us at the mess hall! Anyway, I must hurry! Meena is waiting on the onions to make aloo gobhi!'

'You sang?' Rakesh demanded, turning to Sarojini and grabbing her by the shoulders. 'I thought I explained to you that if you got caught it would be the end of our lives on the army base!'

'I didn't sing!' Sarojini protested, trying to wriggle away, but Rakesh tightened his grip.

'Really? So why is it that they want you to sing in front of all of the officers in Lucknow?'

'It's just singing, Rakesh! I think you are making too much out of this!'

'Singing first! Dancing next, and then what? Returning to being a *devadasi*!'

Sarojini stopped trying to break free from his grip and looked him in the eyes. 'Rakesh, I left that life behind me to start a new one with you. I would not do anything to hurt you or us!'

'I thought I could get my hair put up like this,' Meena explained to the hairdresser in town, unpinning her tresses and holding them up. She and Sarojini had come into town to have her saree blouse stitched and they'd called in at the hairdresser on their way home so that they could agree on a hair-up before the ball.

The hairdresser sat her down on a chair, then lifted the heavy tresses and squealed. 'Oh, madam, there are lice in your hair! All over! Look! One just fell to the floor,' she screamed, stomping on it with her slippers.

'The children!' Meena cried. 'They get them from school and they give them to me! This is the fifth time this year – I can't get rid of them!'

'Well, madam, I can do it,' the hairdresser said. 'But it will take two hours a week for the next three weeks. I can kill these little pests! Leave it to me! We can start right now.'

Meena looked at Sarojini. 'You don't mind, do you? Why don't you go and have a look at the saree shops? You haven't got a saree to wear yet for the ball!' When Sarojini nodded, Meena strode towards the basin and sat down. 'Kill 'em!' she told the hairdresser.

Sarojini smiled and walked out into the autumn sunlight. It wasn't a particularly warm day, so it was quite pleasant to stroll about town. And it was even lovelier to be out of the army barracks. She was hardly getting out at all now, after Rakesh's edict.

As instructed by Meena, she went to look for a saree. Not that she had any money, but it was nice to look. She looked in this shop and that, wrinkling her nose at what was on offer, walking the length and breadth of the saree district until she found herself back at the store where the other army wives had bought their sarees.

'Sir, I don't know if you remember me,' Sarojini said, approaching the elderly nawab. 'I came in a few weeks ago with some friends.'

'Of course I remember, my dear,' the portly gentleman replied, bowing graciously. 'How could I forget? I sold more sarees that day than I usually do in a week!'

'Do you think I could have a look at that saree?'

The nawab did not have to ask which saree she wanted to see.

'Why, of course, madam. Though I will confess that you are not the first woman to fall under her spell.'

'Why do you call the saree a *her*?'

'Madam, this is no ordinary saree,' the nawab replied, gently unrolling it and draping it on a high cupboard. 'When I bought this saree my luck changed. Just before I bought it, there had been terrible trouble between the Hindus and Muslims here in Lucknow. Lootings. Riots. Did you hear about Lucknow down south?'

Sarojini nodded.

'I know we Muslims aren't supposed to go into Hindu temples, but when my wife and I dropped our son off in New Delhi to catch a flight to Australia, I stopped by a temple and I prayed,' the nawab said. 'I prayed for something to keep us safe. And a few days later, this pregnant girl turned up. Ever since I put her saree up in my shop window, not a single thug has darkened my doorstep. Not a one. Shops on both sides have either been burnt or looted but not mine. My wife now does not even like for me to loan it out for weddings. She says it makes her feel unsafe. It's magic.'

Looking at the saree, Sarojini could understand. It was fluidity and beauty married into one. And it was delicately finished too. There wasn't a single thread out of place and every stitch of embroidery was perfect. Quite unconsciously, she recited lines from a favourite poem, describing the great Ganges, and how she transformed India as she flowed from the Himalayas down through the plains and on to the ocean, how she brought grace and knowledge to all of humanity through her life-giving force.

'You know Makhanlal Chaturvedi?' the nawab asked with surprise.

Sarojini nodded again. 'I love his poetry,' she said. Mamaji had taught her girls not just to read and recite poetry, but to understand it.

And *nawab* quoted back the Urdu translation of *The River Ganges* by Robert Southey which Sarojini countered with *A River* by A.K. Ramanujan.'From Mysore are you?'

'Of course, the birth place of the greatest of Indian poets!'

'Come, madam, come!' The nawab invited her into his home. 'You must meet my wife.' Sarojini was nervous, but she followed him upstairs. 'Just my wife and I left,' he explained as he wheezed and coughed his way up. 'Our only son emigrated to Australia about five years ago. He is an engineer.'

'Aisha,' he called out into the roof garden as they reached the top of the stairs. 'I think there is a young lady you ought to meet.'

Aisha turned out to be the nawab's bedridden wife and a retired literature teacher.

'I am so sorry to intrude on your tea,' Sarojini immediately apologised, seeing two cups set out, but the nawab, Ali Khan, had hurried to fetch a third already.

'This young lady is knowledgeable about poetry,' he proudly announced as he returned, setting down a fine china cup on the platter. 'A great admirer of Makhanlal Chaturvedi!'

'I admire a great many of the Indian poets. T.N. Srikantaiah, G.S. Shivarudrappa, Suryakant Tripathi Nirala,' Sarojini protested shyly.

'Have you read any Urdu poets?' Aisha asked curiously.

The next hour and a half was the best hour and a half Sarojini had had since coming to Lucknow. Conversation and tea flowed easily. Aisha turned out to be a scholar of Urdu classical literature. 'The problem is that the young of today watch too many Bollywood films. All they want to see is Amitabh Bachchan and his ladies singing and cavorting on screen! No substance, no poetry.'

Sarojini disagreed. 'But that is where the Indian culture is great, Madame! Song and dance is as natural for us as eating and laughing!'

'Please explain to me, child – where is the culture in half-clad women cavorting on screen?' the lady demanded.

Sarojini gave her a treatise on Bharatanatyam and why dance was an important part of Hindustani culture. 'How can you know the beat and rhythm of poetry if you have not felt it yourself? Music and dance go together naturally and with them comes poetry!'

'So, you've studied the classical forms of dance, then?'

'Indeed I have, Madame. I have studied Bharatanatyam, Odissi, Kuchipudi, Mohiniattam and Kathakali. But Bharatanatyam is what I am really good at.'

'Could you dance for us one day?' the lady pleaded. 'I can't go out now that I am bedridden, but I would love to see you dance!'

'Rakesh! Look!' Sarojini squealed, waving the thin leaf of paper at him. Rakesh had just come in from work with the post, and the novelty of receiving mail had already put a spark in Sarojini's eyes, even before she had opened it and learned the news.

'Shhh . . . the neighbours might hear,' Rakesh admonished.

'Kalpana, Keshto and Abhay are being stationed up here in Delhi!' she said.

Rakesh just grunted again, going out to the bathroom to splash some water on his face.

'Did you know?' she demanded.

'Of course I knew. Abhay is a smart man – I expect he'll be promoted again in the next few years. And Kalpana has done her best to help him. I heard that she held a lavish party for all the officers at the base and a visiting general from New Delhi was very impressed.'

Sarojini rolled her eyes at the implied criticism. She did not and could not entertain, because Rakesh shadowed her every move when they were out and about. How could she even make friends if he would not let her talk to anyone?

'Now, remember what I told you,' Rakesh had said to her outside the mess hall at the last officers' dinner. 'Don't mention anything about your old life in Mysore. I've told everyone that you were orphaned as a child and raised by your uncle and aunt. And that you had a falling-out with them over our love marriage.'

No one knew that Sarojini and Rakesh were not actually married.

It had not ended there. He'd followed her around, listening in on her conversations and correcting her or even changing the subject altogether.

'How is your daughter doing?' Sarojini had asked Meena Singh. 'Did you try the boiled *neem* leaves mixed with turmeric for the rash?'

'That is what we have doctors for!' Rakesh had interrupted. 'Don't waste time with Ayurvedic medicines. I know so many people who waste years with that nonsense only to have their illnesses cured in days by proper western doctors. Take her to the army base hospital,' he said.

'How's the saree blouse stitching going?' she'd then turned

to ask Babitha. 'Do you need me to come and help you pin it one afternoon?'

'Please, Sarojini, that would be lovely,' Babitha had said. 'You know I get so lonely in the afternoon.'

'You do know that Mrs Sunila's parents own the largest tailoring store in Calcutta, don't you?' Rakesh interjected. 'Sarojini hasn't ever sewn a thing in her life! You are better off getting Sunila to help you!'

Sarojini had been infuriated at that. 'Rakesh! You have no idea what I have done or not done in my life!' she'd said when Babitha left to talk to someone else. 'Mamaji made sure we were all self-sufficient. I bet I can sew better than Sunila. No one has ever waited on me hand and foot,' she'd snapped, pointing towards Sunila, who was sitting about while her husband ferried drinks and nibbles to her like a devoted slave.

'So you think you are an educated woman? An intelligent woman? Intelligent women don't sing and dance. They go to school and to college,' he'd jeered. 'Oh, come now, don't get sulky. I was just trying to help. Did you really want to spend afternoon after afternoon helping that airhead with her saree blouse?'

'Actually, I did!'

'Well, I don't want you getting too close to her anyway. I may have to reprimand her husband soon if his performance doesn't improve, and I don't want you getting involved with my work!' he said before stalking away.

Sarojini could not relax after that. She sat in a corner and thought instead, while Rakesh socialised. He came over halfway through the night to speak to her. 'I am so happy to see you sitting here by yourself. It is so becoming of a good wife. Women should know their place!' He looked across the room at Meena Singh and frowned.

Sarojini had followed his gaze across the crowded room to see Meena and Lieutant Colonel having a good laugh with a few of the officers. They leant close to each other while they talked, and started and finished each other's sentences. There was a true camaraderie there.

Across the other side of the room, she saw the young Nagina girl and her husband, deep in conversation. Not for the first time, Sarojini wondered why she'd run off with Rakesh. While they appeared to have so much in common, in actual fact they didn't.

She was still asking herself that question now.

'Do you mind then?' Sarojini asked as she served Rakesh dinner.

'Mind what?'

'If I go visit Kalpana once they come to Delhi. It takes only a few hours by train.'

'Sure . . .' he said without much interest.

'Won't you come with me? Abhay was such a good friend to you.'

'The only reason I was friends with Abhay was because he had that picture of you,' Rakesh replied, absently picking up the paper. 'He is such a high caste bore . . .'

Sarojini rolled her eyes. She'd known Abhay for a good many years and knew that he treated the Dalits and the Shudras he came across with kindness and compassion. He never objected to their presence, nor did he have any issue with Sarojini's background.

'So you aren't coming even to see Keshto?'

Rakesh shook his head. 'Why would I want to see him? He's a child. I only pretended to be interested in him to get you to notice me.'

'May I borrow an umbrella?' Sarojini asked, her teeth chattering.

'Come in here and dry yourself off first!' Ali Khan insisted, bundling her through the saree shop and up the stairs. He had her seated in front of his wife, towelling her hair dry within minutes. 'I thought you were in New Delhi.'

'I was. I just got back,' she sniffled into her chai. Over the past few weeks, she'd developed quite a friendship with the nawab Ali and his wife Aisha.

'So why didn't you catch a tuktuk from the station to the barracks, *beta*?' Aisha demanded.

'I spent a great deal in New Delhi . . . I ran out of money.' How could Sarojini explain the scene at the station just before she'd left for New Delhi? 'Five hundred rupees? Is that all you are giving me?' Sarojini had asked Rakesh.

'That is enough for a ticket,' he'd grunted as he drove off, calling out, 'I am running late for my meeting with my junior officers.'

So Sarojini had done the entire trip in the third-class carriage, wedged between a cage full of chickens and a monkey catcher with his three pet monkeys.

'Surely your husband would pay for it, wouldn't he?' Ali Khan demanded. 'When my Aisha was well, why she used to use all the household money and then come home in a tuktuk! Oh, I used to smile. It is a husband's privilege to indulge his wife.'

'Errr . . . anyway, how are you feeling, Aisha?' Sarojini replied, deftly changing the topic – or so she thought.

'I am well, *beta*, but you haven't yet answered my question – why didn't you catch a tuktuk from the train station to the barracks?'

'It was just that I bought so many things.' Sarojini smiled brightly at them both.

'But that is the same bag you took to the train, *beta*,' Ali Khan said, touching it lightly, only to have it topple over. 'I helped you select it, remember.'

'Remember I took all those sweets and toys for Keshto? That's why the bag is empty now.'

'And you bought him even more toys?'

'Of course,' Sarojini said.

'*Beta* . . . do you think we haven't noticed? That you eat your fill when you are here, like you've been starving. That is why I always have Ali bring so much food when you come. The week in New Delhi was good for you. Your face has filled out a little,' Aisha said kindly. 'Is your marriage all you make it to be?'

The tears that Sarojini had shed on the long train ride from New Delhi came back in force. 'I don't want to go back to him,' she sobbed. 'I should but I don't.' Sarojini chose not to reveal the fact that Rakesh had kicked Pranay the kitten so much for eating its fill that it too had run away.

'Why, *beta*, why? Does he hit you?'

'No! Never!' she cried. 'I don't exactly know what it is, but I know I am not happy with my life.'

And maybe it was the trip to New Delhi that had shown her what happiness really was. What her life could be, rather than what it was.

Kalpana was deliriously happy, of course. Keshto was a robust young lad with a cheeky grin and strong set of lungs he was not averse to using. Kalpana had found the only way to make him quiet was to outsing him. Mother and son would belt it out until Keshto gave up and started to dance instead.

'What if you are overheard by your neighbours?' Sarojini had worried.

'So what if they overheard us?' Kalpana replied, puzzled.

'What if they found out? You know?'

'Found out what?'

'That you had been a . . . you know . . . ?' Sarojini had whispered.

'What? A *devadasi*?'

'Won't it ruin Abhay's career?'

'I don't think so anymore. It probably won't affect his career at all. If anything we'd get invited to more parties! If it became a problem for Abhay, we'd just return to Mysore. He can get a good job in a company after having been a captain! We've decided we don't care if we are discovered. All that hiding and lying was exhausting us!'

With Abhay's connections and caste, it would be easy for him to have a successful career outside the army. And his love for Kalpana was stronger than ever. He came home each day bounding with energy, wanting to spend every second before bed with Keshto and Kalpana. There was laughter and smiles. He took pride in the fact that he was the only person who could convince Keshto to have a bottle or make him go to sleep. Watching the three of them together convinced Sarojini that there was something very wrong with her relationship with Rakesh.

'He supports my family, Aisha. I cannot fault him for that,' she said now.

'But he only gives you fifty rupees a week for groceries?' Ali spat in disgust. 'You can barely buy three hundred grams of gourds for that!'

'But it is only me I need to feed. Rakesh eats at the mess hall.'

'*Beta*, have you told your parents about this? Surely your father can have words with Rakesh. He has your dowry and he is still answerable to your parents.'

Sarojini shook her head. 'My father died when I was about two and my mother lives in rural Gokak. She would no sooner speak to him than God.'

'What about your brothers, surely they can speak to him.'

Again, Sarojini shook her head sadly, stifling sobs.

'Was it a love marriage?' Aisha asked. 'Is that why your brothers will not interfere?'

Sarojini nodded shakily.

'Do you still love him?'

'Aisha, he was the only person in my whole life who ever told me that they loved me. Not my parents. Not my brothers. Not anyone. I don't want to lose his love! And if he loves me, why does he treat me like this?'

'Sarojini, *beta* . . . have you heard of the story of Shazia Muna Khan?' Aisha asked.

'No.'

'She was the wisest and first wife of King Sheer Abdullah Khan. In those times, young girls were betrothed early. So when they finally got married, there was no excitement, there was no energy in their marriage. Indeed, six years after their marriage, she was still a virgin!'

Aisha had Sarojini's complete attention, so she continued.

'So one day, Shazia disguised herself as one of the dancing girls in the harem and went to him. She refused to let him see her face but danced for him until his mind and body were on fire. But she would not let him touch her. Not for seven nights. And on the seventh night, they were together, but only with a veil covering her face. Then she disappeared. It was as if she vanished into thin air.'

'A year later, Shazia came back as a dancing girl and danced for the king again. Again she danced for seven nights, and on the seventh, they were together. This continued for several years, until the king was desolate without the dancing girl. He no longer had interest in anything or anyone else.'

'Why are you doing this to me?' the king demanded of

Shazia. 'Why do you leave me alone and without love? Do you not know I love you?'

'Shazia knew that she'd got into the king's heart. Finally. So she took him by the hand to the harem compound, where she took her veil off.'

'I have been here all along, my darling,' she said. 'You only had to go into your home to find all the love you need.'

'So what are you saying I should do?' Sarojini asked Aisha. 'That I disguise myself as a dancing girl? Rakesh would kill me!'

'No, I am telling you that you should make that man sit up and take notice of you!' Aisha declared. 'And I know just the way! Ali, I think it is time we lent that saree to this young lady!'

The Brigadier's Ball was held at Qaisar Bagh Palace. Built in 1850 by Wajid Ali Shah, she was grand and opulent, and a decaying mess. The British had attacked in 1858 on some trumped-up pretext and partially destroyed her. Battle-scarred and pockmarked, in the daylight she looked in a sorry state. But at night, she glowed and blazed forth in all her long-ago grandeur, thousands of lights outlining the building like the setting sun, hiding her many deficiencies.

The army had even gone as far as to roll out a red carpet by the main entrance. This was where the officers waited for their wives, who were, of course, running late. There was hair to be put up, make-up to be applied and sarees to be draped, when all the men had to do was pull on their trousers and shrug into their jackets.

'I ran out when Meena wanted me to start helping her with the pinning!' Lieutenant Colonel Singh laughed into his tumbler of whisky. 'I don't understand it! These women wear sarees every day of every week. They wear them to work, they wear them to bed, but every time they have a special event they panic!'

'Says he who needs help tying his turban! And that is only five yards of cloth, while a saree is six!' Meena retorted.

'But you do look pretty, my dear,' Lieutenant Colonel Singh smiled. 'Speaking of which, where is your beautiful wife, Rakesh?'

Rakesh shrugged. Sarojini had been very secretive since she'd returned from New Delhi. Her mysterious smiles caused him to be extra suspicious. He'd seen it all before. His mother had done exactly the same. Many times. To the many suitors who'd fallen from grace.

She'd be sweet as honey to them at first. Like a butcher in an abattoir, gentling the terrified animals and winning their confidence – right before bringing down the axe.

Rakesh felt like one of those animals. Wary and terrified. The only thing that kept the gut-gnawing fear at bay was the fact that Sarojini could not leave. Quite literally could not leave. She had no money and no way to get back to the protection of Mamaji in Mysore.

Comforting himself with that fact, Rakesh started to pace. He was one of the very few officers left outside, and all of the others were single men, laughing merrily and getting heartily drunk on the free-flowing liquor. He would tear strips off Sarojini the next day. Tardiness was unacceptable in the army. He was rehearsing his speech with his back turned when a silence spread among the young men.

He turned to see his Sarojini come through the Mermaid Gate, to the east. As she floated magically beneath the arch of pure marble, it was as if one of the mythical mermaids carved into the stone above had come to life. He held his breath, as did all the other officers. Could it really be Sarojini?

'Oh my goodness!' Babitha squealed, coming out to greet her friend. 'How did you convince your husband to buy that saree for you? It cost 75,000 rupees!'

'No, Babitha, the nawab and his wife kindly lent it to me for the night,' Sarojini said, waving to the couple who had just dropped her off. Aisha waved back from the car window as they drove away, her face alight with joy.

'Well, what do you think?' Sarojini asked, pirouetting in front of Rakesh. In the shadows she could not quite see his face.

'Who cares what he thinks?' Babitha cried. 'Come, Sarojini! You will be the envy of every woman here tonight!'

And she was. They all wanted to know who in town had draped her saree and stitched her blouse. 'My goodness – it is a cross between a dancer's saree drape and a classical *nivi*,' Meena Singh said, trying to figure out the folds and pleats of the drape without unravelling Sarojini in front of all the guests at the ball.

'I say, my dear, I can never lift my arms when I wear a saree jacket! Is this the brassiere cut?' Mrs Benares even deigned to ask. The wife of the highest-ranking officer at the barracks, she never spoke to the wife of any man below Lieutant Colonel, and Sarojini flushed with pride.

'You must be very proud, son,' the Brigadier said, coming up and thumping Rakesh furiously on the back. 'A beautiful and accomplished woman is an asset to any man!'

Giddy with all the compliments she had received, Sarojini did not think twice when the band struck up but went straight out onto the dance floor. This was her night. She would do it. She would find a way into Rakesh's heart – a way for him to accept her as she was.

Music and dance came as naturally to her as breathing, and she could keep up with any beat. As she swayed and sashayed to the music, the bandmaster recognised a talented dancer and picked up the pace, urging his musicians on and pushing them to give their all.

After months of unhappiness and uncertainty, Sarojini felt a flood of joy as her body moved to the music's powerful rhythm. Before long, the entire officer corps and their wives had surrounded Sarojini and were watching her dance, but she barely noticed. Movement made her free – it was how she expressed herself. This was what she had been born to do, what her long years of training had prepared her for. She was truly herself when she danced, and it felt good – very good – to be reminded of who she really was.

When the music stopped, it was not because the band-master or audience wanted it to, but because the maître d' had kept sending nasty glances at the maestro, eventually sending a messenger to say that if they did not get a move on, the first course would be ruined!

Sarojini stopped to applause that shook the crystals on the chandelier above. She struck an artful pose, like one of the statues adorning the walls of the Hindu temples of Karnataka, lifting her arm so that the *pallu* of her saree cascaded down her back like a waterfall.

There was stunned silence. As she'd danced, no one had really taken notice of the *pallu* of her saree. But now they could see it. And it was breathtaking. The rubies of the eyes of the peacock flashed fire and a dazzling light reflected off the sapphires in its feathers, making it almost difficult to look at. More than one devout Hindu in the room wondered whether they were perhaps in the presence of divinity.

'Not even the *devadasi* of Orissa, Karnataka or Tamil Nadu could dance as well as that,' the Brigadier roared, clapping approvingly. 'Bravo! Bravo!'

As the crowd dispersed, Rakesh strode onto the dance floor and dragged her off.

'I say, I do hope the major is not going to be an idiot and chastise the poor girl,' the Brigadier observed.

Rakesh pulled her by the arm out onto the verandah, away from the other guests. His face was contorted with rage, but he kept his voice low. 'I cannot believe you could do that to me! After everything I have done for you and your family!'

'Tell me, Rakesh, what exactly have I done to hurt you?' Sarojini asked quietly.

'How dare you! Is this how you repay my kindness? By ruining me?'

'Rakesh . . .'

'Women!' he cried. 'You are exactly like my mother! Now everyone will think that you are somehow connected with the *devadasi*. Only they can dance like that!'

'Rakesh, I am not connected to the *devadasi*, I am a *devadasi*.'

'Yes, I know!' he hissed. 'Nothing more than a common whore!'

Sarojini looked at him for a long moment. The pain of the final realisation was overwhelming. She had almost convinced herself that she loved Rakesh. She'd wanted to believe that someone could love her and she could love him in return, but she could no longer fool herself. The truth had struck her that evening as she'd stood in front of the mirror and seen herself, resplendent in the saree. She looked like a goddess. She was the goddess.

Draping that saree had been almost an ecstatic experience. From the first tuck she'd felt an inexplicable joy. A wonder. A love. As she'd pulled the saree around her waist, she'd thought of her life and all that she had learned, from her early days in the hamlet of stunted coconut trees to her time with Mamaji at Moona Mahal. As she'd pleated the *pallu*, she remembered the men in her life – Harindra, the young man she'd taken on in the slums, Karuna the dwarf and then Rakesh. And when she draped the second drape around her body she knew. She knew she had control over her life. Unlike the many thousands of women who had no control of their sarees or their lives, Sarojini had control. Indeed that was what the *devadasi* were famed for. Their ability to control their emotions and to be with their human partners.

As she arranged the *pallu* artistically over her shoulder, she'd believed it at last. Believed in her heart and soul that an ordinary life was not hers to be had.

Whatever her path might be, she was a true daughter of Yellamma and she would dedicate the rest of her life to the goddess. Rakesh could be a part of that life or choose not to. She had danced, showing him her true self, hoping he would find it in him to accept her as she was – but he could not. Without looking at him, Sarojini turned and started to walk towards the Mermaid Gate.

'Where are you going?' Rakesh called out. 'Come back! Come back right now! You are mine!'

'How can I be yours when I belong to the goddess?'

'But I love you!' Rakesh cried, the reality of what was about to happen nearly crushing him.

'That may be true, Rakesh, but I love myself more,' Sarojini said firmly before stepping away.

Walking into the darkness of the night and all the way to the nawab's home, Sarojini's heart beat firmly and fiercely. Whatever the future might hold, Sarojini had no fear. Unlike millions of women across the world, Sarojini had a choice.

# The Fall

Mumbai, India, and
Melbourne, Australia, 1997

Madhav loved India, he was sure, more than his own mother. The soil of Hindustan itself was holy. From the deep brown of the fertile plains of the Punjab to the deserts of Rajasthan and the snowy heights of the Himalayas. Holy. And her rivers. Oh, her rivers! The Ganges, the Mahanadi, the Yamuna and the Saraswati! All heavenly flows that brought grace, intelligence and life. The work of the gods themselves.

Yet Indians were defiling her. Inch by inch. Day by day. They talked on cellular phones – he was sure it was making the holy Indian air impure – and they drove cars, the noise drowning out the sound of the Vedas. Even the cows were not getting the respect they deserved! Why just last week he'd read that some American food chain was being allowed to set up in India. Of course they weren't going to serve beef, but they did elsewhere!

But soon he could escape the noisy chaos of Mumbai. He just needed to get through the ordination ceremony unscathed and he could go to a temple. A quiet and peaceful temple where he could be at peace and work. He had his heart set on Varanasi, where the mighty Ganges made its way from the western Himalayas down to Bangladesh. There he could spend his days in prayer and contemplation and impart the wisdom of the Vedas to the ignorant masses.

It was all just a matter of hours away. And everything was going perfectly. The principal of the seminary had ordained Madhav first, ceremonially dragging his five fingers dusted with *vibuthi* across Madhav's brow and dotting his forehead with vermilion.

'Our youngest graduate. Not even twenty-three yet!' the old pundit announced with pride to the audience filled with parents and siblings. 'Came to us when he was only seventeen and demanded entry. For four days he slept on the stairs outside my office to prove to me he was ready.'

All the other students rolled their eyes. They'd all heard the story before of course and some could even recite it in their sleep. Some did indeed recite it softy under their breaths.

'Madhav heard the call of God not when he was teenager or even when he was a boy, but when he was a baby! He'd already memorised half the Puranas before he even came here!'

Even the worst of his detractors had to concede that Madhav had something of the divine in him, though. When he chanted the Bhagavad Gita his pronunciation was perfect, his intonation poetic, and if you closed your eyes, you could almost imagine that you were privy to the conversation between the Pandava Prince Arjuna and his guide Krishna before Arjuna started a war with his brother.

But the applause that had greeted Madhav when he received his Brahmin thread was muted. Neither his parents nor siblings were there. 'Poor orphan boy,' more than one mother observed, the lonesome look on his face piercing their hearts.

When the ceremony was finished, the other students' parents swamped Madhav. A pundit of his calibre would be a rich man one day, and the mothers wanted him for their daughters.

'No, aunty, no . . . I cannot possibly visit Uttar Pradesh,' Madhav protested, looking over one lady's shoulder to see her daughter hovering close behind. 'I do not believe in marriage for myself!'

And then there were the fathers, who would not leave him alone, trying to extract promises from him to visit them in the city later in the week. 'Come, *beta*, come. I know many good people who would be interested in a promising young man like you.'

'No, sir no, I do not attend homes or private businesses. If you want your family or business to succeed, then you must do good *karma*. Have you done good deeds? Abstained from doing evil?'

'What a devout pundit,' more than one parent observed. 'Rare to find one so pious these days.'

'He must come from very good stock,' another added. 'It is such a pity he is an orphan.'

'But he is *not* an orphan,' one irritable graduate pointed out, as a look of horror dawned on Madhav's face.

A flashy new Jaguar had just pulled into the temple grounds. As his fellow students and their families looked on, his mother and sisters stumbled out dressed in clothes more suitable for a Bollywood cocktail party than an austere Hindu seminary graduation!

Madhav rushed from the seminary to the principal's office all in a dither. He should have been the first among the students to receive his posting. Temples from all over India vied for graduates from this seminary – that was why he'd chosen this seminary from the thousands all over India. But his parents and siblings had been impossible to get rid of. 'Why are you here? How did you find out?' he'd demanded of his mother in a stern undertone.

'Vinod told me,' his mother smiled, before defying Hindu custom to kiss her son fulsomely on his cheeks.

'Vinod the gardener?'

'Yes, he saw the notices up on the gates and he told me! We were on our way back to London and we thought we'd drop in. Now introduce me to your friends, *beta*!'

Pinky Patel was a born networker, and so was her husband.

His father was already working the reception hall. 'Suresh Patel . . . I am sure you have heard of me . . . realtor to the stars! He shook hands with the other parents western-style, handing his business card over and flashing a megawatt smile.

Meanwhile his sisters were walking around the shrine room, chattering to each other in Hinglish and exclaiming over the little statuettes. 'How quaint!' they said to each other.

'You aren't supposed to touch them!' Madhav snapped, following them and smacking their hands away. 'It is disrespectful!'

The principal, Reverend Srinivasan, overheard him. 'You speak English?' he demanded.

'But of course! He was born in Belsize Park and grew up there, until he got this crackpot idea he wanted to become a pundit!' his elder sister replied, half in Hindi, half in English.

'Then Daddy bought his business here, so now we spend half our time here and the other half back in London,' his younger sister explained.

'I am so sorry,' Madhav said as he walked into the principal's office later.

'Sorry for what, *puttar*?' the ancient principal asked.

'For my parents . . . for being late.'

'Your parents are your parents, child. They make you who you are. But I am glad that you were late.'

'Why, venerable sir? Is there a problem with my posting to Varanasi? I spoke with the trustees of the temple there just last week.'

'Yes, they were impressed . . .' the Reverend Srinivasan said. 'I just finished speaking to them myself. I was glad you were late because I got to speak to them myself finally.'

'Why did you speak with them, sir?'

'Well, young man, I needed to get their permission to release you.'

'Release me from what?'

'Why, release you from your posting in Varanasi. To send you abroad! When I told them that you spoke fluent English, they agreed entirely with me! See, we have so much trouble finding pundits to tend to the Hindu flocks who live in foreign lands.'

Madhav felt faint. He was being sent back to gloomy England he felt sure! There he'd have to do poojas and chant Vedas for a bunch of young Anglo-Indian kids who rocked up to temple half-stoned or straight from the pub.

'So is it to be the temple in Willesden, East Ham or Merton?' he asked.

'Ferntree Gully,' Reverend Srinivasan replied, pronouncing the English words with a great deal of difficulty.

'Ferntree Gully? I can't remember a Ferntree Gully anywhere in England,' Madhav replied, feeling very puzzled.

'No, silly boy. It is in Australia. In Melbourne, to be precise. We have a sizeable Indian population there now and they are crying out for pundit!'

The flight to Australia was awful. It took him five hours to fly from Mumbai to Singapore and then six hours from there to Melbourne. It took five hours just to fly from the top of Australia to the bottom of it! You could almost fly from London to Mumbai during that time if you had a good tailwind!

Madhav spent the whole time with his nose glued to the window, looking at the landscape below. The scenery was singularly uninspiring – a relentless mass of pale brown earth with not a river or range of mountains to break the monotony. He saw the odd lake or waterhole, but there was nothing, nothing, to compare to the mighty rivers of India.

He was picked up from the airport by a young man named Kumar, but he pronounced his name 'Kuma', without any 'r' at the end. Apparently these Australians did not pronounce the 'r' at the end of words– and sometimes they didn't pronounce the end of a word at all. A television was called a 'telly' and university was called 'uni'. Kumar told him all about it on the long drive from the airport in Tullamarine in the west to Ferntree Gully in the east.

Madhav could barely understand one in three words the friendly young man said. Once they'd got off the freeway and onto the surface roads, he'd felt a jolt of familiarity at the names of suburbs – Brunswick, Fitzroy and even Bayswater – but soon he realised there was something quite wrong.

'Where are the people?' he asked of the jolly Kumar.

'Yeah ... you'll get used to it,' the young man told him, taking his eyes briefly off the road to look at the tired pundit.

'Used to what exactly?' Madhav asked worriedly.

He could see suburb after suburb of tidy houses but no people on the streets. In India, the streets were positively crawling with people. People going to get their groceries, people going to work, people going to each other's houses, people, people, people. And cows. And dogs. And everything in between. London had been similarly busy, though perhaps without the cows.

'Australians don't get out and about much,' Kumar told him. 'Especially not around here. In the inner city you'd see bikes and trams, but out here in the sticks people just get in their cars to go to the shops. It must seem a bit strange to you – I know it freaks me out whenever I go to India and see all those people.'

'But I've come to Melbourne, correct? The second largest city in Australia?'

'Yeah,' Kumar replied. 'But the population of Melbourne is only about four million.'

Madhav gasped. 'So much space for so few people?' He thought about London, with its population of twelve million, so much smaller than the city they were crossing now, and Mumbai, which was even smaller, with over twelve million people.

'Yes, as I said, you'll get used to it. I struggle whenever I go home to India now – it's like everyone is living on top of each other!' But as Madhav looked out at the deserted streets, he doubted very much he would ever get used to it.

The leaves on the gum trees that surrounded the temple were a drab green and the dry earth below them a dull brown. It was as if a veil of colourlessness had been thrown over the Australian landscape, dimming and muting everything in sight. Sure the Dandenong Ranges were pretty enough; but compared to the majesty of the World Heritage listed Western Ghats that surrounded Mumbai, they seemed like little mounds of dirt.

And the temple itself, Sri Ganapathi Vinayaka temple, was uninspiring. Only a single spire of statues over the doorway! Why even the temples in London made more of an effort!

He went to sleep in his little room in the rectory of the Hindu temple feeling very miserable that night. Not only had he had to leave his beloved India, he'd come to a country bereft of people, colour and life.

Ferntree Gully Sri Ganapathi Vinayaka temple was not actually located in Ferntree Gully. The real estate agent had lied to the group of Indian businessmen he'd brought to view the site. 'Prime real estate!' he'd told them, carefully putting his thumb over the part of the contract where the address was written. The five-acre parcel of land was actually in Boronia, a somewhat seedy suburb to the north-west. The address wasn't the real problem, though – the problem was the Rebels Motorcycle clubhouse on the property that backed onto the empty paddock.

The local residents had been trying to get rid of the bikies for quite some time. Their first salvo had been a petition for that little bit of land to be zoned for industrial use. 'Let's see how long they'll last with a chemical factory on their doorstep!' Yet no chemical plant or industrial development eventuated. Local business leaders had a healthy fear of the Rebels. For a long time the paddock just attracted the local bogans, who used it as a comfortable spot to smoke ganja and dare each other to knock on the door of the clubhouse. 'I dare ya, Simmo! I dare ya to knock on the door or you're a faggot!'

When it became known that the group of Indian business-men were considering building a temple there, the residents were deeply conflicted. While they did not want foreigners and their strange gods moving into the neighbourhood, they did not want the paddock left empty, either. It was just begging for some tool to toss a cigarette butt in at the height of summer and all of the Dandenongs would go up in flames!

'It's the lesser of two evils really,' the head of the residents' group had said when he rang the real estate agent. 'We'd much rather a Hindu temple than bushfires.'

Madhav had been looking forward to the peace and quiet of the temple in Varanasi after the noise and congestion of Mumbai, but here on the outskirts of Melbourne he felt quite isolated. The temple received only about ten visitors a day, and sometimes not even that many. The chief pundit, Reverend Shastri, told him that it was much busier on weekends and festival days, and his heart sank. It was exactly like the temples he knew back in the UK – visited only on weekends, as a social activity.

There was a half-hour walk from the temple down the hill to the shops and the train station, and the shops themselves were not particularly inspiring – a milk bar, a charcoal chicken shop and a lacklustre hardware store that existed mainly because it supplied hydroponic equipment to the Rebels. Madhav did not exert himself much to go to the shops – not because he didn't want to, but because he got seriously sunburnt the first time he tried.

'The Australian sun is not like the Indian sun,' the chief pundit had told him, handing Madhav a hat and a tube of papaw cream. 'I know you probably spent your entire time in Mumbai without needing protection, but the sun here is evil. It will kill you with cancer!'

After that, Madhav was almost too terrified even to leave the shaded compound of the temple itself.

To make matters worse, the chief pundit took a holiday almost as soon as he'd arrived, before the end of his first week. 'Very good. Very good,' Reverend Shastri said, packing his bags for Delhi. 'You are a graduate from one of the best Hindu seminaries in India! You know what to do,' he insisted.

So day after day, Madhav found himself confined to the temple with no one for company. Staring at the walls. Lighting and rearranging offerings. Going over and over the liturgy in the cramped little office until he thought he'd go insane.

But there was a reason that Madhav confined himself to the office. It was not strictly true that he was all alone at the temple. For every morning, like clockwork, a car rolled into the compound and dropped a woman off at the doorstep of the temple. She was very elegantly turned out, her saree immaculately draped and her long grey hair pinned carefully into a bun at the back of her head. She was quite delicate, though, as if many years of malnutrition had robbed her of her vitality.

He had been friendly at first, talking to the woman, inviting her in, but she only nodded silently as she got the broom from the closet and started to sweep the compound. She attended every pooja though, standing at the back of the room and rocking in prayer, her lips moving in silent benediction. She even did most of the decorations in the temple, organising the trays of fruit for offerings but promptly stepping away before the sacred fires were lit. She was definitely useful, and Madhav would have been glad of her company, if only she weren't so morbidly silent.

It was during a pooja that Madhav became aware she was not quite right in the head. A young couple had requested a full fire pooja, with sacred fires lit in all the sanctums, asking Madhav to beseech the gods on their behalf for the husband's success in a job interview. They had paid handsomely for it too, a whole two hundred dollars, which was a lot for a migrant family.

The silent woman had not been in the rectory when Madhav started preparing for the ceremony, lighting the fires with great pomp and getting everything ready. He'd been discussing the significance of the fire pooja with the young couple when she came back in. She'd taken one look at all the fires and started to scream – unholy screams that had literally made Madhav tremble with fear – and then ran outside still screaming.

'Stop! Stop!' Madhav yelled at her, trying to manhandle her back into the temple. But he could not get through to her. She kept screaming and sobbing for a good forty minutes before falling into a dead faint.

When the car came to pick her up several hours later, Madhav crossly confronted its driver, a young man. 'Your mother had a nervous breakdown today! She screamed and screamed until she fainted!'

'She is not my mother,' the young man replied, wearily getting out of the car. 'Where is she?'

Madhav grudgingly took him to the rectory, where the woman was still asleep on a very uncomfortable sofa.

'She can't come here if she is mentally unstable,' Madhav said. 'This is not a lunatic asylum!'

'Did you have a fire pooja today?' the young man asked.

'Yes – we did. Why?'

'Next time just tell her and she'll stay out of the way. She can understand and speak when she wants to,' the young man said, shaking her shoulder. 'Aunty Nila, Aunty Nila, wake up . . . it's me, Aravinda.'

She looked at him, confused.

'I'm Renuka's nephew,' he said. 'You've been living with us in Australia for some time now. She forgets everything when she's had one of these episodes,' Aravinda explained for Madhav's benefit.

'The answer is no. You can't extend Hindu religious studies every Sunday by an extra four hours.'

'But . . .' Madhav protested; despite having been at the temple for nearly six months now, he was nowhere closer to having the management committee on side.

'But nothing,' Ananda, the chair of the board of trustees spluttered. 'For most of these kids, Sunday afternoon is the only free time they have! If we try and keep them in on Sundays as well, we'll have a mutiny that would make Mangal Pandey proud!'

'My girls have no time, *nah*,' Mrs Vasundaram huffed. 'Monday night is maths tuition, Tuesday night is remedial lessons in English, Wednesday night is music, Thursday night is science tuition and on Friday night I look over all their homework and set them extra lessons they have to fit in on Saturday before or after swimming.'

'Do your girls go to Professor Srilal for maths tuition?' Ananda asked.

'Yes. He was the dean of mathematics at Lucknow University, but he drives taxis now.'

'You should try Vivek Banerjee,' another trustee interrupted. 'My Preethi was only getting eighty and eighty-five for her maths tests and two weeks with Professor Patel and she is getting perfect scores.'

'Was he teaching at Delhi University?'

'No, at the University of Bangalore . . .'

'Is he driving cabs?'

'No, he is working in Delights of Delhi in Doncaster as a waiter.'

Madhav rolled his eyes. The trustees spent more time gossiping than discussing any temple business.

'I also wanted to ask about Nila Mendis,' he said, interrupting. 'Is there anyway we can prevent her coming to the temple every day?'

'No, *puttar*, no . . . we cannot ban Nila Mendis from coming to this temple,' Reverend Shastri interjected kindly. 'I grant you it is difficult with her loitering about, but she is truly harmless, son.'

'Just ignore her,' Ananda advised.

Madhav was not pleased, but he had more important questions. 'Fine – but what I really wanted to talk to you about was Varalakshmi Vratham.'

Again Ananda looked sternly at Madhav. 'As I've said before, if we were to celebrate every festival for the 330 million deities in Hinduism, neither you nor I would have a moment to spare!'

'But Mahalakshmi Vratham is not a festival for a local deity. It is a pooja for the goddess Laksmi! It is celebrated all around India!' Madhav insisted.

'It is a pooja practised at home by housewives. They fast, they decorate the house, they chant some *gathas* and that is it. There is no need for the temple to get involved,' Mrs Vasundaram chided.

'So what is the point in women doing the pooja in the home if they spend the rest of the evening gossiping?' Madhav said angrily. 'Families must come to the temple after their offerings at home!'

'It is none of our business what they do at home after the pooja,' Reverend Shastri said, starting to sound a little impatient now.

'But it *is* our business. The Mahalakshmi Vratham Pooja is an essential pooja in the Hindu calendar! It celebrates the goddess Laksmi and her bountiful benevolence! Do you know the tale of Charumathi?'

A set of blank faces greeted him.

'Charumathi was a Brahmin woman who lived in Kundina in the kingdom of Magadha. She was a good woman. She was a devout woman. She fasted when she should and she prayed three times a day. So one day, Mahalaksmi came to her in a dream and asked her to worship her by saying special secret prayers on the Friday before the full moon in the month of Sravana – July. She did as the goddess asked, and she found that all her worldly desires were fulfilled.'

He had their attention, at least for a moment.

'Her children did well, becoming educated pundits, and her husband's business – well, it flourished. So after that, year after year, more and more women would join Charumathi to chant the special secret prayers that Mahalaksmi had told her. *Padmaasane Padmakare sarva lokaika poojithe Narayana priyadevi supreethaa bhava sarvada,*' Madhav recited.

'Let me conduct this service. Let the families come here after they have their poojas at home and we'll chant the special prayers. All we need is some money for *kalanas* and some decorations,' he continued.

As soon as he mentioned money, Ananda looked at the time on his watch and Mrs Vasundaram started to put away her notebook and pens. In desperation he blurted, 'I'll pay for it then! Take it out of my pay! Just let me do this pooja.'

Ananda relented. 'It is his money after all,' he said, looking first at Reverend Shastri and then at the other board members.

'What utter nonsense – we women are too tired after fasting and making sweets for our families to come to this silly pooja,' Mrs Vasundaram grumbled.

'You have to do the decorations all by yourself,' Reverend Shastri warned. 'None of the committee will help and it all has to be finished by ten pm. I do not want to have the police turn up!' The chief pundit stood and stomped off, muttering to himself. 'Those police come here thinking they can get a two for one – hassle us while raiding the ganja growers out the back!'

On the afternoon of the Mahalakshmi Vrata Pooja, nothing was going to plan.

'Here! Idiots! The *kalanas* don't go there! And have you filled them with anything yet?' Madhav asked. His helpers were the lad who had driven him to the temple that first night, Kumar, and his trusty sidekick Gohar.

'Filled them with what?' Gohar asked.

'Rice, you idiots!' Madhav yelled,

'Look here . . .' Gohar started, but Kumar stopped him with a murderous glare. Gohar knew the deal. Madhav would allow the two of them to stay in the rectory at the temple each Friday and Saturday night for a whole month. 'A whole month, remember,' Kumar muttered. 'A whole month of being able to go out and drink as much as we want and walk home! Imagine that! Our mothers will never find out.'

Yes indeed, the pundit was enabling two young Indian men to go out on a Friday night to the most dubious nightclub in the eastern suburbs of Melbourne, Stylus, to get legless, so that they would help him with the decorations for the pooja!

'You need to fill the pots with rice and a mirror, and decorate them,' Madhav explained, pointing to a picture in an illustrated Hindu theology book. 'Then you'll need to put the buntings up and put the betel leaves out!'

On and on this went all afternoon. At just after five, Madhav caught Kumar and Gohar walking around with crowns of coconut husks on their heads, having mock battles with the fake bronze swords that were supposed to be the goddess Laksmi's husband's weapons. Half the decorations were not yet up.

'What are you doing?' he cried. 'Get back to work. People will start to come a little after six.'

'Nah . . . people won't come anytime before seven,' Kumar said. 'People have to go home, have dinner and make their kids do their homework before they jump in the car and drive for three-quarters of an hour to come here.'

Madhav collapsed to the ground and held his head in his hands. He should never have thought he could pull off a festival like this. Not so early in his career. Maybe he should tender his resignation and go back to India.

It was then that he noticed something. From in between his fingers.

'What have you drawn on those clay pots?' he demanded.

'You told us decorate them like the ones in the pictures,' Gohar protested pointing to the Hindu theology book.

'See, we have drawn them exactly like the symbols in the book,' Kumar said. The book had a picture of a pot with only a part of the symbol showing. And Gohar and Kumar had copied it exactly.

'You bloody fool! You have drawn half a bloody swastika!'

'As in *Heil Hitler*?' Gohar demanded, sticking his arm out in a Third Reich salute.

'No, as in a real swastika!' Madhav cried. 'The swastika was and is the Hindu symbol for goodness! Wipe those symbols off right now and start over again.'

In desperation, he closed his eyes and begged the goddess Laksmi for help. Any help. But as he opened them again, he felt that the gods had really deserted him, for Nila Mendis was just being dropped off in the courtyard.

'If you can keep your aunt at home just for that day, I would be most grateful,' Madhav had begged her nephew, but clearly his pleas had fallen on deaf ears.

Reverend Shastri emerged from his office and took the young pundit by the arm. 'Good lord, lad! You are going to conduct your first major pooja and we haven't even talked yet!

Come! Come!' he insisted. 'We need to discuss the order of service, the prayers list and specific people to thank. We cannot forget the board of trustees – it is, after all, due to their benevolence that we are all here.'

Madhav's interview with the chief pundit lasted a good hour and a half. Reverend Shastri insisted on not only determining the prayers but also checking his pronunciation of the more arcane words. As Madhav finally rushed to his room to change for the ceremony, he was grateful that Mahalakshmi Vratham Pooja was on a Friday night and hopefully not too many people would attend since it was the night for mathematics tuition!

I felt something. Did you feel anything?' one lady whispered. 'I never took the Mahalakshmi Vratham Pooja seriously, but this was truly magical,' another said to a friend as they stepped into the bitterly cold winter night, leaving the warmth and magic behind them. And it *had* been magical.

Lamps had been lit all around the shrine room and lanterns hung high beneath the ceiling. The central walkway to the inner sanctum had been strewn with rose petals and the perfume of sandalwood wafted over it all. And in each corner of the large room, there had been a lavishly decorated *kalanas*, smeared with vermilion and draped with hundreds of necklaces and jewels. The whole room had reflected the opulence and grandeur that was the benevolence of the goddess Laksmi.

But nothing, nothing, could have prepared them for what happened next. When the new pundit had walked in, followed by Kumar and Gohar, carrying the statue of the deity on their shoulders, everyone gasped. Some prostrated themselves in religious fervour.

The saree draped on the near life-size statue had been a work of art. Not that it was an uncommon saree by any stretch of the imagination – it was just a commonplace Benares silk – but you could have been forgiven for thinking she was real, such was the intricacy of the folding and draping, following her figure as faithfully and surely as if she were alive.

More than one person thought they'd felt the goddess's eyes on them. Some people even swore that they'd seen her move, such was the elegance of the drape of the saree. But everybody knew that the temple was graced with her divine presence when Madhav started to chant.

During the whole two-hour service not one person walked out, fidgeted or even stirred, spellbound by the magic of the prayer service. But the real magic started several days later.

'Guess what? My Srinivas got a job!' one woman cried on the phone to another. 'We went to the Mahalakshmi Vratham Pooja and we made a vow. The very next day he got a call for the interview, and two days later – a job! He has been looking for three years now!'

'My daughter is pregnant,' another cried at a large afternoon tea party. 'They have been trying for six years and finally she is pregnant. I made a vow at the Mahalakshmi Vratham Pooja!'

'We were struggling to make ends meet,' a young mother confessed to a friend at her mothers' group. 'The rent is so high and babies cost so much money. But my husband just called me and told me he just got a promotion! I think it's because I made a vow at Mahalakshmi Vrata Pooja the other week.'

Rumours and whispers started to sweep through the community. What started as a quiet conversation here, a telephone call there or a friendly exchange somewhere else soon turned into a raging fire. An Australian bushfire almost. Vows and dearest dreams were coming true all over the place. Businesses were succeeding, jobs won and women falling pregnant.

People had been to the Ferntree Gully Sri Ganapathi Vinayaka temple before and made umpteen vows, but nothing had come of it. Something had changed. And it had to be that new young pundit. What else could it be? It had to be that young man who prayed so earnestly. And everyone had heard the voice of the Mahalaksmi Devi when he led the prayers that night. No one could doubt that.

Ever since the Mahalakshmi Vratham Pooja, Madhav had been swamped. There had been a series of near miraculous changes in some lives and people were now flocking to the Ferntree Gully Sri Ganapathi Vinayaka Temple to get their cut of divine intervention.

'Punditji, I have problems with my mother-in-law. *Aii!* Day in, day out she is criticising me. The food I cook is not good enough. My children are not respectful enough. Now my husband is ganging up with his mother against me,' the young woman wept.

'My wife . . . I think she is having an affair,' a man cried.

'My son is thinking of marrying an Australian girl. I have no problem with her. But her mother, well, she has pink hair. I am so scared my grandchildren will have pink hair too!' another lady confided.

People came from all over the state. Indian doctors from Echuca, Hindu devotees from Warrnambool and even hippies from an ashram in Daylesford. They all came to him seeking advice, spiritual solace, and in every instance – help!

Madhav tended to them all. He doled out wisdom based on ancient Hindu scripture, soothed their troubled minds and did poojas for them.

'Listen to your mother-in-law. Does she have a point? Is your cooking good enough? Are your children respectful? Hinduism teaches that it is the responsibility of the woman to be a good wife. A good daughter-in-law. Are you being that?

Now I will do a pooja. We will beseech the goddess Sita for you. We must ask her to help you to be a good wife,' Madhav advised.

'If your wife is having an affair, you have every right to take her back to India and divorce there. Come back to Australia with your children. Adultery is against the *dharma*!' he advised sternly. 'I will now do a pooja for Lord Ganapathi and ask him to find you a good wife. A homely wife,' he said.

'I am not worried about your son's mother-in-law's hair as long as your daughter-in-law is a good Hindu. Ask her to come to the Hinduism course I am teaching every Sunday night now. She needs to understand the ancient tradition she is marrying into,' he replied.

But what had changed the most was the relationship between Madhav and the board of trustees. Even the chief pundit had a new respect for the young man, who now seemed indispensable to the running of the temple.

At the next board meeting, Madhav brought up the subject of a break.

'What do you mean you need a break?' Ananda spluttered.

'I work from six in the morning until ten at night. I need more than an hour's lunchbreak,' Madhav clarified.

'Of course,' the man sighed.

'Oh, thank goodness,' Mrs Vasundaram gasped. 'It was just that we thought you might be wanting to take a break to go back to India.'

'No, no . . . I have work to do here,' Madhav said. Yes, God's plan was very clear to him now. He realised why he had been sent to this land. It was to bring Hinduism to these people. He finally understood his journey. From London to Mumbai, and now to Melbourne.

'But I need some help. I need someone to help me with the poojas and to help me set everything up,' he continued.

'Would you like us to send for someone from India?' Ananda asked.

'No. Why not ask Kumar and Gohar? They have holidays coming up from university next week. Could they help me?'

'We do not have any money to pay them,' Mrs Vasundaram protested.

Madhav stared straight into her eyes. 'We do not have money, madam? Really? Everyone of my poojas costs twenty-five dollars. I also know that you buy cheap fruit from the markets for the actual offerings. Since my pay hasn't increased and the number of people who come has increased many fold, what is becoming of all that extra money?'

Ananda and the other trustees bristled.

The trick to haggling is to know when to up the ante. 'And I hear that they are looking for a new pundit for the temple they are building in Seaford. I hear that it is by the beach and there would even be scope for having water poojas!'

'But of course we can get Kumar and Gohar to help. We'll even pay them the minimum wage!' Mrs Vasundaram said quickly. 'Did you know they don't even pay minimum wage at Delights of Delhi in Doncaster? I heard they got raided by Immigration!'

'I heard they got raided by the health authorities,' Reverend Shastri interrupted.

'No, no, it was Immigration! All those international students working overtime!' Ananda said.

'So, you agree then? That I can have Kumar and Gohar to help?' Madhav said.

'Yes – just for the school holidays to start with.'

Kumar and Gohar weren't bad lads – they just weren't smart lads. Kumar had earned sufficient marks to get into engineering, having been tutored during his primary school and high school years, but he was floundering at university

Gohar was cut from a different cloth altogether. The youngest of four children and the favourite of his grandmother,

he'd been indulged beyond belief. When he'd struggled at
school, mainly due to laziness rather than lack of intelligence,
his grandmother had blamed it on a poor horoscope which
would right itself with age.

'Let the boy be,' she would croon, pushing another laddoo
into his mouth. 'He'll grow up when he needs to. I'm leaving
him my property in India. Go back home, my son, and enjoy
the good life in the Punjab. Marry a rich girl and have plenty of
servants! Why should he do chores around the house?'

They were not quick learners, and Madhav was often impatient with them, but Nila Mendis was there to show them what
to do and guide them. Kumar and Gohar were not as grateful
as they should have been, and often tormented Nila. They
took indescribable pleasure in repeatedly asking her questions,
knowing she was reticent to speak.

'So what is your name, Aunty?'

'Where do you live, Aunty?'

'Can we have a look at your underskirt, Aunty? Is it red
or blue?'

'If you show me your underskirt, I will marry you. Please let
me marry you?'

Madhav did nothing to stop their nonsense, hoping she
would grow tired of their teasing and not come back one day.
She was the sole nuisance in what was fast becoming a perfect
life for Madhav. She was there. Always there. Looking at him
with those beady eyes.

Madhav never saw it, but in the privacy of the shrine room,
Kumar and Gohar's relationship with Nila Mendis was something altogether very different. The boys were immensely
thankful to Aunty Nila. She'd saved them more than once.
When tasked with a serious job or in a moment of crisis, Nila
was as lucid and sensible as anyone else – in fact she could
speak plainly and well, as she'd demonstrated on the night of
the Mahalakshmi Vrata Pooja. When Madhav had disappeared
into the chief pundit's office, she had taken charge.

'Boys, come here,' she'd commanded in a voice that brooked no dispute. 'Now I want you to put away those silly swords and help me fill these pots. And put those buntings up again. Do it properly this time!'

Before they knew it, the room had been entirely redecorated. But where Aunty Nila had really shone was when she'd draped the saree on the statue of the deity, whispering prayers under her breath. The boys had seen her magic there . . .

While Madhav had actually conducted the poojas and offered counselling, it was Nila who'd made sure everything went smoothly, praying alongside the pundit in the inner sanctum. So while the miracles were attributed to Madhav, it could be argued that they would not have occurred without Nila.

Madhav remembered the first time he ever heard a prayer; it was to the Lord Ganesh and it was while he was in his mother's womb. Yes, truly. Why would a Hindu priest lie? He was about six when he was finally able to ask his mother about it over breakfast.

'Mama . . . what were you doing in Aunty Preethi's house the night Uncle Jude had his heart attack?'

'I can't remember, *beta*,' Pinky Patel had fudged as she strapped her youngest daughter into a high chair and poured cereal into the bowl of her older daughter, who was watching TV. 'It was a long time before you were born.'

'But Mama, you remember everything.' Madhav had rolled his eyes. 'You even remember who sewed your mother's *lengha* for her wedding.'

'I was there because Preethi called all upset. Her mother had called her from India saying that she'd heard from Aunty Pimmi that Uncle Hithesh had heard from his cousin that . . . *beta*, how did you know that I was at Aunty Preethi's house? You weren't even born!'

'I remember,' he'd confessed. 'You caught the tube from Holland Park to Monument, but you got worried when you changed over. Then you went up Angel and walked to her house through the markets . . .'

'Yes . . . it was the end of spring and I bought . . .'

'Some apples. Green apples. Yuk!' Madhav had gagged. 'I fell asleep once you got there, though . . .'

'I was chatting to Aunty Preethi . . .'

'I always slept when you gossiped.'

'I wasn't gossiping!' Pinky protested.

'I had just woken up and Aunty Preethi begged you to help her with the pooja . . .'

'Yes, she'd just found out that Uncle Jude was still in contact with his girlfriend in India! And she wanted to pray to Lord Ganapathi to get her out of the way!'

'But you prayed wrong and Lord Ganapathi got everything out of the way,' Madhav whispered. 'He almost got Uncle Jude out of the way.'

Pinky Patel collapsed quite nerveless onto a high stool near the breakfast bar.

'Mama . . . I hear God, Mama. I hear him speak to me some times.'

'What does he say to you?' Pinky demanded.

'He is not a he, Mama . . . oh, sometimes he is a he . . . and sometimes she is a she . . .'

'So what does he or she say to you?'

'Nothing much . . . she is there sometimes when I am scared of the dark. He helped me with some bullies in the park the other day. But they are very happy when I pray. I can feel them smile.'

Pinky had started to panic. 'You don't listen to them, *nah*! Never listen to them! They are bad voices.'

'No, they are good voices. They are gods!'

'No, *beta*, no. You must not listen to them!' she'd pleaded.

'But can I speak with them?' he begged. 'I love talking to them.'

'How do you talk to them?'

'I pray . . . *Shri Mahaganapatim Bhajeham Shivatmajam Sanmukhagrajam*.'

'And they hear you?'

'Of course . . . They hear everyone who prays to them.'

'But they don't always answer prayers.'

'That has to do with karma. If you have really bad karma they cannot help you. But they do listen. They try to help all the time. They say they like it when I pray. They like to do things when I ask them to do things. Remember that time when we were at the park and I lost my toy car? I prayed and we found it days later?'

Pinky nodded. It had been nothing short of miraculous that the toy car had been left on the top of the swings. And she had to admit there was something very compelling about Madhav's voice. He was not an ordinary little boy. From his earliest days, people were drawn to him just to listen to him speak.

'Don't listen to them, though . . . you only listen to Mama and Papa,' she'd insisted. 'And don't tell anyone what you've told me today!'

'But I can still pray?' Madhav had demanded.

'Yes, *beta*,' Pinky had conceded shakily. She would simply have to ensure that he got involved in sports and so many other activities that he forgot his religious leanings. And parties. She'd make sure he went to plenty of parties.

But try as she might, she could not stop Madhav from praying. In the early hours of the day or in the dead of the night, she'd find him in prayer, his lips moving silently, his eyes half closed. She was sure he was the only teenager in England who did not have to be told to get up off the couch and away from the TV!

'So what do you see or feel when you pray?' one of his sisters had asked in frustration the day he'd left England for India. It had been six months of constant fighting for the entire household. His mother and father had vehemently opposed his decision to become a pundit and had fought him all the way.

'Everything . . .' he'd whispered. 'I see everything. Adithi . . . you don't understand. I feel God. I feel what they are feeling. And it is magic. My body feels light. I go to another place.'

'So you are saying it is like drugs?' she'd whispered, looking sideways at her parents. They were too busy fighting to have overheard her.

'If you'd only spent more time with the boy, *nah*!' Pinky screamed.

'No! It's all your fault,' Suresh raged back.

When Adithi looked at Madhav, she wished she could dissolve herself into magic too.

Madhav had one afternoon per week off. The forty-hour week and trade union movement had not quite made it into the Hindu establishment. The trustees insisted he work like Indians back in India. All the time.

But he'd been living in Melbourne for almost eight months now and he desperately needed to get some new underwear. So he was on his way to Boronia. While the temple was technically in Boronia, the high street which served as the suburb's mercantile hub was a good five kilometres away and accessible only by train. The nearest station to the temple was Ferntree Gully.

The ticket counter was closed when he arrived. So was the milk bar which sold the scratchy version of the tickets. 'So what am I to do now?' Madhav growled to himself.

He was still standing there debating what to do when a mother with three children came along. He'd seen them often enough. They lived about ten minutes away in a house that looked as if it should be condemned. The eldest, whom Madhav supposed to be about six, was nose deep in a book. The middle child was a little girl of about four and the youngest was a snotty-nosed tot trapped in a very rusty pram.

The mother took a deep drag of her cigarette before she walked through the open turnstile onto the platform. The guilty way she kept looking at the ticket counter made it clear that she didn't have a ticket and had no intention of buying one either.

When the train rumbled along the tracks, he decided to take

his chances with the ticket inspector, promising himself that he would buy a ticket at the other end.

Only the ticket counter at the other end was closed as well. He could not blame the Met – Boronia was a singularly dreary suburb. He made his way along the narrow strip of shops, passing a string of drunks and drugged-out people squatting on the pavement and carefully picking his way around them. He held his sarong close to his legs as he strode through the car park to the Big W behind it. He did not approve – how could he?

These people were given money to live on by the state and then wasted it on alcohol and cigarettes. They needed to go to a country like India to see poverty. Real poverty. Where children were forced to live on mountains of garbage to eke out a living. Ten families living in a single room. Hunger. Desperation. That was real poverty.

What he saw at the large department store only went to prove his theory.

The mother and her three kids had followed him to Big W.

'Mum . . . can I have this book?' the young boy asked.

'How much is it?' his mum grunted, her young voice already coarsened by years of smoking.

'Ten dollars.'

'You're kiddin' me, right? I ain't got enough money to feed youse!'

'But Mum, it's a really good book!' the boy said. 'Please?'

'Go on, piss off . . . and you, Angel, stop smacking your little brother!' she snapped as she went up to the counter and spent fifty dollars on a carton of Benson & Hedges. 'Full-strength, please,' she said.

Madhav quickly bought six pairs of underwear and was hurrying to the till to pay when the young boy noticed him.

'Why is that man wearing a skirt?'

'It's not a skirt, it's a sarong,' Madhav corrected him.

'Yeah, like your uncle Phil wore on his beach trip to Thailand,' his mother interjected.

'But we're not at the beach,' the little boy pointed out.

'That's because they're different,' his mother said.

'How?'

'They just are. They eat curry, so that keeps them warm . . .'

'But he's wearing a jacket.'

His mother took a look at Madhav and quickly looked away. 'Stop asking questions,' she said, dragging the little boy away.

The mother and her three children followed him back onto the train back to Ferntree Gully. The little fellow was enthralled by Madhav, now peeking over his seat to stare at him.

His mother did not stop him. She was too busy keeping the other two from hurting each other. 'Angel, I will wallop you if you don't stop buggin' Dylan!' she kept shouting. So it was while all this commotion was going on that the ticket inspectors came through.

The inspectors worked their way through the semi-packed carriage full of children returning home from school.

'Tickets, please,' they called, stopping when they came to the young mother.

'Don't have any,' she snapped belligerently.

'Why not?'

'Because the stupid counter was closed.'

'Well, you'll just have to pay the fine, then,' the young officer told her, opening his pocketbook.

'That is just fuckin' stupid,' the woman said. Her son and daughter drew close together to protect themselves from the oncoming war of words. 'This is fuckin' stupid is what it is! I tried to buy tickets but there was no one there! I have no fuckin' money to pay a fuckin' fine!'

On and on the altercation went. The mother would not give an inch and neither would the inspectors, the argument spilling onto the platform at Ferntree Gully, where Madhav quickly slunk away, his heart beating rapidly at the narrow escape he'd had from paying a $120 fine.

*Abishekam* was an essential part of Hindu priests' daily rites. Each deity in the shrine had to be bathed in a concoction of milk and ghee and finally washed with rosewater while Reverend Shastri and Madhav chanted mantras in the early hours of the morning.

'*Om Sri Ganapathis Ram . . . Om Sri Ram . . . Om Sri Ram . . .*' Madhav muttered as he handed the *kalahasas* of milk to the chief pundit. His stomach rumbled quite loudly. Normally the *abishekam* would have long been completed. But not today.

Cold bitter winds and rain had lashed Melbourne the night before. For hours the wind and rain had howled through the Dandenongs, the surrounding ghost gums creaking and cracking and shedding their limbs. Madhav and the chief pundit had spent the night huddled in the part of the rectory furthest away from any large trees, but at around midnight an almighty crash was heard from just beyond.

'Lord Ganapathi save us!' the chief pundit had cried, running to see what had happened.

It was a large gum tree and it had fallen in between the rectory and the temple proper, damaging nothing of importance but creating quite a hindrance. Had it not been for the Rebels in the shack in the adjoining paddock, Madhav and Reverend Shastri would have been trapped.

'M'name is Clint,' the chief Rebel had drawled, walking in with a chainsaw just after dawn. 'Guess you'll be wanting that tree removed, huh?' he'd said, stating the obvious, before setting to work with six other similarly tattooed men. As much as Madhav had wanted to send the man packing, he couldn't. He really needed the tree removed. He needed the temple set to rights because he'd received a very important call a few days ago.

'Yes, this is the Reverend Madhav Patel at the Ferntree Gully Sri Ganapathi Vinayaka temple,' he'd answered.

'Hi, my name is Kylie, and I'm calling from the *Australia Today* program on Channel 6. We've had reports that miracles are happening in Ferntree Gully and we'd like to send a reporter out to talk with you.'

'I don't know about miracles, but we are devout Hindus here,' Madhav had told Kylie pompously. 'What exactly have you heard?'

'We've got reports of three women falling pregnant after visiting your temple. Two of these women had been through multiple rounds of IVF and failed.'

'They were lucky,' Madhav said. 'These things happen.'

'Then there was a child who had glaucoma and it has disappeared. Can you explain that?'

'Did the child have treatment at a hospital?'

'I assume so.'

'That is most likely the cause of the cure, then.'

'I'd still like to come out and speak to you anyway,' Kylie had pleaded. 'Either way, it will be good publicity for your temple, and the work you are doing in the local community.'

'I will have to consult with the board of trustees before I allow a camera crew onto the temple grounds,' Madhav said. He was very excited at the thought of being on TV but didn't want the woman to know it.

'Oh, think of it,' Mrs Vasundaram had cried excitedly. 'We'll be the leading Hindu temple in all of Australia soon! Wait till I tell my mother back home in India!'

'Do you need a trustee to be there on Thursday? I can take the day off,' Ananda had offered.

'No . . . I think I will be able to manage,' Madhav had replied.

So now Madhav was desperately trying to finish the *abishekam* and get ready before the people from Channel 6 arrived. The falling tree had been inconvenient, but the bikies had sorted it out and now he could get on with preparations for the filming. He was expecting Kumar and Gohar to arrive any moment to help him set up.

That was when the phone rang out in the rectory. Madhav dashed out to answer it, wondering if it might be the television crew calling. 'It's me, Kumar,' a rusty voice sounded down the line. 'Look, Gohar and I can't come today. Our car was crushed by a tree.'

'But . . .'

'But nothing, mate,' Kumar said sullenly. 'I just had that car resprayed. I'm completely gutted!'

Madhav hung up on him and started to panic. He could finish off the preparations for the camera crew on his own, but what was he going to do about Nila Mendis? He didn't want that crackpot about when he made his TV debut and had been depending on Kumar and Gohar to keep her out of the way!

Steeling himself, Madhav changed into a lungi and an elaborate sarong. Once it warmed up in the shrine room, he would strip down to his sarong and Brahmin thread, but not yet. He wanted the Australian audiences to see a proper Brahmin priest as he should be seen.

'So, do you need the firewood, or should we take it away?' Clint asked as Madhav came out of the rectory.

'I thought you'd left!' Madhav cried.

'Nah . . . just went out for morning tea. Had some scones and jam from the bakery.'

'Don't worry about it. We've got a TV crew coming in about ten minutes, so I will arrange to have the wood cleared up later.'

'It's all right, mate. We can take care of it now – won't be long. It's the least we can do,' Clint assured him, as the other Rebels got to work stacking the wood.

Madhav could not exactly demand they leave after they had been so helpful, so he left them to it and rushed to front of the temple just as two large vehicles bearing the Channel 6 insignia came driving up.

'Just as well we had the four-wheel drives,' a blond woman called as she jumped out of the first car. 'Fallen trees everywhere! I'm Kylie – are you Madhav Patel? I hope you are, because we want to get this story filmed today and air it tomorrow!'

'Yes, I am Madhav Patel,' he replied, feeling ill. From the corner of one eye he could see the Rebels coming around the side of the temple with their chainsaw, and from the other, the rusty car belonging to Nila Mendis's nephew. He closed his eyes in horror and opened them again, only to see the little white boy from the train walk into the compound.

'I thought I'd find you here!' the boy called out, seeing Madhav.

Madhav watched the report with the chief pundit on the television in the rectory.

'. . . and now to the outer eastern suburbs of Melbourne, where miracles are taking place,' said the presenter. 'Infertile women have fallen pregnant. The long-term unemployed have found jobs. A child with glaucoma has been cured, and even a cat who'd been missing for two years has been found safe and sound. More from "Weird and Wonderful" reporter Kylie McLean in Boronia,' she finished.

The chief pundit did not look impressed.

'Sri Ganapathi Vinayaka temple was always just another Hindu temple among the handful of Hindu temples here in the cosmopolitan heart of Melbourne,' Kylie opened, walking towards the camera. 'But earlier this year everything changed when a British-born holy man or sadhu took over the running of the temple.'

'Meet Madhav Patel. He was born in the UK and had been offered a place studying medicine at Oxford when he ran away from home to join a Hindu seminary.'

'It isn't easy to join a Hindu seminary,' Madhav explained on camera. 'You have to sit exams testing your understanding of Sanskrit and Hindi. These were especially difficult since I had been entirely educated in the UK.'

'Madhav says he first heard the gods speak to him in his mother's womb,' Kylie's voice continued, as viewers were shown a montage of Madhav walking around the temple grounds and praying.

'Since arriving in Melbourne, direct from the seminary in Mumbai, Reverend Madhav has been credited with bringing about miracles.'

'We have been trying for fifteen years to have a baby,' a middle-aged Indian woman explained on camera. 'The doctors had given up. But we went to the Mahalakshmi Vrata Pooja and four weeks later we received the amazing news!'

'My son Srinath is a qualified engineer. Graduated top of his batch at university. Worked for a few years but lost his job. Could not find one for another six years. So I made a vow at the Mahalakshmi Vrata Pooja and two days later he got called for an interview and now he is employed at the Met driving trains,' another parent said gleefully.

'The doctors wanted us to consent to laser surgery. They found glaucoma in our daughter's eyes,' a father said tearfully as his child played with her puppy in the foreground. 'But we went to the Mahalakshmi Vrata Pooja and made a vow. Two days later she had another scan and there were no traces of the glaucoma.'

'So how do you do it?' Kylie asked Madhav. 'How do you bring about these miracles?'

'I don't bring about miracles. It is God who brings about miracles,' Madhav told her.

'Which god? I see so many gods here that I don't know which one to choose.' The camera panned around the temple, showing the hundreds of statuettes.

'Hinduism has over 330 million gods. You choose the god who is right for what you need.'

'So which god would I go to if I wanted a new car?'

'It does not work like that. You have to have true belief in your heart when you approach God. What you give out is what you get.'

'Is that like karma?' Kylie asked.

The camera cut to a heavyset biker covered with tattoos, having a chat on a stump with his mates. 'Isn't karma like when you kill a fly and get reborn as a dog?' he asked.

'The laws of karma are a lot more complex than that,' Madhav said. 'Karma is about intent. It is determined by all of one's thoughts and acts, not odd acts of thoughtlessness or cruelty,' Madhav's voice chimed in.

'Are you saying that killing a person is permissible then, as long as you don't do it often?'

'No, killing is never permissible. All Hindus should practice *ahimsa* – non-violence.'

'You don't eat meat?'

'Never.'

The following scene showed the glamorous Kylie in the shrine room proper, perambulating and bowing to the various gods.

'So every day of the week, you'll find this young holy man beseeching God on your behalf. All it requires is that you come here with twenty-five dollars and a plate of fruit, and all your wishes will come true,' the voice over read as the camera showed Madhav smearing Kylie's forehead with vermilion.

'Can the gods taste the fruit?' Kylie asked.

'Of course not.'

'Then why offer it? Isn't it a bit wasteful?'

'It is about giving something to receive something in return.'

'So why come to a temple to do an offering? Why not do it at home?'

'Of course you can do your offerings at home. That is completely up to you. But here at a temple you have people – pundits – who pray to God all the time. God is more likely to visit a temple than your house.'

'So, it's like going to a party. You know the gods are more likely to be here, so you'll get a chance to talk to them.'

'Yes,' Madhav had replied, distracted, not realising what he had just agreed to. Brendan had come rushing in carrying one of the mock swords from the Mahalaksmi pooja. Madhav was very relieved when he spotted Nila swiftly take the little sword from the boy.

'Will there be another grand party soon, when the gods will preside again?'

'There are no parties here!' Madhav huffed. 'We have poojas. That is when we commune with God!'

'So when is the next major pooja?'

'At Navaratri, when we worship the triple goddess, Durga-Amman, the great mother, Mahalaksmi, the goddess of abundance, and Saraswati, the goddess of wisdom.'

'So there you have it folks, come to Ferntree Gully Sri Ganapathi Vinayaka during Navaratri and all your dreams will come true!'

The chief pundit was horrified. It took six weeks for Madhav to recover from watching the report, and several months before he could be persuaded that the television itself was not an inherently evil invention.

'The Navaratri pooja will be big this year. We have to start planning now. It is September now and November will be upon us before we know it!' Ananda, the chair of the board of trustees, declared.

No longer were committee meetings poorly attended and barely listened to. It was serious business now. The temple now had three full-time staff on top of Madhav and the chief pundit. Kumar and Gohar were now priests in training and receiving a youth allowance.

After the *Australia Today* story, people were flying in from as far away as Brisbane and Sydney to visit the temple, in numbers worthy of a smallish pilgrimage site in India. A few entrepreneurs had even set up shop on the little grass knoll near the temple, selling hot chips, drinks and cheap fruit.

'We'll need a budget for the Navaratri festivities this year,' Mrs Vasundaram said, looking at her notes. 'I think five thousand dollars should cover it all?'

'Five thousand won't cover the basic necessities,' Madhav countered. 'We'll need to have at least 200 litres of milk for the *abishekam* over nine days and two truckloads of fruit. Not to mention at least twenty cartons of camphor, as well as vermilion paste, turmeric paste, rose water and *vibuthi*!'

'Don't you just take ash from a burnt tree for *vibuthi*?' a new trustee asked. His name was Narayan and he had only recently come to Australia.

'It is actually cow dung incinerated with sandalwood,' Madhav explained.

'And you smear it all over your forehead?' the young man asked in horror.

'Madhav is right – we'll need more supplies,' said Ananda. 'I just heard from the Hare Krishnas. They will be coming in force during Navaratri.'

'That'll be a thousand extra pilgrims!' Reverend Shastri gasped.

'No, an extra two thousand at least. Their movement is quite large here in Victoria.'

'Oh my God! How are we to accommodate such a number?'

'I have already contacted the seminary in India and they are sending extra pundits out to help us,' Madhav said. 'It is the Navaratri pageant I am worried about,' he continued.

'We usually don't have a pageant,' Ananda said.

'We will have over three thousand people attending. What do you suppose we do with them? Have a Bollywood dance-off on the lawns? We need a pageant!'

'On the last night, like in India!' Reverend Shastri seconded.

'With large floats on trucks. We'll bring out the statues of the Durga-Amman, Mahalaksmi and Saraswati Devi dressed like the queens of the heavens!' Madhav insisted.

'But . . . a pageant? It'll cost money, and we'll need to get the council's permission,' Mrs Vasundaram said. Some of the other trustees nodded.

'Mrs Vasundaram, isn't your daughter sitting her final exams for university entrance this year? Didn't you just buy a new business, Mr Ananda? And you, Mr Govinda, you've not been in Australia a year. Aren't you thinking of buying a house? You all want the gods to hear your prayers and answer them, to give you their blessings, but you must also give to the gods in return!' Madhav said. Even the most miserly trustees were moved by his speech.

'It will be my pleasure to donate the saree for the Durga-Amman statue,' Mrs Vasundaram declared. 'I saw a beautiful saree in Clow Street in Dandenong on the weekend.

My daughter is studying for the VCE this year, and by the grace of Durga-Amman, she will be a doctor!'

'My wife and I will donate a thousand dollars for a saree for Mahalaksmi,' Ananda said. 'We've just opened a restaurant in Surrey Hills, and by her benevolence, it will be successful.'

Madhav waited for someone to take up the cause for Saraswati, but there was silence. 'Is no one going to take up the goddess Saraswati's cause? No one?' he asked.

'We really don't have the money,' Narayan confessed shamefacedly. 'My wife and I have only been here a year and we are desperately trying to save money for a deposit for a house.' The other trustees nodded; their situations were similar.

'It is traditional that the sarees are donated by the trustees of the temple,' Reverend Shastri chided. 'It is a great honour and a privilege to do so.'

'Perhaps the saree can be donated by the visitors to the temple?' Madhav suggested. 'I'll go into Dandenong and find a saree, and then we'll place a donation box in the shrine room and get people to chip in for it. That way everyone will have a hand in the blessing.'

There were ways and means of persuasion open to a priest not available to most. Especially so in the case of Madhav, as he was the person everyone came to see. Had the Reverend Shastri been at all an egotistical man, he would have thrown a tantrum worthy of a toddler, but he was quite happy to be relegated to a junior role as Madhav took on more and more of the services. Some people even walked rudely away from the older priest if he dared to touch their offering plate. 'We came here to see the miracle maker,' they would mutter, and not too softly, either. Madhav barely had time to catch his breath from when he started in the morning until he fell asleep.

But the young pundit's passion for the gods could not be doubted. He had placed a large donation box in the temple with a sign on it that read: 'Target $50,000 for Saraswati's saree'.

What? Who'd pay $50,000 for a saree?

Of course the trustees had raised merry hell about it. 'What? Fifty thousand dollars? That's enough to put a deposit on a four-bedroom house!' Govinda had protested.

'They are robbing you blind!' Mrs Vasundaram had cried. 'Take me to the people trying to sell you this saree at once and I will have words with them! Trying to rip off a Hindu priest and a nice young man like you! Imagine that!'

So Madhav had trooped the entire board of trustees off to a private home in the south-eastern suburb of Bentleigh one overcast Sunday afternoon, leaving Kumar and Gohar in charge of the temple.

'I looked in every shop on Clow Street in Dandenong but I could not find a saree that was appropriate,' Madhav said, knocking on the door. 'Then quite by chance someone mentioned that Feroz Khan had recently returned from India, where he had packed up his father's saree store in Lucknow.'

'We are going to buy a saree from a Muslim?' Govinda squealed in the background.

'We are all children of India,' Reverend Shastri rebuked.

When Mr Khan answered the door, he greeted them quietly, ushering them in and apologising for the mess. 'We've just moved here,' he explained.

Mrs Vasundaram sniffed. The house was in fact in something of a state, with boxes and piles of clothing covering every surface.

'You moved here from India?' Mr Ananda asked eagerly.

'Oh no . . . we've lived in Australia for about fifteen years now. We've just moved down from New South Wales.'

'From Sydney?' Mrs Vasundaram asked. 'I know many Indian Muslims in Sydney. Do you know Zia Ali Abdul from Andhra Pradesh? A doctor from Hyderabad. Surely you must know him?'

'No. We lived mainly in country New South Wales . . .' Feroz Khan said.

'And what did you do there?' Mr Ananda asked.

'I worked for the Snowy Mountains Hydro-Electric Scheme,' he said, looking distinctly uncomfortable as his effusive wife came bustling up.

'Why are you standing in the doorway in the cold, *nah*? Come in! Come in!' she welcomed. 'I am boiling water for chai, and I have some laddoo and muruku here as well. Come in! Sit! Sit! Sit!' she cried. 'I suppose you have come to see the saree?'

'Of course,' Mrs Vasundaram replied. 'It's just that fifty thousand dollars . . .'

'. . . is far too much for a saree!' Mrs Khan agreed heartily. 'See, I told you, Feroz. No one will pay you fifty thousand for it! No one will pay that much money for a saree. Not here. Not anywhere!'

'But the valuer told us that the saree was worth at least seventy-five thousand!'

'How on earth does a saree cost that much money?' Mrs Vasundaram demanded. 'Is it made entirely out of gold?'

'Can we see the saree?' Madhav asked softly.

'Come with me,' Feroz Khan said, and they followed him along a little corridor to a room in the back of the house. 'You'll understand why we keep it under lock and key,' he said as he knelt by a heavy iron trunk bolted to the ground and locked with two heavy padlocks. Mrs Khan handed him the keys, which she kept on a heavy gold chain around her neck, and he opened the lid of the trunk.

In the bright afternoon sunshine streaming through the impossibly grubby windows, they saw the saree, a beautiful shimmering golden white, lying on top of a bed of other sarees.

'Don't touch it,' Feroz growed at his wife. 'You've just been in the kitchen and you may have oil on your hands!'

He took it out, carefully unfolding the layers of tissue paper protecting the fabric, then laid it out on the large Persian rug on the ground, rolling out the ornate *pallu* to awed gasps all around.

'The valuer counted over three hundred sapphires alone in the peacock,' Feroz announced proudly. 'And the rubies used for the eyes are worth five thousand dollars.'

'The thread used to embroider the bottom edge is dipped in gold,' Fatima Khan added. 'We think there's about a kilogram of twenty-four-carat gold in this saree.'

Mrs Vasundaram gently lifted the *pallu*. Yes, it was heavy, but the weight was evenly distributed so that it flowed like a silk ribbon in the air.

'We had an Asian art expert look at it too. He says this saree is priceless. He could not identify the silk used, it is so rare. He thinks it may have come from a boutique sericulture farm in China or even Burma.'

'Who or what could have inspired such a beautiful saree?' Mr Ananda mused.

'It could only be Saraswati Devi,' Reverend Shastri proclaimed. 'They are her colours. Golden white with blue. The peacock is her totem animal. And the fluid design represents the river, her gift to the world, the wisdom that quenches the fires of ignorance. She is that which knows and knows that which needs to be known.'

After that, there had been no debate about the temple acquiring the saree for the Navaratri pageant. 'It is an investment,' Narayan insisted. 'In ten years, we'll be able to sell it to a museum for twice the money we paid for it!'

So every time Madhav did a pooja now, he would look meaningfully at the donation box. The message was clear. Twenty-five dollars paid for the offering plate, but the quality of the service was dependent on the amount deposited in the box. Coins bought only a lacklustre performance. Green ten-dollar notes and orange twenties guaranteed a little more energy, a little more effort. But multiples of the mustard-coloured fifty-dollar note would result in chanting of such passionate frenzy that even the laziest gods in the heavens above would be obliged to take notice, even if it were just to find out who was disturbing their rest.

To gain favour with the gods, first one must gain favour with their emissary. And their emissary was Madhav. So the people grudgingly parted with their money. Most of the pilgrims were new immigrants, still in the habit of converting dollars into rupees. Yet they were desperate. Desperate for jobs. Desperate for secure accommodation. Desperate for new lives in this new country. Which was why they parted with their money.

'Why did you become a priest?' the little Australian boy asked seriously. He pushed back the pair of glasses perched on his nose and stared intently up at Madhav.

'Because,' Madhav retorted. It was lunchtime, the only spare half-hour he had in the day, and he'd much rather spend it reading the newspaper in the rectory or calmly composing himself, preparing for the busy afternoon. But no, he could not have any peace because he had a little white ant. Kumar and Gohar were there too, sprawled on the couch watching the tiny television, the noise making it even harder for him to concentrate.

'Because of what?' the little fellow asked. 'Because you get your food for free and it's all cooked for you?'

Madhav looked at him, confused, putting down his week-old copy of *The Times of India*.

'That's what my mum says. That youse live off the hard work of other people. That youse should work hard like everyone else.'

'Firstly, Brendan, it is *you*, not *youse* . . .'

'But—'

'If you want to converse with me, you will use the Queen's English. Secondly, we do not live off the hard work of our parishioners. You see what I do here. You have watched me work – though I have noticed you aren't spending as much time in the shrine room as you used to.'

'Aunty Nila told me it would be better if I did some work while I was waiting for you. She's got me cleaning the grounds while you pray. But that's only in the afternoons. She makes me read and do maths in the morning. She says I should be at school.'

'Then for once I agree with Ms Mendis. Why aren't you at school?'

'Because me mum had a fight with me class teacher. Miss Carlie says I can't come to class without lunch and wearing the same clothes all week. She says by end of the week I'm putrid. Then me mum waited for Miss Carlie in the car park and put dog shit all over her car, and now she doesn't let me go to school.'

'Shouldn't the welfare authorities be involved?'

'Yeah, a lady from the department comes every week. But she says me mum is on the line but never over.'

'Over what?' Madhav asked cautiously.

'Over the line where they'd have to take me, Angel and Dylan and put us in foster care.'

Madhav didn't know how to respond, but Brendan didn't wait for an answer. He had lots more questions.

'Anyway, what I wanted to ask was why do youse never eat meat? I love meat. I love spag bog. I have it most nights. Me mum says that she can feed us kids for twenty dollars a week by just giving us spag bog.'

'Don't you have any salad or vegetables?'

'Nah . . . that's why Miss Carlie me teacher said my farts stank. No vegetables. I told Aunty Nila and that's why she sends me in here to have lunch with youse . . . you . . . so I get me vegetables. Aunty Nila says she's praying for my mum to find a husband. She says if she was married she'd have someone to look after her, and then maybe she could do a better job of looking after us.'

'Nila Mendis should mind her own business,' Madhav muttered.

'How would she know?' Kumar laughed. 'She's never been married!'

'Who'd marry a complete nutter?' Gohar said.

'No, she's been married before and she even had a daughter,' Brendan insisted. 'She only went nuts after they took her daughter away.'

Kumar was interested now. 'Do you know why they took her daughter away?'

'Her husband wasn't like her . . . she said he was a Tameze, or something like that,' Brendan replied.

'Tamil, you mean? Nila was married to a Tamil man?' Gohar asked. 'But isn't she Sinhala?'

'Yes, she is Sinhala,' Madhav replied. 'Her nephew has told me a little about her. But how are we to know if anything she says has any truth to it? She barely talks, and when she does, it's utter gibberish!'

'That's because you don't talk to her properly,' Brendan said. 'You have to speak to her when it's quiet or when she's preparing a pooja. She speaks all right then.'

'What would you know?' Madhav said abruptly, standing up to rinse his cup and plate. Looking out over the courtyard, he saw Nila out in the grounds, weeding and tidying up. It was nothing specific but any normal person could tell that she was not quite right in the head. There was something quite manic about her. Even from this distance it was plain that there was something strange about her. It was nothing he could put his finger on, though.

As Madhav stepped out into the afternoon sun, he recited a little prayer in his head, not for the first time, beseeching the gods to remove both the pestilential Brendan and the lunatic Nila whose behaviour he found completely and utterly embarrassing. All he wanted was peace and quiet to do his work.

It took a while for Madhav to notice him. He looked as if he was about thirty, handsome and very out of place. He loitered around the back of the shrine room, looking at this and looking at that. He'd arrived first thing in the morning but it was lunchtime now and he had not yet got around to doing a pooja, though he did have a little bill in his hands indicating that he'd paid for his plate of fruit to be offered.

If he was still there at afternoon tea time, Madhav decided, he would speak to him himself.

The man *was* still there at teatime – only to Madhav's eternal consternation, Nila got to him first! How dare she converse with a pilgrim? It was the job of a priest to welcome a new parishioner and make them feel welcome – not the local nutter!

'Good afternoon!' Madhav rushed eagerly forward, throwing back his scalding tea in one swallow. 'Welcome to the Ferntree Gully Sri Ganapathi Vinayaka temple. How may I help you?' He rudely turned his back to Nila, dismissing her.

The man bowed deeply to Nila as she scurried away.

'Look, I was going to come up and make my offering,' the man replied quietly. 'It's just that . . . em . . .'

'Yes? God makes no judgements, *puttar*,' Madhav said.

'Well, I haven't been to a Hindu temple for a long time and I don't speak Hindi.'

Madhav looked him over closely. He could well be a Hindu from the south of India, although with his fine features and medium-brown skin he could be from anywhere.

'Yes, most of the pilgrims who come here are from north India, but the gods have no idea of north, south, east or west. We welcome one and all.'

'I am not Indian,' the man replied shyly.

'Sri Lankan Tamil then?' Madhav volunteered brightly, putting an arm behind the man and guiding him towards the shrine room. 'My name is Madhav, by the way.'

'My name is Mahinda. And no, I am Sinhalese.'

'Ah, yes, we have a lot of Sinhalese Buddhists come here. They go to the temple to do their meditations and then they come here for help from the Hindu gods!'

'Nothing changes,' Mahinda whispered softly, offering Madhav the slip of paper with his donation written on it.

Madhav took the little slip of paper and almost whistled softly under his breath. This man had brought five hundred dollars' worth of offerings. 'What am I praying for?' Madhav asked, even more attentive now.

Mahinda looked sad for a moment, gazing out a distant window to the gum trees swaying in the wind.

'I don't have any family, you see . . . I am praying for peace of mind. That is what I would like the gods to give me. Some peace of mind.'

There was something about the man that moved Madhav, and it had nothing to do with the cheque he had just signed. He beseeched the gods passionately, asking that this man be granted whatever he desired.

After a good quarter of an hour of chanting, Madhav ceremonially circled the holy flame around Mahinda's head seven times before smearing his brow with *vibuthi* and dotting a bright dash of vermilion on the centre of his forehead with his thumb.

'So tell me,' Madhav asked when he saw Mahinda drop several green notes into the collection box. 'What do you do?'

'I am a mechanical engineer by training,' Mahinda said, 'but when I immigrated here about ten years ago, I purchased a textile processing mill here in Melbourne with the help of an old friend. Mustafa Mohamadeen from Andhra Pradesh . . .'

'So you are a textile wallah then, like Mr Mohamadeen? All of India knows him!'

'Err . . . no. I produce fine wool-blend fabrics for suiting. My mill is one of the last woollen textile mills in Australia.'

'Curious. Our people are rarely so passionate about wool,' Madhav remarked as the two men left the shrine. 'We are usually more passionate about cottons and silks.'

'There was once a time when all I could think of was creating the finest silk,' Mahinda replied in a soft voice that spoke of a pain beyond human understanding. 'To create a silk so fine and pure because it was made without killing a single silk moth.'

'Thirty, forty, forty-five!' Mr Ananda counted the stacks of hundred-dollar bills rolled into bundles of five thousand dollars and tied them together with heavy-duty rubber bands. 'We've got a month to go but I think you'll be able to raise the final five thousand dollars required in the next week or so.'

'And how are you going with the Navaratri celebration planning? Are the floats to your liking? We've conferred with the council and everything will be fine with them,' Narayan added.

'We've also organised a television crew from Channel 6 to come for your pageant. They will also televise the pooja,' Mrs Vasundaram added.

At the mention of Channel 6, Reverend Shastri frowned, but he said nothing.

'The vermilion and camphor have been ordered and I went down to Dandenong Market to discuss the fruit order. They will be bringing a ton of fruit before the first day of festival and half a ton after that for your poojas,' Gohar chimed in.

'Have we looked into the *vibuthi*? We need pure *vibuthi* for all of Madhav's poojas,' Mr Ananda declared.

'We ordered as much as we could from Varanasi,' the chief pundit declared. 'But they could only spare 250 kilograms.'

'That is not enough. Madhav will need at least twice as much for the number of people attending. They won't be happy with a small dot – they'll want him to dust their entire heads!'

Mr Ananda said. 'No, Madhav will need more than 250 kilos!'

'And where do you suppose we get all this *vibuthi*?' Reverend Shastri asked. 'I have tried all our regular contacts, but there isn't much they can spare.'

'I will go to India myself then!' Mr Govinda declared. 'I will burn the cow dung myself if I have to! Anything for pundit Madhav!'

'But aren't you still saving for a house, Mr Govinda?' Kumar asked. 'Or have you found one already?'

'No, *beta*, no. We get outbid at every auction we go to. House prices are going up and up, but our savings are not. I am not worried, though. Madhav has promised to do a pooja for us. I am sure we'll find the right place soon,' Mr Govinda replied. 'And you, Kumar? You'll be off to India next year yourself to start your training at the seminary – and I hear your mother is arranging a marriage too!'

'Actually, Madhav is doing a pooja for me, so that this arranged marriage won't come off so quickly!' Kumar laughed. 'This is why I am helping him so much with his Navaratri celebrations! So he'll ask the gods to help me!'

'I am very grateful for the pooja the pundit did for me,' said Mr Ananda.

'Yes, congratulations on your restaurant being featured in *The Age*, Mr Ananda!' Mrs Vasundaram said politely. 'It's quite a feat to be declared the best Indian restaurant in Melbourne only six months after you open.'

'Thank you,' Mr Ananda replied, not quite able to look Mrs Vasundaram in the eye because of her sad news. 'And how is your daughter? Is she much better now?'

'Oh, you know how these things are – she'll get better in due course,' Mrs Vasundaram replied. The rumour was that her daughter had suffered a breakdown while studying for her exams. The young woman had spent an entire day crying in bed and hadn't been to school for a whole week now. 'Madhav said that he'll do a pooja and everything will be set right.'

The man at the centre of all this discussion was quiet. Unusually quiet. Something peculiar had happened that morning. Actually he'd been feeling it for some time, but this morning he had finally realised what it was. He'd started his morning prayers and he'd not felt that familiar presence. That presence that had been with him all through life. It was as if his best friend had suddenly left him and he didn't know why. He'd used his precious lunchbreak to go into the inner sanctum and pray again – but yet again, he hadn't felt that familiar presence. What had gone wrong?

'Excuse me? What?' Madhav asked as he heard his name being called.

'When are you going to take your money to the Khans for the saree?' Mr Govinda asked.

'In a fortnight,' Madhav replied. 'We need extra locks fitted here at the rectory before I'll bring that saree back to the temple.'

'Good, good. We don't want your saree to be stolen,' Mrs Vasundaram said.

'It is not my saree, Mrs Vasundaram. It is a saree for Saraswati Devi.'

'No, *puttar*, it is your saree. You raised the money, it is for you to do as you wish,' the Reverend Shastri said. 'You are the one buying this saree for Saraswati Devi and it is your contribution to this temple.'

Madhav smiled weakly. Perhaps the gift of the beautiful saree might persuade Saraswati and her fellow gods and goddesses to come back and commune with him once more.

Feroz Khan and his wife Fatima were as different as two people could be. Feroz was a taciturn man, quite content to live and work in rural New South Wales. Indeed, he'd been eager to get as far away from civilisation as possible. It had been in Cooma in New South Wales that the Khans had met another South Asian family, the Gamages from Sri Lanka. Albert was an engineer on the project along with Feroz. Drawn together by a shared cultural heritage, they'd found comfort in each other's company as they explored a strange new land and new way of living.

'You cannot imagine how glad I am that Anoja met another Asian woman,' Albert often said to Fatima. 'I was surprised as anyone when I received the telegram from my father-in-law saying that I was the father of twins! And Anoja certainly needs your help with them! Especially since her own mother died not a month after they were born.'

'Yes, this is good practice for you when your time comes. If you can cope with my twins, especially Marion here, then you can cope with anything,' the vivacious Anoja added. She often left the twins in Fatima's care before she went off to some party or other. It was just as well that Fatima had no children of her own, for she could not have mothered the twins so well if she had – and the poor things needed her.

But unable to cope with the isolation of rural New South Wales, the Gamages had decamped to the bright lights of Sydney within just a few years. By then Fatima had become so attached to Ryan and Marion that she'd make the five-hour trip to Sydney every three months to visit the children.

Eventually, though, it came to the point that Fatima could not bear the bitter cold winters of Cooma and drudgery of carrying all her spices and Asian provisions on the train for the five-hour return trip. 'If you want hot chapatti, you can drive to Sydney and bring the *atta* flour yourself!' she had said to her husband. 'God help me, but this is the last time I explain to someone on the train what I use aniseed for!'

'Shall we move to Hobart, then?' Feroz had suggested.

'No! I want to go somewhere where there are other Indians! People like us.'

Melbourne had been the compromise. It wasn't as busy as Sydney but it certainly wasn't quiet like Adelaide. Mostly Feroz had definitely not wanted to move anywhere in the vicinity of Anoja Gamage. Albert was a good friend, but Feroz could not bear his vulgar wife. Fatima, on the other hand, found Anoja amusing, and her love for the children meant that she was willing to overlook some of their mother's more irritating behaviours, in order to maintain the friendship.

The year the twins turned seventeen the family came to Melbourne in the September school holidays and stayed with the Khans for a week. It was a shock for Fatima to see how much older and taller they were and how grown-up they looked, and she realised that they weren't children anymore.

'Here, Marion,' Fatima said fondly, opening a trunk full of fabrics several days after they'd arrived. 'I think you'd love this saree.' She pulled out a length of bright blue fabric and draped it on the girl.

Marion had grown up into a serious young woman. Tall, dark and willowy, she looked nothing like her parents. 'She takes after Anoja's late sister, Nila, but I can't explain the height,' her father had laughed.

'My brother Manoj is tall,' Anoja would snap. 'But it's a pity all that height is wasted on Marion instead of Ryan.

My darling Ryan is smart, though – if only he will score well enough to get into medicine!'

'You should go and make a vow at the Hindu temple in Ferntree Gully,' Fatima suggested. 'They say the pundit there is a miracle maker. Feroz is giving them one of his father's most valuable sarees to use in the Navaratri celebrations.'

'I am not giving it to them, dear, I am selling it to them,' Feroz corrected.

'Well, I don't know why you just don't give it to them. We have enough money for our needs and we don't have any children to leave an inheritance to!'

'I do not believe it is appropriate to give such a valuable garment away for nothing. People don't appreciate these things unless they have to pay for them,' Feroz said.

'Uncle Feroz, can I have a look at it?' Marion asked.

'Of course, my dear,' he replied as Fatima unlocked the trunk.

'Don't you get any ideas,' her mother butted in when she saw Marion transfixed by the beautiful saree that was emerging from the depths of the trunk. 'Can you imagine, Fatima? She wants to study fashion design and she's been begging us for the past year to let her transfer to a technical college!'

Unbeknown to her parents, Marion often took the train into the city to visit the New South Wales Art Gallery. It was one of the few places she'd found peace in her life, wandering the quiet rooms, looking at the paintings on the walls, no critical voice sneering at everything she did. It had been an exhibition on South Asian textiles that had sparked the short-lived debate about going to art school.

'It is nursing for you, girl! Three years of a proper university education is all we'll pay for!' Anoja had snapped.

'Anoja, she does have a gift for drawing,' Albert mumbled now, and glanced at Fatima, wondering if she might back him up. Nearly eighteen years of marriage had almost completely cowed him.

'What gift? What utter nonsense!' his wife said.

'Here,' Feroz said, holding the saree up and breaking the tension. 'Here it is.'

Marion was spellbound. The jewels on the saree sparkled in the morning light as she came forward to touch the fabric reverently, her eyes drinking in the beauty and fingertips absorbing the magic. There was something aching familiar about this saree. It was almost as if she had seen it before.

Madhav was on tenterhooks. He kept fingering the tatty fabric pouch in the front knot of his sarong, feeling for the edges of the piece of paper. It was the cheque for fifty thousand dollars, the hard-earned money of thousands of pilgrims donated to buy a glittering saree for the goddess Saraswati.

'We'll bring the saree to the temple ourselves,' Fatima Khan had assured him on the phone last night. 'I have some friends who want to make a vow at your temple for their children's education.'

'Friends of yours will always be welcome here! And don't worry about bringing anything for the pooja. I will do it for free,' Madhav had promised.

But they were running late. Fatima had promised to be here by nine in the morning but it was already half past ten. Madhav had wanted them to come early because he planned to keep the saree from everyone until the day of the Navaratri pageant and have a grand unveiling. He'd especially wanted to keep it from the lunatic Nila, who'd pawed and fingered the sarees donated for the goddesses Mahalaksmi and Durga-Amman.

'Get your filthy fingers away from that silk,' Madhav had finally growled in frustration.

Nila Mendis had slunk away then, looking quite sad and withdrawn.

She was out in the courtyard beyond the temple now, though, playing with Brendan, and seemed happy enough. It would seem that Brendan had been evicted entirely from school and spent his days wholly at the temple, going home at night only to sleep.

'Me mum don't care,' he'd mumbled.

'My mother does not care,' Madhav had corrected him perfunctorily. 'But you can't live here. This is not your home.'

'It's a lot more quieter than home,' the boy had replied evasively.

'How are things at home, *puttar*?' Reverend Shastri had come right out and asked. The old man's keen eyes had taken in the boy's second-hand clothes and grubby skin.

'It's all good!' Brendan lied glibly.

He spent much of his time at the temple with Nila. She put up with him far more willingly than Madhav did – in fact she seemed to enjoy his company – but she insisted that he read to her every day and work through some maths problems. But Madhav never understood how she persuaded the little boy to do things, as she never spoke.

'Where *are* they?' Madhav grumbled under his breath as he saw Nila and Brendan walk into the rectory to stay out of the sun. 'Typical Sri Lankans. Always late!'

He walked into the shrine room and took out the cheque to look at it again. It had taken the teller at the ANZ branch in Croydon a good hour and a half to count the money. But every dollar had been accounted for. Madhav smirked remembering the scene at the bank.

'What are you going to buy?' the teller had asked. 'A car? A caravan? A massive diamond ring?'

He'd been evasive. 'Oh, with the price of things now, fifty thousand isn't going to buy much.'

Madhav was so lost in his reverie that he didn't realise that Fatima had arrived with her friends until she tapped him on his shoulder.

'We are here,' she declared proudly.

'Oh, welcome! Welcome!' Madhav cried.

'And here is the saree,' Fatima said. She turned to a tall, dark, willowy girl in the background, who stepped forward, right into the spot where the skylight shone a beacon of daylight into the temple. She was carrying the saree.

'No need to finalise the transaction so fast!' Madhav insisted. 'You mentioned something about a pooja. Let's do that first and then we'll settle things. Who are we doing it for?

A diminutive woman bustled forward. She was attractive, though inappropriately dressed for a temple visit, in tight leopard print leggings and a rather revealing top. In the foyer beyond, Madhav could see the spiked stilettos she'd left behind.

'It's for my son, Ryan,' she replied, pushing forward a pudgy youth with a pudding bowl haircut. 'We want him to get into medical school.'

'Don't forget Marion,' Fatima insisted, pushing the willowy girl forward. 'She'll be doing the exams too.'

'Let's start, then. I'll need the children's birthdates and places,' Madhav said, turning to light some camphor for the sacred fire. And as he turned, he saw Nila and Brendan walk into the shrine room through the back door.

'Quick, give me the saree,' he blurted to Marion, snatching the box from the girl's hands and striding into the inner sanctum of the shrine room, where Nila could not and would not follow. Taking it out of Nila's sight and grasp the answer to all her unspoken questions. Definitive proof that her beloved husband Raju did not die.

A sudden gust of wind roaring through the Dandenongs extinguished all the lamps in the temple. The great chamber was plunged into a profound darkness except for the single beacon of sunlight where Marion stood. An unnatural silence fell.

'Rupani?' an unfamiliar voice called from across the large hall.

Madhav turned around to see a look of untold terror cross the face of Fatima's friend. 'Come, we must leave at once.

Now!' she shouted, grabbing her son and daughter by the arm and running out.

Nila ran after them, but the great length of the large hall gave Fatima Khan and her friends a head start. By the time she stumbled down the steps, they were already seated in their car and about to drive away. Nila flung herself onto the boot of the sedan, trying to stop them from reversing out of the car park.

'You have to go!' Anoja screamed at Fatima. 'Now!'

'How?' Fatima demanded.

'Just drive over the gardens!'

As the car lurched forward over the newly landscaped gardens, Nila fell to the ground, but she picked herself up and stumbled after them, running down the hilly road until she could no longer keep up, then collapsed onto the side, screaming and wailing.

'Come back!' Madhav screamed at Brendan, who'd given chase after Nila. 'She's crazy!'

'She's not crazy!' Brendan screamed back. 'I know crazy. I live with it!'

The nine extra *pusaris* arrived in Melbourne and Madhav met them with great ceremony at Tullamarine Airport. 'Welcome, welcome!' Madhav rushed forward with garlands.

After the initial introductions, everyone moved *en masse* to the cars, the nine men separating into vehicles according to their levels of seniority. The older pundits got the plum seats in the better cars while the younger ones had to be content with Kumar's rust bucket.

'Please,' the right honourable Srinivasan said to Mr Ananda, whose front seat he was graciously offered, 'I would prefer to ride with young Madhav here. After all, he was the best student I had at the seminary in Mumbai.'

'So, Madhav, how are you settling into Melbourne?' the Reverend Srinivasan asked as soon as they cleared the parking tollgate. 'I was worried when I sent you over here to Melbourne but I have heard rumours that you are quite respected as a miracle maker. Is that correct, *puttar*? Have your prayers to the gods been answered?'

'Of course they have, sir,' Kumar replied for him. 'Why just last month we heard that a woman who could barely walk for years is now taking up swimming.'

For the next hour Kumar extolled story upon story of people who'd had their dreams come true after Madhav prayed on their behalf.

'My favourite of course is the little girl who was cured of blindness,' he said.

'To be clear, Srininvasan sir, the girl wasn't blind. The doctors suspected early stage glaucoma. But it could simply have been an error in the test they did,' Madhav muttered irritably.

'Of course that would not be your favourite miracle,' Kumar teased. 'And we all know what you are most proud of achieving.'

'I am not particularly proud of one miracle over another,' Madhav retorted. 'I am not even convinced I brought about any of these miracles anyway!'

'Sure you did!' Kumar said. 'How else could we ever have got Nila Mendis out of the temple? The Ferntree Gully Sri Ganapathi Vinayaka temple is now a lunatic-free zone!'

'What? What is this, Madhav? Have you driven a lunatic out of the temple? You know that is forbidden!' the aged pundit demanded of Madhav.

'I have not driven anyone out of the temple!' Madhav cried. 'She just hasn't come back after she had an altercation with someone who came to the temple for a pooja.'

'Nila Mendis versus a Toyota Camry – Nila Mendis scores zero and Toyota Camry scores one!' Kumar laughed.

'Stop it! The poor woman could have been seriously hurt. The gravel burns on her knees and hands were terrible. I am quite worried about her!'

'Brendan's worried about her too. He asked his mum if he could go visit her, but she said no,' Kumar added.

'Who is Brendan?' the elderly pundit asked.

'Brendan is the little Australian boy who sometimes comes to temple,' Madhav replied.

'Good, good! Good to know you're bringing Hinduism to the people of Australia!' the pundit crowed excitedly. 'Many of our young pundits were little boys when they first heard the call.'

'He hasn't been coming much lately,' Kumar pointed out.

'When Nila Mendis stopped coming, Brendan stopped too,' Madhav said with a heavy heart. Since the incident with

Nila Mendis, Madhav had been feeling extremely out of sorts. If he'd felt he'd lost his way previously, he knew he had now.

'Nah! Brendan not coming has nothing to do with Nila Mendis,' Kumar said. 'I walked past the house the other day on my way to the shops and his mother has a new boyfriend. A real idiot. Told me to go back to where I came from. I doubt he'd let Brendan come. Bloody racist Australians!' He glowered as he shifted gears to get up the steep hill. 'They piss their money down the drain and take drugs.'

'Most Australians are fine people,' Madhav objected. 'Good, decent, hard-working people who have welcomed us to this country. And someday Brendan will be like that. A good man.'

'I doubt it – look at his parents. He'll be just like them,' Kumar smirked as he looked out the window. They were about to pass Brendan's house now. Madhav had an awful premonition. The first sense of the divine he'd had in weeks.

'Hey, there's an ambulance parked at Brendan's house,' Kumar said. 'Bet his mother has taken an overdose!'

'Stop! Stop the car!' Madhav shouted.

Kumar pulled over as Madhav bolted out the door. 'Don't get involved! They are the Dalits of Australia!' Kumar yelled as Madhav ran to the ambulance.

'What? What happened to him?' Madhav demanded as a stretcher carrying the young boy was wheeled out the front door. His mother came out too. She looked too drunk to stand up straight, although she was carrying a baby in her arms.

'How am I supposed to leave these brats and come with youse?' she demanded.

'We'd much rather you not come, Miss,' the ambulance driver said.

'Where are you taking him?' she demanded.

'To the Monash Medical Centre. They are the best in the world at treating third-degree scald wounds.' That was when Madhav looked down to see Brendan's legs covered in bandages. Even through the thin gauze, he could see the raw burns, and where the white flesh was showing through.

It was the night before the big Navaratri pageant and Madhav felt as if his head was about to explode. It had been nonstop ceremonies and events for the past seven days and he'd barely had time to stop to draw breath. Yet he had to do what he had to do.

'Come, Kumar, we must go,' Madhav insisted, manhandling the young lad off the couch where he lay sprawled. Madhav did feel stirrings of pity in his heart. They'd both been up since three in the morning and everyone was exhausted. 'Look, we'll stop by the shops in Clayton and see if we can get some fresh laddoo. Would you like that?'

'Hmm . . .' Kumar grunted.

'I'll even buy you a lassi.'

'Hmm . . .' he grunted again.

'Okay. We'll go and see Brendan, and while we're at the hospital, I'll make Brendan let you play with his PlayStation.'

That was enough to get Kumar up off the couch and out to the car. Madhav followed him a few minutes later, first taking the time to go into his room and fetch the cheque that he had to give the Khans. He felt as if he could not dress the deity in the saree meant for her unless he'd given the money for the garment in return.

'We have to go to the hospital first,' Kumar insisted as they started driving down Ferntree Gully Road towards the hospital in Clayton. 'Visiting hours finish at six, but we can go to the Khans' place any time.'

Madhav groaned. It would be another fight to get Kumar off Brendan's hospital-issue PlayStation in the recreation room.

The Monash Medical Centre was a large teaching hospital in the south-eastern suburbs of Melbourne and was a state-of-the-art facility. To Madhav's eyes it looked more like a hotel than a hospital – it certainly put the NHS hospitals of London to shame with its wide clean corridors and brisk staff who rushed about doing their work.

'Hey, Brendan,' Kumar greeted their young friend as they entered the rec room, which was kitted out with computer games, PlayStation consoles and all manner of gadgets to keep the young patients entertained while they were receiving treatment. Brendan was slumped on a wheelchair with his legs raised, playing computer games.

'Hey, Madhav! Hey, Kumar! How are you?' the young boy replied cheerily. 'I hoped you'd come today, but I wasn't quite sure because of all the Navaratri celebrations.'

'What do you know of Navaratri?' Kumar asked.

'Well, der! I've been around the temple for months now. Are the poojas going well? And how is the preparation going for the pageant? I am so sad I'll miss it all tomorrow.'

'The doctors have said you can come out for the evening to watch the pageant. It's been all organised,' Madhav said. Indeed he'd had a lengthy conversation with the head of paediatrics assuring the man that Kumar would pick the lad up before the pageant and bring him back after.

'Nah . . . they've changed their minds,' Brendan replied with a grimace as he moved painfully. 'They're in there talking about it right now.' He jerked his head towards the little meeting room on the other side of the corridor.

Madhav let Kumar and Brendan get on with killing some poor aliens or some such nonsense and went across to knock on the meeting room door. Sharon, Brendan's mother, seeing that it was Madhav, let the young man in before resuming the argument she was having with the doctor and the physiotherapist.

'I can't afford private physiotherapy. I guess he'll get what he gets,' she rasped.

'The more intensive the physiotherapy he receives at these early stages, the better his recovery will be. With three extra sessions a week, Brendan would be out of here within a couple of months instead of six.'

'I can't afford sixty bucks a pop three times a week,' Sharon insisted. 'I can barely put food on the table as it is!'

'Anything extra would be great,' the physiotherapist insisted. 'Even a single extra session a week would be a huge help.'

'Nah . . . he just gets what he gets,' the woman said.

'Mr Patel, how can we help you?' the doctor asked, turning to Madhav.

'I was just wondering why Brendan said that he could not come to the pageant tomorrow night. I though we'd settled it. Kumar from the temple will drive him there and back again.'

'It's not the coming or going, Mr Patel, it's just that he needs a long physiotherapy session in the heated pool and the only time we can schedule it is in the evening.'

'Ain't it strange? The boy burnt his legs with hot water and now they're using a hot pool to cure him,' Sharon chipped in. She didn't add that it'd been her fault that he'd burnt his legs in the first place. Not many six-year-olds would be able to drain hot spaghetti unsupervised.

'Can't he attend another session? Navaratri only comes around once a year and it is very special,' Madhav pleaded.

'I'm sorry,' the doctor said, 'but we need to get him into all and any sessions we can get.'

Something started to burn in Madhav's heart. What was happening to Brendan was not right. A child's recuperation from a horrible accident should not be dependent on what his parents could afford.

'Come, Kumar, come!' Madhav insisted an hour later, when visiting hours were nearly up. 'We must go! We have to get back to the temple in time for the evening ceremonies after we give the Khans the cheque!'

'But you promised me laddoo and lassi,' Kumar said as they walked out of the hospital. 'The Indian shops are just around the corner.'

'Oh, come on then,' Madhav said grumpily. 'But we need to hurry.'

Only Kumar could not quite decide on which sweets he wanted. He stood there with his nose plastered to the glass behind which rows and rows of brightly coloured sweets were displayed to the great joy of the shoppers. 'I must have some laddoo. I love burfi as well. And they have excellent gajar halwa here. Have you tried it, Madhav? Maybe I'll get some sandesh, too.'

'Whatever you get, make it quick,' Madhav growled as the shop assistant poured out two bright orange lassis into tall plastic glasses. Madhav hurried from the queue, as all the Indians in Melbourne seemed to have congregated in the sweet-shop to get their festive sweets. In the crush he almost missed seeing a familiar face.

'Arjun . . . is that you?' Madhav asked, spotting Nila Mendis's nephew.

'Oh yes,' the young man replied distractedly. 'But my name is Aravinda.'

'So how is your aunt? We haven't seen her for quite a while.'

Aravinda sighed deeply. 'She is not at all well. She's had a complete breakdown. She and my Aunt Renuka return to Sri Lanka tomorrow.'

'll tell her you came to see her when she is better,' Renuka said as she led Madhav and Kumar into the tiny lounge room.

'But why can't I see her?' Madhav insisted.

'Because she is not up to it,' Renuka told him. 'I don't know why Aravinda invited you back here.'

'She was fine when I left,' Aravinda replied as he came into the lounge carrying a tray of tea things. Their living space was small even by Indian standards – just two rooms connected by a dingy living room, spilling over into a tiny damp kitchen. No natural sunlight. No natural ventilation. 'She even got up this morning and made her own breakfast.'

'You know she can change from minute to minute,' Renuka said as she wearily sat down. She was precise and elegant in her movements, dignified despite her present poverty. 'Though I haven't seen her this bad for a long time.'

'She's always been bad,' Aravinda retorted. 'And I still don't understand why you will insist on taking care of her. She is no blood relative of ours!'

'Aravinda . . .'

'Renuka, *nanda*, you have to put her in an asylum and be done with it. She is not our flesh and blood and she has nothing to do with us. I have no idea how I allowed you to convince me to let you come and stay with me!'

'She is more than flesh and blood . . . she is my very life,' his aunt replied softly. 'You did not know her before, when she

452

was not crazy. The most talented saree weaver you have ever met. If she was still herself today, we would not be worthy to have her set foot in our house.'

'She wasn't born crazy?' Madhav asked.

'Good heavens, no! She was sane as you or I,' Renuka replied. 'And a very talented saree maker, skilled in the *pancha dakshata*.'

'So what happened? What made her go crazy?'

Renuka stared at the wall for a long moment. The pain in her eyes palpable.

'It was me,' Renuka confessed, tears starting to drip from her eyes. 'I destroyed her life. Because of my jealousy and greed, her husband was murdered and her parents stole her newborn child. The gods have punished me, though. Everything I set my mind to from that point on was a disaster. Every business venture. Every relationship I ever had after that ended in disaster. My family chased me away because they thought I was cursed!'

'Then one day I was visiting the last of my relatives who would give me roof space when they took lunch – *dhanay* – to an asylum in the hill country of Sri Lanka. And that was when I saw her. My old friend from the weaving mill. They had her chained to the wall naked. That is what they do to the mentally ill in Sri Lanka.'

'What? What happened next?' Kumar asked, horrified.

'I knew what I had to do. I had to make reparations. I took her home with me and I looked after her. Things started to change then. I got her some treatment and slowly she started to improve. My family started to speak to me again.'

'So what are you doing in Australia?' Madhav asked.

'We came here so I could work,' Renuka explained. 'Although my family supports me, I no longer want to be dependent on them. I am still an excellent dressmaker. So I have been working here illegally sewing saree blouses and the like so I could save enough money to go back home and buy a little house. That way Nila and I can live peacefully by ourselves.'

'So why are you going back? Plenty of people work here illegally for years!' Kumar exclaimed.

'Because she needs medication. Truly, this is the worst I have ever seen her. I cannot take her to the doctors here because we are illegal immigrants. I need to take her back to Sri Lanka. Look, if you are really quiet, I will show you,' Renuka offered.

Standing up, she gestured for Madhav and Kumar to follow her and cracked open the door to one of the other little rooms. The diminutive woman who'd been the bane of Madhav's life was now in a straitjacket, lying sedated on the bed.

'We can sedate her enough to take her on the plane and back home,' Aravinda explained.

Renuka sighed. 'We were so close.'

'Close to what?' Madhav asked.

'Having enough money to build a house and maybe start a little business. I thought we could set up a little sewing business when we got back,' Renuka said. 'All I needed was enough money for two sewing machines and a small house. I have saved ten thousand dollars in the last two years and another five thousand would have been perfect.'

'It is very commendable that you are looking after your friend,' Madhav said as both Aravinda and his aunt Renuka showed him and Kumar out. 'You are making a lot of good karma. Wholesome deeds that will bear fruit in the next life.'

'No,' Renuka insisted looked at the young pundit in the eyes. 'I am just making amends. This is my penance. The gods, they can see. They see when we try and right the wrongs we've done.'

It was the perfect spring evening for a pageant – about twenty-five degrees, with a light easterly wind. It was just as well there was a cool breeze, for there were thousands of people, both

Australian and Indian, mingling in the crowds. The mayor of the City of Knox was riding on the first float in the pageant, mounted on the back of a large flatbed truck. It depicted the myth of King Rama and his queen, Sita, who was abducted by King Ravana of Lanka, with an epic battle scene forming the backdrop. There were loud cheers and applause as it went by.

As the float passed out of view of the crowd, the mayor thankfully collapsed onto a chair and loosened his hot red mayoral robes. He'd had a rich meal of dosai, sambar and chutney with the assembled VIPs in the rectory before and was feeling decidedly unwell. 'I just hope you don't get sick on the float and make a fool of yourself,' his wife had scolded him. 'You know you can't eat spicy food.'

'But darling, have you tried those doughnut-shaped *vadais*? They are divine!'

'Yes,' the woman confessed greedily, stealing another one of the deep-fried doughy snacks from the table. 'I suppose it is a matter of getting used to it. That boy certainly has,' she remarked, pointing to Brendan, who was sitting happily munching away on a plate of *uppuma* and chutney.

Brendan was still thinking about food when Kumar wheeled him out to the stage set up for the VIPs in front of the temple. 'Do you think I could take a bag of *muruku* with me to the hospital? I just love *muruku*.'

Kumar was too excited to reply, though. 'Look, Brendan, look!' he cried, pointing to the second float coming down the road. This one was in the shape of a lotus flower and the pundits were sitting on the petals. 'There are the pundits from the temple! Wave!' he said.

Brendan was too caught up watching the pageant to take up the issue of *muruku* again. Drummers and fire dancers paraded gaily down the street, the light breeze keeping them cool as they performed and the crowd cheering them as they passed.

'The Rebels Motorcycle Club!' Brendan squealed as the bikies from the back paddock rode up on Harleys. 'Woo hoo!'

he screamed with joy as the younger members did tricks and stunts. 'I'll never be able to ride like that,' he whispered to Kumar, looking at his legs.

'Why not?' Kumar demanded.

'The physiotherapist said . . .'

'Oh, I wouldn't worry about what the physiotherapist said,' Kumar told him. 'Madhav's looking after everything. That's why you could come tonight.'

'What?' Brendan asked, confused.

'Oh, look, the Mahalaksmi float!' Kumar shouted, and started to cheer 'Mahalaksmi! Mahalaksmi!' along with the crowds.

The float itself was truly magnificent. In the centre of a massive paper lotus stood a seven-foot-high statue of the deity. It had taken twenty strong men to lift her from the temple and place her on the float. The petals of the lotus were gold and red, and around the goddess were symbols of fertility and abundance – stalks of rice, coins of gold and large urns of milk.

'She who was with us at the time of the beginning of the universe and will be with us until the very end,' the chief pundit of the temple boomed in a massive voice. 'All hail Mahalaksmi!' he shouted as all the pilgrims let out a mighty roar of '*Om Sri Mahalaksmi Devi*' as the driver of the float flicked on the lights.

There was an awed silence as everyone took in the majesty of the deity. Resplendently dressed in a magnificent red and gold silk saree, she was abundance, fertility and goodness personified. Even from a distance people could see the intricate gold embroidery and rich tapestry that clothed her glory.

Next came Durga-Amman's float, decorated entirely in yellow and orange. Garlands of marigold were hung from a lintel and young boys flung cut halves of lemons and limes at the crowds.

'She who is invincible and gives us strength to face life!' the senior pundit visiting from India boomed. 'All hail Durga-Amman!' he roared as the pilgrims joined the deafening refrain of '*Om Sri Durga-Amman*'. This was the cue for the float driver to switch on the light, and again, there was a stunned silence.

This time the deity was dressed in a bright yellow saree and draped with hundreds of gold necklaces. In her many hands were miniature weapons made of solid gold. Many pilgrims made vows to her there and then, asking her to remove obstacles from their paths, convinced their lives would change for the better.

Then the final float started down the hill. Some who saw it coming thought it was just a leftover float of no consequence and started to make their way to the main temple to complete their offerings and be on their way back home. It was only when the float reached the VIP stage that people realised – this was the goddess Saraswati.

The float was very modestly decorated. Just garlands of orange blossoms that permeated the evening air with a sweet but uplifting fragrance. The seven-foot deity at the centre of the float looked as if . . . What? Could that be possible? Was she just dressed in a plain white cloth? It looked like a rough calico!

'She is all that is wise and pure,' Madhav called from the float.

A murmur of disapproval spread through the crowd. Hadn't everybody contributed handsomely for an extraordinary saree to be draped on Saraswati? What was this?

'What happened?' Brendan demanded of Kumar.

'Wait, you'll see,' Kumar smiled back.

'She who is wise and pure has no need for finery or riches,' Madhav called. 'She is that which is grace. And grace requires no embellishment. It took me a while to understand that. The gods do not need money or fancy offerings. Just sincere prayers. They always listen to prayers that come from the heart. So please join me,' he implored. '*Om Aim Saraswatiye Namah*.'

The pilgrims were angry. They did not join in his chant. What had happened to all their hard-earned money? Had he swindled them?

Madhav looked at the angry pilgrims and then up at the sky to send a quiet prayer heavenward. Out of the corner of his eye he saw a plane streak by. Perhaps it was the one carrying Nila Mendis and her friend Renuka home to Sri Lanka.

Yes, he was happy. Deeply and supremely happy. For deep within Renuka's handbag was a cash cheque for twenty-five thousand dollars. Enough for her and Nila to start a new life and for Nila to have the care she needed.

He'd asked Kumar to take him into the city that evening after visiting Nila. He'd walked several miles along the Yarra River to the heart of Melbourne, then sat by the banks at the Arts Centre and watched the schoolboys row as trams rattled past on their way to St Kilda. He breathed in the city air and his mind was no clearer than muddy Yarra flowing in front of him.

Then he wandered back along the length of the river, to Abbotsford, until he'd come to an old ramshackle building. 'Abbotsford Convent' the sign read. Divinity had a strange way of attracting the divine. Perhaps Jesus's mother Mary was not that different to Mahalaksmi, Madhav had thought as he crossed the cracked and abandoned courtyard. Then he'd sat down by the river, plunged his feet in the murky water and meditated.

*Samadhi* had not come easily to him but he'd persevered for what seemed an eternity, though time no longer seemed to have a meaning, leaving his body and connecting with that part of himself which was the purest.

And that was when he realised what he'd have to do.

'Let me know if you need more money,' Madhav had insisted. 'Make sure Ms Mendis gets the helps she needs.'

'Weren't you raising money for the Saraswati deity's saree?' Aravinda had asked at the doorstep as Madhav handed the cheque to his aunt Renuka. 'Won't the temple trustees be furious with you?'

'No, they won't. The two chief pundits and I spoke to them this morning. We told them about the importance of charity as a Navaratri tradition,' Madhav said. It hadn't really been so easy to convince the trustees, but the other pundits had agreed with him. Charity was more important than sarees.

Since no one was joining Madhav in chanting, he strode forth and slowly sat cross-legged in front of the deity on the float. He closed his eyes and prayed to the gods who'd deserted him, hoping they would finally come to his aid.

'*Yaa Kundendu tushaara haara-dhavalaa, Yaa shubhra-vastra'avritaa*

*Yaa veena-vara-danda-manditakara, Yaa shweta padma'-asana*

*Yaa brahma'achyuta shankara prabhritibhir Devai-sadaa Vanditaa*

*Saa Maam Paatu Saraswati Bhagavatee Nihshesha jaadya'apahaa.*

*Shuklaam Brahmavichaara Saara paramaam Aadhyaam Jagadvyapinim.*'

'She, who is as fair as the Kunda flower, white as the moon, and a garland of Tushar flowers; and who is covered in white clothes;

She, whose hands are adorned by the excellent veena, and whose seat is the pure white lotus;

She, who is praised by Brahma, Vishnu, and Mahesh;

O Mother Goddess, remove my mental inertia!'

No one joined him after the first repetition of the prayer, but by the third or fourth time he repeated the mantra one or two people chanted along with him. Madhav felt the gods' holy presence, and the people's anger dissipated in the wind. Soon every one of the pilgrims joined in the chanting. Standing on that hillside in Ferntree Gully, thousands of people beseeched the great Saraswati for wisdom, peace and grace.

'So what did he do with the money we raised for the saree?' Brendan asked Kumar when he put the young boy in the car to drive him back to the hospital.

Kumar smiled. 'Don't you worry about that! You just focus on getting your physiotherapy. Twice a day for the next three months and you'll be walking before you know it!'

# The Finishing

Melbourne, Australia, 2010

Not many people could see the difference between Eggshell beige and Portobello beige. In fact, the director of medicine and the director of nursing had had an all out fight in front of the interior designers who were managing the refurbishment at St Jude's about it.

'There is no difference! I do not know what you are talking about. It just looks like yellow to me!' the director of medicine had spat.

'We have dying patients on this ward! I would much rather that our patients die in a warm environment rather than in a cold colour!' the director of nursing had returned fire.

The interior designer had just looked at me in desperation. She was tired of the incessant arguing and the politics behind something as simple as a colour choice.

'Why don't we go for Ecru beige?' I'd suggested coming forward. 'It sits in between those colours and straddles both.

The directors had agreed with me for the simple reason it allowed them to agree on something that had not been suggested by either one of them personally. Egos saved and reputations untarnished. Not many in the medical profession would actually know even if I did, that Ecru beige was exactly the same shade of beige the walls were currently painted in. People only need to think that they've had some input to a change to feel that they've had some influence.

Besides, it suited me to maintain the the colour scheme. It worked well for me for another reason; I'd spent the last five years stacking the clothes in my wardrobe exactly with that shade of beige. Pants, shirts and jackets – all in varying tones of off white and bone. On any given day, I could easily blend into a wall or curtain at the hospital without being noticed at all.

Perhaps that was why the consultant cardiologist brushed so hard against me as he went past. He didn't realise I was there against the back drop of the freshly painted wall. Only his bump sent the pen I was holding to sign off on the report flying across the page. His arrival on the ward had the same effect as opening the arctic-cold morgue downstairs, a pool of spreading icy silence like an invisible force field around him. I actually saw the duty nurse shiver as she stood up primly and dutifully followed him through into the ward. Even she didn't realise I was there, because no one bar me saw the stabbing motion she made to his back as she followed him though.

I hit print on the report and sat down to sign it again when Kristen the graduate nurse tried to perch her petite *derrière* on the chair I was already sitting on. Again I smudged my signature on the report. 'Oh, sorry Mare, I didn't see you!' she chirruped brightly before turning to one of her colleagues and continuing. 'They are just adorable aren't they? Why do these things happen to people like them? Good people, you know? I just don't get it.'

'They are really lovely people. And she is so beautiful.'

'They don't seem old either. I bet she is no more than forty-five if she was a day, but it's hard to guess his age though. I must check her charts!' Kristen continued.

The ebb and flow of the conversation continued around me as if I didn't exist as specialist after specialist, physician after physician walked into the ward and out again all morning.

'Oops . . . sorry . . . Did I make you do that?' the young intern apologised as he bumped into me and made my pen fly across the report I was signing for the third time that morning. I generally don't mind my invisibility; actually I quite enjoy it, except for instances like this when I have to redo whatever

I was doing. Signing a cause of death report is never a trivial matter.

'It's quite okay, Luke, no harm done,' I said with resignation as I hit print on the report again.

'I don't know how I didn't notice you sitting there,' he said. 'It's not like you're small or anything, Dr Gamage . . . Marion . . .' he stuttered as I unfolded my six foot frame out of the rickety office chair to get the fresh report from the printer. 'I mean how could anyone not notice you . . . I mean . . . Sorry . . .'

'It's quite okay, Luke,' I repeated looking down at the five-foot-five young man. He had a bright crop of red hair, cerulean blue eyes and a tubby paunch from having spent the last five years tied to a desk studying. There could be no greater contrast to my lean frame and dark colouring.

He stomped off abruptly though when a few nurses strolled in, tossing his head arrogantly and muttering something under his breath. Apparently there had been a spat between young Luke and Kristen last week and the dust hadn't quite settled yet. Not that the nurses noticed his rude leave taking. They were too busy gossiping about the latest arrivals on the ward. Rumours were running wild about the newest addition to the palliative care ward, a couple from India who'd sought last-ditch care in Australia.

'Wonder how long they've been married.'

'This is such a tragedy. Old people dying is fine; but she is so beautiful. I wonder if she was a Bollywood star. She certainly looks beautiful enough . . .'

I wanted to point out that death didn't differentiate between the ugly and the attractive. It was the one certainly that awaited all of us; the rich, the poor, the famous and infamous alike. But I held my tongue and listened absently as I finally signed off on the death report. The family hadn't requested any follow up. They just wanted to bury their twenty-year old son who'd died of testicular cancer.

I put the report in an envelope and slid it into the out tray, then stood up to go on my rounds. I'd been on Christmas holidays up in Cairns for three weeks and I didn't know any of the newcomers.

'How was your break, Mare?' Kristen asked as she faithfully trailed me out of the nurse's station into the ward. 'Was Paris all it was cracked up to be?'

'I went to Palm Cove, not Paris,' I replied wryly. 'How are you Mrs Goldenblatt?' I asked the octogenarian sufferer of liver failure cheerily. If spirit and strength of will were the only requisites for organ donation, Mrs Goldenblatt should have received one two years ago; but the lady was kind as she was determined. 'Leave the organs for young ones – not old foggies like me,' she'd insisted.

'Well enough to go to a disco!' she joked back.

Palliative care is the death stop. None of my patients have any hope of recovery. It was my job to make sure the end was as painless and as peaceful as I can make it. I am under no illusion that the end is easy. I've seen people fight the end; gasping and hawing for their last breath as if . . . well . . . as it were their last breath.

'Everything's looking good, Mrs Goldenblatt,' I assured the lady checking over her vitals which were those to be expected of a person dying slowly. 'Is there anything we can do for you?'

'Nothing m'dear . . . nothing,' the lady replied lying back. Even the brief examination had tired her out. The end wouldn't be long, though these things are hard to gauge. I've seen people who'd I'd been sure would pass in hours hang on for weeks. And people who'd be spry pass in minutes.

There are fifteen patients currently in situ on the ward and the Nairs, the couple from India, were the fifth in order of room number for me to visit.

'Good morning, I am Marion Gamage and I am the doctor on duty this morning,' I said, briskly walking in. Mrs Nair was lying in bed, looking out the window.

'It would be a good morning if I could get up and go for a walk in the sunshine,' Mrs Nair replied.

'Let's see if we can organise for one of the nurses to take you out,' I said, looking over her charts.

'Oh, Mr Nair will take Mrs Nair out,' Kristen the nurse interjected.

'Your husband will be visiting today?'

'He doesn't just visit,' Kristen said with a smile. 'He's staying with her. I doubt I've met a more loving husband in all my life.'

I took a quick look around. The exclusive private hospital room was standard issue, but it somehow had a homely feel about it. The odd saree print cushion here and a bright bunch of gerberas sitting on the windowsill over there. It was as if the Nairs had taken it on as their own home and added touches to define it as theirs.

I smiled and helped Kristen sit Mrs Nair up so that I could check her breathing. Yes, the woman was in the last stages of terminal myeloma, but chest infections in a hospital environment had a nasty habit of hurrying up the end.

'You are kind,' Mrs Nair remarked as I warmed the chest piece of my stethoscope in the palm of my hand. I was listening carefully for any fluid in the lower parts of the lungs when I noticed the yellowish tinge to Mrs Nair's fingernails.

'We should check on your liver function, Mrs Nair.'

'Oh, don't worry about my yellow fingernails,' she laughed hoarsely. 'It's just turmeric from years of eating curry with my fingers!'

'I thought as much, but I should still check.'

'Are you Indian?' Mrs Nair asked eagerly.

'No, Sri Lankan,' I confessed.

'My husband is Sri Lankan, too. He's lived in India now for nearly thirty years now, but he still loves *paripu*.' Mrs Nair sighed wistfully. 'I had the cooks learn how to cook it especially for him. Even I learned how to cook it!'

'And it's the only thing you can cook,' a gentleman teased, coming out the bathroom from the adjoining door.

As I turned to smile in greeting, I was thankful for the years of my medical training. For that and that alone stopped my smile from faltering. Mr Nair was horribly disfigured. Scars covered most of his face and neck. I could hardly see his right eye for the scar tissue that covered it. I quickly looked at his arms peeping from his long shirtsleeves and they too were covered with scars. From his strained gait, I assumed that the scarring extended down his back and legs.

'Raju, she's Sri Lankan,' Mrs Nair told her husband.

'Oh, I came here as a baby. I don't even speak Sinhalese,' I said.

'You're Sinhala, then?' Mr Nair asked.

'Yes,' I confirmed before moving back to Mrs Nair. The bright summer Melbourne sun filtering through the east-facing window must have caught Mr Nair straight in the eye because I heard a sudden hiss of breath from him. 'Sorry,' I apologised. 'Kristen, could you bring the blind down somewhat? I think Melbourne is the worst for sun in the eye of all the Australian cities – it's like you are being blinded with clarity!'

'It's not the sun, child. Where in Sri Lanka are you from?' he demanded. There was a strange urgency to his question that made me uncomfortable, and I didn't like the way he was looking at me.

'I was born in Badulla, but my family is from Colombo.'

'Where in Colombo?'

'I can't rightly say. I've never been back,' I said evasively. Doctors were trained not to reveal too much of their lives or to get involved with their patients. 'Someone will come and take your bloods shortly and I will be around this afternoon to check on you again, Mrs Nair.'

Mr Nair limped to the door with Kristen and I. 'How is she doing? How long do you think she has?' he asked in a soft voice.

'I wish I could give you a definite answer, but I can't. Your wife is too unwell for you to take her back to India, but if you have family who could come and visit, then I suggest they do so in the next few weeks. She may have only weeks or a month at the most.'

Raju Nair sighed deeply. 'Yes, perhaps it is time I sent for our son.'

I t didn't take me long to understand why all the nurses were absolutely enamoured with the Nairs. They were a charming couple. Absolutely divine.

She, Shanthi Nair, was sweet as sweet could be – never demanding, never complaining. Kristen, the nurse, had once walked into their room to find the couple rugged up with all the spare blankets and woollen caps from the cupboard despite the balmy weather outside.

'Why didn't you tell me the air conditioning was on the blink again?' she had asked seeing them huddle together for warmth.

'Oh, we didn't want to bother you,' Mr Nair had insisted.

'I have never really experienced a winter. I've lived all my life in Tamil Nadu, where it is warm all year round. I may never really experience the cold again,' Mrs Nair had giggled. 'Oh, how I wish I could see snow.'

When Mrs Nair had indicated she'd like to see a zoo for the last time, Mr Nair had paid for two nurses to travel with them to Parkville. Not only that, he'd also paid for an extravagant banquet meal at the Langham Hotel for the nurses though neither he nor his wife could join them. He ate whatever she ate, which was bland hospital food. 'I don't even want her to think of all the spicy food she so craves. What if she smelt it on me?' he said.

She was just as devoted to him. 'He needs to rest. Please? Can we have a larger bed?' Mrs Nair had begged and begged

until the hospital administration had relented and procured a
queen-sized bed for them to share. 'We have not slept apart in
thirty years!'

And both protected and coddled the other to a ridiculous
degree.

'He doesn't like watching TV, so don't worry about bringing
around the DVDs,' she explained to the volunteer who brought
the library cart.

'She hates stupid storylines, so I don't watch TV. Why
aggravate her? She is a sick woman.'

'He adores gingernut biscuits. Could you please bring extra
when you have them?'

'I am neither here nor there on gingernut biscuits. But they
helped her when she was having chemotherapy, so I pretend
I like them so she'll have some to keep me company,' Mr Nair
explained.

It made the nurses laugh. 'They are so sweet to each other.
So rare to see these days,' the director of nursing said one
morning at the staff meeting.

'So when is their son arriving?' Kristen had asked. 'If he
looks anything like his mother, he'll be hot!'

'I don't know that he'll be coming soon,' I told her.

'Why?'

'Because he doesn't know his mother is sick.'

Raju Nair had sought me out in my little office to explain.
'Our son Lucky has been living in the UK for some time now –
he runs the European arm of our business,' he'd said.

'What kind of business?'

'All kinds of textiles now, but we started with sarees. We do
everything from coarse woven cotton to fine silk sarees.'

'Sarees? I love sarees. Don't know how to wear one, of
course, but I love looking at them.'

'Bring one in one day and I can show you. I used to be quite
a dab hand at draping them,' Mr Nair had laughed.

'You were saying about your son?' I'd reminded him,

embarrassed at the thought of being dressed by a complete stranger.

'Yes, well, when we got Shanthi's diagnosis, the oncologists in India assured us that with treatment she would have between three and seven years. So we didn't want to worry him. We didn't expect things to progress so quickly. Lucky will be devastated now.'

'I understand Mrs Nair was only diagnosed six weeks ago?'

'Yes. She'd been feeling under the weather for quite some time, though. We were in Europe visiting Lucky over the summer. She was so busy fussing with him and fussing with me that we hardly noticed she was not as active as she used to be.'

'And you came here immediately for treatment?'

'Yes. We didn't want to go to the UK because Shanthi didn't want Lucky to see her sick. But if I know my son there will be hell to pay now. He simply adores her and it'll kill him that he's missed spending the last few weeks with her.'

'Is that why you haven't called him yet? Because you are scared?'

Raju Nair had nodded sheepishly.

I gave him a long stare. 'Call him. Do it. I would want to know if something like this was happening to my parents.'

'So you are close to your parents then?'

'No, not at all,' I replied softly. 'My mother hates me.'

'Would you like to go to the movies on Saturday night?'

'Why?'

'Because I want to watch a movie and I thought you might like to, too?'

'Can't you go with one of your friends? What about that mate you go to the footy with? What's his name?'

'Jimmo? We've been seeing each other for two years and you still can't remember my best friend's name?' Simon asked.

Simon and I were sprawled out on my bed in my apartment on Malvern Road. Outside, I could hear the rattle of the iconic old Number 5 tram as it made its way into the city. They always brought out the old bone rattlers when the temperature went over thirty-six degrees in summer. The modern air-conditioned trams didn't have the stamina of the old models, wilting and dying in the heat.

'We aren't exactly seeing each other,' I replied moving aside from under him.

'What would you call it then? Maybe it's time we got serious. We are getting to that age, you know,' Simon added.

'And what age is that?'

'I'm thirty-six . . .'

'But I'm only twenty-nine . . .'

'Perfect for an old fella like me,' Simon smiled.

'Simon . . .'

'Come on, Marion. Don't you think it's time we started

perhaps seeing each other outside this room? I can hardly remember what you look like with clothes on!'

'We just had dinner and I was completely dressed while we ate,' I protested.

'That's not what I mean and you know it. Come on, Marion. At least meet some of my friends.'

I looked at Simon Stuart for a moment. He was perfect. Quite literally perfect. Six-foot three to my six-foot frame. One of the very few men I actually had to look up to. A doctor. Funny. Sweet. We'd met during my first week at St Jude's, though it'd taken some time for things to get started.

'I kept meeting this beautiful woman, but whenever I turned to look for you, you'd melted away somewhere,' Simon had said to me on our first date.

'So, you'll come to the movies?' he asked again.

'Hmmm . . .' I mumbled hesitantly. 'When?'

'How about next Saturday? Jimmo will be there with his girlfriend, Carla, and Bingo too, I think . . .'

'Who's Bingo again?'

'Bingo – Brett Dingman – he's the engineer who did St Jude's building audit last year.'

'Why do all your friends have such stupid names?' I asked.

'Don't you get "Mare" all the time?'

'Only from the nurses.'

'Jumped-up bunch of nannies!' Simon snapped. 'Did I tell you what that cow Angela on ward twelve did today?' he asked before launching into a long diatribe against the entire nursing sorority.

'If something goes wrong, it's my neck!' he grumbled as he climbed out of bed and pulled on his jocks. 'Who does she think she is? Did she do five years of study? No. I did. A three-year degree and they bloody think they own the world.'

I made conciliatory noises as I handed him his clothes. A doctor he might be, but he had the attention span of a Cavalier King Charles spaniel. Before he knew it, I'd got him dressed and through the door without him even realising I'd engineered him leaving.

I mulled over what to do with Simon as I padded through to the kitchen to grab a glass of water.

Whatever might be said about how invisible I am, the same could not be said about my apartment. Within the safety of these four walls, I didn't try to hide my true self. I'd painted the walls in bright colours – reds, blues and rich oranges – and put lush wool carpets on the warm wooden floors. I'd found the most colourful paintings I could find and hung them on the walls. I crossed to the French doors that led to my rooftop garden and tried to open them, but they were stuck. Again. So I picked up the hammer and gently tapped them open to let some fresh air in. Part of the doorframe crumbled away. I would soon have to have the frame replaced for the third time in as many years – it was just that the rising damp from the butcher's shop below was unstoppable.

'Why do you live in this dump?' my mother demanded the one time she visited. 'And how do you deal with the noise from the trams all night?'

Yes, living in the apartment over a butcher shop on the corner of Glenferrie and Malvern Road was not what people expected me to do, not with my extravagant doctor's salary, but I wouldn't move for love nor money. 'How do you stand the smell?' more than one of my colleagues had demanded when I'd told them where I lived. 'The Meat Works? That has to be one of the oldest and dingiest butchers in all of Melbourne. I think my great-great-grandfather bought his chops there!'

'They're very clean and I'm almost never there when they take deliveries.'

People looked doubtfully at me – but they did not know my secret. Not many people knew, actually. Except for my landlord and the real estate agent. For across the rooftop courtyard was a sizeable room made almost entirely of glass. A greenhouse. 'A bunch of hippies grew weed here during the sixties,' the real estate agent had explained. 'You don't have to use it, but it's on the lease.'

I had taken it on gleefully. It was perfect. A perfect sanctuary for me. A place for me to indulge my unfulfilled dream of being a fabric artist.

The news of impending death had strange effects on people. Some people sobbed. Others took the news calmly, only breaking down later in the privacy of their homes. Then there were those for whom death was a relief, or even a blessing, especially if they or their loved one had been ill for a long time. It could be hard to predict – but Raju Nair had been right when he said that his son would be furious when he finally learned that his mother was dying.

'How long has it been going on for?' I demanded that afternoon as I came in for my shift.

'He came in last night. They hadn't told him it was a hospital when they told him which address to go to,' Kristen replied in a hushed undertone. 'I heard them start arguing just before they closed the door at about ten pm.'

'When you said St Jude's I thought it was a resort city, like St Barts!' the young man's voice had echoed down the hall.

'And he's had all the oncologists in there?'

'Yup. We put them in the family meeting room. He's even called in several specialists from the US and UK.'

'Damn it, this is why people are supposed to have these conversations before they get to the palliative care ward rather than after,' I said looking down the corridor to see dying patients either sitting up in their beds listening eagerly to the muted argument.

'Oh, don't be such a spoilsport Mare. For most of our patients this is the best fun they've had in weeks! Months even!'

Over the next hour or two, I heard snippets of conversation through the swinging doors of the meeting room as specialist after specialist trooped in to explain Mrs Nair's diagnosis and the prognosis. I did not actually see the Nairs' son, rather I heard his raised voice as doors opened and closed.

'Is there no cure?'

'Are you really the best oncologist in Australia?'

'What about alternative treatments? Have you considered those?'

'Did they have a break for lunch?' I demanded after a while. 'His mother will be exhausted.'

'Oh, Mrs Nair is resting in her room,' Kristen replied, pointing down the corridor in the opposite direction. 'He's in there with his father. And yes, he called for lunch from Quaff's and they delivered it within half an hour.'

'All the same, the prognosis is pretty clear. She's not well and won't get any better. Asking questions and shouting isn't going to change that.'

'Come on, Mare. You'd be the same if you found out your mother was dying. Wouldn't you move heaven and earth to try to save her?'

I paused for a moment before answering. I'd seen Kristen's mother pick her up after a late shift. Mrs Donovan always came with snacks for her daughter and told anyone who'd listen how she never wanted her precious child to have a car crash after a stressful shift. Kristen probably hadn't spent most of her rebellious teenage years vacillating between wanting her mother dead and feeling guilty for having those awful thoughts.

'If I found out my mum was dying, I'd want to spend as much time as I could with her instead of arguing with doctors,' I said, not wanting to reveal much of myself, then stalked off to do my rounds for the afternoon.

I took my time with it, too. I wasn't in a hurry to meet the young Mr Nair, so I had a few lengthy chats with patients. Some of them found the muted sounds of the argument raging away disturbing – but not for the reasons I'd expected. 'I have six children, doctor. I raised six children. But no one comes to see me. Mrs Nair raises one child and he comes halfway across the world to see her. Mine just live down the road,' Mrs Shepard complained tearfully.

'Some of us are lucky with our children,' Mr Owens called from the other side of the ward.

'And some of us are lucky with our parents,' I put in firmly, just as a Code Blue buzzed through the ward. 'Room 35!' the nurse shouted as she rushed past me with the crash cart. I quickly caught up to her and we burst into the room together.

'She was fine just a few seconds ago,' the old woman's granddaughter cried. 'Then she started to shake!'

I moved swiftly so that I could examine the elderly lady. It was Mrs Goldenblatt. She'd had a seizure – a massive stroke, judging by the blood pooling in the whites of her eyes. The fetid smell of faeces filled the air. I quickly felt for a pulse. It was there, but extremely weak.

'What are her instructions?' I asked, looking up at the nurse.

'What do you mean, instructions?' her granddaughter demanded.

'To resuscitate or not to resuscitate.'

'Ignore what she said. Do what you have to do to save her! Now!'

'She's left non-resuscitation instructions,' the nurse confirmed, whipping Mrs Goldenblatt's chart from the end of the bed and shoving it under my nose.

'I don't care about those instructions! Resuscitate her now!'

I gently took the young woman's hand and placed it in her grandmother's. 'You're Jemima, aren't you? Her youngest granddaughter? Your grandmother spoke often about you.' I tried to speak as gently as I could. 'Your grandmother left very clear instructions that she did not want to be resuscitated. Please. Come. Sit with her. She's only got moments left.'

The nurse and I sat with Jemima until Mrs Goldenblatt drew her last feeble breath and the calm of death took over her face. I don't care what the medical books say about death being the cessation of brain function – it happens when the soul leaves the body. You can feel it happen as sure as you can feel a cold breeze on your face. Death is as real and tangible as birth.

'Time of death, 4.45 pm, Tuesday, 12 January 2010,' I called softly to the nurse. 'We'll go and inform the rest of your family,' I told Jemima, who was sobbing into the crook of her grandmother's neck.

I was so focused on what I had to do next that I almost missed the tall man standing by the side of the door. It was only when he spoke that I noticed him.

'I don't care what my mother's instructions are. You will resuscitate even if she is on her last breath,' he said.

'And you are?' I asked in confusion.

'Laksman Nair. Lucky.'

The damn thing about international patients' families was that they hung around all the time. They didn't have local homes to go back to. It drove hospital staff nuts. Simon always complained that it was a pity that St Jude's hadn't installed a swimming pool, private gym and twenty-four-hour bar with *à la carte* room service when they'd opened their doors to international patients five years ago.

'St Jude's will be like those resort hospitals in Thailand. Five thousand for a boob job and ten thousand for your alcohol bill, thank you.'

I didn't argue with him, though I didn't agree. It was different for Simon – he was a generalist, and most of his patients weren't dying. In the palliative care ward it made perfect sense for families to want to hang around and I didn't see a problem with making their time as pleasant as possible.

But by the end of the first week of Lucky Nair's stay in Melbourne, even I was praying for a bit of divine intervention in the shape of a pub that would get him out of the hospital even for an hour a day so that *I* could get some respite.

'Her pain medication was five minutes late. She is dying, you know.'

'She needs to be sat up more. Can we get fluffier pillows?'

'I have had better food on airplanes! Who does the catering for this hospital?'

The nurses who'd once swooned at his dark good looks and cultured accent took to hiding in the double-locked medical storeroom when they heard the soft tread of his expensive shoes on the vinyl in the corridor. 'There's no space left in here,' Jodi said, shooing Kristen away one afternoon when three nurses had scooted in there. 'Try the broom closet!'

I couldn't hide, of course. As the senior ward doctor, I was obliged to be available at the nurses' station if I were not doing my rounds. But by the end of the week, I'd developed a migraine from gritting my teeth, dealing with young Mr Nair.

'May I call you Lucky?' I'd asked him politely early in our acquaintance.

'Mr Nair will do,' he'd cut back. 'So what about her pain medication?'

'Well, Mr Nair, you'll find that your mother has a self-activated morphine dispenser that allows her to manage her own pain medication.'

'What about the pillows?'

'There are fifteen luxury Sheridan pillows in the top section of your mother's wardrobe. Have you run out of those?'

Lucky had shaken his head sheepishly.

'Try those first, and if you still need more, I'll get house-keeping to drop off a few extras.'

'But what about catering? The food is atrocious!' he'd fired back.

'Mr Nair, the food at St Jude's is supplied by some of the best caterers in Australia. Your mother receives nutritionally balanced meals that she can easily keep down. I know it is bland. I know it is boring. But plain food is best when you've just finished radiation therapy,' I explained patiently.

'Is that it?' Lucky demanded.

'If you have any special requests, I can have the chef come and speak to you.'

'No, I wasn't talking about the catering,' Lucky said. 'Is there nothing else other than radiation? Nothing more we could do for my mother?'

'I saw you speaking with the oncologist and the radiation

therapist. They are both world leaders in the treatment of myeloma. Did they speak to you about any experimental treatments?'

'Yes, but they also said that my mother probably would not do well with them at her age!'

'That is a fair point. Even young, fit people in the prime of their lives struggle with chemotherapy.'

'Why is that?' Lucky had asked, cocking his head to the side. In the dim light of the nurses station, I could understand why he had sent the nurses into a dither. He was a strikingly good-looking man with the most penetrating set of eyes I had ever seen.

'Chemotherapy is really a contradiction in terms,' I explained. 'We inject people with carcinogenic chemicals, hoping that those chemicals will kill the cancerous cells before the patient becomes too ill to continue with the treatment. Until better treatments are found, that's our only hope.'

'That's it then. I am going to lose my mother,' he'd sighed, looking down at his feet.

'Mr Nair, losing a parent is one of the most difficult things anyone of any age ever has to confront. I am so sorry for what you are going through. We have a grief counselling service here at St Jude's and I would be happy to arrange an appointment for you. There is also a chaplain service and I can organise a session with a psychologist if you wish.'

Lucky looked up angrily. 'Look, I don't need your pre-prepared grief counselling spiel here. I need the truth!'

'And you would have heard the truth from the oncologist yesterday. I cannot add anything more to that.'

'So what kind of a doctor are you anyway?' he demanded, looking down his nose at me.

'I am a palliative care specialist,' I replied. Somehow the derision in his voice had got under my skin. 'I tend to people while they are dying. I make no promises other than to look after my patients until the very end.'

'Have you lost a parent?' Lucky demanded.

I pressed my lips together. I wasn't going to talk to him about my parents.

I prepared for the twentieth of every month with a great deal of trepidation. In fact I even started taking a half-dose of Valium and cancelling any interfering appointments.

'What do you mean you're not having dinner with me? It's Valentine's Day, for God's sake!' Simon cried in an aggrieved tone down the line when I told him I was unavailable.

'It's too close to the twentieth of the month, remember?'

'Oh . . . PMT. Well, you'll have to make it up to me. Come with me to the Moonlight Cinema at the Botanic Gardens with Davo and his bird Susan. We'll make a party of it.'

I agreed reluctantly, promising myself I'd find an excuse not to go closer to the date. It was time to break off my relationship with Simon altogether. He was asking things of me I couldn't give him. Not in a million years.

And the diagnosis of PMT was not far off either. Rather than it being pre-menstrual tension, though, it was pre-mother tension. For it was on the twentieth of each month that my mother called. From wherever in the world she might be. That simple call was sufficient to trigger a depressive episode so severe that I always ensured I was rostered off work that day.

To mitigate the effects of her call, I usually spent the morning of the twentieth in my studio. I was working on a Japanese-style mural – a four-metre by two-metre red flame of a fabric painting with a gold Japanese maple leaf motif. It'd been inspired by a lecture about Lafcadio Hearn, the great twentieth-century orientalist and Japanophile at the Wheeler's Centre I'd attended. I'd bought one of his books – *Kwaidan: Stories and Studies of Strange Things* – simply for the kick of being terrified by Japanese ghost stories in my flat above the meatworks.

But that morning I could not concentrate, my hand constantly darting towards the phone and my heart in my mouth. I'd tried to pin my mother down to get her to agree on a time to call me, but she wouldn't agree to that. 'I raised you for eighteen years and you want me to make an appointment to call you?' she'd asked, incredulous.

By half past ten that morning, all the cups of chamomile tea I had been drinking conspired against me and I bolted to the loo. And as always, my mother had perfect timing and called me midstream. I literally ran to get the phone with wee dripping down my legs and onto my jeans, then sat gingerly on the edge of my hammock to talk to her, thinking of all the hundreds of time in my life that my mother had me wetting my knickers.

'Now, can you explain to me why your father's HDLs are up?' my mother opened. 'And the doctor said that my blood pressure is a little on the high side too. What do you think I should do about that?'

'Can you get your doctor to email me your test results?' I sighed, looking up at the sky. 'I've given him my email details before.'

'Oh, we've changed doctors,' my mother replied airily.

'Why? I thought you loved James Hodges. His practice is within walking distance of your place and he bulk-bills.'

'But we're seeing Brently George now. He is the Peraras' and the de Silvas' doctor and it's nice to go as a group to see him.'

'Mother, you are not going to the doctor to have a pedicure,' I groaned. 'You should not be shopping for doctors. You should have continuity of care. That's important at your age.'

'Well, there would not be any issue of continuity of care if your brother had become a doctor instead of you!' my mother roared. It would have been unethical for Ryan to treat my parents, just as it was for me, but rationality wasn't a character trait my mother was known for.

I sighed. In twelve years the conversation hadn't changed. Twelve years since I'd been accepted into medical school instead of my twin Ryan.

'What if she gave up her position in medical school for Ryan? Can't we swap one child for the other?' she'd demanded of the dean of admissions at Sydney University. The dean politely refused to see her ever again.

However, halfway through first year, my anatomy teacher caught me crying while dissecting an arm. Perhaps it was the fumes of the chloroform used to preserve the cadavers that finally loosened my tongue and had me pouring out a lifetime of grief to her.

'I'm sleeping in the garage now. She won't let me into the house anymore,' I sobbed.

The professor had gone away and a few weeks later I'd had a meeting with her and the course convener.

'We can organise for you to receive a full scholarship and you can live on campus at one of the colleges. Would that be preferable to staying at home with your parents?' the course convener had asked.

I'd nodded, taking with both hands the opportunity to escape my tormentor. I told my mother that living on campus was a condition of the scholarship, but she didn't care, as long as she didn't have to pay my fees. As soon as I graduated, I moved to the colder but more comfortable Melbourne, where I could be close to my aunt Fatima, an old family friend who'd cared for me when I was a child – and been more of a mother to me than Anoja ever had.

I stayed on the phone listening to my mother rant until she was spent, which was a good thirty minutes later. I did not argue or try to interrupt. When she was done she hung up.

I curled up like a ball in the womb-like confines of the red hammock, taking comfort from the feel of the roughly hewn cotton fabric against my skin. I couldn't ever remember being held by my mother – and she actually boasted about the fact.

'I never cuddled Marion as a child. I only ever picked her up to change her nappies. One day she cried for five hours straight. After that she stopped crying. Altogether. She's never cried since.'

Pressing my face against the bright red of the hammock, I wished I could cry. Perhaps then I could actually feel my heart beat just for once, instead having to rely on my stethoscope for proof.

'I know some of you are not keen,' the director of medicine informed the staff on the palliative care ward. 'But the Nairs are willing to pay you double-time and a half for in-home care until Shanthi Nair passes.'

Such arrangements were not uncommon. Families sometimes wanted to be in more familiar surroundings to help ease the passing of a loved one. It was not unusual for people to come into a palliative ward and then go home if the end became a protracted process. And in Shanthi Nair's case, it was fast becoming clear that that was how things would pan out. She'd rallied extremely well once her son had arrived. While she was not well enough to return to India, she did not require the constant medical care needed by a person about to die.

In these cases, St Jude's provided an in-home service complete with twenty-four hour nursing care and a doctor on stand-by as well. Only this time, nursing staff were proving difficult to get. I wasn't surprised.

'You won't have to go far,' the director of nursing rushed to assure the mutinous group of nurses. 'Mr Nair has secured a beachfront house in Brighton. It is lovely. I went there myself. Three storeys.'

'He treats us like maids,' Jodi said furiously.

'He won't even look us in the eye, ignores us and just barks orders at us,' Kristen seconded.

'Mr Nair? I don't believe you. He's lovely!' the director of nursing said. 'And you will have the top floor to yourselves with your own private balcony and a private swimming pool – you certainly won't be treated like maids.'

'We're not talking about Mr Nair, we're talking about his son Lucky!' Kristen retorted. 'I am not going to that house to work for him!'

Several other nurses nodded in agreement, their arms crossed militantly across their chests. Both the director of medicine and the director of nursing looked beseechingly at me. I was standing at back of the room with my back to the wall. I felt like I should join the protest too. I had been on the receiving end of Lucky Nair's rude behaviour too and I'd had enough.

'It's too cold in here, doctor. Fix it.'

'The tap in the bathroom is broken, doctor. Fix it.'

'The coffee in the cafeteria is bad, doctor. Fix it.'

I sometimes wondered whether he thought my name was Doctor Fix It. And he seemed to see past my invisibility cloak, which irritated me no end.

'You are a very attractive woman, you know,' he observed in the corridor one day. 'Never mind the drab clothes you wear.'

'I am a doctor, not a fashion model,' I'd slapped him down. 'And shouldn't you be visiting your mother and not perving on her carers?'

' "Perving" is not exactly what I'd call it; rather a car crash you can't help look at!'

He'd then disappeared into his mother's room before I could think of a suitable retort.

'Come on,' I said, trying to rally the troops. 'You know this isn't for him. It's for her. Mrs Nair is the one dying.'

'Look, I feel for her, but I'll be damned if I'll be treated like shit by her son,' Jodi said.

'Jodi, what are their options? She won't last the ten-hour flight back to India. They're not Australians, or even permanent residents, so they don't qualify for Medicare. Should we let them go and tell them to find agency nurses for themselves?'

There was a rumble of discontent. Agency nurses were regarded with more than a mild degree of contempt.

'Yes, imagine that. That wonderful woman is dying, too shy to ask for pain relief even when she's suffering, and you want to put her in the hands of contract nurses?'

'Okay!' Jodi agreed. 'I'll go, but I want you at the house when I'm there!'

'What do you mean?' the director of nursing asked.

'I will only work for the Nairs if Marion is there with us!' Several other nurses nodded their agreement.

'But Dr Gamage must be here on the ward. Doctors do two visits a day to support external patients, but that is it,' the director said.

'Then we won't go.'

The director of nursing and the director of medicine briefly spoke to each other before turning to look at me. 'Marion, will you do this for us?' the director of medicine pleaded. 'Lucky Nair has promised a hefty donation to the hospital. Enough to fund several research scholarships.'

'Excuse me? You want me to go and live at the Nairs?' I demanded.

'Please?' the director begged. 'It'll be like a holiday by the beach. We'll even pay you double-time.'

I straightened my shoulders to refuse. Goddamn it, I was doctor, not a nurse, and I opened my mouth to say as much when I saw old Mr Nair. He'd escaped his son's clutches momentarily and limped painfully out to the little balcony for a breath of fresh air. He was such a sweet old man. So kind and gentle. I watched as he gallantly stood aside for two elderly ladies coming in from the balcony.

'Okay,' I agreed softly, though the words sounded strange even to my own ears.

learned more about family living in the brief time I spent with the Nairs in Brighton than in my entire previous dysfunctional personal life before that. I also learned that Lucky Nair wasn't such a big arse after all. Perhaps.

For one thing, he'd moved heaven and earth to find his parents a comfortable home. 'Oh, *puttar*,' Shanthi Nair had gasped, seeing the elegant Victorian house on the tiny rise at the end of Cole Street in Brighton.

'I knew you wouldn't want one of those glass and concrete houses,' Lucky replied softly, pointing to the postmodern crimes against aesthetics that flanked the Victorian masterpiece on either side.

'Look at the gardens,' Raju Nair said as the medical transport personnel wheeled Shanthi in through the cottage garden filled with roses, lilacs and geraniums in full bloom.

It was not a bad place to spend your last days really. The 'library' was as large as my entire apartment and the windows overlooked expansive lawns onto the beach and Port Phillip Bay just beyond. People were making the most of the hot weather with the distant hum of jetskis and sailors calling out to each other from their sailboats.

I could not fault Lucky's sense of what was appropriate either. 'I've had them convert the library into Amman's room. My parents will sleep in there. I've also had them place the nurses' station in the dining room adjoining that. There is a little sofa bed in there and a sealed closet for all the medication.'

'So where are we supposed to sleep?' Jodi asked grumpily.

'On the second floor. Whoever is on duty will have use of the master bedroom, and Dr Gamage can have the use of the second room.'

'And where are you sleeping?'

'There is a little attic on the top floor,' Lucky said. 'It doesn't matter where I sleep.'

'Because he'll most likely sleep at the foot of our bed,' Shanthi called out weakly.

'And we'd only just succeeded in booting him out too!' Raju laughed.

'You still sleep with your parents?' I asked with a smirk.

'I moved out of their room when I was sixteen!' Lucky said.

'Because you went to London for your studies,' his mother reminded him. 'Doctor, the night before he went, he slept between his father and I like he was a baby!' Mrs Nair laughed.

'Call me, Marion, please,' I said.

'Such a pretty name for such a pretty girl,' Mrs Nair sighed, making me feel very uncomfortable.

'I swear I've seen your face before,' Raju said for the hundredth time since he met me.

'Yes, you do look so very familiar to me too,' Shanthi seconded.

'Are you sure you don't have any relatives in Tamil Nadu?' even Lucky asked. 'Have you ever been to India?'

'No,' I muttered. 'I have never been to India, or even back to Sri Lanka for that matter.'

'You haven't travelled much then?' It was Lucky's turn to smirk now.

'I go overseas at least twice a year for medical conferences so I make sure I see much of where I go to,' I replied. Yes, I feel uncomfortable with my lack of worldliness. 'You've travelled extensively then?'

'These two dragged me everywhere and anywhere. But I would have preferred a brother or sister,' he returned glaring at his parents. For their part they just rolled their eyes. 'Do you have any brothers or sisters?'

'Yes,' I admitted brusquely before helping Jodi to set up all the equipment we needed – heart rate monitors, resuscitation carts and a drip line while a friendly argument broke out amongst the Nairs about the sibling they never provided for Lucky.

'So, are you close to your siblings?' Shanthi asked me as we worked. 'Do you have brothers or sisters?'

'A brother.'

'Older or younger?'

'A twin.'

'You are a twin? Oh, how wonderful! You must be so very close.'

'What does he do?' Raju asked. 'Is he a doctor like you?'

'No. He moved to Sri Lanka last year and works for my uncle's business.'

'Oh, what kind of business does he run?' Lucky asked arrogantly. 'I have some interests there too.'

'My uncle runs a waxworks,' I replied, but was cut off by Raju, who was looking curiously at his son.

'Since when have you developed an interest in Sri Lanka?' his father asked.

'Since I lodged legal claims for the old saree mill in Panadura six months ago. That was why it took me a few days to get here from London. I stopped in Sri Lanka *en route* to finalise the deeds – I would never have done it if I'd known why you were asking me to come – but the courts found in our favour. The squatters have been kicked out. Appa, the saree mill is ours again.'

'Are you even Sri Lankan?' Lucky asked, eyeing my dinner plate with distaste. It'd been about a week since we'd all moved into the house in Brighton and the peace was, at best, tenuous. The nurse on duty took one look at him as he strolled into the kitchen from the laundry and bolted out of the room with her salad, leaving me alone with him. By and large the nurses had taken to eating their meals in the sitting room upstairs and avoiding the surly Lucky altogether.

'I'm brown, aren't I?'

'So what is that you're eating then? Burnt meat and boiled vegetables. Why aren't you eating the food the caterers dropped off?'

'Because I've been working at St Jude's for almost four years now and I've eaten that food on rotation so often it makes me gag.'

'Can't you cook?' he asked grumpily as he helped himself to some food from the fridge. He'd got in contact with some local Indian caterer and they kitted out the fridge every couple of days with foods whose sumptuous fragrances nearly made me swoon.

'Clearly not, since all the food I eat is raw,' I said sarcastically, pointing to the medium-rare lamb cutlets and crisp wok-tossed vegetables on my plate. Oh, the man was infuriating, but I'd be damned if I'd eat my meals like the nurses, in solitary confinement.

'So why don't you eat the food I have had the caterers deliver? I understand that the Australian nurses may find it a little spicy but you should be fine with it,' Lucky said, sitting down with a plate of biryani, lamb curry and a glass of red wine. He was dressed in a pair of camel-coloured pants and a charcoal T-shirt. He'd just come back from a swim in the bay and had a shower, and there was water still clinging to his hair.

'Because it's a free country and I can do what I want to do. That includes eating what I want to eat.'

'India is a free country, only our women aren't as opinionated as you!'

'Clearly you must have failed history in high school if you

think all Indian women are meek and subservient. Remember Indira Gandhi? And isn't the chief minister of Tamil Nadu a woman too? Jayalalithaa? Hardly a bunch of wilting flowers your country has produced.'

'The current chief minister is a man – but yes, Jayalalithaa was the chief minister for Tamil Nadu for a long time,' Lucky said, looking impressed. 'You are quite worldly for an Australian. Very few people outside India know much about its politics.'

'Why do you suppose Australians are ignorant? Australians are among some of the best-travelled people in the world.' I looked daggers at him and made a neat cut into my meat.

'Eating with utensils is like making love through an interpreter,' Lucky said, quoting the great traveller Ibn Battuta as he mushed his rice and curry into little balls before depositing them elegantly in his mouth with his lean fingers.

'You must have some experience with that, since you'd probably only score women who don't speak the same language as you,' I tossed back.

'Oh, the lady has a temper! What next? What insult will you hurl at me now?'

'Would it matter? It's not as if anything will make a dent in that thick head of yours!'

'No – that is true. I am blessed with a self-confidence that could not be shaken even with a sledgehammer. But it is clear I have chinked your amour.'

'I don't have any amour to chink,' I hissed.

'Oh, please! I've never seen anyone so guarded.'

'Enjoy your dinner,' I snapped, snatching my plate to eat in peace in my study.

My mother's house had been a curious place. She was ashamed to be Sri Lankan, yet she aspired to be 'someone', a luminary within the Sri Lankan community in Sydney. Ryan and I spent most of our childhoods being stationed outside Sri Lankan community meetings while mother attempted to get onto some committee or other.

'Stupid curry-smelling Lankans. Bloody useless, the lot of them,' Anoja would complain, mere moments after having begged herself a lunch invitation from the high commissioner's wife.

When I left Sydney I left all that baggage behind me. It'd been a long time since I'd been a part of any scene, and I rarely had to confront the fact that I was even Sri Lankan. I could go for weeks forgetting I was any different to anyone else, until I'd see my dark skin against the paleness of one of my patients.

But working at close quarters with the Nairs, I felt the distinction between myself and the other Australian nurses acutely. Not that the Nairs discriminated against them in any way – in fact Raju and Shanthi went out of their way to be hospitable to them – it was just that they were more comfortable with me and were more likely to lapse into uncomfortable family conversations in my presence. And to their son's sadistic pleasure, his parents loved to drag me into the conversation too!

'Could you please tell my mother that there is nothing wrong with going for a swim at six in the morning and that walking through dew will not kill me?' Lucky said one morning coming in from the beach. 'You're a doctor. You understand germ theory. Could you speak to her?'

'I have no desire to see anything more of Australia before I die, Laksman. I am quite content to be here with your father and you. Tell them, Marion. Tell them that I am in no state to be travelling anywhere,' Shanthi insisted.

'Don't you think he works too much? Tell him, Marion – tell him to take a break. He's been working all night! Tell him he'll have a heart attack by the time he's forty and hasn't even had any children!'

But being so close to them allowed me to experience some of the most touching moments I had seen in my life. Lucky cuddling up with his mother at any given opportunity. The entire family lying close together on Shanthi and Raju's big bed, as if to store up skin memories for when the mind memories eventually faded.

And when Lucky was not spending time with his mother, he was furiously working on his plans to resurrect his father's business in Sri Lanka. I heard snatches of his conversation, though I didn't understand much.

'Guru Hirantha died a few years ago, but Guru Sakunthala and Guru Sindhu have indicated that they would love to return to the mill.'

'Have you found Guru Lakshmi?' his father asked.

'Not yet, but I am still looking. Hey, have you done your stretches? Come. Have you done them? Tell him, Marion. You're a doctor. Tell him he needs to do his exercises daily!'

'Which brings me to another important point,' Shanthi interjected bossily. 'It is time you got married. Find a good woman who'll look after you and your father. Tell him, Doctor, tell him that it is time to settle down. We've put the feelers out, Lucky. There are several good prospects for a bride for you.'

I smiled evilly at Lucky's discomfort, chiming softly in with. 'Yes, Lucky, it is time to make some woman very un-lucky!' I whispered so only he could hear and smirked at his discomfort.

'If I have told you once, I have told you a million times, I will not get married to some Tamil Nadu princess with a penchant for shoes, sarees and the use of my charge card at Selfridges,' he told his parents.

'Not all Tamil Nadu women are like that!' his mother protested. 'There are educated women in Tamil Nadu who'd want nothing of your money!'

'That is where you are wrong, Amman,' Lucky snorted. 'If they are educated, they are worse. Then they will abandon everything to make money themselves!'

'You are my son, but you are an idiot!' his mother rebuked

him. 'Don't be a woman-hater just because you don't want to get married.'

'If you don't want to marry an Indian girl, why not a foreigner?' Raju asked. 'You know we would not object.'

'But why do I need to marry? Why can't I just stay the way I am for the rest of my life?'

'But we would rather you have a partner in life. Someone you can depend on. Someone who will love you and look out for you,' Shanthi said. 'Don't you agree, Doctor?' she asked.

'Entirely. I think it's high time your son had someone to keep him in line.'

'Exactly! So have your parents arranged a marriage for you yet?'

'Mrs Nair . . .' I said.

'Call me Aunty . . .'

'Err . . . okay . . . Aunty. Like Lucky, I have no interest in getting married. I'm quite happy as I am.'

'What is this nonsense! What do your parents think of this?' Shanthi cried. Now it was Lucky's turn to smirk.

'I am not very close to my family.'

'But you are such a lovely young woman! Your parents must be odd people!'

'Amman!' Lucky gasped. 'You can't say that to a stranger!'

'Marion is not a stranger. She is a good Sri Lankan woman. A person of subcontinental descent! And I am dying and I can say whatever I want.'

'Shanthi, don't interfere,' Raju said, but his wife took no notice.

'Yes, your parents must be very odd people. I stand by what I say. Any parent would be proud to have such a pretty and intelligent girl for a daughter. And if you were my girl, I would have married you off within days of you graduating from medical college!'

'Well, I should be thankful for small mercies then,' I parried with a smile.

'So, do you have a boyfriend?' Shanthi insisted.

'Sort of.'

'Sort of? What does that mean? Tell me you aren't one of those women who likes other women. Unnatural, if you ask me.'

In the background, both Raju and his son were giggling.

'No, I am not gay, and, yes, I have a boyfriend,' I confessed reluctantly.

'What sort of a man is he?'

'He is a fellow doctor.'

'Indian or Sri Lankan?'

'Australian, actually.'

'Well, that is of no use,' Shanthi Nair said. 'You want a good Indian or Sri Lankan man who'll understand your culture.'

'Or both,' Raju suggested. Which was when I noticed him glancing slyly between his son and me.

How I ended up on a crowded tram on a scorching Saturday afternoon filled with drunk cricket supporters, a basket full of food on my lap and an even larger parcel of silk paintings next to me is, quite frankly, beyond me.

'Smells delish, love,' a middle-aged man slurred happily.

I smiled politely and ignored him. I'd been too busy to remember to cancel my movie date with Simon and couldn't think of a convincing excuse to get out of it at the very last minute. To add to my woes, Raju and Lucky had been there when I'd taken the call from Simon confirming the night. 'Simon, I've been working really hard lately – I'm really not up to seeing you tonight,' I'd said.

'My dear, why don't you leave early!' Raju had insisted, interrupting my conversation. 'Kristen is an extremely competent nurse and Shanthi has been doing so well.'

'You can't let the doctor go early to see her boyfriend. This isn't a prison, and we don't allow for conjugal visits,' Lucky butted in.

'You aren't too old for me to take you across my knee, Lucky!' his father had replied angrily before apologising profusely to me. He now insisted that I leave early. 'Please, doctor. As a way to say you forgive us for our rude son.'

Since I was pretty sure Simon had overheard the whole conversation, I couldn't tell a bare-faced lie and pike on him. So my plans to have a lovely afternoon down on Smith Street in Collingwood riffling through yards and yards of silk had been totally scuppered.

It got worse as I was halfway home from Brighton, when Simon had texted me to pick up a picnic basket from the food hall at David Jones. 'It's not out of your way, hop off the tram on Bourke Street, and Bob's your uncle, you've got food for us all!'

So now I had not only a large silk painting with me on the tram, but an extra large picnic hamper as well. By the time I made it to the fabric warehouse after getting off the tram and trudging down Smith Street in the heat, my temper was fuzzier than my curly hair.

'Eh, Missy! I thought you were going to miss our appointment today,' a squeaky voice greeted me from behind the counter.

'Have I ever missed one of our appointments? Hey, where is everyone?'

'It's well after six, Missy Marion – everyone has left. I keep shop open especially for you,' the office manager said.

Nimal was a very small man – long-term malnutrition during his childhood in Sri Lanka was to blame. I'd first met him during a psychiatric consult when I was an intern. He was being treated for post-traumatic stress disorder. It'd taken him about twenty years, but he'd learned to talk properly again after having become a psychosomatic mute after witnessing a violent incident when he was just a child.

'So, so . . . show me,' he demanded in his heavily accented English. He still seemed unsure about using his voice.

I needed no second invitation and immediately laid out the fabric paintings. If my work as a doctor was a labour of love, them my fabric painting was a labour of joy. I'd painted a series of stylised ducklings and little goslings. Perfect patterns for a child's layette or bedcovers in bright tropical colours. As always, Nimal showered me with heartfelt compliments. I loved to show him my work.

'Where is the boss?' I asked as he measured out ten metres of silk as barter. I designed and painted silk templates for the textile manufacturers to take back to Sri Lanka, and they kept me supplied with silk.

'He is upstairs talking to another businessman,' Nimal replied, carefully folding the silk. 'Where are you going after this? Do you want to join Mahinda Sir and I for dinner?'

'I am going to a picnic, so no, but thank you,' I replied, retying my ponytail and turning my face towards the fan in the corner. Despite the high ceilings in the warehouse, the heat was oppressive. Sweat trickled down my back and arms.

'And she doesn't like curry,' a familiar voice mocked from above. I looked up to the mezzanine level to see Lucky come down with Mahinda, the owner of the warehouse.

'Lucky, I didn't know you knew Marion,' Mahinda said. 'It was her fabric paintings I was showing you. She's our freelance fabric designer.'

'But she's a doctor,' Lucky said, puzzled.

'No, she's the best fabric designer we work with. Completely self-taught!'

'What are you doing here?' I snapped at Lucky. 'Did you follow me?'

'Of course not! I have business with Mahinda here. He's helping up me set up a silk farm in Sri Lanka.'

'Oh!' I replied, feeling a little foolish. 'Well, then, I'll see you in a few weeks, Mahinda, and I will see you, Lucky, on Monday at the house,' I said, quickly grabbing my things and bolting out.

As I struggled down Smith Street to catch the tram back down St Kilda Road to the Botanic Gardens, I saw Lucky drive past in his BMW in the other direction.

As I waited for the tram, I wondered how such lovely parents as Shanthi and Raju Nair had produced such a douche-bag for a son. I mean really. He was such a pompous tool. I stood there thinking about suitable retorts to cut him down, then I thought about just ignoring him. Yes, I decided. I would ignore him.

Which is why it took me forty minutes at the tram stop to realise there were no trams coming past, on either side of the road. I looked at the Metlink app on my phone and there it was in bright red letters – all tram services had been suspended.

What was I going to do? The open air movie at the Botanic Gardens was going to start in a little over forty-five minutes and I hated being late.

I looked up and down Smith Street hoping for a cab but there were none to be found, just lots of people starting to stroll out onto the street now that the heat of the day had passed. I was starting to panic when I heard a beep behind me.

'Come on. Get in,' Lucky said, rolling down the window to treat me with a blast of cold air from inside his car.

'Why?'

'I'll take you where you want to go.'

'I'm just waiting for a cab,' I said loftily.

'You'll be waiting for a long time. Traffic is blocked up for ten kilometres both sides,' Lucky informed me, tapping on the radio.

'How did you get around?'

'GPS.'

I am many things – introverted definitely, aloof most likely, even cold maybe. But stupid I am not. 'Fine then,' I muttered gracelessly as Lucky popped open the boot so I could put my things in it.

'Where to?'

'The Botanic Gardens. They're having an Audrey Hepburn movie marathon tonight.'

'I love Audrey Hepburn too!' Lucky smiled at me genuinely for the very first time.

'This is so gay,' Simon observed and not for the first time that night.

He and his mates Davo and Bingo had polished off a six-pack of stubbies each and it wasn't hard to tell.

'Why is it black and white? Couldn't they colour it in?' Bingo slurred.

'Ran out of money, mate . . .' Davo chimed in.

Davo's and Bingo's partners had switched off too. Jenna was tweeting updates on her phone and Carly was only half-watching the movie as she spent the rest of the time swatting away mosquitoes.

But I loved Audrey Hepburn in *Sabrina*. I felt myself tearing up when Sabrina's young heart was almost broken by the philandering younger brother – why could she not see she was meant for the older workaholic brother and not the younger one? I taken by surprise when I felt a gentle nudge the dark – it was Lucky, offering me his handkerchief.

'I don't cry,' I muttered.

'Didn't think you could,' Lucky snapped back. 'But it'll help you get that bit of dirt you've had stuck in your eye since we got here.'

I still couldn't believe he'd invited himself along.

'Hi, I'm Lucky Nair,' he'd said, introducing himself to Simon while helping me unload the picnic hamper from his boot.

'Fine set of wheels you've got there,' Simon had drooled. 'Is that an M Series Sport?'

As they started talking about cars I tuned out, until Simon squealed like a girl. 'You've got freebies to the Grand Prix? You shitting me? Grandstand? Mate – come watch the movie with us!'

I sent Simon a death stare but he blithely ignored me. In fact he ignored me for the rest of the night; more interested in Lucky's knowledge of European automobiles than me!

So what was supposed to have been a romantic movie outing for three couples ended up being the three girls serving food and wine to the boys while they argued over the cars they would drive if they could.

'My mate's got an Audi TT. The problem is that it's not steady. They spin out really easily,' Davo opined.

'You want to try the Skoda, mate. Built by Volkswagen, only half the price,' Bingo chimed in.

'Can't go past a BMW, I say,' Simon said.

I didn't get it. A car was a car was a car. I got a Toyota soon after I'd graduated from university and I'd driven it ever since.

'I'm heading out to the track on Phillip Island on Tuesday. I have three BMWs back in India and the MD called me and asked me to come and test-drive another here,' Lucky had said. 'Come with me. We'll go for a spin.'

'Excellent! I'll call in a sickie at work,' Simon said.

But as the evening progressed, I could not help but notice the real difference between Lucky and Simon and his mates. While Simon and his mates lolled around like overgrown adolescent boys discussing cars and the footy, Lucky did not think twice about joining the girls' conversation.

'Can I help you serving those mussels? Here you go, all you needed was a dash of lemon.'

When Jenna moaned about a dress she'd love to buy but couldn't because she felt it was more suitable for a younger woman, he interjected. 'Don't let adolescent girls define fashion. You are a grown woman. You define what younger women wear. Women of age and experience should be leaders, not the other way around.'

And in the final scene of the film, when Sabrina left New York on a ship bound for Paris with her heart broken, I felt Lucky move closer. My 'boyfriend' was snoring, sprawled on the grass like a lump. Lucky didn't touch me or anything – he just let me know he was close.

'You don't have to drive me home,' I insisted as he poured Simon into a cab and sent him on his way.

'Come on, I'll drop you off on my way. It's not out of the way. It's been good for me. I haven't watched an old movie for a while. With all that has been happening, I'd forgotten how much I love simple things.'

'Just enjoy your mum while she's with you, Lucky. Just enjoy her. But don't stop living. You've spent the last three weeks constantly at her side – it's good you got away for a while.'

'Actually my dad texted me to say thank you for allowing him and mum some private time,' Lucky giggled as he put his car into gear and drove back onto St Kilda road.

'It must be lovely to be a part of such a loving family. To have grown up with parents who love each other so much,' I whispered softly in the darkness.

Lucky turned to stare at me as he stopped at a traffic light. The lights from the Shrine of Remembrance cast odd shadows around us. 'Dr Gamage, all that glitters is not gold,' he said softly.

could still remember the first time I got a stick of crayon and a bit of paper. I must have been about four. Oh no! Don't get me wrong. I didn't have a deprived childhood or anything. My father Albert was Director of Engineering and Infrastructure at Sydney Rail and my family was never short of money. My brother Ryan studied at one of the most exclusive private schools in Sydney while I went to a state school not far from home.

It was just that my mother loved my brother much more than she loved me. She bought all the crayons and toys for Ryan and she'd never let me play with his things. I still remember sitting in my own playpen longing to touch the colourful toys in his – but being never allowed to. Whenever my father would object to her treatment of me, the row she created was unimaginable.

'Albert, don't you dare speak to me of treating her well!' my mother would scream. 'I brought her to Australia, didn't I!'

'You couldn't exactly leave her behind, could you?' my father would reply; only to unstopper a torrent of rage.

'There I was pregnant and you'd run off to Australia. Bigger than a house. Not that my mother would let me out at all after you left. Made me go up to Badulla for the entire pregnancy.'

'That was because the air up there was good for you . . .'

'Stuck out in the middle of nowhere! And then I became a mother of two! I told Mother I could not care for two children. I told her that I should leave that one behind in Sri Lanka,' she shouted, pointing at me. 'But Mother insisted I take both with me! She got cancer, but instead of growing a tumour she grew a heart! She even brought the baby to the airport and made sure I got onto the plane with her.'

'How could she not, Anoja? Marion looks exactly like your sister, and she was lost in that bus crash! Your mother would have wanted the best for her!'

'My sister? She dies and everybody forgets what a hag she was! Ugly! Were you in love with that ugly witch, too?'

My father gave up after a while. Years later I found out that my father had seen a psychiatrist about my mother's attachment problem. The psychiatrist had said that it was extremely rare for a mother to attach to one twin and not the other. To be a normal and loving mother to one child and abusive to the other. I suppose he thought the problem was not with the mother but with the child. Me. I learned very quickly not to be seen or heard. Being shouted at every time you speak does that to you.

But I remember the crayon and paper day like a ray of sunshine after weeks of rain. We'd just moved to a new house and we had paper left over from wrapping the crockery. There must have been a family of children living in the house previously, because I found the crayons at the back of a cupboard. I smuggled a lovely long strip of paper out into the backyard and I drew. Flowers. Horses. Dogs. Rainbows. Cats. Anything and everything. Fitting as many pictures as I could onto that bit of packing paper.

My absence must have been noticed eventually because I remember my mother's reaction when she found me. 'What's this?' she'd mocked. 'What use are tiny pictures? No one can see them! Stupid girl! Albert! Look at this stupidity your daughter has created!'

My father hadn't totally given up on me by that stage. After my mother had stomped off, he'd pulled me onto his lap and asked me to explain to him what I'd drawn.

'I like to draw long pictures. Pictures you can wrap yourself in,' I told him.

'You really do take after your Aunt Nila, Marion. She was a saree maker, darling. And a fabulous artist. Such a tragedy she died in that bus crash,' my father had sighed. He told me all about her. How kind she was. How gentle and sweet.

That night I dreamt that my Aunt Nila was my mother instead of Anoja. Only beside her was a man engulfed in flames. Behind them was a beautiful lady in a white saree. Her face was covered with tears. The beautiful lady looked at me beseechingly, as if she was trying to promise me something. She didn't speak to me, but told me things, things I have forgotten, but the one thing I do remember was her telling me that my mother loved me and all would end well.

But the magic of drawing with a simple crayon never has left me. And the nastier my mother got, the more I would draw. Hiding in the toilet or out the back in the shed. Creating unending reams of colour that my mother would use to line the bins. It was a habit that stayed with me, though I eventually swapped crayons and pencils for ink and paints. It'd amused my fellow medical students no end that I often spent the night before a big exam in front of an easel painting.

Which was why I was painting today. With wild abandon. Splashing colours on a canvas with feverish intensity. Lucky Nair had been impossible to deal with lately.

'Aren't you supposed to be double-checking all the medication you give my mother?' he had asked, coming in on Jodi and I while we were checking the locked bar fridge containing the opiates.

'What do you think we're doing now?' I'd asked, turning to show him the clipboard with the drugs list the pharmacist had dropped off.

'How should I know what you are doing?'

'If you don't trust us, why don't you check it yourself?' Jodi had returned fire stomping off in anger.

'She is a mite tetchy,' he observed.

'The nurses who work here are trained professionals. As I am. Believe it or not, we care for your mother and we are doing our best to help her.'

'If you really want to help her, you'd help me find a cure for her,' he growled back

'I am so sorry, Mr Nair, but there is no cure for your mother,' I told him gently.

'What? What about this? Have you read about the powers of fruit juice?' he'd demanded, whipping out his paper-thin laptop. 'Look! Look at this! This is why I got my mum out of that hospital. At least here I can get her to try some alternative therapies.'

Out of compassion, I'd taken his laptop and sat at the little desk by the sideboard to look at what he wanted to show me.

'All I can see are plans for a saree mill and some designs for a saree,' I told him.

'Oh, sorry. Here it is,' he said, flicking to the right window. 'See, they are saying that goji berries have worked wonders with patients with myeloma. And there are these sulfur springs I want to take her to in New Zealand. If you would just speak with her . . .' he pleaded.

'But she does not want to do any of that, *puttar*,' a deep voice answered, as Lucky's father came into the corridor, softly closing the door. 'Doctor, she's asleep,' he said, answering the question clearly written on my face. I was concerned that Shanthi might have been distressed by our argument.

That was when I heard a sob. Within a blink of an eye, Raju Nair moved fast to engulf his son in his strong arms. 'Let her go, *puttar*. Let nature take its course. She fights pain almost constantly now. Let her go.'

'But what if I'd been a better son? Would she listen to me if I'd been her real son?' Lucky cried. The pain of losing his mother was ripping him apart.

So having loving parents is as painful as having abusive ones, I thought.

'I doubt you could have been a better or more real son to us,' his father whispered, joining his son in tears.

The second universal truth that Jane Austen failed to acknowledge was that a visit from the in-laws must always elicit panic cleaning. Gauri, Raju's sister, was coming to visit and the entire household was in a state of uproar.

'Have you put out the flowers? And is there a statue of Ganesh?' Shanthi called out weakly. She'd had an amazing rally when Lucky had arrived but looked as if she was fading fast again. Her sister-in-law was flying in from London to spend what little time she could with Shanthi. But her deteriorating health didn't stop her from worrying incessantly about their visit.

'Make sure you've wiped down the bathroom. Have you checked the sheets, Raju? You know how particular your sister is about sheets!'

Raju and Lucky rolled their eyes. Not only had the cleaners done a thorough job, but they'd spent the last few hours 'Indianing' the house – placing little Hindu statuettes about the place and fanning incense through the rooms.

'Gauri is very religious. She'll be wanting to know why we haven't been doing poojas every hour,' Shanthi groaned.

'Praying twice a day is quite enough, all things considered,' Raju replied wryly.

'Maybe we should get a pundit to come and visit while she's here. Have either of you contacted any of the Hindu temples in Melbourne?'

Raju and Lucky looked guiltily at each other.

'What are you going to do when I die? Have you not organised anything?' Shanthi cried, only to fall silent at the thud of closing doors and the sound of someone coming up the driveway.

'Quick! Positions everyone,' Lucky cried as I dashed to the head of the bed and Raju sat down next to his wife.

Since Lucky had accepted that his mother would die and not recover, he'd become much easier to live with. 'I just thought you'd given up on her. I guess I just needed to accept the truth,' he'd confided in Kristen, Jodi and I one afternoon. 'I am so sorry.'

'My dearest sister, I cannot believe the tragedy that has befallen you,' a voice called down the hallway.

'Come in, come in,' Shanthi cried as a tall woman with burnished ebony skin burst into the room.

'How could the gods do this to you? Why does tragedy always befall us?' Gauri cried, falling dramatically into her brother's arms. 'Is there nothing to be done? What have the doctors said? How long do you have left?' Gauri asked tearfully.

'The best person to talk to is our doctor,' Raju said. 'May I introduce you to Marion Gamage? She is the doctor in charge of Shanthi's case.'

I went to shake hands with Raju's sister as she wiped the tears from her eyes, but as she looked at me she started visibly.

'Have we met before?' she demanded. 'You and my daughter could be sisters!'

And when I looked across the room to the young woman now lounging on the couch and checking her phone; I had to concede that the resemblance was startling. We both had the same high cheekbones, wide set eyes and broad shouldered frames.

'I am certain we have never met,' I insisted haltingly.

'I have asked the questions. The resemblance is startling, I agree,' Raju interjected before I could answer. 'But Dr Gamage is of Sinhala descent and I cannot find any relations. Her family are from Badulla and her parents' names are Albert and Anoja.'

'Raju had Sindhu check if the Gamages were even distantly related to the Mendises – but even he cannot find a connection,' Shanthi added weakly. 'I am sure Sindhu knows all the

Mendis families on the island personally now that he has been harassing them for nearly thirty years.

'Mendis is such a common name,' Gauri remarked. 'My secretary counted 20,000 Mendises in the Colombo district phone book alone!'

I ignored them and spoke to their mother. As Gauri turned back to me, I explained Mrs Nair's diagnosis and prognosis. 'Your sister-in-law has a particularly aggressive case of myeloma. All we can do is make her comfortable now.'

'Have any poojas been done?' Gauri demanded.

'We've been more focused on spending time with Amman,' Lucky replied. 'Time is precious and it is all we have left.' He pointed to the crosswords in the corner and a box of Scrabble.

'Pity there isn't a box of Monopoly there,' Sally, Gauri's daughter observed nastily. 'Because that'll be what it'll be when you die, Aunty. Lucky will get everything and we'll be left with nothing!'

'Quite a step up for a low born brat,' her brother David added.

'That is quite enough!' Gauri snapped. 'Your aunty is dying and you'll keep your mouths shut!'

'How? How can you say that Amman?' David demanded. 'You too will be destitute because everything will be left to this bastard son of the kitchen maid!'

I t only took three days in the company of Lucky's 'cousins' for the nurses and I to start feeling sorry for Lucky. Within five days, any one of us would have happily stuck them in the back with a scalpel.

'That is it!' Kristen growled at me at the nurses' station. 'If that cow makes another dig at Lucky about eating in the kitchen because his mother was a maid, I am going to stick her with a fork.'

'Make sure you stick it in deep and turn it slowly so it hurts,' her mother drawled from behind as Kristen and I nearly jumped out of our skins.

Kristen made a hasty excuse and hurried away leaving me alone with Gauri. You would have needed a chainsaw to cut the tension. What could you say to a person who'd mothered such two awful people?

'I need to explain my children,' Gauri said looking at me sadly. 'It's my fault they are the way they are. My ex-husband raised them mainly while I was busy setting up and running my business empire. He was a refugee who'd fled the '83 riots in Sri Lanka and everything he did was clouded in hate. And he taught them hate, too.'

From the other room, we could hear the roar of the Play-Station game that David had been told repeatedly to reduce the volume to while his aunt was resting. And on the lawn Sally was exposing her already dark skin to dangerous levels of UV light, lolling about in a bikini reading the latest copy of some fashion magazine.

'You need to tell her to put on some sunscreen,' I yelped. 'The Australian sun is very dangerous. One good sunburn is all she needs!'

'And Lucky, too. Look, he is out there on the beach too. In this heat!' Gauri grumbled heading out with a can of spray on sunscreen. 'Can you give him this hat, my dear? He is the light of my brother's life and I do not want him to burn in this ridiculous Australian sun.'

I could hardly refuse – I'd taken the Hippocratic oath, after all – so I plopped on an extra-wide-brimmed sunhat myself and trotted down to the beach where Lucky was fossicking in a little rock pool.

'Here, your aunt sent you this,' I said, handing him the hat.

'Could you hand me that bucket? I do believe that it is a baby spider crab. Must have got caught when the tide went out. Appa will be so happy to see it,' Lucky said, catching the little crab with a net and putting it in the large bucket. 'Don't worry, little one. We won't eat you. We'll look at you and put you back.'

I rolled my eyes. 'Are you a marine biologist as well as a textile mogul?'

'I'm neither, actually,' Lucky laughed. 'I fell in love with the sea when I was a child. My dad grew up next to the coast, so he made sure we spent a great deal of time down by the coast every year too. But I'm not a marine biologist – and I won't be a textile mogul forever, either. When my father dies, Sally and David are bound to contest his will and I will lose my share of the business.'

'Surely they cannot contest a will that has been written in sound mind.'

'You forget that the case will be heard in India. Judges can be bought with a hefty bribe or two. My heritage has never been a secret. High born judges would delight in taking me down a peg or two.'

'But Raju Nair is your father – doesn't caste come through the paternal line? Does it matter who your mother was?'

Lucky gave me a sad smile. 'Did you think my father cheated on my mother with the maid? Raju Nair is not my father. I am no blood relative to either one of my parents. I am the son of the scullery maid and a railway worker. My mother was working for my grandparents when she abandoned me.'

I couldn't hide my shock.

'Don't worry. I have come to understand her decision – I accepted it a long time ago. She was pregnant with my sister and my biological father's family were trying to force her into an abortion. I am sure you've heard of the Indian tradition of female infanticide.'

I nodded. 'How old were you when she left you?'

'I was about eighteen months old, my parents think. They don't have a birth certificate or anything like that. I tracked my mother and my sister down a few years ago in a little town north of Delhi. They live in an ashram devoted to the goddess Saraswati. My mother stole an elaborate jewelled saree from my father – from Raju – and sold it so she had enough money to enter the ashram for life.'

'Don't you hate her?'

'How can I, Marion? If she hadn't abandoned me, I would never have had the life that my parents have given me. I could never have had their love and their care. No one could have loved me as much as they do.'

'It must be wonderful to be loved by two people so clearly in love with each other,' I said.

We'd been walking up the beach the long way to the house. Why we were doing that I wasn't quite sure.

'They're not.'

'What do you mean they're not?'

'They're not in love with each other. That's not quite right, though. My mother is in love with my father – she has been since she was a girl – but he does not love her.'

'Don't be stupid! Blind Freddie can see that they love each other!'

'They love each other, yes, but my father is not in love with my mother, and he never has been. He is still in love with his first wife. In fact my parents were never legally married. My father refused to marry my mother. They were married by Hindu decree, using the rites reserved for a second wife. But they are not legally married. Which was why the courts never allowed them to formally adopt me.'

'I don't understand.'

Lucky opened his mouth to explain, only to stop as a terrified scream ripped through the air. 'Marion! We need you!' It was Gauri's voice, and I broke into a run. My sunhat got caught by the wind and blew out into the bay.

'What?' I panted as I reached her on the front lawn. 'Shanthi was stable just before I left – what has happened?'

'It's not Shanthi! It's my brother! He's had a bad turn.'

It didn't take long for the paramedics to arrive but by the time they did come, I'd stabilised Mr Nair and had him comfortably resting in a cool bath.

'It's all my fault,' Raju kept repeating. 'The doctors keep telling me of the importance of hydration but some days I just forget.'

'I need a full analysis of his electrolytes and do a full blood chemistry as well,' I barked down the line to the pathology lab. 'And call the results through to me!'

The problem had not been so much stabilising Raju but rather dealing with a hysterical Sally and David.

'What is to become of us if Uncle dies?' Sally screamed.

'We'll be in the gutter that is what will happen! Is he dying? Is he already dead? Why do these things always happen to us?' David cried, the console of his PlayStation still in his hands.

'Because you are a pair of nasty brats!' their mother snapped at them closing the door as Lucky and I carried Raju into the

room from the deck where he'd collapsed. Only David and
Sally barged in, following us.

'His breathing in fine but his heart rate is fluctuating,'
I observed urgently as Sally started to sob uncontrollably and
David started to pace the floor. I looked for symptoms of what
was wrong – strapping on the blood pressure cuff and putting
on the electrodes from the heart monitor that Jodi wheeled in.
'Does your father have hypotension?'

'No.'

I gently prised open his mouth. And his skin temperature
was skyrocketing and his tongue was swelling. 'He is dehy-
drated. We need to get some fluids into him and cool him down
quickly. Lucky, run a tepid bath quick!'

While Lucky was running the bath, Gauri and I undressed
Raju. Even in full crisis management physician mode, I could
not stop my sudden intake of breath at seeing the scarring on
the older man's body. 'Dear God in heaven, who did this to this
poor man?' I asked as Lucky bodily lifted his father and gently
lowered him into the bath.

The passage of decades had healed the burns to a certain
extent but the muscle atrophy through the scar tissue was clear.
And no one could lose that much of the top three layers of their
skin and not live in near constant pain.

'You did,' David accused in a deadly voice.

'Leave it!' Lucky roared. 'I am warning you just the once.
Leave it well alone!'

'Or what? You'll hit me? I've had boxing lessons since the
last time,' David growled, throwing a few mock punches in
the air.

'No, I will hit you,' his mother snapped instead. But by then
Raju had revived somewhat. I ignored David altogether and
bolted into the other room to get an IV drip line and all the
equipment needed to place the cannula.

'Do you know what you are doing?' Sally asked me, seeing
that I was struggling to get a vein inflated enough to take the
cannula.

'Incompetence! Without us they would not know what to do! No wonder Sri Lanka is going to the dogs now that the Tamils have left!' David smirked.

Again I ignored them and focused on my work. Tightening the pressure strap to finally locate a vein on the back of Raju's un-burnt hand. I only looked up when Raju had sufficient fluids to be revived.

'Leave him in there,' I sighed collapsing beside the bath. 'I should have thought of it. Anyone with burns to over 50 per cent of their body is susceptible to rapid dehydration. I'll keep an eye on him from now on.'

'Why? So you can kill him again?' David interjected.

In that instant, something inside me snapped. David was rotund but small, and I used my height to intimidate the bully.

'I have never hurt anyone in my life. Whatever your problem is – take it to a shrink!'

'You don't intimidate me, you stupid Sinhala cow!' David roared back charging at me only to be confronted by the rock solid Lucky.

'Shut it, you little turd, before I crack your jaw like I cracked your ribs when you were ten!'

'Why are you defending this Sinhala bitch! You know she was responsible for what happened to your father?'

'How? Your uncle sustained his injuries in an accident!'

'What accident?' Sally asked. 'There was no accident. My uncle was set upon by a bunch of Sinhala thugs and set alight deliberately. Murderers, the lot of you!'

In spite of everything, the end was very quick. Gauri had packed her children and herself back onto a plane. She left to catch her plane home to the UK tearfully, hugging her sister-in-law close. 'Thank you, Shanthi. Thank you for everything.'

'No, *akka*,' Shanthi Nair had wheezed uneasily. 'I owe you everything that has been good in my life.'

Over the next week Shanthi deteriorated rapidly. Jodi and I took turns to monitor her around the clock. One night I fell asleep slouched in a chair by her bed and woke to the alarm on her heart monitor beeping. Shanthi's heartbeat had slowed right down but she was still lucid.

I woke Lucky and Raju up quickly. 'You may only have a few minutes with her.'

'Amman? Amman!' Lucky cried. 'Don't leave me! I can't have another mother leave me!'

Shanthi used what little strength she had left to turn her head beseechingly to her husband. Raju enveloped his son in his arms.

'Let her go, *puttar*. Let her go. You were the best thing that ever happened to her. Happened to us, our dearest boy. Without you, we would never have learned to love. Let her go with love.'

Raju and Lucky sat on either side of Shanthi and held her hands. Raju opened his mouth and started to chant in an unsteady voice. '*Om Visvam vishnur-vashatkaro bhutbhavy-abhavatprabhuh bhutkrd bhutbhrd-bhaavo bhutatma bhutab-havanahVishwam . . .*' When he faltered, Lucky joined in.

'*Bhaavo, Bhootaatmaa, Bhoota-bhaavanah, Pootaatmaa, Paramaatmaa, Muktaanaam.*'

'What are they saying?' Jodi asked.

'They are reciting the thousand names of the god Vishnu, so that no evil or harm befalls her as she crosses over to the gods,' I said. Lucky had explained this to me a few days ago when we'd gone for a stroll along the beach for some air.

When the end did come, it was soft and gentle. I was sure Shanthi held Raju and Lucky in her celestial arms before she flew across the bay into the heavens above in the cool minutes of that autumn morning.

While father and son grieved, I gave Shanthi a sponge bath,

like I would a baby. Then, as I'd been instructed to by Gauri, I smeared holy ash all over my patient's body.

Unlike the thousands of deaths that I'd officiated at, I actually went to the funeral this time. I saw Raju prise his wife's mouth open and fill it with raw rice. I stood behind Lucky as he pressed two gold coins into the palms of his mother's hands. 'To pay the ferryman, Amman,' he whispered softly, tears streaming down his face. 'Do you remember how you always gave me extra money for the school canteen?'

Gauri had not been able to make it back to Australia, so I accompanied Raju and Lucky to the crematorium in Carlton. The father, son and I piled Shanthi's body with sweet-smelling flowers – pungent late summer roses, gardenias and jasmine. I don't know how on earth Lucky found jasmine at that time of year, but I knew it'd been his mother's favourite flower.

After the cremation, I hadn't had the heart to drive them back to the great big house in Brighton, so I took them back to my place instead.

'It's not very big. It's quite old actually. Not very glamorous,' I stuttered as I took them in. A sum total of two people – my mother and Simon – had been inside my apartment, and they'd both disliked it.

Neither Lucky nor Raju answered, following me like blind men seeking light up the narrow flight of stairs. I took Raju into my bedroom and drew the curtains, turning down the covers on my bed for him lie down and have a rest.

I left him alone and went to join Lucky in the living room, but I didn't find him there. He wasn't in the little room where I kept my computer and paperwork, either. I felt a cool breeze waft through the apartment. Panic gripped my heart as I realised he was in the rooftop courtyard.

'I can sand that door back if you have some sandpaper,' Lucky said as I rushed out. He was swinging in my hammock. 'Though I can understand it if you'd prefer to leave it as it is. The door to my office in India has an uneven hinge. I know I should get it fixed, but there's a certain . . . I don't know . . . charm in having to shove a door open.'

'Look at this,' I said to him, pointing to a loose concrete paver. 'I can't bear to have it fixed either. See, if you sit on the hammock and rock your foot on the paver like this, you get this amazing swing. Try it.'

'You're right. It's perfect,' he agreed, swinging himself gently. 'This whole set-up is perfect, actually. You should have had my mum over here when she was alive – she would have loved it.'

'What? The view of the tops of the elm trees? The tram powerlines? And can you hear that? That's the butcher down-stairs sawing through a cow!'

'No, she would have loved that if you look up, all you see is the blue blue sky. And she would have loved that your studio is just across the way. Perfect place for it really. Nothing but sunshine for inspiration!'

I looked at him, terrified.

'And no, I didn't go in. My father is an artist – hasn't painted much since his accident, but he still dabbles here and there. I know better than to barge in on an artist's studio. You only ever go in when you are invited.'

'Thank you,' I replied. 'Most people don't understand.'

'No, they don't,' Lucky agreed. 'People live mainly on the surface. Flitting like butterflies. But people like you, creative people – they need to sit, absorb and reflect. I guess that explains why you chose palliative care.'

'Really? I thought I chose it because it was one of the least popular courses on offer!' I laughed, but I was fascinated by Lucky's insight. Simon always joked that the only reason I'd chosen palliative care was because of the light workload.

'No diagnosis. No risk. You just get to sit there and dream,' he'd mocked more than once.

Lucky laughed. 'I had a look at some of your fabric paintings before I came out. They're beautiful, Marion. What are your plans for that side of your life?'

'Perhaps when I retire I can do it full-time. Plenty of doctors have gone on to creative careers after medicine.'

'Why practise medicine full-time, though? Surely it's not just for the money.'

'Partly that, and the other part is my parents.'

Just then my phone rang, the sound of the ringtone so foreign that I nearly jumped out my skin.

'Marion! Marion!' my mother screamed down the line. 'You have to come to Sri Lanka! There has been a fire at your uncle's factory. Your brother and your uncle are dying!'

White was an impossible colour to wear in Colombo. So were taupe, camel and all of the neutral-toned clothes I possessed. I couldn't even walk from my room to breakfast without getting smudged with something. The problem is the humidity combined with the residue from all the diesel fumes; it leaves a grimy coating on everything from the walls to the pot plants.

Now I finally understood why Sri Lankan women wore such brightly coloured sarees. The yards of cotton are easy to wear in the horribly humid weather and the bright colours hide the grime. When all my clothes were covered in grease, I found myself at a boutique called Barefoot, looking for a pair of trousers.

'No, madam,' the softly spoken but steely-eyed sales assistant had insisted as I naturally drifted towards the lighter colours. 'Those colours are not for you. They are good for old people going to temple. Madam, you are a beautiful lady of good years. Come, come with me.'

What was a lady of good years?

He waved aside all of my concerns, insisting that I try on soft brushed cotton skirts and blouses of the brightest of bright hues. I ended up buying them simply because the fabric felt so luscious against my skin.

'See, madam, you are beautiful now. And you must be trying a saree, too. It is very easy. See – knot, drape, pleat, drape another one time, put fall over your shoulder and finish off,' the young lad had explained, deftly draping a saree over my skirt. 'Very simple, madam. Very simple.'

I'd been so excited by how easy it looked that I'd bought a saree in a shade of iridescent blue. It had a taupe border, though – I couldn't help myself. But after spending about ninety minutes trying to drape the saree on myself, I had only given myself a headache and had to concede that I perhaps did not have the dexterity required.

'Marion, your uncle and brother are dying and you are playing dress-ups!' my mother snapped, walking in on me.

'Ryan is not dying and there is every likelihood that Uncle Manoj will recover as well,' I murmured before donning a pair of linen pants and following my mother out to visit them both at Nawaloka Hospital – an expensive resort-like facility whose menagerie of peacocks on the front lawn gave the elegant splendour of St Judes a run for its money.

'Your brother will never be able to walk again!'

'Mum, he has burns to less than ten per cent of his body. He just needs to shake himself out of this apathy he is in.'

When we arrived my uncle's doctors told us his recovery was not proceeding as fast as they'd hoped, but that it was only a minor setback and there was no need to worry.

'What? What do you mean my brother's recovery is not going as planned? You said that he should be fine to leave within a few weeks?' As my uncle's only living relative willing to tend to him, my mother had taken the role with gusto. My mother's other brother Herath had long been estranged from the family and my uncle's ex-wife and children wanted to have nothing to do with him.

'Such setbacks are normal, Mrs Gamage,' the chief of the burns unit, Dr Gurusinghe, had insisted.

But my mother completely ignored him, instead turning to the British volunteer doctor beside him. 'Is it normal? Is the treatment plan this local doctor is following any good? How do we know my brother will recover?'

The doctor looked at me confused before turning to my mother. 'It is perfectly normal for tiny infections to take place if you've suffered significant burns. Your brother was very lucky. He sustained significant burns but is still well enough to sit up and have a joke with the nurses,' he said, pointing to my uncle. 'And I am here to learn from Dr Gurusinghe, and not the other way around,' the doctor said. 'This man wrote the book on treating burns victims. He saved so many people during the war.'

'Dr Gamage,' Dr Gurusinghe spoke to me quietly, 'Your uncle is on the mend and your brother is doing very well. Can I interest you in some volunteer work?'

'Where?'

'As you've probably heard on the grapevine,' he said, jerking his head towards the nurses, 'I am out of favour with the government. They cut funding to my burns clinic in Kerid-amadu. We need some generalist doctors to help. Would you be interested in coming up with us for about a week?'

'Sure, I am on extended leave, and I'd be more than happy to come up. I don't think Ryan needs me,' I replied. Ryan was sitting in his bed at the other end of the ward being fussed over by our mother. By the looks of it, he wasn't enjoying our mother's presence any more than I was.

Dr Gurusinghe told me that there was an orphanage attached to the hospital, so when I got back to the hotel that afternoon I ducked back into Barefoot to buy some handmade toys.

'These toys will last those children for a lifetime. Made from the best Sri Lankan cotton!' the familiar sales assistant smiled brightly, his eyes widening as I paid the two lakh rupee bill without batting an eyelid. I was finally using the money I had saved on rent for something worthwhile. 'We are the last true fabric weavers left on the island,' he added.

'Not for long,' an even more familiar voice observed from behind.

'Lucky! What are you doing here?' I cried delightedly. 'How are you? Where is your father?'

'Appa is back in Panadura. And I am here to meet someone you know!' Lucky smiled, pointing over my shoulder to the courtyard cafe behind the shop. Sitting sipping coconut water from a *kurumba* was the fabric merchant from Melbourne, Mahinda Ratnayaka.

'How are you going?' I greeted my old friend. 'And what are you doing here?'

'Same as you, though, I understand you've pipped me to the post and bought out all the soft toys in the store!' Mahinda smiled warmly back.

'I'm heading up north tomorrow. I want to spend a few days volunteering at one of camps, so I thought I'd buy some toys for the kids.'

'We'll meet you up there, then,' Lucky grinned.

'Why? I understood that there is nothing much to see up there yet.'

'We're not going up there on holiday, my dear! We are going up there to work! And we are taking with us something worth more than gold,' Mahinda said, opening the little box he had on the seat next to him. 'These are *Bombyx mori* moths. Your friend Lucky and I are going to set up a sericulture farm. People up north don't need charity. They need development.'

'Never in my wildest dreams,' I murmured as I stood at the summit of the rock citadel Sigiriya looking out over the northern plains.

Lucky came to stand next to me. 'I had heard of this, but even I am . . .'

'Speechless?'

Yes, the amazing rock citadel of Sigiriya was perhaps one of the few things that could silence the loquacious Lucky. And rightly so.

Most of the fortress had been built around 477 AD by Prince Kashyapa.

'They say the prince built this on the run after murdering his father,' I told Lucky, looking through my guidebook. 'Good thing he took some architects, artists, builders and landscapers with him.'

If the summit of the rock was impressive, with its twin swimming pools carved out of solid granite for the king and queen, it was nothing in comparison to the extensive gardens in the surrounding area complete with water fountains and a water feature mirror that reflected the paintings on the rock itself.

'You don't say,' Lucky said, helping me scramble over some rocks. It was fortunate I'd gone with Lucky because I was terrified of heights. Without his gently coaxing and encouraging me, I would never have made it up.

In the end, it had been fortunate too that Dr Gurusinghe and I had decided to hitch a ride with Lucky, or we would never have made it through the checkpoints. 'Do not doubt for a moment just how corrupt everything here is,' the doctor had said after Lucky handed over yet another 'facilitation' payment.

'Where we are going is about three hours north of here – be prepared to enter hell on earth,' Dr Gurusinghe said coming up to us on top of the citadel.

'And we grew up four hours east of here in Nayaru,' Mahinda said, coming up to us and pointing to the lush jungle as Nimal stood silently by him. Nimal had become quieter and quieter the further north we went. 'We used to have watch-towers around the perimeter of the village. The jungle used to teem with wild elephants and leopards.'

'The sea off the coast was very rich once,' Nimal added softly. 'Not like the seas down south or to the west. Fresh bream, Spanish mackerel, prawns, cuttlefish.'

'And crabs, don't forget the crabs,' Mahinda added.

'Didn't Vannan teach you how to swim by pushing you out of an *oruwa* into a part of the lagoon full of crabs?' Nimal said.

'Yes, drowning was not the only incentive I had to start to learn to swim. Fast!'

'Not much fish in the sea in these parts anymore. The Sea Tigers planted sea mines and poisoned stretches of the coast,' Dr Gurusinghe said. 'The animals suffered more than the people through this godawful war.'

'I just don't get it,' Lucky said. 'About half the population of Colombo is Tamil and there doesn't seem to be any overt tension now.'

'How much do you know about the conflict here in Sri Lanka?' Dr Gurusinghe asked, turning to Lucky and me.

'Not much,' I replied. 'I grew up in Australia. I knew there was conflict here, but I only ever heard the Sinhala side of the story. Every time there was a bomb blast, my parents would glue their ears to the BBC World Service and then call Sri Lanka to make sure everyone back here was safe – so I only ever heard that the Tamils were bombers and killers.'

'Same here,' Lucky confessed. 'We lost all our property here in the Black July riots in eighty-three. Quite a few workers at the mill were killed. My parents had several families stay with us in Kanchipuram, but they left not long after. My dad refused to support any militants and set the dogs on the money collectors when they came to the gate.'

'You are a Tamil – didn't you feel any sympathy for the cause?' I asked, surprised. After having seen Mr Nair's wounds, I had developed a dislike of my own people.

'Yes and no,' Lucky shrugged. 'I understood that the Tamil grievances had just cause but my father abhorred the LTTE and their tactics. And he drummed it into me that the average Sinhala person was no more responsible for the government's discriminatory policies than an average Tamil person was responsible for the acts of terrorism in Colombo. Bombing temples and buses is not the way to win friends and influence people.'

'And he'd be right,' Dr Gurusinghe said with a firm nod. 'You must understand that this was not a grassroots conflict in many ways. Sinhala and Tamil people have lived side by side for centuries.'

'I grew up here in the north,' Mahinda confessed. 'My best friend and all the people I knew were Tamils. Good people. Honest people. Kind people.'

'So why? Why did this all happen?' I asked

'Because Sinhala people let power go to their heads when they finally gained freedom from the British and the Tamil people became militant when they lost their position of privilege,' Dr Gurusinghe replied.

'No one will ever know who threw the first stone. It hardly seems to matter now,' Mahinda added, looking sadly into the distance. 'So many people dead. So many lives destroyed.'

'And for nothing,' Dr Gurusinghe observed very sadly. 'There is actually no genetic difference between the Sinhalese and Tamil people. We have more in common racially, culturally and religiously than any other two races on the planet – yet we have nearly almost destroyed ourselves over perceived differences.'

'Are you looking forward to seeing some of your family up here again? Maybe even your best friend? Now that the war is over, maybe you can track him down,' Lucky asked, trying to dispel the gloom that had descended.

'I lost my entire family in one of the massacres,' Mahinda said. 'My father, grandmother, my six brothers and sisters were hacked to death. And my best friend Vannan led the attack on the village.'

It took me a couple of days to get used to working in the squalid conditions in the camp. Actually, it was two days before I could even walk through the ward without being sick to the stomach.

'I wish I didn't need to leave you here by yourself,' Lucky had groaned, seeing me looking grey in the little lean-to kitchen with my morning cup of tea.

'She should be fine today,' Dr Gurusinghe said, coming through. 'It usually takes doctors about three days to get used to it all. Marion was able to do a few sutures yesterday, and we'll get her doing field evacuations later today.'

'I'll be fine,' I reassured Lucky. 'Besides, this is not as bad as Menik Farm.'

'No, you're right, this is not as bad as Menik Farm,' Lucky agreed.

'And you two saw it during the dry season,' Dr Gurusinghe added, stirring his three teaspoons full of sugar into his tea. 'During the monsoon season the main road through the camp turns into a river.'

'Whose bright idea was it to build a refugee camp so close to three rivers?' I asked. It had simply been appalling.

'The government – who else?' Dr Gurusinghe muttered angrily. 'Three generals complained. Three field marshals sent communiqués to army high command. No one listens. I became fed up and quit. Now, I run my clinics without government interference doing what I want to do.'

'Anyway, I'd better head off with Mahinda,' Lucky said, reluctantly squeezing my shoulder. Their van had just pulled up the muddy driveway. 'I'll see you tonight. Maybe we can head off to town and get some dosai?'

'Sure, sure,' I said before steeling myself to walk through the wards.

The wards were beds made from what the locals called *booru andang*. 'Keeps the sanitation costs to a minimum,' Dr Gurusinghe had explained. 'Just boil the cloth that hangs between the coconut wood frame and it's all fine.'

I was rather sceptical about it all, though the locals didn't have much choice. The hospitals up north in Jaffna were overflowing and it took several hours driving along dirt roads to get to Trincomalee, the next closest town, by which time a seriously injured person would be dead.

Taking a deep breath, I started my rounds, seeing to children with amputated limbs and people who needed treatment not only for burns but for the shock of losing their hearing.

'That is the problem of landmines,' the good doctor had explained. 'A person loses more than just their limbs – they often lose their sight and definitely lose their hearing. So, this is where I need your help this week. Could you check on the state of people's hearing?'

I sat myself down in a corner of the clinic and had the orderly bring me patient after patient. I'd do an acoustic reflex test assessing how much a person could hear or not. Back in Australia, an audiologist would carry out tests like these, but I'd quickly learned that paramedical specialists were thin on the ground.

I was completely immersed in my work when a commotion started in the courtyard.

'I don't care who he is! If he is hurt, he gets attention here,' Dr Gurusinghe roared as an army truck carrying an injured man pulled up.

'We have instructions to get him to Colombo,' the lieutenant said.

'You bloody fool! This man's femoral artery is gushing blood. He'll be dead before you get him halfway to Anuradhapura!'

To add to the chaos, the man's innumerable children were screaming in the truck.

'Do what you must, doctor,' the lieutenant finally said as I ran to the scene. 'But he has constant military supervision! Constant!'

The man was rushed to the makeshift surgical area while I tended to the children, who were covered in dirt and blood.

'Come, come!' I tried enticing them from the back of the truck with hand gestures. I spoke neither Tamil or Sinhala but put my faith in sign language.

'I speak a little English,' the eldest boy said.

'What happened?'

'My father was clearing some land and there was a landmine,' the boy explained.

'Your father is being looked after by one of the best doctors in the area,' I reassured them.

'I hope so . . .' the boy confessed. 'He is all we have left. Our mother died last year.'

'I am so sorry,' I said, feeling completely inadequate. The youngest child was barely four or five. A big responsibility for a single father, but what would happen to her if she had no father at all?

'I told him not to go!' the boy muttered under his breath. 'But he went to the island anyway!' Since we went back to his home village after my mother died, he's got this stupid idea of starting a silk farm there!'

'Perhaps not too silly. My friend Mahinda has just headed

up to Kattikatal now. He is thinking of setting up a silk farm in that very lagoon!'

The boy looked at Marion with surprise. 'My name is Mahendran. I was named after my father's best friend Mahinda. He was the person who came up with the idea for a silk farm many years ago in the first place.'

'Mahinda,' I approached my old friend diffidently. How did you break it to someone that the person who'd massacred his entire family was just down the corridor? 'I have to tell you something.'

'Yes, my dear?' Mahinda asked wearily. He looked haunted. He, Nimal and Lucky had just returned from their day in Nayaru and were resting in the small mess hall before they headed off into town for dinner.

'How was the trip to your old village?' I asked. This was going to be harder than I thought.

'Like walking back through an old dream that is the same but so different. The village is the same but everything is different.'

'The old school is still there,' Nimal added. 'The waterhole behind it is as filthy as it ever was.'

'But they don't farm tobacco there anymore,' Mahinda said ruefully. 'And all the old Tamil families have left. New families have moved in. I didn't recognise any of the faces in the village. I don't know why I want to build a silk farm up here anymore. There is no one I know who would help. If there was someone, anyone . . .'

That was when young Mahendran came in search of me. 'Doctor, doctor,' the young lad called. Both Mahinda and Nimal turned to look at the boy.

'Who are you?' Mahinda asked. Something in his voice frightened me.

The boy took one look at Mahinda and ran in search of his father, but Mahinda gave chase.

'That was what I was going to tell you,' I called, running after them. 'They brought your friend in this afternoon. He was hurt by a landmine.'

Lucky nearly overtook Mahinda and almost tackled him to the ground, but the older man found a nimble strength and speed no one could have foreseen and swerved to avoid Lucky. But he could not avoid the soldiers stationed at the doorway to Vannan's little room. They'd insisted that he be kept cordoned off from the rest of the patients in the hospital.

I didn't really understand what happened next, because Mahinda lapsed into rapid-fire Tamil and Lucky could only understand and translate for me so much of the northern Sri Lankan Tamil dialect.

'You bloody bastard!' Mahinda screamed in the doorway, straining against the three Sri Lanka Army soldiers holding him back. 'You killed my father! You killed my brothers and sisters. Prema was like a sister to you! You taught her how to walk! You taught my brothers how to swim! You killed my grandmother – and she fed you! For years!'

Vannan sat up weakly in his bed, his five children crowding around him.

'I had nothing! Nothing!' Mahinda screamed, tears pouring down his face. The terrible grief of losing his entire family was still fresh on his face despite the passage of twenty-nine years. 'What do you have to say for yourself? What, you bloody bastard?'

'Nothing,' came the weak voice of Vannan. 'I did what I had to do.'

'You did not have to kill my brothers and sisters,' Mahinda sobbed hoarsely, breaking down on the ground. 'Prema was only seven.'

Vannan got weakly out of bed.

'Stop,' I cried. 'He is too weak to walk. He's only been out of surgery a few hours.'

'Help me,' Vannan ordered one of the soldiers, who wordlessly jumped to attention and did as he was told. 'I have dreamt of the day when you and I would meet. Shivani and I talked about it a lot. The only way I could atone for what I did would be for you to watch me die,' the man said. 'Yes, I killed your entire family. I was there when they hacked down your grandmother and saw your father plead for your brothers and sisters' lives. But the LTTE had Shivani. Her brothers sold her to them and told them that I had local knowledge. They threatened to kill her and the entire village if I didn't join.'

'You should have let them!' Mahinda roared viciously back.

'You are right. I should have let Shivani die,' Vannan agreed in a sad voice. 'Because they killed her in the end anyway. She died in Nayaru Lagoon last year before the Lankan soldiers could save her.'

'We tried, sir, we tried,' the lieutenant said softly. 'Your wife got your children to safety before the LTTE suspected what was going on, but they shot her in retaliation.'

'Why did they kill Shivani?' Mahinda demanded. 'Her brothers were top LTTE cadres and you were one of their commanders!'

'They killed Shivani because they found out that I worked with Vinayagamoorthy Muralitharan and had led the breakaway Colonel Karuna faction.'

'Colonel Jeyam has been working with us for about twenty years,' the Sri Lankan army lieutenant corroborated. 'We could not have won the war without men like him. Men who turned people like Vinayagamoorthy Muralitharan away from terrorism. That is why we need to get him to safety in Colombo. You never know where the LTTE spies could be.'

'Marry me,' Lucky asked me.

'Excuse me?' I asked with surprise.

'Marion, I am in love with you. I want you to dump that idiot Simon and marry me,' Lucky said, shifting his weight from one foot to the other.

'Lucky . . .' I replied, shaking my head and standing up, only to be brought up short when I trod on my underskirt. I carefully shifted the yards of silk and turned to face him, still holding a clipboard I'd been using to check some medial supplies. I had rung my mother several days before and told her that I was extending my stay up north by another week so I could visit Nayaru and do some work there.

'Your brother and uncle are dying and you are gallivanting around. Aren't you ashamed of your behaviour?'

'Mother, I know for a fact that they are not dying. I spoke to Ryan's doctor and he said that Ryan was starting hydrotherapy next week.'

'What about your uncle? Don't you even want to spend time with your dying uncle?'

'I also spoke to the doctor about Uncle Manoj and he said he was doing well. The skin graft operations should take place next week and I'll be back in time for that.'

'Do you have no heart? Don't you care about me?'

Blessedly, the call had fallen out. It happened often in rural Sri Lanka. I realised did not feel any pity for my mother. The horror of confronting true adversity meant that I no longer had any patience for her petty problems. How could anyone really care about a pampered middle-aged woman feeling lonely when there were a dozen orphaned children without anyone to even feed or clothe them?

That was what I'd been doing in Nayaru. Helping out at the orphanage and setting up their food program.

'Thank you, my dear, for your help in the field hospital, but I think your skills would be better used at the orphanage,' Dr Gurusinghe had said kindly when I'd managed to lose my lunch after seeing another landmine victim. Years of working in the quiet confines of the palliative care unit had in no way prepared me for seeing the horrors of bodies ripped apart by landmines. 'At the rate you are going, we'd have to hospitalise you for dehydration!'

Another outcome of visiting Nayaru was that I was now forced to wear a saree. Vannan's mother had not left the area, and upon hearing that Mahinda was back in town, she'd descended on him like a hurricane. She sobbed for several hours the first time they met, telling her side of the tale of what had happened over past two decades.

'When the LTTE were bad, we yearned for the government. When the government is bad, we yearn for something else. This is our fate. To be always suffering,' she cried. 'I lost two sons. I know one died but the other one was taken away by a group of men in a white van about ten years ago.'

'Was that Krishna?' Mahinda had asked aghast.

'Yes,' Vannan had replied. 'The tricky thing is that no one knows who it could have been. It could well have been the government or the LTTE.'

'What is being done? Surely news of these injustices must be reported overseas?' I'd exclaimed.

'There is precious little international intervention can do now,' Dr Gurusinghe said. 'Sri Lanka has aligned itself with China and Pakistan. Many of the western nations have lost any clout they had in Colombo through their tacit support of the LTTE.'

Vannan's mother stopped paying attention then and turned to the only other woman in the group. Me.

'So, is this your daughter?' she asked Mahinda.

'No . . .'

'Your wife, then. She is a little young to be your wife but she is a doctor, a medical person like your mother, and she will bear you good children.'

'I never got married,' Mahinda confessed. 'I just couldn't. What could I give a woman? I have spent the last twenty years just looking after Nimal and myself. I have never really left Nayaru. Marion is a good friend, though.'

'What is this friends?' the elderly woman demanded. 'Men and women aren't friends. They are married or related!' There was a fierce glint in her eye. I suddenly understood where Vannan got his tenacity and courage from.

So when Vannan's mother decided that Mahinda and I should get married, she executed her plan with military zeal. And the first part of her strategy was that I looked the part of a potential bride. Every morning Vannan's mother would arrive with one or more of the village women to dress me.

'What? Wear cream pants? Pants? You are a woman, not a man!' she insisted, speaking through one of the village girls who had a modicum of English. 'And light colours are only for funerals!' she'd insist before wrapping me in the most sumptuously colourful yards of silk and before thrusting me in Mahinda's face.

'I am so sorry,' Mahinda would mouth. But behind him, Lucky did a fair imitation of a stunned mullet.

'You er . . . you . . . er . . . look beautiful,' he stammered.

'You've cavorted and partied with Bollywood stars and this is a simple village woman's saree. I cannot believe you are amazed by this,' I told him.

'Well, I am. I think you are beautiful, but I'll be damned if I have to stand here and defend myself for saying so!' Lucky had snapped before stomping away. Only he'd come back not long later with his unexpected proposal.

'It's the saree, isn't it?' I asked.

'No, Marion, I love you and I want to marry you.'

'Oh, Lucky . . .'

'I'm in love with you and the thought of you marrying someone else is tearing me into shreds.'

'You know I'm not going to marry Mahinda, don't you? He and I have been friends for years!'

'I know you won't marry Mahinda. But you may marry Simon eventually. I love you, Marion. Please marry me.'

'Simon and I broke up just before I left Australia. But I don't even know you, Lucky.'

'What do you mean, Marion? You and I shared a house for close to two months. You saw me through losing my mother. I doubt you could know me any better.'

'But you don't know me,' I pointed out gently.

'You know, I used to think that I didn't know you – that you were an incredibly cold fish – but you've changed. No, Marion, you haven't changed – I suspect you've always been that way. But now I've seen the side of you that you hide so well.'

'I don't hide anything!'

'Oh really? I never saw you really smile until I saw you with the kids here at that orphanage, and I don't mean just pulling your lips apart to show your teeth. I mean really smile. And when you do, the entire room lights up. And when you're talking with the villagers here, that cloak of invisibility you've wrapped around yourself drops away. I see you, Marion. I see the kind, sweet and generous woman you are. And I want you. I want you as my wife.'

'I can't be your wife, Lucky. You don't understand. I am broken. I must be. I have to be.'

'Why, Marion? Why must you be broken?'

'If my mother couldn't love me, surely I must be broken.'

The coastal hamlets of Sri Lanka had been a safe haven for bandits, pirates and all manner of miscreants for thousands of years. Which was why the Sri Lankan navy had long had a presence in the Jaffna peninsula, to ensure that pirates did not harass the local fishermen. Unfortunately the eastern coast of Sri Lanka did not prove to be a safe haven for me. In fact Sri Lanka as a whole was not an ideal retreat for people who like to avoid issues and hide from themselves. Perhaps it was the dense population, perhaps it was the mosquitoes that make silence impossible because the constant slap-slapping required gives a person's location away, or perhaps it was the universal trait of nosiness that marks all Sri Lankans whether they are Sinhala, Tamil, Malay or Burgher.

'So tell me about your parents?'

'Surely you must be an orphan or your family would have arranged a marriage for you by now!'

'Are you sure you are Sinhala? You look Tamil to me.'

'You must be Tamil.'

'Sometimes you look Tamil. Sometimes you look Sinhala.'

'Why aren't you married?'

These questions were repeated over and over again as I travelled down the east coast from Trincomalee to Batticaloa then down to Matara. Dr Gurusinghe had decided that we would take the coastal road back to Colombo, explaining that he wanted to visit some of the more remote hospitals, making the return journey twice as long. And everyone, from the driver of the van to the busboys at the guesthouses, wanted to know all about me.

Whenever I managed to get away from nosy local inquisitors, I ran into Lucky. A man who could, in fact, give the Spanish Inquisition a run for its money. I avoided him by pleading tiredness, headache or work, but my luck ran out when I got to the southern city of Galle, just a day's drive from Colombo.

'You've avoided me long enough,' Lucky said as he spied me at the reception of the hotel. Galle is a prosperous southern city with bona fide five-star hotels. I'd had my first hot shower in days and was feeling blissfully clean. 'Can you please explain to me how you are broken?'

The foyer was packed and I wasn't going to open up to him there – and certainly not in front of Dr Gurusinghe.

Lucky turned to him. 'Dr Gurusinghe, Mahinda and Nimal have decided to have dinner in their rooms. I asked if they didn't mind if I took my fiancé out for a romantic meal,' he explained tightly.

Dr Gurusinghe looked between Lucky and I.

'But we are not engaged!' I snapped. 'We aren't getting married. I told you. I cannot. I am broken.'

'Please explain,' Lucky pleaded. 'If you are rejecting my proposal, you must at least explain yourself.'

He took my hand and led me outside, and we made our way to the ramparts of Galle Fort by the dwindling light of dusk. A sea fortress built by the Portuguese some six hundred years ago, its fortified battlements were the perfect place for quiet discussion.

'My parents never loved me,' I told him. 'Not my mother. Not my father. I have vague memories of my father holding me as a child but my mother never did. They never smiled at me. They never comforted me. They just looked through me.'

'Are both your parents back in Colombo with your brother?'

'My parents live quasi-separated. By and large Dad lives in a flat and appears for command performances for when my mother needs a social crutch. My mother destroyed him too.'

'So she loves Ryan but not you?' Lucky asked curiously.

'She dotes on Ryan. She adores Ryan.'

'Have you thought that it could just be a boy versus girl thing? I saw it a lot back in India. Sisters of my friends were ignored. And you know my own family history.'

'I thought that might be it too, for a long time. But it's more than that,' I explained, stopping to lean against one of the battlements. Below the waves crashed relentlessly against the fort. 'My mother actually hates me.'

'So you think that just because your mother couldn't love you, you aren't worthy of love?' Lucky asked.

'It's not just that,' I said. 'I don't know how to love anyone else. And I don't want to hurt you.'

'Is that what you are afraid of? That you won't love me properly and hurt me? Marion, I love you. And I know you love me too!'

'I don't love you,' I said.

'Oh, is that why you always look after me, then?'

'It's because I'm a doctor. It has nothing to do with love.'

'I grew up in a home where kindness and simple caring turned into the most devoted love possible between two people. My mother started by simply caring for my father and their love grew from there. It wasn't romantic love but it was devotion and loyalty. Give us a chance, Marion. Please. I have enough love in me for both of us.'

Perhaps it was the moon glistening in the dark over the Indian Ocean down below. Or perhaps it was the pungent aroma of the *vadai* seller's cart going past that made me quickly look in his direction. It could have even been the mosquito that bit me on the back of the neck just that second. But I did nod and that was all Lucky needed.

'So they've almost finished renovating the main salon. We've started working on the main weaving halls already. They should be ready in time for the grand opening in three weeks,' Lucky said excitedly as he dragged me around the compound in Panadura by the hand.

'And this will be where we'll live!' he crowed, pulling me into the grand residence that was being rebuilt.

'Lucky, careful you don't get too attached to this place. Sally and David could take it from you,' I counselled him.

'I'll have everything I need in life if I have you,' he smiled in return as he twirled me around the spacious formal living area.

'And I thought you could have your clinic here and your studio there,' he suggested – pulling me into an anteroom just off the side of the house and showing me a larger space overlooking the river. 'Mahinda and I will have to conduct more and more business together, so I imagine we'll spend half our time here and half our time in Australia.'

'Slow down! My head is spinning!'

'I intend on keeping it spinning!' he cried. 'Say yes. Say you'll marry me on the day of the grand opening!'

'But that's just three weeks away! We haven't worked anything out. I don't know how I will work if we're going backwards and forwards between Australia and Sri Lanka, and we haven't even told our families yet!'

'And that is the easy part to fix,' Lucky cried now, pulling me out of the house into the main compound.

The compound itself was a hive of activity. Local *basunnaha* in sarongs were darting about carrying around tools and supplies. A whole batch of saree weavers had come over from India and they were setting up looms in the long galleries which would soon be filled again with local saree weavers, creating soft supple silk to be worn against the skin.

As Lucky pulled me across the compound, I dug my heels in for a moment and stopped to look around; taking in the old house that was being done up for a party like a grand old dame.

'This is beautiful,' I said softly. 'And I know this is a bizarre thing to say, but I feel like I know this place.'

'Of course you know this place,' Lucky gloated. 'I am Hindu. I believe in reincarnation. I know we have been together before. I am an Indian Saliya and you are a doctor from Melbourne! What are the odds? I bet we've been here together before!'

He dragged me on down the path. 'My dad is in one of the teacher's bungalows. The same one he lived in when he was a teacher. He insists he'll live there and not up in the big house. He's even started painting again!'

'What's over there?' I asked, pointing to an open amphitheatre.

'Oh, you'll love this,' Lucky cried, pulling me in that direction now. 'Appa told me that it should be here and when I had the *basunnaha* dig, they found this!' he cried happily, showing me an excavated statue of the goddess Saraswati. Behind the statue was a freshly rebuilt dais for her to be placed on.

I knelt down to look at the statue. It was almost perfect, barring the odd knick and scratch.

'She was not damaged by the fires after the riot at all,' Lucky observed in a reverent voice.

'That is because she is perfect and beyond human harm,' a familiar voice said calmly.

'Mr Nair!' I cried, standing up.

'It's Raju – or have you forgotten, my dear,' he said with a smile, opening his free arm to give her a hug while leaning heavily on his cane with the other.

'The statue itself is about six hundred years old. My great-great-grandfather brought it home from Tamil Nadu when he went there to get married. Apparently my great-great-grand-mother had to leave her trousseau behind to make space for the statue and was not too happy about it!'

'Good that you bring up the discussion of a trousseau,' Lucky said smugly. 'Because Marion will need one soon!'

'Why, my dear!' Raju cried. 'I had no idea! Where is that boyfriend . . . err . . . fiancé of yours? Simon?'

'Appa! She's not marrying him!' Lucky cried. 'You said that you didn't like the thought of Marion marrying a man who could not hold his drink! You said that! That night I came back from the open-air cinema! You said Marion should be made to see sense!'

'So who is she marrying?' his father asked with a cheeky glint in his good eye.

'Your wonderful son!' I replied, surprising myself.

'I thought as much,' Raju laughed, hugging us both. 'Congratulations the both of you! Congratulations! Oh, Lucky, your mother would be so happy! It was her dying wish that you would marry this wonderful girl! We must meet with your parents, Marion,' he said excitedly. 'Soon. Custom is that the groom visits the bride's family.'

'My mother is here in Sri Lanka, as is my brother,' I told him. 'But there really is no need for any ceremony. I am more

than happy for any meetings to be low-key affairs. And the
same goes for any wedding. Quiet and simple.'

'What nonsense! My aunt Gauri will arrive tomorrow and
she'll want to meet with your mother,' Lucky insisted.

'Yes, Gauri will want to meet your family!' Raju agreed. 'We
cannot be backward about these things. Marriages are important and they need to be contracted properly. Lucky, we'll need
to hire some caterers. We need to take thirty-two varieties of
sweets with us.'

'And fresh buffalo curds and treacle. Is that a custom in
Sri Lanka as well?'

'Yes, it is! And three vats of turmeric. We do not want to
offend the Gamages!'

Father and son launched immediately into organising the
initial meeting while I started feeling ill.

'Which day can we meet with your mother, my dear?'

'Day after tomorrow would be best,' I replied. 'My uncle is
having his skin graft operation tomorrow and he should be out
of the woods by then, so please come and visit my mother and
I at our hotel then.'

In the end it was three full days before Lucky and his father
could come and visit with my mother and I. And it wasn't at
the hotel either, but in intensive care unit at Nawaloka. My
uncle's skin graft operation had gone horribly wrong.

'I don't understand how it happened,' I explained to
Lucky on the phone. 'I was in there with Dr Gurusinghe. The
operation itself was a success, but things went really badly in
recovery. I just don't understand how the necrotising fasciitis
got into the sterile environment. I watched them clean everything down with alcohol before they brought him in.'

'The what?'

'Necrotising fasciitis – flesh-eating bacteria. Because his
skin was already compromised, it spread like wildfire. I can't

bear it, Lucky. He is in so much pain. Our only hope is that he dies quickly.'

'My father and I will come. You and your mother need us,' Lucky said quickly and hung up before I could respond. No, my mother did not need company. She only needed a punching bag and I was providing that already.

'It is all your fault this happened!' my mother had screamed at me in the ward that Ryan was in. My mother had been instructed not to visit my uncle in the sealed ward. 'Your fault!'

'How, Mother? How can I be accountable for a bacterial infection?'

I could totally understand my mother's distress, though. Morphine and painkillers could only numb the pain of being eaten alive so much. My uncle's screams of pain had faded over the hours, not because of the pain relief he'd been given but because he was too exhausted to go on.

'What did he do to deserve such a thing?' I muttered softly, looking through the glass into the sealed room. My uncle was in complete isolation, attended by doctors and nurses in biohazard suits.

Her mother looked at me for a long moment and appeared as if she were about to say something, but stopped. 'I have to go to the bathroom,' she muttered, and walked off.

So I was sitting with Ryan when Lucky and his father came.

'Ryan,' I said, standing up. 'This is my fiancé, Lucky, and his father, Raju Nair.'

'I didn't know you were engaged,' my brother said, turning to look at me. 'Nair? Is that Tamil?'

Lucky kissed me on the lips. 'Sorry, darling, Appa's paintings from India came. I had to see to their unloading before we came.' He turned and held out his hand to my brother. 'And yes, I am Tamil.'

'I don't have a problem with it, but you'll forgive me if I hurry to the other side of the ward when my mother finds out,' Ryan joked.

'I am sure my son will do his best to charm your mother,' Raju said, shaking Ryan's hand too. 'Now, tell me, how are you going with your rehabilitation? As you can see, I have been severely burnt, too.'

For the next quarter of an hour, Raju listened to Ryan and his fears about his recovery, then gave him some advice. 'Focus on what you want to achieve. Have one ambition. I had a single ambition and that was to weave a particular saree in the memory of my first wife.'

'Who are you and why are you speaking to my son?' a shrill voice asked. 'Marion, who are these people you've brought to speak to your brother!'

We'd been so caught up in conversation we hadn't seen my mother come into the ward.

'Amma, this is my fiancé—' The rest of my introduction was cut off when Raju Nair turned to stare at my mother.

'You!' he cried, blinking hard, as if to get the dust out of his eyes. 'I have finally found one of you!'

'And who are you?' my mother asked.

'Raju Nair, Nila's husband!' he roared.

As Raju stood up, my mother turned on her heel and ran.

'What's going on? Who is Nila?' I asked Lucky as we pursued Raju and my mother down the hallway. Raju must have been in pain, but he ran so fast that we could barely keep up.

'She was Appa's first wife,' Lucky explained, looking confused.

'Nila is the name of my mother's sister who died in a bus crash!'

Mother stopped just outside the sealed door to her brother's room as Raju advanced on her menacingly. 'How did you kill her?' he shouted.

And as she cowered from him, Raju looked up to see the name of the man kept under strict quarantine. Manoj Mendis.

He moved swiftly to get into the sealed room but I moved quicker. 'He has necrotising fasciitis – if you go in there you'll get it too! It is a flesh-eating bacteria and the pain is impossible to bear! It will kill you, Raju.'

Raju hit at the glass panes with his cane. 'What did you do to Nila? How did she die? Tell me where her grave is!'

'He can't speak,' I told Raju. 'He himself will probably die in the next day or so.'

'You! You must tell me where Nila's grave is!' Raju said, turning to my mother.

'My sister died in a bus crash. There was no grave,' mother replied in a little girl voice.

'Oh God!' Raju cried, sinking to his knees. 'So it was true. My poor darling girl.'

'Can someone explain to me what's going on?' Lucky shouted.

'Your Aunt Nila was my first wife,' Raju said, looking at me. 'That man dying in there was the man who doused me in petrol and burnt me in revenge for marrying her.'

'My family did this to you,' I said softly.

'It was all Nila's fault! If she hadn't run off to become a saree maker, all of this would never have happened!' my mother shrieked, close to hysterics. 'Because of her I met Sunil and because of that . . .'

'You had me,' Ryan said softly from behind. A nurse had wheeled him in. 'Yes, living in Sri Lanka has been very enlightening. There are no secrets here, Amma. Uncle Manoj got very drunk one night and confessed that some up-country tea planter was my father and not Albert Gamage.' He turned to Raju and Lucky. 'And the other thing my uncle confessed was that his sister Nila didn't die. That's all a lie too. She is alive and living in Negombo.'

I was completely frazzled by the time I got to Katunayake International Airport. The car I hired to take me to the airport broke down four times. Yes. Four times.

First it had stalled not far from the hotel. Bizarrely, it had stopped right in front of the Sri Ponnambalavaneshwarar temple. So while the driver fixed the car, I wandered into the shrine room, offering a short prayer to the gods asking them to stop the pain in my heart.

'We can't marry,' I'd said to Lucky after Raju had acquired my aunt Nila's address from Ryan. 'You know it won't work. Not with this between us.'

'What do you mean? This has nothing to do with us!'

'No, it has everything to do with us. Every time your father sees me, he will be reminded of the fact that my mother and uncle hurt him.'

'Marion, that is just an excuse and you know it! You've wanted to find an excuse to go back and hide in Australia and you've found it,' he'd accused.

That night back in the hotel, I'd booked the first flight back to Australia. I wasn't sure if I would stay in Melbourne when I got back. Perhaps I would move up to Cairns or somewhere up north.

My phone rang for the hundredth time that day and I switched it off without looking. It was probably my mother calling to tell me of my uncle's death, but she needn't have bothered. I was glad he'd died, uncharitable though it might have seemed. He'd finally paid for his crimes.

The car broke down three times more, each time in front of a Hindu or Buddhist temple. I supposed it to be a sign. Maybe I should look into religion. Women fresh out of relationship break-ups did that kind of thing.

By the time I finally got to the airport I knew Lucky and his father would be up in Negombo. Just ten kilometres north of the airport. Lucky's father would at long last be reunited with his first wife, my aunt. And she would love Lucky. Lucky was an easy person to love.

I was feeling so numb that I nearly missed the call for my flight. I was sitting in a stupor until one of the ground staff came up and got me. 'Are you Dr Gamage?' she asked. 'We've been calling for you for the last ten minutes. Can you please board?'

I'd walked onto the plane with lead feet. Was my real name even Gamage? What was the name of the tea planter who'd sired me anyway? I made mental note to call Ryan once I got home. I needed to find out about our father.

The flight attendant helped me to my first-class seat as I placed my oversized sunglasses on my face to shade my eyes from the light. I couldn't cry but I still needed to grieve – to feel the pain even if I couldn't express it. The plane pushed off and had started to taxi down the runway when out of the corner of my eye I saw an approaching tank. An army tank and, judging by the dented panels, it had seen action too.

'Is that normal?' I asked the attendant as the airplane came to a screeching halt.

She did not respond but rather hit the panic button immediately.

'Get down! Under your seats!' she called through the cabin. 'We are about to have a hostage situation.'

The lady next to me snarled. 'Bloody Tamils. The war is bloody over but they still try to ruin our island.'

I saw the pilot come out of the cockpit and have heated words with the flight attendant before opening the door.

Everyone on the plane was agog to see what was about to happen next. Stairs had been hurriedly wheeled to the plane and now someone was climbing them, carrying a large square object. Incredulous comments flew about. 'They stopped the plane so that someone could transport a painting?'

It was Lucky.

'They said you were up front,' he huffed as he stood the large painting in the aisle beside him and took a deep breath.

'What are you doing here? I'm going back to Australia.'

'Wait a second,' he replied, breathing in deeply. 'Have you ever wondered why everyone in my family thought you looked familiar?'

'Coincidence?'

'No. It was because of this,' he explained, pulling off the dust cover to reveal the painting. It was a near life-size painting of a woman standing in a river dyeing a saree. Her resemblance to me was uncanny, though there were some clear differences. The woman was not tall, but her eyes and jawline were identical to mine.

'Did you paint that?'

'No, my father did,' Lucky explained.

'He's fast.'

'No, he isn't. He painted this thirty years ago. It's a portrait of his first wife, Nila.'

I didn't understand what he was saying.

'Anoja was never your mother. Your mother has just arrived on the tarmac,' Lucky told me with shining eyes. I looked out the window to see a diminutive woman being helped out of the army tank by Raju.

I did not think as I rushed down the stairs and across the burning hot tarmac and into the arms of the woman I'd seen at a Hindu temple in Melbourne many years before.

'Oh, my precious girl. My precious Marion,' Nila cried, running to me, with Raju limping slowly behind. And for the first time in thirty years, I cried.

When I'd 'agreed' to Lucky's moonlight proposal on the ramparts on Galle Fort, it'd been madness. Absolute madness. How could I agree to marry a man I barely knew? I knew better than most how awful a bad marriage could be. I had always assumed that Albert and Anoja hadn't known each other well enough before they were married.

So looking back years later, I realised that I fell deeply in love with Lucky in the weeks after I met my biological parents. I finally got to know him through one of the most difficult times in my life. Everything I knew about myself and my life had been turned upside down in a matter of moments, and it took time to make sense of it all.

Lucky took it in his stride. His kindness, gentleness and intuitive knowledge of what needed to be done showed me the man he truly was.

My mother could not stop clinging to me. 'I didn't even get to hold you properly,' she cried, her dark eyes constantly brimming with tears. 'I went into labour late one evening and had you only four hours later. I fell asleep with you in my arms and you were gone when I woke.'

My father, Raju, was equally affectionate, kissing me on my forehead and hugging me when my mother could bear to let me go.

'My beautiful, beautiful girl,' he'd repeat over and over again.

And it was all too much. I'd lived all my life without love or affection – and I could not breathe. I could not run away, lest I compounded the hurt felt by my parents, but I could not stay either. Which was when Lucky would step in, carefully disengaging me from my parent's clutches, claiming his rights as a fiancé and taking me on long walks, down to the river and beyond. And sometimes even into town in Panadura, to the huts along the beach where the vendors sold hoppers and curries.

'I don't know how to do this,' I confessed. 'I don't know how to be a daughter to them.'

'You *are* their daughter,' Lucky replied, holding me gently. 'Just be yourself.'

'How do you know so much, Lucky? How do you know what to do?'

'Because I have done this myself,' he reminded me. 'I went in search of my biological mother, remember? I found her. And my sister. The first few months of our relationship were diffi-cult. I didn't need her as my mother. I already had one. But I needed her all the same. We had to find a space that was right for us. Just do what comes naturally.'

What would have come naturally for me would have been to run and hide, but Lucky did not let me do that either.

'Oh, come now. Surely you can't be afraid of a tiny woman and a disabled man?' he'd laugh before gently dragging me to my parents' little bungalow and leaving me there in awkward silence until I learned how to be around them. Getting to know them. Understanding their story and mine.

'My mother . . . sorry . . . your sister hardly ever spoke of her family. I never met her parents or your brothers until Uncle Manoj got hurt,' I told Nila one evening.

'I am not surprised,' Nila said. 'We are not a particularly nice lot. Manoj and Rupani got along best, I suppose.'

'Why do you call her Rupani? Her name is Anoja.'

'Rupani was the nickname I gave her as a baby. It means *she who is beautiful.*'

'That was one of things that made tracking your mother so difficult,' my father explained. 'Everyone knew that Manoj became involved in politics, but no one could tell me what happened to the sister Rupani because they all knew her as Anoja.'

'They were my mother's favourites,' Nila said. 'Rupani always detested me and Herath has not had anything to do with us since he went to university.'

'Was Uncle Manoj really that evil? Did he have any good qualities?'

'If he had any, I don't know of them. Mrs Vasha, our neighbour, always said that if she knew he'd turn out the way he did, she would have stuffed him in her sewing bag after she'd helped with his delivery and drowned him in the canal.'

'Why aren't you angry? Both of you?' I'd demanded.

In some ways I resented the ease with which the two of them had fallen back together as if they'd never been apart, finishing each other's sentences, both quietly content to do whatever the other was doing, chatting or laughing at silly jokes as my father painted and my mother designed some saree or worked on a piece of embroidery. That they were two halves of a whole no one could doubt. Sometimes I felt like an intruder in their happy party.

'Darling, why should we be angry? Never in my wildest dreams could I have imagined that I would see my precious Nila again in this lifetime. And not only that, I found I had a daughter. A beautiful, intelligent and wonderful daughter,' my father replied, stroking my face.

'What about the time you have lost? What about the lives you should have had? Both of you suffered terribly. Aren't you angry about that?'

'My precious angel, don't forget yourself. Do not forget yourself,' my mother whispered, kissing my cheek. 'I cannot imagine that you'll ever forget the pain of your own childhood. But please, do not destroy your present happiness by thinking of what could have been or should have been.'

'I didn't know you were a Buddhist philosopher,' Lucky chimed in cheekily, coming into the room with some snacks and breaking the tension. 'Why aren't you wearing a yellow robe?'

'I was quite mad, you know,' Nila confessed. 'I completely lost my mind for many years. Within the blink of an eye I saw my husband burning, I lost you, my darling Marion, and I lost my craft. After I came back from Melbourne, we lived near a temple for a while. Not a common end-of-the street temple but a meditation centre. I visited them often, and by their example, I learned to gain control of my mind. I learned to let go of the memories and live in the present.'

'Maybe I should go there too,' Raju said. 'Perhaps all of us as a family. It will help us heal.'

'Aren't you Hindu?' I'd asked, confused.

'Honey,' Lucky said, taking me by the shoulders and spinning me around so I could see the amphitheatre through the window and statue of the goddess Saraswati which still lay on the ground. 'That is the goddess Saraswati. The patron goddess of all artists and craftsmen. The patron goddess of the Saliyas. She is also the goddess who protects all Buddhist pilgrims. She understands that their quest to understand their minds and spirit is the only way her holy water can douse the fires of ignorance.'

'When we seek God, we only find ourselves,' my mother added as evening closed in properly.

'And in finding ourselves and quieting our minds, we find the divine within ourselves,' my father finished.

'We only have the comfort this world can give us, Marion. You have endured enough in this lifetime. Happiness is as much a decision as it is a consequence of external factors. Make the decision to be happy, Marion,' Lucky said.

And I knew that I could not have found a better man. A better partner. And perhaps in time, I would be convinced that Lucky was the part of my soul that had always been missing.

Everything had been going so well I was convinced that something was about to go wrong. It had to go wrong. Such a streak of good luck could not be sustained.

'I don't understand why you could not choose a saree from our own mills for the wedding,' my mother grumbled good-naturedly as she went about tidying the room. 'Your father, mother and husband-to-be are all saree makers, and you insist on having a saree sent over from Australia.'

'You don't understand, Amma, this saree is perfect. I saw it when I was about seventeen. I fell in love with it there and then. It belonged to an old friend of my parents . . . er . . . an old friend, and it is beautiful. Fatima Khan is flying it over especially!' I replied. 'You know, I brought it to the Hindu temple the day I saw you in Melbourne!'

I was sitting in what should have been my childhood room. My mother had stitched my saree blouse and underskirt from some vintage silk in the stores, choosing the fabric using the tiny silk scrap Fatima had sent ahead. Such was the worth of the saree that Fatima was hand-delivering it from the vault in Melbourne.

'You would not believe it, Mum, but the saree has real sapphires and rubies on it. It is beautiful,' I cried as I twirled around in my saree blouse and underskirt. The hairdresser clucked her tongue as a pin fell out of the elaborate up-do she'd created. I sat back down on the seat for her to reinsert the pin and for the make-up artist to finish her work. In the mirror before me was a woman I did not recognise. My life was brimming with colour.

'You are beautiful,' my mother told me, kissing me on the cheek. She herself was dressed to the nines in a burgundy silk saree with a dramatic gold border.

'What are they doing?' my mother exclaimed, looking out the window to see a positive sea of waiters walking around with drinks and refreshments for the hundreds of wedding guests. 'Are they serving the samosas already?'

'They've brought out the champagne too,' I said. 'That's supposed to be for the toast!'

'I'll attend to that,' my mother said and stepped out. 'Send me a message as soon as your saree arrives. I want to dress my daughter for her wedding!'

As the hairdresser and make-up artist left too I looked out the window onto the lawn and amphitheatre just beyond. The mill was safe now – Lucky would never lose it. Though his right to it might be challenged, mine could not. I was Raju Nair's daughter by birth. It felt right to be celebrating my marriage to Lucky here.

My parents had invited hundreds of people. Friends. Family. Business associates. I'd even met a one-eyed merchant called Mustafa Mohamadeen who was a close family associate just the day before.

'Mustafa Mohamadeen is helping us set up our online business,' Lucky had explained. 'He has to be the finest trader south of New Delhi!'

'I can find you anything you want, my dear!' the old man had boomed. 'Sarees, stereos, iPods, iPads. I get them cheap from China these days. But m'dear,' he'd said, pulling me aside. 'What I can't sell you is happiness. I've known Lucky since he was but an *achaa* baby. He is a good man. Treat him well and he will love you like a queen.'

And it was a riot of colour out there. People were dressed so brightly it looked like a carnival. Women in bright blues, purples, reds and sunny yellows mingled happily with men dressed in crisp sarongs and tunics. Yet in among all that colour the large statue of the goddess Saraswati stood out like a beacon. The ancient statue had been lifted and placed on the dais the night before.

'The trick is the prayer,' the dwarf weaving master had said, and he'd muttered something under his breath as fifteen men, including Lucky and her father, had hefted the ancient white stone sculpture onto its side and then up to the dais. Men had tried before but had been unable to make it shift at all.

'Or perhaps the trick is your amazing strength,' his exquisite wife had smiled. Sindhu had been a lifelong friend of my father's. He and his amazingly beautiful dancer wife, Sarojini, were an incongruous pair, but I had to concede that they were a well-matched couple.

'I don't believe in such things as soulmates,' Sarojini had confessed over dinner the night before, 'and certainly not love at first sight. The first time I met Sindhu I did not appreciate his worth, but the second time I met him, while working as a dancer in Mysore, I realised I'd met my match. See, I'd learned to love myself by that time and I could truly accept his love then.'

'Love – isn't that what we all live for?' said the Hindu priest who'd be conducting the service that day. Madhav had been the pundit at the temple in Melbourne I'd visited many years ago. 'In our search for God what we truly seek is a source of unconditional love. Yet the best source of unconditional love is ourselves.'

Everyone seemed to have an Australian connection, and a connection to each other. It'd been a surprising evening all around. Lucky and I had expected to make a great many introductions, only to find out that everybody already knew everyone else somehow.

Madhav was now a guru at the ashram Lucky's biological mother and sister lived in as well. He even knew Mahinda!

'Why I never!' the holy man kept repeating. 'Nila used to come to the Hindu temple in Boronia many years ago! And I must tell you, your mother saved me!'

'How so?' my mother had asked with a laugh. 'I was quite mad, you know. Madhav gave Renuka and I the money to return to Sri Lanka so I could get treatment. It was he who saved me!'

'Quite the contrary, my gracious lady. It was you who saved me. You made me face my inhumanity. You challenged my arrogance. Your humanity made me a better man!' the pundit said, kneeling and touching my mother's feet with his forehead. 'Forgive me, mother,' he'd begged. 'I feel it is more than a coincidence that I would end up leading the ashram where your mother is a chief disciple, Lucky. The great goddess Saraswati is at work here.'

Lucky's mother had smiled. She had flown over from India along with Madhav and Lucky's sister, Radha, for the wedding.

'I believe it be Ma Savatri work,' Pilar had added in a soft voice. She was very shy and hardly spoke to me, but she'd brought me a beautifully woven cotton saree as a wedding present. 'I not rich woman. I gives you what I can. Makes my Laksman happy man. I is so happy he marry educated woman.'

Radha was an accomplished young woman herself. 'I will be singing with Sarojini as you walk down the aisle. My gift from the goddess is my voice.'

Out of the corner of one eye I saw Vannan and his brood arrive. The ex-LTTE cadre leant heavily on his crutches as his children looked uncertainly around. My mother came forward and warmly welcomed them, pointing the children in the direction of other children present and Vannan in the direction of the karaoke machine my cousin Ryan was setting up.

Ryan and I are closer now that we aren't brother and sister. The truth about our relationship finally set us free to enjoy each other's company, as cousins should. Spending time with

Ryan, I realised how destructive Anoja's relationship with him had been.

'Do you think any of us survived unscathed?' Ryan had asked me one afternoon. 'I couldn't protect you from her! I was powerless! And I was supposed to have been your twin brother, your protector. What kind of person did that make me?'

But Ryan seemed happier now. He too was spending a great deal of time with my parents, realising that a lifetime of hatred could be erased by a faithful heart.

Indeed, looking out over the lawn, I could not believe that there had been a civil war in Sri Lanka at all. Sinhala, Tamil, Burgher and Muslim people were mingling happily in the throng, waiting for the blessed occasion to start. I understood, then, how small the differences are between us. All people just want to get on with their lives and care for their children. Nothing more, nothing less.

I heard a sharp rap at the door. Fatima Khan had finally arrived. 'Come in!' I cried happily, but to my surprise it was not Fatima but an unknown lady with an alabaster complexion who came in. 'I'm sorry, I thought you were my aunty Fatima!' I exclaimed, feeling naked in my skin-tight midriff-baring saree blouse.

'I know Fatima well. But she has gone to speak with your mother,' the lady replied as she laid the large box containing the saree on my bed.

I did not need an invitation to pounce. Taking off the cover, I looked reverently at the beautiful golden white saree that lay in the nest of white tissue paper.

'Just like I remembered it,' I whispered softly.

'Come on, let's drape it on you!' the lady said.

'Oh, my mother wanted to do that. I'd better send her a message.'

'Your mother is otherwise occupied,' the lady said. 'I believe your Aunt Gauri has just arrived, and it is many years since they have seen one another. Besides, we need to hurry. The ceremony starts in twenty minutes!'

I did not argue as the lady took the saree out of the box and expertly draped it on me.

'Marriage is not an easy undertaking, my child. Gautama Siddharta likened it to living together with a drunk elephant. But with a kind heart and open mind, victory will be yours, child,' the lady assured me.

'Who is Gautama Siddharta?'

'The man who became the Buddha, you gorgeous girl!' the lady smiled. 'Wisdom, patience, compassion and kindness. Keep those close to your heart and you will not fail.'

'Have you been married?' I asked the lady. She was of an indiscernible age. Strikingly beautiful. Radiant. Dressed in a white saree rich with embellishments but subdued all the same.

'I am married to what I do,' the lady replied with a smile. 'Which is just as important. Now look,' she instructed, turning me to face the mirror. 'Don't you think you look like a goddess?'

I was speechless. I was covered in white but glowed with colour. Something about the border of the saree made me think of my long walks along the river with Lucky. There was something in the wave and form of it and the exquisite jewels that swished around my feet that spoke of flowing waters.

The lady pinned the *pallu* of the saree to my shoulder. As I turned, I saw the elaborate peacock sewn entirely of sapphires and with bright red rubies for eyes. The lady arranged it on my arm like a cascading waterfall.

'Go quickly, my darling!' The lady hurried me as the clock in the main house chimed five o'clock.

'Aren't you coming with me?' I asked.

'I am never apart from you,' the lady called as I heard my mother come in search of me.

'Marion, I completely lost track of time!' my mother cried, coming down the corridor. 'Lucky is waiting for us.'

'I am already dressed,' I called back, hurrying out of the room, grabbing my posy of lotus flowers from my dresser on the way.

'Oh my,' was all my mother could say when she saw me, covering her mouth with her hand to stop herself from crying.

We could not stop because the Reverend Madhav had started the chanting for the wedding. As we walked down the aisle to where my father and Lucky were standing, whispers rose around me. My mother's friend Renuka looked as if she'd seen a ghost.

'Where did she get *that* saree? Is it possible?'

'It is only possible because miracles do happen,' Raju Nair said in a firm voice that carried over the noise of the chattering crowds. 'My precious child,' he whispered in my ear as he handed me over to Lucky, who was already seated in front of the sacred fire.

Even the Reverend started dramatically when he saw me wearing the saree.

'How did you get that saree? And who draped it on you?' he demanded.

'The saree belongs to Fatima Khan,' I explained in a faltering voice, pointing to Fatima sitting in the front row. 'And a strange lady came and draped it on me.'

I looked past the holy man to see the statue of the goddess Saraswati behind him, carved six hundred years previously into solid white granite. The goddess was identical to the lady who'd just been with me. Identical in features. Identical in grace and form. Identical in radiance.

Madhav gave me a steady look. 'I am not sure who that saree really belongs to anymore, but I do know that it is draped on you in what we call the *devi* style. A style only used by the gods.'

'Perhaps Marion has just met with the gods,' Lucky said, beaming at me, as a divine peace spread like a pool of liquid joy through the amphitheatre and beyond. 'Marry us, holy man, because I want one of my seven lifetimes to start now!'

# Glossary

**Abishekham** (Hindi/Tamil) Libation of the deities in milk and rose water

**Achaa** (Hindi/Tamil) Expression of surprise or delight

**Achiamma** (Tamil) Grandmother

**Aibuwan** (Sinhala) No exact English equivalent – a greeting of welcome or good day.

**Aiya** (Sinhala) Older brother

**Akka** (Sinhala) Older sister

**Alarippu** (Tamil) 'Flowering bud'. Traditionally the first dance piece that Bharatanatyam dancers learn and perform in this type of classical dance recital. It is an invocation piece, symbolising the offering of respects to both God and the audience.

**Amma/Ammi** (Sinhala) Mother

**Ammachi** (Tamil) Mother

**Ana** (Tamil) Older brother

**Anay** (Sinhala) There is no direct English equivalent, but is almost like saying 'pretty' in 'pretty please'.

**Anay ba aiyo** (Sinhala) 'No I cannot'

**Anujate** (Kanarese) Sister

**Appa** (Tamil) Father

**Arari** (Kanarese) Boyfriend

**Arrack** (Sinhala) Sri Lankan whisky made from the fermented sap of coconut flowers, sugarcane and grains.

**Ashwagandha** (Hindi) Indian ginseng

**Baana** (Hindi) Weft threads

**Bahasa** (Hindi) Language

**Bala** (Sinhalese/Hindi) *Sida cordifolia* – used extensively in herbal medicines.

**Balli** (Sinhala)  Bitch

**Banderi** (Telegu)  Female monkey

**Bao** (Chinese)  Boon

**Basunnaha** (Sinhala)  Tradesmen

**Beedee** (Sinhala)  A noxious Sri Lankan cigar.

**Beta** (Hindi)  Child

**Brahmins** (Hindi/Tamil)  Caste of people who are traditionally the custodians of the temples and are priests.

**Bung** (Sinhala)  Mate

**Burfi** (Hindi)  A sweet confectionery from the Indian subcontinent. Plain burfi is made with condensed milk and sugar and cooked until it solidifies.

**Burgher** (English/Sinhala)  Eurasian descendants of Portuguese, Dutch and English colonists who have intermarried with Sinhala and Tamil people.

**Chai** (Hindi)  Tea

**Chakra** (Hindi)  Traditional Indian spinning wheel.

**Cheek** (Sinhala/Tamil)  An expression of disgust.

**Chettie** (Sinhala)  Merchant

**Dalits** (Hindi)  People of the untouchable caste.

**Deepavali/Deevali** (Sinhala/Tamil/Hindi)  Hindu festival of lights celebrating the victory of good over evil.

**Demala** (Sinhala)  Derogatory reference to a Tamil person.

**Devadasi** (Tamil/Hindi)  Handmaidens of the gods.

**Devarige biduvadu** (Kanarese)  A ceremony dedicating a young girl to the life of a *devadasi*.

**Deyo Buddhu sale** (Sinhala)  'Oh my dear Buddha'

**Deyo Buddhuhamduruwanay** (Sinhala)  'For the love of the Buddha'

**Dhoti** (Hindi)  Sarong-like garment worn around the waist for men.

**Dosai** (Tamil)  Pancakes made from crushed pulses and rice.

**Duwa** (Sinhala)  Daughter

**Faluda** (Sinhala)  Sickly pink drink made of rose essence, jelly, *casa casa* seeds and milk.

**Ferenges** (Hindi) Foreigners

**Gamanayaka** (Sinhala) Village headman

**Gani** (Sinhala) Woman

**Gharwali/s** (Telegu) Madam/s in a brothel

**Gokshura** (Sinhalese/Hindi) *Tribulus Terrestris Linn* – a known aphrodisiac.

**Govigama** (Sinhala) Caste of people whose chief occupation is that of farmers.

**Gulab jamun** (Hindi) A milk-solids based dessert, similar to a dumpling.

**Hastas** (Tamil) Expressive hand movements in Indian dancing.

**Hirja** (Hindi) Transgender/transsexual people.

**Hoppers** (Sinhala) Crisp bowl shaped breads made from rice flour and coconut milk.

**Idali** (Tamil) Steamed cakes made from crushed Urdu grains.

**Iskolay mahathaya** (Sinhala) School teacher

**Jogti** (Kanarese) Usually retired *devadasi* who work in temples as oracles. They go into trances and have prophetic visions.

**Jowar** (Kanarese) Sorghum

**Kaai kani halwa** (Hindi) Indian sweet that from sweetened grated vegetables.

**Kaalai va nakkan** (Tamil) No exact English equivalent – a greeting of welcome or good day.

**Kalamkari** (Hindi) A type of hand-painted or block-printed cotton textile, produced in parts of India and in Iran.

**Kalhasas** (Hindi) Clay pots

**Kapuwa** (Sinhala) Matchmaker

**Karana/s** (Tamil) The 108 key transitions in the classical Indian dance described in Natya Shastra. *Karana* is a Sanskrit verbal noun, meaning 'doing'.

**Karawe** (Tamil) Caste of people whose chief occupation is that of fishermen.

**Karma Sutra** (Hindi /Tamil) A treatise on healthy living that also provides a guide on good sexual health.

**Kiri hodi** (Sinhala) Creamy coconut milk curry made with spices, thick coconut cream, onions and spices.

**Kohomba kolla and lime mixture** (Sinhala) A home remedy made of Indian lilac and lime used to lighten skin.

**Kohu** (Sinhala) Straw

**Kos** (Sinhala) Jack fruit

**Kovila** (Sinhala) Hindu temple

**Kshatriya** (Hindi) A caste of people whose are traditional occupation is that of potters.

**Kumhas** (Hindi) A caste of people whose are traditional occupation is that of potters.

**Kurumba** (Sinhala) King coconut

**Laddoo** (Hindi) *Laddoo* is made of flour and sugar with other ingredients that vary by recipe. It is often served at festive or religious occasions.

**Machang** (Sinhala) Mate

**Malli** (Sinhala) Younger brother

**Malu ambul thial** (Sinhala) Dry fish curry cooked in pepper, curry powder and curry leaves.

**Mam** (Tamil) Mother

**Mamaji** (Hindi) Mother

**Mangala sutra** (Tamil) The necklace that is draped on a woman during a marriage as the symbol of the nuptials.

**Marcel** (Tamil) Father-in-law

**Marmee** (Tamil) Mother-in-law

**Mata lajai aiyo** (Sinhala) 'Oh, I am so embarassed'

**Modalali** (Sinhala) Shop keeper

**Muddu** (Kanarese) Darling

**Muruku** (Sinhala/Tamil) Crisps made from chickpea flour.

**Nangu** (Sinhala) Younger sister

**Navaratri** (Hindi) Festival dedicated to the worship of the goddess Durga.

**Nawab** (Hindi) Honoured merchant

**Nay** (Sinhala) No direct English equivalent, but similar to 'eh' at the end of a sentence to denote a question.

**Nivi** (Hindi) The style of saree most commonly worn today with the pleats tucked into the waist band and the fall draped over a shoulder.

**Ossareeya** (Sinhala) A style of saree that originates from the central highlands of Sri Lanka. The pleats are fanned over the hips instead of being tucked into the waist band.

**Pallu** (Hindi) The fall and most ornate section of a saree.

**Pancha dakshata** (Sinhala) Five skills

**Paripu** (Sinhala) Lentil curry

**Pattam** (Telegu) The last step before becoming a fully-fledged *devadasi*.

**Perehera** (Sinhala) A grand pageant held in Kandy, Sri Lanka, where the tooth of the Buddha held in the citadel is brought out and taken on elephant back throughout the city.

**Pippalyadi yoga and japa** (Hindi) An Ayurvedic concoction for contraception.

**Pol sambol** (Sinhala) Coconut sambol

**Pooja** (Hindi/Tamil/Sinhala) An offering to the gods.

**Pooroochen** (Tamil) Husband

**Potta** (Sinhala) The fall and most ornate section of a saree.

**Puranas** (Hindi) Ancient Hindu texts eulogising various deities.

**Pusari** (Sinhala) Hindu Priest

**Putta/Puttay** (Sinhala) Son

**Puttar** (Tamil/Hindi) Son

**Ra** (Sinhala) Sri Lankan moonshine which is made from fermented toddy.

**Sadhu** (Sinhala/Tamil) Holy man

**Saliya** (Hindi) Caste of people whose chief occupation was as weavers.

**Sambar** (Sinhala/Tamil) A soupy curry with a tamarind base made with pumpkin, eggplant, drumsticks and tomato.

**Sambol** (Sinhala/Tamil) Spicy condiment

**Sangeet** (Tamil/Hindi) An important musical function before a wedding.

**Sani** (Tamil) Faeces

**Shah** (Sinhala) No direct English equivalent – an expression of admiration and approval.

**Sharada Navaratri** (Tamil) A festival celebrating the Goddess Durga.

**Shatawari** (Sinhalese/Hindi) A species of asparagus found in the Himalayas and Sri Lanka.

**Shodi** (Tamil) Gravy in a curry

**Shudras** (Hindi) A caste of people whose traditional occupation is that of labourers and field workers.

**Suddha** (Sinhala) White male

**Suddhi** (Sinhala) White female

**Suddu** (Sinhala) White

**Tai Hanuman Udho Udho** (Kanarese) 'Praise Lord Hanuman who saved me'

**Thaana** (Hindi) Warp threads

**Thairu** (Tamil) A yoghurt drink.

**Thali** (Hindi) Similar to the *mangala sutra*.

**Thangachchi** (Tamil) Younger sister

**Thosai** (Sinhala) Pancakes made from crushed pulses and rice.

**Vadai** (Tamil) Spicy doughnuts made from crushed pulses.

**Vedas** (Hindi/Sinhala/Tamil) A large body of texts originating in ancient India. Composed in Vedic Sanskrit, the texts constitute the oldest layer of Sanskrit literature and the oldest scriptures of Hinduism.

**Vedda** (Sinhala) Ayurvedic healer

**Vellalar** (Tamil) Caste of people whose chief occupation was as farmers.

**Vesak** (Sinhala/Hindi/Tamil) A festival in May celebrating the birth, enlightenment and passing of the Buddha.

**Vibuthi** (Tamil) Holy ash that is made from incinerating *homa* wood with cow dung.

**Watha rathu malkoha** (Sinhala) Red-faced Malkoha (*Phaenicophaeus pyrrhocephalus*)

# Acknowledgements

This book could not have been written without the consistent and enduring support of Shelagh Louise Reynolds and Leon Gettler. Every time I tried to abandon *Saree*, neither one would let me give it up and kept me going – Leon with his late-night chats on Facebook and reassurances that my voice needed to be heard, and Shelagh, who reminded me that she had earlier drafts if I decided to delete it from my computer.

On editing support – thanks again to the indomitable Monika Smith. There was an amazing confluence of opinion about *Saree* from her and my wonderful editor at Simon and Schuster, Roberta Ivers. Thanks also to Larissa Edwards, Kate O'Donnell and Elizabeth Cowell.

To the people at Beautiful Silks, I thank you for your invaluable advice on the silk making process. And likewise to the Handweavers and Spinners Guild of Victoria for letting me lurk about like some kind of maladroit stalker.

Last but not least, I need to acknowledge the support I received from my beautiful mother, Lalitha Dharmapala, who carried my world on her shoulders like Atlas as I wrote this book.

# About the author

Su Dharmapala is a Melbourne based writer.

She was born in Singapore and grew up between Singapore and Sri Lanka before immigrating to Australia in 1989. She completed her Bachelor of Arts (majoring in French and German) and Bachelor of Science at Monash University in 1997.

After graduating from university, Su has worked in technology for some of Australia's Fortune 500 companies.

*Saree* is Su's second novel. *The Wedding Season* was published by Simon and Schuster Australia in 2012.

When she is not writing, Su is a political junkie with a passion for social justice and food. She lives in the leafy eastern suburbs of Melbourne with her family.

# The story behind Saree

*In ever loving memory of my father, Piyadasa Dharmapala. I still miss you so very much.*

My dedication for *Saree* was the last sentence I wrote, long after the plotting, writing, editing, re-writing and countless hours of staring blankly at a computer screen were done. Yet those last sixteen words undid me more than the original 200,000 words I'd written. I allowed the tears to flow freely and sat there in my study wishing that, even for a brief moment, my father could put his arms around me and I could feel his love again. My father died in 2009 and it has been a very long time.

While it may seem quite predictable that an author dedicates a book to one or other of their parents at some point in their career – mine wasn't a simple dedication to a most beloved parent. *Saree* was my father's story. And because parents give us not just our genetics, but a framework with which we view our lives, this is also my story.

My father was born in Singapore several years before the start of World War Two. Only weeks before the fall of Singapore, my grandfather spirited the entire family across the bridge from Singapore into the jungles of Johor. Dodging aerial raids and sniper fire, my father, his older brother, two sisters and parents made their way on a rickshaw across the treacherous roads of Malaysia.

Once in Malaysia, they eked out a subsistence living on a tiny farm with two other families – living on wild manioc and whatever they could manage to grow, barter and spare from the Japanese officers and escaping British POWs. So, as a young child, my father witnessed more brutality in those

few years than most of us do in a lifetime. He watched as
several POWs were executed in front of his front door and
saw my grandmother almost take a bullet meant to kill my
grandfather.

But he also bore witness to amazing acts of courage and
generosity. The simple act of giving water to Japanese soldiers
meant that vital medicine was provided when children were
sick. Sheltering escaping POWs meant that lives were saved
and, in turn, their own lives were protected.

His experiences of World War Two made my father many
things. A man with boundless generosity – literally boundless. He'd give someone else the clothes on his back if he knew
they needed them. An alcoholic. A man riddled with so much
anxiety that his temper was always trigger sensitive.

He also became a firm believer of karma. Not the trite
interpretation of it as retribution, but a profound understanding of the interconnectedness of the universe and how what
we sow is what we reap.

This belief in karma was further deepened during his
lifetime and became a cornerstone of how he lived his life – and
it fueled his selflessness. He tried telling my brother and me
about the importance of it but we could not see past the need
for Reeboks and Sony Walkmans. That is, until two events
came to pass that shifted our entire perspective.

In 1958 my father was a border at St John's College in Panadura,
when the ethnic tensions between the Sinhalese and Tamils that
had been mounting steadily since Independence escalated to an
all-out pogrom. In retaliation to Tamil thugs cutting off the breasts
of a breast-feeding mother in Panadura and murdering her, Sinhalese thugs dragged a Hindu priest into the main thoroughfare of
the town, doused him in petrol and burnt him to death.

My father had been walking back to the hostel from town
that day and saw the vicious attack. Years later, the memory of
it still had the power to shake him. The horror of it lived with
him for a lifetime. He knew the thug who had done it and like

most, feared for his own life lest it be formally reported. But my father never forgot a name or face.

Not long after the ethnic clashes, my father had to leave school to provide for his family. My grandfather had died and dowries had to be provided for his younger sisters. So he took up his father's trade as an engraver and sailed to Hong Kong to work for the jeweller SPH De Silva. There he grew his trade skills and in the late sixties, Dad's best friend, Chandra, arranged a marriage for him.

'*Machang*, my cousin Lalitha is an awesome girl,' was all my mother's cousin, Chandra, had told my father. So in 1970, after two years of correspondence and one face-to-face meeting, my parents got married. They moved to Singapore and my father set up a one-man engraving workshop on Middle Road, the road that literally ran through the middle of Singapore's then central business district. My brother was born in 1971 and the couple became a family.

Not long after my brother was born, my father spotted an unlikely duo in the *coppi-o* (coffee canteen) shop next door. The older man and younger boy stood despondently looking at the sweet tea and coffee being served, unable to afford it. I never found out why my father struck up conversation with the duo and bought them breakfast that morning. But whenever he spoke of them, he always mentioned that the boy was painfully thin and that he had knobby knees.

My father soon discovered that the older man was a Tamil rubber tapper working in one of the many rubber plantations in Malaysia. And that the young boy had won a scholarship to one of the most prestigious schools in Singapore. They'd travelled over the border the day before to claim the scholarship only to discover they couldn't because they didn't know of any Singaporeans who could vouch for them as guarantors. They'd spent the night sleeping on the doorstep of the coffee shop and were about to start on their long journey back, helpless.

Based on a conversation of no more than twenty minutes, my

father grabbed his wallet, put the closed sign on his shop and went with the man and his son to act as a guarantor for the scholarship. Once the paperwork was done, he paid for their bus fare back to Malaysia and gave them what was left in his wallet. My father lived for the day and never thought much of the future. He mentioned what had happened only in passing to my mother a few months later when he received a Diwali card in the mail from the boy, who was now studying and boarding in Singapore.

I was born in 1974, and in 1982 our family emigrated to Sri Lanka. My father wanted to give us a Sri Lankan childhood and felt that he could not raise his children well in the concrete jungle of Singapore.

I cannot pin down the date, and people become incredibly cagey when I ask them for details, but sometime in 1983 or 1984, we were having dinner when one of my uncles came rushing in, all in a dither. I can still remember what we were eating that night – creamy coconut milk curry with curdled eggs and crusty bread – when my uncle garbled what had happened.

There had been a terrible industrial accident in Panadura. The owner of a floor wax company was being rushed to hospital with terrible burns. The vast vat of wax had caught on fire and had exploded – covering the man first in wax and then broiling him alive, then burning him. No one expected that he would even make it to the hospital alive.

My father asked who the businessman was as he was still very knowledgeable about the people who lived in Panadura. And when my uncle said the name, my father blanched. I can still remember it, even after nearly thirty years – my father going grey beneath his deep dark skin and leaning forward to support himself. Then he took a deep breath and turned to my brother and me and said: 'Children, that is karma at work'.

It turned out that the businessman who was now dying in hospital and the thug who'd doused and murdered the Hindu priest were the same man. The circle was complete. He'd reaped what he'd sowed.

In 1983, my parents and I were in the middle of the Black July Riots. We witnessed first hand the brutality of the pogrom and were amongst the many thousands of Sinhala families who shielded and protected our Tamil neighbours. Moratuwa was one of the few suburbs of Colombo where burning and lootings were limited.

It was clear that the conflict in Sri Lanka was escalating – so we moved back to Singapore in 1985. And my father's business collapsed. The years between 1985 and 1989 were the worst years of my childhood – a hand-to-mouth existence as my father struggled against the increasing computerisation of his trade as an engraver. His prized hand-work no longer held the same value as precision laser-cut engravings. We had to make do with bursaries and scholarships my brother won; he only had a single school uniform, and we wore the same shoes with holes in their soles until the monsoonal rains made them ridiculous.

But in 1987, an old friend of my father offered him a job as an engraver in Melbourne, Australia. It was the hand of the divine to drag us out of the mire. My parents cobbled together the submission fee and we somehow applied for our Australian residency. Only to have tragedy strike again: two days after our medical examination, my father had a serious heart attack.

Singapore did not have a medical safety net. If you could not pay for medical services, you died. The reality was stark. That night, my parents made their way to the hospital in Toa Payoh (the suburb we lived in) knowing full well that my father would die.

As my father sat in that emergency room that night – waiting in an interminable queue – he told my mother how much he loved her. He was instructing her on what to do next and how she should manage when he was cut off.

A nurse grabbed my father from the queue and rushed him into emergency treatment, brushing aside his concerns about not being able to pay for his treatment. As they put the oxygen mask on his face, a doctor with a beatific smile came into view.

'Mr Dharmapala – you wait in no queue when I am on

duty,' the doctor told him. 'And I will take care of all medical expenses,' he assured my father. 'Can't you remember me, Sir? You are the reason I am a doctor.'

The young Tamil boy whose scholarship my father had acted as a guarantor for many years previously saved my father's life that night.

The circle was again complete. The laws of karma are immutable. My father reaped again what he'd sown. Like all the stories in *Saree* – my father showed me that we were all interconnected and part of the one universe.

In 1989 my family and I moved to Australia. And as we flew into the Australian sky on the flying kangaroo, we brought all our hopes and our stories to this land. Over twenty-five years later, I like to believe my brother and I give back a lot more to Australia than we've ever taken. My brother, Sam Dharmapala, now runs a charity out of the Philippines that helps street kids get jobs and provides trafficked women with opportunities to make a living.

And me? Well, I tell stories. I hope my stories make you smile a little, make you sad a little and make you realise that we are all a part of a whole that makes this universe possible. Like threads in a Saree – we all support each other and make each other flow.

Su Dharmapala
March 2015